THE APOCALYPSE FIRE

BOOK TWO OF THE AVA CURZON TRILOGY

DOMINIC SELWOOD

CORAX

Published in Great Britain by
CORAX
London

Visit our author's blog
www.dominicselwood.com/blog

British Library Cataloguing in Publication Data.
A catalogue record for this book is available from the British Library.

ISBN 978-0-9926332-7-1

Typeset in Monotype Dante 11/14
by Corax and Odyssey Books

FOR
DELIA, INIGO, AND ARMINEL

Acknowledgements

As usual, I have a long list of friends to thank for their deep expertise and friendly guidance.

For heroic help with everything from maths to grenades: Dr James Campbell, Rosaria Galeota, Claudia Gold, Charles Pierre MacDonald, Henrietta McMicking, Philip Rubenstein, Andreas Selwood, Rev. Dr Simon Thorn, Tom Ward, and Robin Wilson.

A special thank you to Dr Lindsay G H Hall, Mrs Claire Powell, and Dr Mark Shuttleworth for going above and beyond in their willingness to answer my endless questions.

For artwork: Delia Selwood for Rasputin's soulful sketch of John the Baptist, and Mrs Claire Powell for the extraordinarily cool Aramaic inscription.

Rachel Thorn, for her sure, wise, and speedy editorial hand on the first draft.

Michael Bhaskar at Canelo, for his tremendous enthusiasm, encouragement, and guidance from start to finish.

Kate Hordern, my wonderful agent, without whom none of the fun would ever have happened.

And lastly, Delia Selwood, who has thrown herself into this book at all stages: as inspiration, fellow-traveller, adviser, and critic – and made it better in every way.

D.K.S.
London
1 October 2016

For the LORD thy God is a consuming fire.

DEUTERONOMY 4:24
(traditionally ascribed to Moses)

PROLOGUE

————— ◆ —————

One Year Ago

Tverskoy District
Moscow
Russian Federation

THE HOLY MOTHER was terrifying.

Oleg Antonevich Durov knew it from the moment she had first visited him, many years ago. Yet he had always done what she asked – however awful.

He looked out of the armoured limousine's tinted windows at the stationary traffic around him.

It was going nowhere.

He was late for a meeting at the Ministry of Energy. As chairman of the Oil and Gas Working Committee, he had a big day ahead.

He ordered the driver to stop.

It would be faster to walk.

Stepping out onto the pavement, he unhooked his jacket from the peg by the window, picked up a slim brown leather pouch of papers, slammed the door, and set off on foot.

He walked a block, away from the luxury boutiques, and the incongruous mix of super-wealthy shoppers and tourists keen to be surrounded by the finest Moscow could offer.

As he crossed the road, carefully avoiding the puddles left by the early-morning street cleaners, he was suddenly aware of a storm of small diffuse white light balls darting from behind him. They were travelling quickly, flitting by his feet, hips, and head, then scudding along the pavement ahead.

He listened, horrified, to a low-frequency thundering deep in the earth. It rose to ear-splitting levels, and the ground started to shake violently. A moment later, the sound was joined by a high-pitched rushing, as if he had stepped behind a waterfall.

The noise level mounted until it was thundering in his ears, impossibly loud.

He fell to his knees, terrified he was having a brain haemorrhage. His pouch of papers slid to the pavement, spilling sensitive Kremlin documents and petrochemical reports over the tarmac.

Up ahead, the white lights slowed, centring on one spot, where they coalesced into a shimmering ellipse, then a mandorla.

He watched incredulously as the shape's edges started to strobe and fluoresce with psychedelic pulses of colour, bleeding out into the bland scene of people going about their business.

He stared uncomprehending at the young woman materializing at the centre of the shape, her feet resting on a crescent moon, and her body in front of a blazing sun.

She wore a dress of burnished silver, a starry rainbow sash at her waist, and a hooded cloak of shimmering blue. Her skin was radiant white, and her lips were a glassy ruby red.

He clamped his hands over his ears to shut out the unendurable noise. But it made no difference.

Petrified, he watched in awe as the woman's crimson lips parted, and her voice flowed over him, scalding like molten gold.

He was vaguely conscious of other pedestrians staring at him. Then he realized – as he had on the two ecstatic occasions she had appeared before, many years ago – that he was the only one special enough to see her.

She had chosen him.

It was a private theophany – a sacred gift.

And she reserved it for him alone.

He listened to her words, feeling them penetrate him like heavenly arrows. They speared every cell, breaking apart the individual helix strands of his DNA, fusing with his soul.

His eyes were on fire. He felt himself burning up.

What she commanded was unspeakable. Inhuman. Terrible in its destruction.

He was to be her agent on earth – her amanuensis for the Final Days.

It was all written, in the Bible – every detail of the Apocalypse.

And he understood the ancient prophecies of annihilation in all their terrifying glory.

Deep in his heart, he felt blessed. His knowledge was why the Holy Mother had chosen him.

He was the only one who understood her.

He was the only one she could trust.

DAY ONE

— • ◆ • —

CHAPTER I

Present Day

Cathedral of Saint John the Baptist
Turin
The Republic of Italy

THE FOUR MONKS checked their weapons.

They were ready.

Night had fallen over the Susa Valley, which carved its jagged way through the Alps – from the French border, deep into the mountains of Italy.

At its eastern end, on the northern Italian plain, Giovanni Raspallo looked hesitantly through the ancient low doorway of the cathedral's sacristy.

The moment the black-robed figures appeared in the gloom, he knew he had made a dreadful mistake.

Earlier that morning, a hollow-cheeked monk had approached him gingerly, quietly introducing himself as Father Vasily.

The monk had asked in halting Italian if he and a few brothers from a monastery near Novgorod might have some prayer time alone with the ancient icon of Saints Archelais, Thecla, and Susanna – the tortured virgins of Salerno – whose Orthodox feast day commenced at sunset.

4

As the cathedral's caretaker, Raspallo regularly received requests for favours, and he was usually happy to oblige. Turin was, after all, increasingly expensive for a single man of his age. It was no problem to keep a candle lit, fill a flask with fresh holy water, or leave a favourite rosary lying overnight on the tomb of Blessed Pier. The little windfalls he earned in return allowed him to buy occasional treats for his pair of goldfinches, and when he refilled his empty boxes of table wine to help blur the lonely evenings, he did not always have to buy from the cheapest tap of *dolcetto*.

Now it was dark, and Father Vasily had returned with his three brothers. They were waiting outside the sacristy's side entrance in the cool evening air – just as Raspallo had instructed – unmistakeable in their loose black Russian Orthodox robes and veiled *kamilavka* cylindrical hats.

Raspallo could not immediately put his finger on the problem. But the moment the monks began filing past him into the cramped sacristy – its glass-fronted cabinets filled with the silverware and embroidered vestments he had lovingly tended for decades – he instinctively knew something was very wrong.

As he closed the thick wooden door behind them, his head exploded in a bolt of burning white-hot light, and he was suddenly falling in a juddering searing paroxysm of agony, as if an archangel's fiery sword was splitting him open.

By the time his gnarled back hit the smoothed terracotta flagstones, his aged muscles were spasming wildly, and a suffocating bile was rising in his throat.

His eyes rolled back into his head, preventing him from seeing the two slender copper wires now embedded in his chest, or the lithium power magazine in Vasily's hand remorselessly pumping out fifty thousand volts.

Raspallo tried to scream, but the overpowering electrical interference was jamming all neural pathways in his jack-knifing body.

After five terrifying seconds, the current shut off, and he went into deep shock, shaking uncontrollably.

Before he had time to understand what was happening, Vasily reached down and yanked out the barbed taser darts, roughly ripping his flesh.

With no let up, another of the monks crouched in front of him and, without warning, punched him hard in the larynx. As the fresh pain and nausea tore through his neck and chest, a hand grabbed his head, and he was aware of something being slipped over it.

He struggled to understand why he could feel straps being fastened at the back of his skull. But his thoughts were cut off by the excruciating pain of his front teeth breaking as a metal block was hammered into his mouth with the heel of a palm, filling his throat with blood and shards of enamel and dentine.

Now he screamed – with all the force his convulsing body could summon. But the solid metal gag filling his mouth absorbed all sound.

"Be calm, and you won't get hurt," a voice grunted.

Raspallo struggled to process the words as he fought to absorb the violence of the onslaught.

Two of the monks approached and grabbed him under the shoulders, dragging him face-down across the floor, then out into the incense-heavy cathedral.

The fourth, with a wide pockmarked face, was already in front of the control panel regulating the building's fourteen discreet high-definition day-night security cameras. He tapped rapidly on the screen of a tablet he had jumped into the RJ45 maintenance port, temporarily disrupting the image feed for fifteen minutes while the system registered it was going offline for a software update.

As the two monks carrying Raspallo pressed deeper into the cathedral, he could tell from the patterns of marble hexagons in the floor that he was being taken down the candle-lit nave, towards the high altar.

Through the intense pain, he struggled to understand what was happening.

This made no sense.

The icon of Saints Archelais, Thecla, and Susanna was in the southwest corner of the building – in the opposite direction.

He began to struggle wildly, lashing out with his arms and legs to break free from his captors' crushing grip, but a numbing punch to the top of his spine turned his skeleton to rubber.

Why were they doing this?

Were they here to kill him?

He struggled to raise his head, looking frantically for solace to the images and sculptures of saints and angels gazing down from the walls and ceiling. But all he saw near him was a bloodied and tortured body cruelly nailed to a cross, and a teenage girl strapped to a breaking wheel as a Roman soldier shattered her bones with a hammer.

He started to retch with fear.

As they carried him to the chancel, his eyes were drawn upwards from the altar's six immense gold candlesticks to the towering rotunda, with its awe-inspiring cascade of ever-grander altars, one behind the other, fading into the cavernous gloom.

Surely God would not allow murder here, in this holy place?

He was numb with terror.

The men turned left, up the north transept, and Raspallo suddenly understood why he had been unnerved when the monks entered the sacristy.

It was obvious now.

They were not men whose bodies had been blunted by years of still-ness, prayer, and fasting. They were straight-backed, athletic, and mus-cular.

Their faces were wrong, too, with short fresh beards, instead of untended straggly wisps of pious neglect.

As the group approached the cluster of side chapels lining the north wall, Raspallo caught sight of the first-floor triforium balustrade screen-ing off the grand royal box. It was where the counts of Savoy once heard Mass, basking under the colossal gold, red, and white sculpture of their royal coat of arms.

The monks stopped and, with a shattering realization, Raspallo under-stood what they wanted.

"*Smettete lo —*" he bellowed, but the sound died in his mouth, absorbed by the solid metal gag.

Up ahead, Vasily strode to the side chapel beneath the royal box, expertly assessing its floor-to-ceiling glass screens. Behind the partition was a long low altar in front of a thick red curtain, and on the cloth was hung a large indistinct photograph of a man's head. It had an oddly elongated face, with high cheek bones, long hair, a full beard, and deep haunting eyes.

Vasily confidently opened the sliding glass screens, stepped into the chapel, and grabbed hold of the red curtain. He tore it down with a sin-gle tug, dragging the beguiling photograph to the floor with it.

They could all now see that the curtain had been hiding a large glass case, twice the length and width of a man, and more than eight inches deep. It was mounted on an adjustable metal trestle frame, permitting it to lie horizontally or be flipped up vertically. Bizarrely, it was plugged into a bank of hi-tech computer equipment.

Although Raspallo had never been allowed behind the curtain before, he knew exactly what the case was, and what the electronics, cables, and tubes were for.

The glass was hollow, and the machinery humming beside it twenty-four hours a day regulated the artificial atmosphere inside it at a constant temperature and humidity, ensuring it was anaerobic and anti-bacterial, 99.5 per cent argon and 0.5 per cent oxygen.

It was not the sort of technology normally found in a church. But then, the thin piece of fragile ivory-coloured linen it was protecting was not in any way ordinary either.

Raspallo could not see the ancient piece of textile. But he knew exactly what it looked like.

Every detail was burned into his mind.

He had marvelled over it during the official exhibitions in 2010 and 2015, when several million people had visited the cathedral to shuffle past a special display. In the evenings, when the crowds had left and the building was dark and quiet, he had stood before the relic, drinking in its wonders. He had stared at it so long he could now close his eyes and recall intimately the faint sepia-coloured image of the front and back of a viciously crucified man, disfigured by hundreds of wounds and blood stains.

As Vasily approached the sacred glass reliquary, Raspallo felt a fresh surge of fear.

Why was he being made to watch what they were doing?

The two monks dropped Raspallo to the floor. The stockier of the two grabbed his trembling wrists, then expertly bound them with a zip tie under his right knee, trussing him up into a position that left him unable to move.

Both monks then bent down and took weapons from their small black backpacks.

Raspallo was not a military man, but he had done his *naja* service forty years ago, and he could recognize a mini submachine gun – not that he had ever seen one so small, or with such malevolent futuristic lines.

He coughed to clear the blood from his throat, only intensifying the throbbing and burning pain in his mouth as his whole body starting to convulse uncontrollably.

The tallest of the monks moved quickly back into the church and took up an observation position from where he could see the sacristy's door and his comrades. Another of the monks remained between Raspallo and the side chapel, training his evil-looking weapon directly on the caretaker.

Vasily bent over an open black backpack and pulled out a rectangular machine with wide hooped handles. Without warning, he flicked its power switch, and the noise of the two-thousand-watt engine reverberated off the smoothed floor and walls, shattering the great temple's hush.

Raspallo was drenched in sweat, staring at the chainsaw.

Surely they weren't … ?

He had seen films.

His eyes widened as the monk stepped towards him, but it was only to pull a protective pair of glasses from his bag, before slipping them over his eyes.

Throwing a threatening glance to Raspallo, Vasily strode over to the hi-tech display case, peered down for a moment at the bulletproof glass, then lowered the savage-looking circular saw blade.

Raspallo gazed on impotently, rage now mixing with the terror.

This was sacrilegio.

It was an outrage.

The sacred linen was not just another object in the cathedral, like one of the many censers, candlesticks, or valuable paintings.

It was the most famous relic in Christendom – gifted to the Holy Father himself by the last king of Italy, whose family had preserved the ancient cloth for five hundred and thirty years.

At the other end of the side chapel from Vasily, the pockmarked monk had pulled a grey rubber-ribbed laptop from his bag, set it onto the end of the glass case, and hooked it up to a matching satellite phone.

The monk closest to the caretaker prodded him in the gut with the tip of his gun's barrel, then shoved his hand deep into the older man's back pocket, pulling out a battered wallet. He tossed the brown leather bundle over to his comrade at the laptop, who flipped through its meagre contents, before pulling out an official *Carta d'Identità*.

Raspallo watched in confusion as the monk held the official green and brown card up against the laptop's screen, scanning its biochip, barcode, photograph, and signature. Then he began typing quickly, muttering as his gloved fingers raced over the soft rubber keys, each marked with a letter from an alphabet Raspallo did not recognize.

The noise from the power saw was getting louder as Vasily scythed its diamond cutting edge effortlessly into the polycarbonate-reinforced glass, ripping an ugly gash deep into the display case.

The caretaker stared with incomprehension at the laptop screen, but could only see line after line of tiny white letters and numbers on a solid black background. It looked nothing like the brightly coloured webpages he normally saw on the tourists' tablets and phones.

"Your *Uni Banca* account shows you withdrew your entire life savings yesterday," the pockmarked monk at the keyboard announced with a heavy Russian accent to Raspallo. "Nineteen thousand seven hundred and fifty Euros. And the flight manifests from Turin Sandro Pertini airport record that you boarded an Alitalia flight this evening to Paris, where you will soon land, before being safely logged through local border control at Charles de Gaulle."

Raspallo did not understand.

Why would he be in Paris?

What did that mean?

The monk looked across at the caretaker with mock admiration. "Congratulations, Signor Raspallo. You just committed the crime of the century. Singlehandedly."

He had?

Raspallo shook his head.

It was they who were the criminals. Not him.

"Don't worry," the monk continued. "They're never going to find you." He closed the laptop, clicking it shut. "We'll make all necessary arrangements."

The caretaker watched the industrial cutter cleave through the final section of glass, and an entire corner of the protective box clattered to the hard floor tiles.

Raspallo could no longer feel his limbs, and there was nothing he could do as Vasily shut off the power saw and reached his hand into the case's jagged opening, laying a rubber mat over the cut glass edge, before carefully starting to pull out the fragile piece of linen.

Tears pricked the back of his eyes. As well as terror and outrage, he now felt shame.

This desecration was his fault.

It was all down to his greed.

He had let these monsters into the cathedral.

He had let everyone down.

Vasily nodded at the monk nearest Raspallo, who bent down and sliced open the zip tie securing the caretaker's wrists.

Raspallo stretched out his trembling leg as the blood began to flow back into it, but the monk hauled him to his feet, and dragged him stumbling over to Vasily, who seized his wrists, and began stamping his palms down onto the shiny glass surface of the case.

Raspallo's broken body was no match for the younger man's strength, and he could only watch in horror as Vasily steered the back of the caretaker's left hand towards the destroyed corner of the case, then purposefully ground the exposed flesh hard against the jagged glass, which tore effortlessly through the skin and deep into the blood vessels beneath.

Raspallo bellowed in shock and pain as the blood started to run freely from his lacerated flesh into the interior of the empty display case, but the gag in his mouth muffled all noise, leaving the scream echoing around his head.

The sight of so much blood made Raspallo lightheaded, but Vasily quickly pulled the caretaker's mangled hand out of the display case, and began expertly applying a field dressing to the multiple wounds, catching the rest of the blood, preventing any more from dropping onto the case or the floor.

The caretaker was hazily aware that the remaining monks had finished packing away the gear, and were now looking at their leader expectantly.

On Vasily's signal, two of them grabbed Raspallo again, and began dragging him over to the ancient temple's west end.

Confused, the caretaker looked about groggily, until he saw that the tall monk who had been guarding the sacristy was now over by the west door, standing beside the cathedral's ornately carved great stone font.

As the group approached, the tall monk pulled on the ancient iron chain mechanism, hoisting the basin's heavy wooden lid high into the air.

Raspallo stared in confusion.

They had what they came for.

What did they want with the font?

The monks steered him up to the great stone bowl, then pushed his chest up against the exquisite carving of the tree of life.

Raspallo stared around, uncomprehending, until a hand grabbed hold of the back of his head and pushed it downwards.

The instant his face hit the icy water, he shouted for all he was worth, but the sound was lost in the cold darkness of the vast stone chalice.

It was then that Raspallo finally understood.

They had allowed him to live for a purpose.

And now he had performed it.

He screamed again, but too late realized that the precious air he had wasted was the last he would ever have.

He thrashed from side to side as violently as he could, but the arms pinning him to the font and holding his head under the holy water were made of steel.

With a primal terror flooding through him, he knew for certain he was dying.

A swirling purple spot appeared at the centre of his vision and began to grow.

Time seemed to slow, and he could sense his strength ebbing away as his ears filled with a roaring noise.

The spinning dark purple cloud now filled his vision, glittering and shimmering with pinprick explosions of light.

Instinct finally overrode his brain. He sucked in wildly though his nose again and again, drawing oblivion deep down into his drowning lungs.

As total darkness descended, he went limp, and his life flowed out into the baptismal waters.

Then nothing.

The monks opened the sacristy door and admitted two men dressed as dustmen, who quickly put the caretaker's lifeless body into a large wheelie bin, then pushed it outside to a waiting rubbish truck.

The monks did not need to clear away anything. Raspallo's skin and hair had been building up around the cathedral for the past few decades. There was no specific evidence of murder. The only signs of any crime the *Polizia* would find were Raspallo's fresh fingerprints and blood all over the shattered empty glass display case.

When the monks were done, Vasily ushered them out of the building, before closing the sacristy door behind them, and locking it from the outside with Raspallo's key.

They all slipped into a nearby Mercedes, whose engine had been running all the while, and sped off into the night, carrying in a silver suitcase one of the world's most famous relics.

---◆---

CHAPTER 2

10b St James's Gardens
Piccadilly
London SW1
England
The United Kingdom

AVA WOKE WITH a start, instantly on her guard.

She glanced at the glowing red digital readout of the radio by her bedside.

It showed 2:04 AM.

Straining to listen, she heard the sound again.

It was coming from down the hallway.

Fully awake now, she reached under her bed and felt for the loaded Ruger LCR she kept taped there.

She was well aware that the weapon was unlicensed and she should not have it. The days when she had operational permission to carry a firearm were long gone. But, after recent events, she was no longer going to assume that her past would leave her alone.

In the dark, her fingers found the small cold weapon, and she quickly pulled it free, instantly at ease with its snug fit in her hand.

Listening intently, she heard it again.

Whoever it was, they were moving about in her kitchen.

She pulled on a pair of jeans, softly opened the bedroom door, and moved silently down the hallway, the adrenaline pumping hard.

She did not have a burglar alarm. She did not need one. Instead she had a custom-made solid steel front door.

How had the intruder got in?

The kitchen door was fractionally open, and she could see a chink of light coming from behind it.

She steadied her breathing.

In one fluid movement, she swung the door wide open with her knee and entered quickly, moving past the doorway and out of the line of fire.

Her aim zeroed in on the intruder's heart.

To her amazement, the man was sitting at the kitchen table with a cup of coffee in front of him.

He was also holding a handgun, pointed directly at her.

"Ever prepared, I see." His voice was raspy. The accent was Scottish. Glasgow, if she had to guess.

She took in his features in a split second. Close cropped grey hair. Mid-fifties. A crumpled grey suit he wore every day. A frame that was once fit, now going soft around the edges.

Nothing about his appearance reassured her.

He could be anyone.

The tension between them was mounting dangerously. She locked onto his face, searching for any small sign of his intentions.

His expression was impassive. But there was something else, too – a hint of coldness in his pale eyes. Unpredictability.

"Dr Curzon. My apologies. I should've introduced myself." He rose slowly to his feet.

Ava's adrenaline started to surge.

She did not have a nameplate outside her door.

The man kept his aim on her, and with his left hand reached for his inside jacket pocket.

She focused on both his hands, shutting everything else out, looking for the first flicker of a hostile movement.

"Very slowly," she warned him, pulling the Ruger's trigger a fraction. The diminutive silver cylinder turned in the matt black weapon, cocking the hammer on a fresh .22 round.

Gently, he pulled out an identity card, and held it up.

She could not read his name, but the photograph was a good likeness, and three words stood out in bold capital letters:

MINISTRY OF DEFENCE

"Jack Swinton," he explained. "MI13."

"Get out," she ordered, her voice low.

He nodded. "I know what you're thinking. MI13 doesn't exist. Except," he smiled briefly, "here we are."

From the corner of her eye, Ava caught a movement at the edge of the kitchen blinds, on the road outside.

She stole a glance, and saw a black van parked up. Beside it was a police car, with two police officers inside staring out into the night.

"Imagine MI5, MI6, or GCHQ want to get something done." He was speaking quietly, his gun still on her. "But they don't want the politicians or public to know about it." He paused. "That's what we're for."

She continued to stare at him, unblinking. "I said, get out."

He did not move. "Things have moved on since your day."

She swallowed hard.

"The intelligence services now have to answer openly to parliamentary committees. It's impossible to do anything truly covertly any more. Which is where we come in. The politicians don't even know we exist."

She glanced again through the small strip of window at the squad car on the street. It looked real enough – even down to the bored expression on the policemen's faces at having pulled the graveyard shift.

"The boys in blue riding shotgun out there think we're Customs and Excise," he chuckled.

"You've got the wrong house." Ava nodded towards the door. "I'm not going to tell you again."

He sighed. "Let's do it the long way, then. Dr Ava Curzon. Studied archaeology and ancient Middle-Eastern languages at Oxford, Harvard, and Cairo. Followed your father into MI6. Top recruit in the year. After a flying start, you left – disillusioned – at the start of the Iraq war. You joined the British Museum's Department of the Middle East, where you were later seconded to museums in Amman and Baghdad. Now you're back in London working on Assyrian antiquities damaged by the wars in Iraq."

Ava took a deep breath.

He clearly knew his stuff.

"That information isn't hard to come by." She eyed him closely. "If you know where to look." Her voice expressed a confidence she did not feel.

"Fine," he answered. "Just do me one favour. Look at that."

He nodded towards a piece of paper in the middle of the large kitchen table. She had not spotted it before, lying on the photographs and translations of Mesopotamian funerary carvings she had been working on until late.

She had no intention of moving any closer to where he was sitting. She wanted him – and his gun – at a good distance, where she could see them both.

She glanced down at the paper, and saw it was a montage of photocopied documents reduced onto one sheet. As she focused on them, she realized with a jolt they were all familiar.

And very highly classified.

She stared at her former MI6 'Foreign Office' photo-identity card. Her official MI6 fingerprint card. A shot of the Director-General welcoming her intake of new recruits, taken in his penthouse office at 'Legoland', MI6's multi-coloured headquarters that looked like building bricks from a kindergarten toy box. And her confidential P45 'Details of Employee Leaving Work' tax form, issued by HR without so much as a thank you on the day she left.

Even though the photographs had been taken a while ago now, she still looked pretty much the same. Dark hair – still in a ponytail – and brown eyes with gold flecks. It was a good look for the line of work. She could pass convincingly for English, European, or Middle Eastern.

It took her a moment to notice that there was also a shiny brass key resting on the sheet of photographs. As she recognized its familiar shape, she realized that unlike the identical one she always carried, the copy on the table was still shiny, and tagged with a label bearing an alphanumeric code.

"The Firm keeps a key to all doors it installs," he explained. "Your father had this flat done. Late 1990s, wasn't it? I'm sure you know how these things work."

She glanced down again at the key.

Her father had the door installed during a particularly nasty operation in which his safety was deemed compromised. She remembered it well. However, as far as she was aware, she had the only key.

She looked up slowly and met his gaze. "I'm giving you a final warning."

"You recently helped a senior MI6 officer and an American DIA agent deal with a group of very bad people, and there were some – how shall I put it? – unexpected funerals."

She froze, not believing what she had just heard.

Knowing about her past was one thing.

But no one knew about that.

She could sense the hairs on the back of her neck prickling.

That information was beyond classified.

It did not exist.

Beads of sweat started forming in the middle of her back.

Had details leaked out?

Was that what this was?

Payback?

She stared at the muscles around the man's eyes, fractionally tightening her grip on the Ruger's trigger.

Were loose ends being cleaned up?

The barrel of his gun moved almost imperceptibly.

In the split second it took her to breathe out and start squeezing the trigger all the way, she registered that he was lowering his gun.

"Do I have to go on?" he asked, placing the weapon onto the table.

Her palms were moist.

Was this a trick?

"Look, we just really need your help," he persisted, placing his gun on the table. "If I was here to harm you, we wouldn't be having this conversation."

She looked down at the photographs and the key.

What he said made sense.

He was going to a lot of trouble if he had just come to kidnap or kill her. He could have done that while she was asleep.

"I'm sure you've got hundreds of good people." She relaxed her finger and gently lowered the Ruger to her side, every fibre of her being poised for a fast reaction if he tried anything. There were still a dozen ways he could attack. His gun was in reach. So was the coffee mug. There was a knife block behind him.

"Take me off your list," she ordered. "I'm a museum archaeologist now. Nothing more. And that's how I want it."

He slumped back down into his chair. "We can talk about that." He picked up the piece of paper and key, and slipped them back into his pocket.

Glancing up, his eyes rested on a large pair of framed photographs on the wall beside her. One was of Lawrence of Arabia in the 1930s. He was somewhere in the English countryside, wearing British Army uniform, sitting astride a sleek vintage motorcycle. The photograph next to it was of Ava, parked up beside a medieval castle somewhere, leaning against an identical black and chrome motorcycle.

"From what I see," he continued, "I think you'll like MI13. Not very conventional. Not many rules."

Ava glanced out of the window at the squad car. The policeman in the passenger seat was checking his watch.

"It's not going to happen," she answered. "I'm done with all that. I'm sorry you've wasted your time."

He scrutinized her face closely for a few moments, before reaching for the mug of coffee and taking a mouthful. "You'll appreciate, I'm sure, that the current climate with Russia is more tense than at any time since the Wall came down in '89. With everything now going on in eastern Europe and Syria, anything the Russian military does out of the ordinary is therefore of the utmost interest to everyone."

He rubbed his hand across his face. "So here's the thing, Dr Curzon. Would you have any idea why a Russian military unit would heist the Turin Shroud?"

Ava stared at him in disbelief.

That's what this was about?

The Turin Shroud?

"If you're interested, get dressed." He stood up to leave. "We've got a mobile unit outside."

--- · ◆ · ---

CHAPTER 3

10b St James's Gardens
Piccadilly
London SW1
England
The United Kingdom

THE STREET OUTSIDE Ava's house was deserted and quiet. Even though it was summer, the temperature had dropped, and she could see the dew condensed on the iron railings.

Swinton approached the blacked-out van, and Ava followed a few steps behind, still on her guard.

The vehicle's side door slid open, and any lingering doubts she had fell away as she looked inside.

Instead of the usual sparse metal interior, she was greeted by an operations centre lit by LEDs from multiple banks of electronic equipment and several rows of screens.

Swinton nodded for her to climb in.

With a mounting sense of excitement, she stepped up into the van, and Swinton followed, pulling the door shut behind him. He tapped twice on the metal bulkhead separating off the driver's compartment, and the van began to move.

"Show her," he instructed a curly haired man in joggers and a t-shirt sitting at the controls, his lightly bearded young face illuminated in the electronic glow.

The tech began typing quickly, and a large video image appeared, spread across the entirety of the six screens mounted in a three by two configuration on the wall above him.

A series of time counters was running along the bottom of the footage, which appeared to show the inside of a rectangular building.

It took Ava a moment to realize it was a large Italianate church, viewed from a ceiling camera looking directly down.

There was no sound to the footage, but she could clearly see a group of black-robed Orthodox monks dragging an incapacitated elderly man down the nave towards the altar at the east end.

"Turin Cathedral. Five and a half hours ago. Twenty-one forty-five local time," the tech announced.

Ava watched the screens closely, as two of the monks opened bags and took out weapons.

The tech froze the image and rolled a trackball, zooming in on one of the short angular submachine guns until it filled all six screens, clearly showing the Cyrillic military lettering stamped into the chassis: ПП-2000.

"Russian," the tech announced. "PP-2000. High precision. Manufactured by KBP Instrument Design Bureau. In wide use across law enforcement and elite military units in the Former Soviet Union."

A cold sensation gripped the base of Ava's stomach as she saw in her mind the embassy building in Addis Ababa.

Bad memories.

She pushed them away. They were not going to help her now.

"Spetsnaz?" she asked. She recognized the style of the operation. It had the stamp of Russian Special Forces all over it.

Swinton nodded. "That's our working assumption."

"And they're just letting the cathedral's CCTV roll?" She did not buy it. "Unlikely, isn't it?"

He shook his head. "They did a thorough job. The cathedral's integrated surveillance system was comprehensively disabled at the time. The feed you're watching is from one of our own cameras."

"In Turin?" She raised an eyebrow.

Swinton nodded. "The city's a hub for people traffickers smuggling migrants from North Africa into Italy, across the Alps, and on to the UK." His face was set in a grim expression. "An unpleasant group of

Libyan-Italians do a lot of their business in the cathedral. We like to keep an eye on them, to know when things are about to get busy. It's pure coincidence we have this footage."

On the screen, one of the monks took what looked like a power saw from his bag and moved out of shot.

"You can guess where he's headed." Swinton moved the trackball and the footage began scrubbing forward at double speed.

She nodded. "The chapel of the Turin Shroud."

He stopped the feed to show one of the monks carrying a ribbed silver suitcase away from the chapel, while two others dragged the injured elderly man to the cathedral's great carved font at the far left of the picture. As she watched with horror, the video footage clearly showed them murdering him.

"The Italian *Polizia* discovered the theft soon afterwards, when the cathedral's camera system came back on," Swinton explained. "All hell broke loose. The *Carabinieri* are now involved, and they're working on the assumption that it was an inside job by the caretaker, Giovanni Raspallo. His fingerprints and blood were all over the Shroud's smashed case. Also, he took a flight to Paris earlier tonight, along with all the cash from his savings account."

"Leaving the Russians time to get away before the *Carabinieri* work out they've been had," Ava concluded, watching as two men in fluorescent yellow high-visibility uniforms entered and put the caretaker's body in a nondescript wheelie bin.

"As it happens," Swinton continued, "we're streets ahead of the Italians, because we know who to look for. We've tapped into Turin's general CCTV surveillance feeds, which show the rubbish truck dropping the wheelie bin off at a local Russian restaurant, a known hangout of Kremlin operatives."

"And the snatch squad?" Ava was intrigued. This was beginning to sound like a sophisticated operation.

The tech brought up a selection of still images, showing a black Mercedes at various piazzas, roundabouts, and traffic lights. Each image bore a time stamp within the last five hours.

"They headed north-east: through Milan, Como, and Lugano," the tech explained, bringing up a fresh image. "This is real time. They'll soon be passing to the west of Davos, then probably on to Liechtenstein."

"It's only a guess," Swinton cut in, "but the roads are consistent with taking a north-east route to Moscow via Berlin, Warsaw, and Minsk. If that's right, they're going to be passing through Bavaria this morning."

The tech punched up a map showing the two main routes north out of Milan, separating through Switzerland, and converging again at Warsaw. He zoomed in on the map. "Our guess is they'll be on the E51 out of Nuremberg at around oh seven hundred local time."

There was a pause, during which the tech brought up an image of the haunting face of the Turin Shroud, and began altering the contrast, throwing the dramatic features into ever-sharper relief.

Swinton broke the growing silence. "So, Dr Curzon, you now know exactly what we know." His expression was grave. "Do you want to go and get it back for us?"

Ava did a double take. She was not sure she had heard correctly.

She had assumed he wanted to sound her out on an aspect of the relic, and that she would be back in bed in an hour.

"What? Are — "

He cut her off. "We don't have time. We've wasted enough already. Do you want to get tooled up and go in? Yes or no?"

Ava stared at him in disbelief.

"Unbelievable," she replied, astonished. "I couldn't have been more clear. I left. I'm out. I have a normal job. I don't want anything more to do with you."

But as she said the words, she knew they were not the whole story.

She had left MI6. That was true. And she had been disillusioned enough to cut all ties. In the race to war in Iraq, her advice to be cautious about the aftermath had been ignored. It had left her feeling isolated, and she did not want to be a part of what followed.

But what she also knew was that MI6 had been her whole life, and her home. It was all she could remember from her earliest childhood. It was her father's world, and then it had become hers. Walking out after his death had been the hardest thing she had ever done.

After leaving, she had thrown herself into the role she found at the British Museum. It was a dream job. She got to handle some of the world's most exciting objects, research them, piece together ancient puzzles, and share the results with international audiences.

The Museum had sent her to Amman, then Baghdad, where her role in charge of tracing the objects looted in the war had been a once-in-a-lifetime opportunity for a Middle East archaeologist like her. For seven years she had worked from an office in the Baghdad Museum, where she had thrived on the excitement and danger of living in that ancient city.

But she had never been very convincing at lying to herself.

She had been good at intelligence work. And she missed it. She had even recently started some private investigations of her own, on the side, looking into the flow of looted Syrian and Iraqi antiquities flooding the London market in the wake of the current sectarian anarchy in the Middle East.

Swinton opened an envelope on the console in front of him, and pulled out a small plastic card, which he laid before her.

She looked down at it, taking a moment to register that it showed her name and photograph under the bold words: 'MINISTRY OF DEFENCE'.

"You can stay on full-time at the Museum and do your job there. You'd just be a consultant to MI13. I promise we'll keep you out of the political stuff."

Her pulse accelerated.

Was that even possible?

She took a moment to let what he was saying sink in.

"You'll be part of the team, and have a desk at HQ. We'll call you when we need you. Or," he smiled, "you call us. You can choose what you work on."

She tried to slow her thoughts down.

Was he seriously saying she could do archaeology and intelligence? And it would be up to her what she got involved with?

Her performance reports had consistently said that she needed to watch her reckless streak.

Back in her kitchen, Swinton had mentioned a recent encounter with MI6 and the American DIA. That had seemed exciting at first. But as he reminded her, it had ended in a number of funerals: one of them very nearly hers. When it was over, she resolved that she would never again say 'yes' if her former colleagues from MI6 came knocking.

The van stopped abruptly, and Swinton slid open the side door.

They were at the top of Green Park.

In the distance, through the trees, she could see the faint lights of Buckingham Palace glinting where the tended lawns met the drama of the Mall.

But much more significantly, immediately in front of her, parked on the grass, was a large helicopter.

Even in the moonlight, she recognized its unique profile, and knew exactly what it was – one of the Special Forces Dauphins from the Army Air Corps squadron at Credenhill, painted in bland civilian colours to deflect attention.

"The pilot will only wait sixty seconds now we're here." Swinton held out the plastic MI13 pass. "You need to make up your mind."

Ava shut her eyes.

Did she want to get involved with the clandestine world of intelligence again? And – more urgently – did she really want to face the Russian military again?

Ever since the incident in Ethiopia she had spent her life avoiding them.

It had been the end of a normal school day. Her father had brought her to the embassy for the rest of the afternoon. At the time she had believed the faded sign on his office door that stated he was in charge of the embassy's passport division. Years later she had discovered that he was a senior MI6 officer. She went to the embassy with him most days after school. It was the only place for her to go. Her mother had walked out on them years earlier.

The first half hour in the tranquil embassy that day had been normal. She had been sitting with her father's secretary, who was helping her with a school project.

Then there was panic. Shooting. Mangled bodies. Dead glassy eyes, and floors slippery with blood. Adults she had counted as friends, slain at their desks.

Years later, she had understood. The Cold War had gone hot in Afghanistan. America and Britain had been funnelling weapons to the *mujahideen* in the front line against the invading Russians. Ethiopia had been part of that lethal supply chain, and the Russians had intervened.

It had left her with psychological scars and unresolved feelings towards infantrymen wearing the hammer and sickle.

She snapped back to the present and stared at the Special Forces helicopter – menacing in the moonlight. She watched the rotors start to turn, feeling herself being pulled in different directions.

But as her mind fixed on the image of Swinton sitting in her kitchen pointing a loaded handgun at her, a feeling of clarity emerged.

He was asking for her help because she had been good at what she did for MI6.

It was true she loved her job at the Museum. But, deep down, she also knew that she wanted more. There was something missing from her life, and – if she was honest – she knew exactly what it was.

She gazed at the card.

Life was short.

Without saying anything, she took it, and caught a flicker of triumph in Swinton's eyes.

For a moment, she felt a rush of uncertainty.

Was this a game to him?

Was there something he was not telling her?

She pushed the thought aside.

Time would tell.

She had made her decision, and the adrenaline was already starting to flow.

Stepping out of the van into the cool night air, she ran towards the waiting helicopter, ducking under the mounting rotor wash as the large cargo door slid open for her.

Climbing in, she saw the impassive faces of the four-man SAS team already strapped into their seats. One had mutton-chop sideburns meeting in a moustache. Two of the others had trendy civilian haircuts. The fourth was nondescript. None of them had shaved for a few days. They were not wearing uniforms – just jeans, hoodies, and cagoules. They could not have looked less military. But the atmosphere of intense focus and planned violence left no doubt who they were.

As the rotors increased speed, an armed woman in the seat nearest the door passed Ava a small khaki holdall. The zip was partly open, and inside it Ava could see a black SIG P228.

"For you," the woman shouted over the noise of the rotors building speed. Her accent was West Coast American. "I'm Mary. Vatican liaison."

Ava nodded an acknowledgement as she took the bag and, for the first time in several years, sensed a familiar tingle.

She felt alive.

―――――――― ◆ ――――――――

CHAPTER 4

La Goutte d'Or
18ᵉ arrondissement
Paris
The Republic of France

AMINE'S BODY WAS strung out with fear.

He sprinted for all he was worth – his only thought to get away from the car.

He had first heard the engine when leaving his mother's apartment. Initially, he simply assumed it was someone else making their way home. But when he realized it was deliberately following a few yards behind him, he knew something was wrong.

He had tried to lose it by turning down a minor side street. But as the car swung around the corner after him, he started to feel real fear.

What did they want?

Had they been waiting?

It was gone 3:00 AM.

With a burst of speed, he started to run.

As he fled down the street, he glanced over his shoulder, and registered that it was a new-looking dull silver BMW, not the sort of banger driven by dropouts looking for easy cash to shoot up and pass out.

Who followed someone at this time in the morning?

There were four figures inside the cabin.

He slammed into the boarded-up windows of a *bar-tabac* that had closed years ago – the rusted metal shutters now daubed with a jumble of aerosoled obscenities in Arabic and French.

He ran faster, smelling the fear coming off his skin.

Bravery did not come naturally.

Cannoning off a wall plastered in tattered posters for North African *rai* dance nights, he bounced headlong into an alleyway, where he prayed the car would not be able to follow.

For a moment, he was overtaken by a cold dread that he might have been funnelled into a dead end. But as he hammered down the dark rubbish-strewn lane, he saw light and an opening at the far end.

Emerging into the deserted street, he continued running as he again heard the car accelerating – this time from a side road.

His body was soaked in sweat.

He scrambled up a graffiti-covered footbridge, and crossed the broad bundle of railway lines pushing north from the Gare du Nord, under the Péripherique ring road encircling the city, and on into the warzone suburbs of the Seine-Saint-Denis.

Jumping down off the last step, he again heard the engine accelerating at the end of the street.

He cursed.

There must be a parallel road bridge.

The adrenaline was spiking so hard he had no idea where he was. The chase was a blur. All he could think of was to keep his legs pumping faster than they ever had.

From the corner of his eye he saw the street sign said he was now in the nineteenth arrondissement. He could not remember ever having been here. This was Belleville – yet another poor immigrant neighbourhood. A distant memory surfaced that it was where Edith Piaf had grown up.

His lungs were burning as he spotted the hills of the Parc des Butte-Chaumont rising to his left.

Up ahead, the car emerged from a junction, with the beam of its headlamps falling full onto his face.

His shirt and jacket were stuck to his back.

He had never known fear like it.

What did they want?

He spotted a gap between a bakery and a café, and darted into it.

Were they after what was in his bag?

He clutched the brown leather courier-satchel closer to his body.

It was impossible.

How could they know?

Arriving at the end of the alleyway, he collapsed against a large metal rubbish bin, sucking in deep lungfuls of air.

Whatever athleticism he had once possessed had long ago dissipated in lecture halls and libraries.

He stared around, petrified, expecting to hear the sound of the engine any time.

Up ahead was a narrow street with a pair of dark green Morris columns placed a few yards apart – their wide advertising-wrapped cylinders rising beneath imposing oriental-rococo domes.

He did a double take, frowning.

Coming from the wreckage of Algeria, he noticed that sort of thing. Two advertising columns so close together was the kind of bad planning that blighted his old country – not what he expected of the Parisian authorities. But as he stared at them, he felt an unexpected tingling.

Recognition.

Struggling to place it, the memories suddenly clicked into place.

He had been here before. Many years ago.

With Sami.

He looked hurriedly across the street, and there it was – the small stone fountain with the bronze mermaid.

Al-hamdu lillah.

Thanks be to God for Sami.

The details were coming back now.

While he had been studying at the Lycée and then the Grande École, Sami had been bunking off, on the streets, soaking up the limited thrills the city's northern ghetto could offer a young Maghrebi outcast.

He and Sami had always been outsiders.

In Algeria, they were reviled as Christians. Now, here in France, in their new life away from the horror, they were shunned as North Africans. No one seemed aware that Algeria had been Christian long before France. Or that Saint Augustine – the most brilliant thinker and luminary of the early Church – had been African.

It did not even seem to make any difference when, years later, he landed a good job at the university, rising to become one of the foremost specialists in his field.

He could never expect to be one of them.

He lurched into the road, his eyes flicking again to the strikingly curvy statue in the fountain.

This was definitely it.

They had laughed at the French back then. Sami and his friends had joked how the streets of Paris had been so poorly built that many had collapsed. There was a time when the Rue d'Enfer – the Road of Hell – had caved in completely.

Reaching the middle of the street, he looked down and saw it.

The next thing he knew, he was on his knees, hooking his fingers into the small holes piercing the elegant wrought-iron manhole cover. He strained, tugging at the metal disc, pulling it upwards with all his might, praying it had not rusted shut – or worse, been welded down.

The metal moved fractionally as he again heard the roar of the BMW's six cylinders accelerating. It sounded closer now – just the other side of a nearby junction.

With a renewed urgency, he yanked harder, feeling the muscles in his back spasming as his whole body willed the metal to move.

And then, suddenly, it was free.

Somewhere nearby, gears crunched and the engine picked up speed.

He hauled the heavy disc to one side, and threw his legs down into the blackness beneath.

Up ahead, the tyres screeched, and his feet found the small irregular ladder of iron rungs embedded into the concrete wall.

He had lost all sense of time, and everything was happening at once.

The headlights were bearing down on him as he stretched for the manhole cover. With a burst of strength born of desperation, he hauled it back into place over his head, hearing it clang into position.

Now he was suddenly in darkness, and shaking uncontrollably.

Sami had pointed out the manhole cover all those years ago, but they had not gone down it together. That was something Sami did with his friends – the secretive army of *cataphiles* who moved about the uncharted city of catacombs.

Here, in the north, Sami had told him, the tunnels and shafts were not sanitized like those in southern Paris, where in the late 1700s around six million corpses were dug out of the city's graveyards, and deposited into the endless miles of subterranean gypsum and limestone quarries. Nowadays, boggle-eyed tourists could pay a handful of Euros to spook themselves in the skull-lined tunnels, but come closing time, the officials made sure everyone was out, before locking the gates for the night and going home to their baguettes and wine.

These northern quarries were very different, Sami had explained. These were not the 0.2 per cent of catacombs that had been made safe. These were unmapped and unknown, unstable and off-limits. Only the *cataphiles* moved about down here – oblivious to the world above – in a shadowy parallel universe of druggies, dropouts, and freedom warriors.

Amine's coordination was gone, and he slid clumsily down the rungs as the pencil-beam shafts of pale light from the manhole cover above became fainter.

His feet eventually hit the wet sludge covering the tunnel's floor.

The air was colder here.

He clutched the leather bag closer to his body.

They were not going to get it.

He could not believe they knew about it. He had told almost no one.

Ahead were two openings into the catacombs. After a second's indecision, he broke into a run again, heading right.

Left was bad luck.

Suddenly hearing a noise behind him, he stopped with a jolt, straining to listen.

Then he heard it again, echoing around the rocky walls.

There was no mistake.

It was the distant rasp of the manhole cover scraping on concrete and grit.

They must've seen him.

Picking up speed, he began to sprint, the fear now a physical lump in his throat.

He was clutching the bag more tightly than ever.

They would not find it.

They must *not find it.*

He could not let them get what was inside the bag.

The catacombs were infinite.

He hurled himself forwards into the darkness, aware now of ominous pale shadows moving behind him, cast by far-off lights. His lungs were on fire, and his heart was pounding too fast.

As he powered blindly ahead into the gloom, he looked back, and saw the shadows on the walls becoming more distinct.

They were getting closer.

He held his arms out and sped up, blocking off the blinding pain from his exhausted muscles.

The next moment, his palms slammed hard into a rock wall, followed milliseconds later by his left knee, then his face.

Whimpering, he slid to the floor, tasting blood in his mouth and throat, aware from the burning in the front of his skull that he had shattered his nose.

Panicking, he struggled to get up, but his left knee was not responding, and below it his leg was twisted at an impossible angle.

He put out his arm to lever himself up, but the moment his hand touched the ground a sickening red-hot sensation engulfed his forearm.

He gazed about wildly, but could only look on helplessly at the grotesquely distorted and elongated shadows on the walls advancing towards him.

Paralyzed, he sat in terror as the beams fell onto him, and the figures of four men emerged out of the gloom.

From their Asian appearance, full beards, knee-length black *kurta* shirts, and drawn handguns, he was in no doubt who they were.

One of the torches picked out a rusty metal gate set into the solid rock wall behind where he was slumped.

He had come to a dead end.

One of the men stepped forward.

He had a long angular face with fleshy lips and oiled collar-length hair. His right eyelid was frozen half closed.

The shadows of the torchlight distorted his features even more, rendering them grotesque. He locked eyes with Amine arrogantly. "Give me the bag," he grunted with a sandpapery growl, pointing at the satchel.

His Arabic was fluent and flawless, but Amine struggled to place it. The man looked Pakistani, yet the accent was something he had not heard before.

Amine shook his head. As he did, a fresh clot of blood and phlegm slid from his nose into his throat. "Please," he begged, replying in the same language, his voice cracking. "Don't kill me." His eyes were filling with tears from the pain of his broken body. "I am a nobody."

One of the men yanked the bag off his shoulder.

Amine felt sick.

The man handed the bag to the leader, who slowly opened its flap. He stuck a hand inside, and pulled out a notebook, followed by a piece of pottery the size of a paperback book.

"Good." He put them both back into the bag, and hung it from his shoulder.

From somewhere deep down, Amine felt a surge of defiant hope amid the senselessness of it all.

Maybe it would be okay.

At least they did not have the letter.

They would never find that.

The leader walked across to the gate, grabbed one of its rusty bars, and rattled it.

The metal stayed firm.

"Crucify the *kaffir* here," the jihadi ordered, his obsidian-black eyes filling with pleasure.

As Amine's brain struggled to take on board the enormity of the words, he looked on in horror as the three men approached.

CHAPTER 5

The Kremlin
Moscow
Russian Federation

ON THE NORTHERN bank of the River Moskva, high above the great medieval tower, the ten-foot ruby glass communist star gleamed in the strong morning sunlight.

Far below, Oleg Durov's car swept through the grand red-brick gate.

In former days, visitors approached the formidable nineteen-towered curtain wall via Red Square and the Place of Skulls. But now all traffic entered at the south-western Borovitskaya Tower, passing directly into the heart of Russia's political machine.

Once past the checkpoint, the limousine moved confidently through the ultra-high-security complex, navigating its way between the five palaces, four cathedrals, assorted historic buildings, and governmental offices.

Durov gazed out of the tinted window as the car passed the Grand Kremlin Palace of the Tsars, now home to the President of the Russian Federation.

He was euphoric.

Today was only the beginning.

In Russia, Italy, and America, they would start to feel it happening.

Thanks to him.

The chauffeur pulled up at Cathedral Square. The oligarch climbed out, and strode between the Cathedrals of the Annunciation and the Dormition, towards a rectangular building. Its unique façade stuck out among the ancient sacred architecture, arresting in its faceted white limestone bricks, each sharpened at the front to an aggressive point.

As Durov approached, the uniformed guard on the door snapped to attention and nodded him through into the oldest set of rooms in the Kremlin.

Inside, General Gennady Zhurikov was waiting in the Faceted Chamber.

The ancient room was dominated by a vast central column supporting four radiating ceiling vaults, each illuminated by a large triple-tiered medieval chandelier.

Zhurikov was gazing at the gold walls and ceiling, and at the hundreds of frescoes and gilded carvings jostling in a riot of exuberant reds, blues, and greens.

Durov joined him, looking around reverentially.

He loved this room above all others.

It filled him with the Spirit.

He stepped over to one of the large windows, transfixed by the sight of the square's gold onion domes blazing in the sun.

There was Grace in this place.

"Do you know why I've called you here, General?" Durov asked, turning after a moment's pause.

The old soldier's jaw was clenched tightly shut – the white hair and eyebrows taking away none of the face's strength.

Durov looked disdainfully at the crisp khaki uniform, medals, and peaked hat tucked smartly under an arm.

He had no time for the Old Guard. The world had moved on. He struggled to believe that there were still many who had not adapted to the changes in 1991, and that Zhurikov was their poster boy.

"You're not still a member of the Communist Party, are you?" Durov's tone was mocking.

The general bristled visibly.

Durov turned his back on the soldier again and looked out of the window, surveying the five mighty cross-topped domes of the Cathedral of the Dormition, where the tsars had all been crowned.

It was sublime – earthly and heavenly rule, operating in unison.

"But you're still a Communist?" he persisted.

The general's anger flared. "As was this country, for the first forty years of my life."

Durov held his hand up dismissively. "And Comrade Stalin was Premier when you were born. But we were a backward nation then, technologically far behind the West and Asia. Now, we're forging ahead. Yet you," he turned to face the old soldier, eyeing the three stars on his epaulettes, "you want your glory days back, heroically fighting yesterday's battles."

Zhurikov was visibly measuring his words. "Russia stands for nothing anymore. You capitalists have pissed away an empire."

Durov walked towards the older man aggressively. "How many barrels of oil do we make now?"

Zhurikov shook his head. "It belongs to the people. It's not your personal casino chip."

Durov ignored him. "Per day, the US and Saudi produce twelve million each. We make eleven million. China and Canada four million each. Iran, Iraq, the UAE, Mexico, and Kuwait three million each. So you see, General, we're a giant."

"And yet," Zhurikov answered, "we're crippled by US and European sanctions. You can't sell it. Our people starve. So what does it matter?"

Durov felt himself getting angry. "Europe is finished," he sneered. "It's a museum. And the American dream is over, stagnating in disposable culture. The world has new markets now – to the east."

Zhurikov looked unimpressed. "You sell to China at forty dollars a barrel? Why bother?"

He did not have time to give the old man a lesson in petro-economics. "The Saudis have floored the price to squeeze Iran out. It's politics. And it's temporary."

The old soldier looked ahead warily. "Why did you call me here?"

Durov was soaking in the sacred images all around.

This was the beating heart of Russia.

Vlast i vera: *power and faith.*

"For over five centuries, much of this nation's most important history has unfolded in this very room, where the disciplines of politics and war have come together many times."

The general glared at him disdainfully. "What do you know of war?"

"That it belongs to politicians, General, not soldiers," Durov retorted. "Wars begin and end with men in suits around tables. Your role is a means to an end. Nothing more. To obey, not to question."

Zhurikov stared at him defiantly.

"Don't misunderstand." Durov moved back towards the window. "A government only stands with an army behind it. We have a mutual self-interest. Which is why you can now do something. For Russia."

Zhurikov frowned.

"Thanks to our strategic placement in Syria, we now have – how shall I put it? – capabilities, in the Middle East?"

"You know very well what the position is," Zhurikov answered quietly.

Better than you, Durov mused. "I wonder what would happen if an accident befell an oil supertanker leaving the east coast of Saudi. Say, en route from Jubail or Ras Tanura to the US?"

Zhurikov's lip curled. "You have assets for that type of operation. You don't need my men … " He stopped, the penny dropping. "Unless you're looking for a scapegoat if it goes wrong."

"The state is shrinking." Durov allowed a note of concern to enter his voice. "It's a sad but inevitable fact. When the dust settles, I sincerely hope you, and those loyal to you, are still serving the motherland."

Zhurikov stared off into the middle distance, his expression twisting with emotion. When he replied, there was steel in his voice. "Without the army, you'd be nothing."

Durov breathed deeply.

How much longer were these Cold War dinosaurs going to last?

"Of course, you're right." He stepped closer. "But, unless I'm mistaken, you're not the army. You're one man."

"As are we all." Zhurikov was now making no effort to conceal his hostility.

"You should have more faith, General." Durov smiled, lightening the tone. "Faith is all."

The corners of Zhurikov's mouth turned down with disgust. "I have found faith to be a poor answer to most questions."

Durov looked over the soldier's shoulder at the icon of Saint George on the wall. The warrior was victoriously skewering the dragon to the floor with his lance, trampling it under his horse's hooves. It was a holy image of sanctity and strength.

It was perfection.

"Then tell me," Durov was genuinely interested. "When you took your first command, did you not have faith in the Politburo? In the Praesidium?"

Zhurikov rounded on him, anger blazing openly in his eyes. "I was commanding Red Army brigades when you were still begging in the forests."

With no warning, Durov strode rapidly over to Zhurikov, only stopping when his nose was level with the soldier's eyes. "You don't want to pick a fight with me," he whispered.

"From what I hear," Zhurikov snarled, "you don't have the balls."

Durov smiled nastily, before grabbing Zhurikov's hand and clamping it over his groin.

The material of the expensive vicuña suit crumpled softly, and Zhurikov's palm and fingers met no resistance as they closed over the empty space over Durov's pubic bone.

Zhurikov pulled away, a look of shock and revulsion on his face as he turned and strode for the door.

Durov watched him stalk out, under the gaze of the holiest saints of Russia. "Be careful, Comrade," he called after him, emphasizing the word disdainfully. "The thing about generals is that it's good for an army's morale to occasionally stumble across a dead one."

---— ◆ —---

Chapter 6

Nuremberg
Free State of Bavaria
The Federal Republic of Germany

DURING THE NOISY and uncomfortable flight in the stripped-down Dauphin, the SAS corporal with the mutton-chop sideburns had been in almost constant radio communication with the Bavarian police's *Spezialeinsatzkommandos* in Nuremberg.

Swinton, meanwhile, had the job of keeping London and Munich happy with the details of the unfolding operation.

Flying fast and low over Franconia, Ava recognized the immense twin spires of Nuremberg's great medieval Saint Lorenz Church. The two vast stone needles came swiftly into view, like a dramatic shot from Riefenstahl's *Triumph of the Will*. But instead of Hitler's corrugated Junkers JU-52 swooping low over the picturesque rooftops, it was a disguised SAS flight, on its way to do what the Regiment did best.

By the time the helicopter came down in a secluded arable farm just east of Nuremberg, there was an armed German police escort ready to ferry them to the freshly improvised roadblock on the northbound section of the E51.

The Bavarian authorities had insisted that they would make the arrests. They would then hand the Russians and the Shroud over to the

British, who would be given clearance to fly them to the British Army facility at Sennelager, an hour and a half north, where Swinton would join them.

Now, parked up on the wide tree-lined Autobahn beside the roadblock, Ava was watching attentively out of the large riot van's grille-covered window, taking in the lengthening queue of cars.

She was acutely aware that she did not know a great deal about modern Russian forces. After her experiences in Ethiopia, she had been content to let others specialize in Russian affairs, leaving her free to focus on the Middle East. The only small concession had been during her first year at MI6, when she had spent two months with the Russia desk, as a compulsory part of learning about the Firm's work.

The attachment had been an eye-opening time.

She had discovered that, despite the end of the Cold War, relations between the West and Russia were permanently strained, and the Russia desk was as active after the fall of Communism as it had been before. As a linguist, she had quickly mastered the Russian alphabet – enough to read names on files and maps – but had not taken it any further. In no time, the two months were up, and since then her knowledge of Russia was pretty much gleaned from newspapers and television.

Nevertheless, she was under no illusions about the current hair-trigger diplomacy between Moscow and Europe. Relations were at breaking point, with heavy weaponry being deployed by both sides across Eastern Europe and Syria. Tensions were genuinely high, even if the politicians played them down. And now, here was a team of Russian Special Forces soldiers pulling off a lethal operation in the heart of mainland Europe.

She looked around. The roadblock was not exactly a hi-tech affair – just a series of red-and-white-striped barriers with the word 'POLIZEI' in large letters, narrowing the traffic to one lane. Behind the barriers, parked up around her, were a handful of police vehicles and bikes.

She watched as the cars on the northbound section of the road slowly approached the improvised checkpoint, where armed German police commandos were stopping any suspicious vehicles.

Before landing, the SAS unit leader had briefed Ava fully. This was a baby-sitting operation, he explained. The orders were to take charge of the Russians and deliver them to Sennelager. If, for any reason, things 'got noisy', Ava and Mary were to keep out of the way and let the men from the Regiment do their job.

Before disembarking the helicopter, all six of them had put on tactical ops waistcoats, and radio headsets tuned into the designated Bavarian police net for the operation.

As Ava watched the three lanes of crawling traffic through the window, she suddenly heard things kicking off.

Bike riders from the German police commandos were several miles to the south, surveying the incoming traffic. They had spotted and positively identified the black Mercedes with its four occupants as it slowed to join the queue for the roadblock.

"*Ihre Papiere, bitte.*" The policeman's voice was coming over Ava's headset loud and clear. "Your papers, please."

There was a momentary silence, broken suddenly by the shrill sound of screeching tyres, followed by four rapid gunshots.

Ava's heart missed a beat.

What the hell was happening up there?

The SAS corporal leaned forward and thumped the padded shoulder of the policeman at the van's wheel. "Move!" he ordered. "Now!"

Ava blocked everything else out and was listening to the scene of chaos unfolding in her earpiece. Multiple voices were shouting in German, and it was not possible to tell what was happening.

Which side had started the shooting?

She tugged her seatbelt to lock it tight as the van accelerated hard, squealing up the Autobahn's hard shoulder.

She had no idea how far ahead the Russians were, but judging by the howl of the van's engine and the speed at which the cars in the lanes on the other side of the barrier were blurring by, she suspected the distance to the Mercedes was diminishing rapidly.

Her backseat view through the armoured windscreen was partially obstructed. But in what seemed less than a few seconds the driver was shouting, and she braced herself as he pulled the handbrake up hard, spinning the van ninety degrees, sending it skidding to a halt sideways across the hard shoulder.

The SAS team had the doors open before the vehicle had stopped. They were pouring out, weapons drawn, and converging on the Mercedes, which had squealed to a halt to avoid the inevitable collision.

Ava had her gun in hand and her own door open a fraction of a second later. There was no way she was going to remain a target in the van. She preferred her chances down on the road.

She hit the ground hard, landing on the rough tarmac in a prone firing position, the SIG aimed at the scene up ahead. As a stream of loud machine gun fire raked the front of the vehicle, something heavy crashed into her legs. She looked back, and saw Mary beside her, a chunky Beretta in her hand, also trained on the chaos up by the car.

The Mercedes's doors were open, and Ava could already see one of the Russians slumped dead at the wheel. The others were taking cover behind the stranded car, while the SAS team was closing in from a variety of directions.

Ava thought she would feel something on seeing Russian soldiers again – some desire for revenge or closure for what had happened in Addis Ababa. But she did not. These were different men. And it was a different time. They were not even in uniform.

It was pandemonium, with members of the public panicking and screaming in their slow-moving vehicles only yards away as the contact escalated.

Glancing back, Ava saw Mary take careful aim and fire. Up by the Mercedes, one of the Russians doubled over as the round ripped a hole in the front of his shoe and tore deep into his foot.

"Which part of the Vatican did you say you were with?" Ava shouted, not quite believing what she had just seen.

"The bit they don't teach you about at Sunday school." Mary grimaced, squinting to take aim again.

Another burst of submachine gun fire hit the van, sending a fresh spike of adrenaline into Ava's system. She knew she was now a sitting duck where she was, and needed to take cover behind the line of stationary cars up ahead.

Scrambling up, she ran crouching as low as she could. To her surprise, she could hear Mary putting down covering fire.

Ava dived behind the nearest car. A fraction of a second later, three rounds bit into the tarmac immediately behind her, kicking up puffs of debris.

She moved forward again, drawing level with a red Saab. One of the SAS men was up by the front wheel. He was positioned low, firing in the direction of the Mercedes.

Ava's heart was hammering as the intensity of the gunfight increased.

Her mind returned to her earlier conversation with Swinton, when he had reminded her of the last operation she had been on. It had ended here, in Germany, with her staring straight down a barrel as a rabid neo-Nazi prepared to execute her.

The middle of the night flashbacks came later.

She blinked the memories away, and focused on just one thought.

Her job was to find the silver suitcase.

The soldier turned and smiled briefly, motioning for her to stay down where she was, at the rear of the car.

She crouched even lower, head down, and the next moment heard a crack and a soft thumping sound. She looked up, and her stomach turned as the large SAS man toppled backwards, glass eyed, an ugly ragged bullet entry hole just above his left eyebrow.

Something inside Ava kicked into autopilot.

She scrambled forward and took up a firing position where the soldier had been, aiming between the cars in the direction of the Russians' abandoned vehicle.

A bullet flew past her head so close she felt the wind whipping her face. A millisecond later, she heard the ping as it ricocheted off a car close behind her.

She returned fire, but the Russian had moved back to a position of safety on the other side of the Mercedes.

Behind her, she could hear more armed Bavarian police arriving on motorbikes.

The noise of the shots coming from all directions was deafening.

Up ahead, a Russian appeared from behind the Mercedes. Without hesitating, she took careful aim, firing two rounds at the same time as she heard others opening up on him. He dropped instantly, his machine gun spraying rounds over the queuing cars as he toppled.

Then, as suddenly as it had all started, it was over.

There was an eerie silence.

Two Russians lay on the road by the car, and one was slumped in the driver's seat. The other had fallen further away, behind the car.

Without pausing, the Bavarian police commandos scrambled to the dead bodies and disarmed them, while the three SAS men moved to the bullet-riddled Mercedes and began going over it.

Ava ran to the driver's side door, her gun still at the ready.

By the time she got there, Mary was a few yards off, behind the car, kneeling beside the leader of the Russians. She had his slim mobile phone in her hand, and a similar-sized object with no keyboard pressed against it.

Ava leaned through the open door and stretched across the dead driver – a large wet patch in his chest soaking his black robes.

She pressed the dashboard button to unlock the boot, and heard the dull click as it sprang open.

Moving round to the rear of the car, she lifted the lid fully.

There, nestling among a selection of clothing and equipment bags, was the silver suitcase she had seen on the surveillance video from Turin Cathedral.

She stared at it in amazement, feeling her breathing quicken, not quite believing that inside it, quite possibly, was one of Christendom's most controversial relics – a treasure the Church never let out of its sight.

Millions of diehard *sindonistas* believed it was the genuine burial shroud of Jesus – the cloth which wrapped his body as he lay in the tomb one Passover Friday sometime in the early first century AD. Others were convinced it was a medieval artefact, produced either as a pious artwork or a cynical fraud. And around the fringes of the heated debate were the conspiracy groups, who remained convinced it was the death shroud of the last Templar Grand Master, Jacques de Molay, or that it had been painted or photographed by Leonardo da Vinci, or some other whacky theory.

She shook her head.

People would believe anything.

Reaching down, she took hold of the case's handle, but without warning her hand was knocked away hard.

Spinning around, she raised the SIG with lightning speed in an instinctive reaction, only to find herself staring into the face of the SAS corporal with the mutton chops.

"Let's be careful, shall we, ma'am?" he suggested, lifting the case free from the car. "Get the lads to check it for booby-traps before you open it?"

She stared at him, wondering what kind of idiot would encase a priceless ancient cloth artefact with explosives. But she slowly nodded. There was no harm in being cautious.

Suddenly, from the corner of her eye, she caught a rapid movement behind them as an engine accelerated aggressively. Her head snapped round in time to see one of the police motorbikes speeding off the wrong way down the line of parked cars.

The rider was dressed in the black robe of a Russian monk.

With no warning, a gun fired beside her.

"*Nicht schießen!*" a policeman bellowed in her earpiece. "Don't shoot!" But no one was shooting any more, as the motorbike was now scything its way between the two lines of stationary cars, and there was no clean shot without endangering the public.

The SAS corporal slammed the boot of the Mercedes shut. He scowled at Mary, who was leaning against the car, the colour drained from her face.

"He had at least two holes in him, and wasn't moving," she answered defensively, heading off the inevitable criticism.

The corporal breathed out heavily, glaring at her.

Up ahead, the other two were loading the body of their colleague into the van, ignoring a German policeman who seemed on the verge of interfering.

Ava fell in beside the corporal as they headed to the van. "Sorry about your friend."

He blinked an acknowledgement before turning to his team mates. "Let's get out of here," he ordered.

"Can you check the case?" Ava asked, climbing in.

He nodded, putting the silver suitcase by his feet.

"Right then." Ava turned to face the group. "As there are no prisoners to drop off at Sennelager, let's scan the case for explosives, then get it airborne and straight back to London."

---— ◆ —---

Chapter 7

Chelobityeva District
Moscow
Russian Federation

THE SNUG-FITTING RUBBER earbuds were sending growling thrash metal blastbeats deep into Nikolay's auditory canals.

He typed quickly, embedding a path through a series of servers buried in the Deep Web, far below the internet's surface, finally emerging into obscure militant chatrooms in Toulouse and Utrecht.

He knew that the NSA would throw immense resources into tracking the origin of the video, so for fun he added an even deeper layer, taking the trail back to a technical academy in Guangzhou, South China. Finally, at the end of the chain, he mapped it to a server in Damascus.

When the *Yanki* finally unravelled it, all fingers would point to Syria, just as he had been ordered.

But what the NSA would never find was the rack under the window behind him.

He turned to look at it, smiling – four independent blade servers, each linked to a bank of stand-alone routers, in turn wired into a phone switcher cycling between a cluster of pay-as-you-go numbers.

The gear was new. State of the art. He particularly liked the part of the deal allowing him to keep it all afterwards.

When he was done, he would only leave it running for two hours. That would be plenty of time for the video to be copied onto mirror sites by its adoring fans, shared on social media, and downloaded onto thousands of smart phones, where it could be passed around freely.

Nothing would point back to him.

He looked out of the dirt-caked window at the crumbling red brick buildings around him. This part of town was a decaying shell, but it served his purpose perfectly.

He had leased the office in the former factory three days earlier. The area was never going to attract the glitzy businesses of Tverskaya Street. Instead, dozens of anonymous corporations came and went in the decrepit building every year, and that was just fine.

Nikolay's company, Volga Trading Solutions, did not exist, of course, except in the online register of the Russian Federal Tax Service. Hacking into their database and adding the company's name had been a lot simpler than the bureaucratic nightmare of actually incorporating a company in modern Russia.

Besides, he only needed the company for a few days, and it would take the tax authorities a lot longer than that to find his alteration to their digital records.

The building's dumpy leasing manager had made a copy of Nikolay's forged electronic ID, scrutinized his shiny new business card, checked the tax register, pocketed the eighty thousand Roubles deposit and first month's rent, and given him the keys.

Easy.

He was not planning on staying around. The manager would soon find the office empty, and simply strike Volga Trading Solutions off his list, before leasing the pokey room to someone else.

As he drummed along nervously to the music on the stained beige plastic desk, he finally saw the confirmation he had been waiting for flash up onto his laptop screen.

A wave of elation surged through him.

He had done it!

The White House's IT security was formidable.

But he was in.

He did not call himself 'Apollo' for nothing. Although the ancient Greek god was widely worshipped as the sun and as the patron of music and prophecy, he was also famed for his plague-tipped arrows.

Nikolay had planned it carefully.

There was almost no way to beat Washington's mainframe security structure. But people, on the other hand, were something else. They disobeyed rules all the time.

It had taken less than half a day to find out the e-mail addresses of eighteen ordinary White House employees: maintenance, secretaries, catering, and other non-political staff. Then he had the slightly more laborious task of mining personal information on each of them, like the names of friends, children, and pets. Fortunately, the internet was one big register of exactly such details.

The rest was kindergarten stuff. Hack one of their friends' e-mail accounts, then send the target an e-mail from the friend attaching what promised to be photograph of a child or pet.

Despite all the warnings people endlessly received about cybersecurity, there was always someone who clicked, even when the e-mail was flagged up as potentially dangerous.

On this occasion it was Jake Buckner, one of the White House's head groundsmen, who was keen to see a picture of his beloved white boxer.

Nikolay smiled. They had learned nothing since the President's e-mails had been hacked in 2014. Also by a Russian.

The moment after Jake clicked on the attachment, Nikolay's code went live in the White House's system, seeping into its petabytes of ones and zeros, allowing him to open up a temporary backdoor disguised as an SSL connection. From there, he eventually found his way to the White House's public website.

Timing was everything. The longer he remained trespassing, the more likely he was to be discovered.

Typing fast, he queued the subroutines, then hit the worn Enter button, simultaneously publishing the film on the servers in Toulouse and Utrecht, and redirecting the front page of the White House's public website to them.

In a final step, he released the social media packet he had prepared, sharing the film simultaneously via a host of anonymous and sockpuppet accounts on the Dark Net, YouTube, Twitter, Facebook, Tumblr, Instagram, and a range of other social and P2P media.

The servers behind him immediately kicked into gear, propagating the film around the internet, sending its message of fear and hate global, switching phone lines and IP addresses every ten seconds, bouncing the messages across six continents.

Within minutes, it would be flying between the accounts of thousands of the world's jihadi sympathizers. In twelve hours, it would be everywhere.

He sat back and picked up a fresh pack of cigarettes, tearing the foil on the top of the soft packet, and tapping one out into his hand.

He swivelled round to look out of the smeary window at the cloud-covered sky.

Right now, anyone logging onto the White House's website would see a desert-based jihadi fighter, complete with balaclava, black-and-white-checked scarf, and AK-47, vowing to bring oceans of blood to the *kuffar* of America.

Nikolay had thought the film was very slick from the moment the contact had given it to him. He had not needed to do much beyond scrambling the insurgent's voice to make it more threatening, and distorting his eyes to defeat any retinal or iris identification.

The Middle East was not Nikolay's fight. But he was being paid very handsomely, and that was the best ideology he knew.

He lit the cigarette and inhaled slowly, savouring the sensation of the nicotine hitting his bloodstream as the pummelling music in his ears rose in a crescendo.

What he did not know was that, at the same moment as he was taking on the White House for his unknown masters, others in Moscow that morning were uploading different jihadi films to other websites, while yet more were unleashing a barrage of social media support from 'lone wolf' militants, all threatening to bring the war directly to American soil.

CHAPTER 8

British Museum
Bloomsbury
London WC1
England
The United Kingdom

THE BASEMENT OF the British Museum was a rabbit warren of ultra-hi-tech laboratories.

Standing in the largest, in its bright lights and purified air, Ava clicked open the catches of the silver case, and thought back over the last few hours.

After refuelling the helicopter in Germany, the team had dropped her and Mary at the large central London barracks of 21 SAS, before returning to base at Credenhill in the Welsh Marches.

Ava was impressed that MI13 had been able to mobilize the Regiment from Hereford at such short notice. Whatever cover Swinton and his colleagues operated inside the Ministry of Defence, they clearly had teeth and could get things done fast. It made a pleasant change from all the paperwork at MI6.

Mary's presence, on the other hand, was still something of a mystery.

Ava could see why the Vatican wanted to stay close to the Shroud. After all, the pope had only been given the relic in 1983, and it would hardly look good if the Church lost it within several decades – especially after the House of Savoy had safeguarded it for over four hundred years. So Vatican involvement made sense. But, so far, Ava had no idea how Mary came to be sitting in an SAS helicopter on an active operation, how she was connected to MI13, or where she had learned to shoot like that. None of it fitted any mental picture she had of the Vatican.

Shortly before landing, Ava had explained to Mary that they needed to get the linen back to the Museum in order to run some basic tests to see if it really was the Turin Shroud.

After a fraught hour of telephone tag, Mary confirmed that the Vatican was happy for the British Museum to examine the cloth and check its condition.

Now in the laboratory, Ava rested her hand on the case's lid, enjoying the cool sensation of the metal. One of the SAS troopers had scanned it for explosives before they took off from Nuremberg, so she was not worried about nasty surprises.

Instead, her heart was beating a little more quickly than usual as she wondered what she was going to find inside.

Would it be the real Shroud? Or did the Church only keep a replica on display in Turin, with the genuine relic safe in a vault deep under the Vatican, or in a secure storage facility beneath the Alps?

She exhaled deeply.

She was about to find out.

Lifting the lid, she peered down into the case.

There, wrapped in acid-free paper, was a neatly folded section of ivory-coloured linen.

She slipped on a white lab coat and a fresh pair of sterile latex gloves, and carefully removed the cloth from its wrapping, laying it out fully on a sterilized glass workbench.

On the other side of the lab, Mary was connecting her mobile phone to the small plastic handheld unit she had pressed up against the Russian soldier's phone back in Nuremberg.

Ava watched her for a moment, noting that Mary's manner was relaxed and confident. She had not really had a chance to look carefully at her before. She had dark hair cut fairly short around a broad face with wide cheekbones. Ava guessed she was in her early thirties.

Turning back to the examination bench, Ava flipped on the powerful lighting underneath it, and stood back to look at the illuminated length of linen.

She noted the scorch-marked holes, the fine herringbone weave, and the world-famous images.

As she took it all in, she felt a familiar sensation building – the thrill of investigating an unknown object, of uncovering its secrets, teasing out its clues, and establishing its history.

The Shroud had always fascinated her. Despite the fact many of her colleagues treated it as a subject for the tin-foil hat brigade, she had long been intrigued by a number of puzzling and unanswered questions it raised.

And here it was. In her laboratory.

She walked over to the computer terminal beside the workbench, and sat down in front of its two large monitors.

Typing quickly, she activated a ceiling-mounted high-definition camera above the workbench, and began to take a series of images.

The first ones were of the whole cloth, and clearly showed the two parallel tracks of irregular triangular burn holes running the length of the fabric. These, she knew, had been caused in Chambéry, in the early 1500s, before the Shroud had been moved to Turin. A fire had broken out in the chapel where it was kept, and molten drops of the protective silver reliquary case had burned right through the fragile linen. Miraculously, though, the damage had not touched the two extraordinary life-size images – the front and back of a man – which showed up on the cloth as faint sepia smudges.

"It's not very clear, is it?" Mary was peering over Ava's shoulder. "I expected the image to be … sharper."

Ava typed quickly, and the image of the Shroud on the main monitor suddenly transformed into a photographic negative.

Mary exhaled sharply as the indistinct brown shadows transformed into striking sharp white-on-black images of a gaunt fork-bearded and pony-tailed man.

"An Italian lawyer, Secundo Pia, took the first photographs of the Shroud in 1898." Ava zoomed in on the image of the bruised face. "This is pretty much exactly what he saw on the negatives in his darkroom. He was amazed, and made them public. No one had ever seen the Shroud like this before. It became world famous overnight."

Mary peered at the screen. "And how come you know about it?"

"My speciality is the ancient Middle East and its religions," Ava flicked to the next image, "which covers most Judeo-Christian religious artefacts – and they don't get much more famous than this one."

She moved a joystick, repositioning the ceiling camera to take close-up shots of individual sections of the linen. "We often get questions about it in my department, especially given our role in the radiocarbon dating."

"You dated it?" Mary looked impressed.

Ava shook her head. "Before my time. In 1988 the Vatican asked the Museum to organize carbon dating. So we set it up with labs in Oxford, Zurich, and Arizona. Each one was given a small square of the Shroud to test to destruction. Completely independently of each other, they came up with a date range of AD 1260 to 1390."

Mary was still behind her. "But don't lots of people say the test was flawed? That the samples were taken from the edge of the cloth, which may have been repaired in the past with newer linen?"

"I wouldn't say lots of people." Ava measured off the size of the man against the markers on the bench. They showed he was around five feet seven inches tall. She switched to a microscope camera. "But you're right. Not everyone accepts the carbon dating."

Mary continued to peer at the image.

"If you're with the Church," Ava spun the chair round to face Mary, "then do you believe the Shroud is the actual burial cloth of Jesus?"

Mary shrugged. "The Vatican has no official line. And anyway, even if it did, who's to say I'd follow it? Gregor Mendel, the biologist who pioneered genetics, was a Catholic priest. So was Georges Lemaître, the professor of physics who invented the Big Bang theory. We don't all turn our rational brains off the moment someone lights some incense." She walked around to the other side of the workbench. "What else do you know about the Shroud? Has anyone ever examined it scientifically?"

Ava clicked a key to focus the macro camera. "The only known scientific examination was in 1978. The team was made up of scientists from NASA, the US Air Force Weapons lab, Los Alamos nuclear lab, several major defence and IT contractors, and even medical and oceanographic computer imaging organizations. They performed a wide range of tests with state-of-the-art equipment: photography, microscopy, X-ray fluorescence, spectrophotometry, thermography, UV reflectance, and a battery of others. They analysed the data for three years, and reported back in 1981."

"Go on." Mary was bending low over the linen, peering at it closely.

"They concluded that the Shroud depicts a man who was tortured, and then crucified, in the same way as the Bible describes the execution of Jesus."

Mary straightened up. "That's not really an answer, though, is it?"

Ava walked over and joined her at the workbench.

"Look." Ava pointed to the hundreds of rust-coloured stains. "These are blood. They show up white on the photographic negative. The team found that they contain biological material – haemoglobin and albumin."

She pointed to the small bloody patches on the front and back images of the head. "For example, this ring of stains suggests sharp punctures to the forehead, side, and back of the scalp."

Mary's eyes narrowed as she focused on the marks, nodding. "The crown of thorns."

Ava pointed to the man's back. "And there are over a hundred blood-stains, shaped like small dumbbells, running from the shoulders all the way to the lower back, and then down the back of the thighs and calves."

Mary followed where Ava was indicating.

"The number, pattern, and direction of the wounds are consistent with whipping, or scourging, with a Roman *flagrum* – a type of flail whip. In this case, the leather thongs seem to have been tipped with sharp dumb-bell-shaped metal ends."

Mary blanched.

"And here." Ava pointed to a large pool of brown staining on the left of the sheet. "This is the man's right side, as the Shroud imprint is obviously in reverse. As you probably recall, the Bible says that the Romans didn't break Jesus's legs, which they usually did to speed up death … "

"But seeing he was already dead, pierced his side with a spear." Mary finished the sentence.

"And here," Ava pointed to the man's left hand, lying over the right one, "is a bloody wound, consistent with nailing."

Mary looked at it, then down at the man's feet, where there was an equally visible mark from a nail through the right foot.

Ava swung a wall-mounted magnifying lens and light down over the Shroud. She motioned Mary to look through it. "Do you see the direction of the blood flow?"

Mary peered closely through the large lens.

"Autopsy experts say that the amount and direction of the blood trickles are precisely consistent with what they would expect from a newly dead and washed body lying on its back. As you can imagine, a living body bleeds much more. This is supported by most pathology experts, who say that the body shows signs of rigor mortis."

Mary looked at Ava in surprise. "You're saying you believe this is the genuine burial shroud of Jesus?"

Ava shook her head. "In my opinion? This is medieval art. Incredibly detailed and immensely skilled. We'd struggle to do it today."

Mary walked back over to the computer and peered at the negative image. "Would it really be that hard to make it? With all our modern technology?"

Ava focused a pair of bright lights on the linen. "The injuries are relatively straightforward." She leant over the bench with a piece of laboratory tape, laying the sticky surface onto a corner of the cloth, then peeling it off carefully. "Artists down the centuries have studied and even dissected bodies. In medieval times, a determined artist would have been able to get hold of a fresh corpse, especially when the Black Death was decimating Europe, which coincides with the Shroud's first appearance. All he had to do was inflict the wounds the Bible described, then observe."

Mary followed Ava to the computer terminal, where Ava pulled up one of the microscope photographs.

"The problem," she continued, "is here." She magnified the photograph until the individual cylindrical fibres of the Shroud filled the screen. "Do you see how the blood soaks through and around the fibres? Just like you'd expect if someone bled onto a piece of linen which absorbed the blood?"

Mary nodded.

"Well, now look at the image of the body." She switched to a close-up of the fibres bearing the sepia-brown image.

Mary peered at the screen. 'I don't see anything."

"Exactly." Ava zoomed out to show the surface of the cloth, then in again. "The 1978 team couldn't find any paint, stain, pigment, dye, or anything that could account for the image of the crucified man. As you can see, the cloth hasn't absorbed any liquid to form the image. The team concluded that it was as if just the very top level of the fibre's individual fibrils – no more than a few microns – was somehow oxidized and dehydrated, lightly changing its colour."

Mary looked baffled. "How would someone do that? Early photography?"

Ava shrugged. "That's the mystery. No one knows. But it's not pho-tography. Or paint. The team found no residues of chemicals, spices, oils, or – apart from the blood – organic traces produced by living or dead humans. The closest anyone has been able to get is with heat and acid. A large number of fans – mainly scientists and artists – have tried to reproduce the physical properties of the image, but no one has even come close to mirroring all its features."

"Seriously?" Mary looked sceptical. "You're saying a medieval artist used a technique more sophisticated than anything known to modern science?"

Ava sat down. "I'm sure someone could work it out if they got to examine and test the cloth really thoroughly. Just because we don't understand something at the moment doesn't automatically make it a miracle, even if some of its features seem inexplicable."

Ava began dragging the images into a folder. "For instance, if you feed an ordinary photograph into an isometric projector – which uses algorithms to map brightness and give an approximation of a three-di-mensional image – the projection it produces is very distorted, because photos don't contain enough visual data of depth and proportion. How-ever, if you feed in a picture of the Shroud's head, the projector's image comes out as a fully recognizable three-dimensional human face."

Mary frowned. "But how's that even possible?"

"I don't know," Ava admitted, "although I'm pretty convinced it's medieval. The carbon dating gives a range of AD 1260 to 1390, and the first time the Shroud appears in history is in a small village in France around AD 1355, which fits exactly. Anyway," she enlarged an image of the Shroud's head on the screen, "if you forget everything, and just focus on the face – on those long square features – any art historian will say it's medieval. It looks exactly like all those statues of imposing biblical prophets on medieval cathedrals."

Mary stared at it, and smiled. "I guess it does. But if the carbon dating's wrong and the Shroud is much older, how come no one knew about it until the 1300s. Surely it would've been one of the most famous objects in early Christendom?"

Ava nodded. "As I say: it's almost certainly fourteenth-century. In fact, a few years after it was exhibited in France in 1350, the local bishop con-ducted an inquiry, and then announced that he'd found the artist who 'cunningly painted' it."

Mary turned, confused. "But you just said it wasn't painted?"

Ava flicked off the screen. "There's a lot about the Shroud we just don't know." She turned off the lights under the workbench. "Anyway, we'd need to carry out a lot more tests to be a hundred per cent certain, but from what I can tell today, this is the same Shroud from Turin that was examined by the American team in 1978, and there's no obvious sign of any damage having been done to it in the last fifteen hours."

"Then I need to get it back to Turin." Mary pulled out her phone. "They'll close off the chapel for maintenance while they mend the case. The cloth needs to be back in place before anyone suspects it's gone."

"You might consider a few more alarms and some independent cameras," Ava suggested. "The linen is fragile, at least seven hundred years old, worth an astronomical price on the black market, and needs a lot more protection than it had yesterday."

Mary's phone buzzed, and she glanced down and scrolled through the incoming message. "While we're tackling difficult questions, here's one for you. Why would the Russian team that stole it have been led by Major Yakov Lunev, a seasoned Spetsnaz Special Forces officer?"

Ava tried to hide her incredulity. "Are you seriously getting this level of detail from the Vatican?" She found it difficult to keep the surprise from her face. "What exactly is Vatican Liaison?"

Mary nodded distractedly. "I sent a dump of data from his phone back to Rome. Apparently Lunev reports to the GRU."

Ava frowned.

Russian military intelligence?

She knew all about them. Whole teams at MI5 and MI6 tracked the GRU day and night. They were less well known to the public than the KGB – now renamed the FSB – but were older, bigger, and far more active.

They were also a lot more dangerous.

What did the GRU want with the Shroud?

"Lunev's phone shows a large number of calls to a big dacha on the Black Sea. It's owned by an oil oligarch named Oleg Antonevich Durov, who's heavily connected in the Kremlin."

Ava's mind was whirring.

The Kremlin?

She had assumed the heist was arranged by one of Russia's organized crime gangs employing a group of soldiers moonlighting on the black market. But if the Kremlin was involved, that cast a whole different light on it. The modern Kremlin was an exceptionally sophisticated and dangerous organization.

"And," Mary looked up from her phone at Ava, "Major Lunev is probably now well on his way back to Moscow. He knows exactly what you and I look like, and it won't take the Kremlin long to realize that we were with the SAS team for a reason, and that we almost certainly now have the Shroud."

Ava turned to look at the image of the mutilated body laid out on the bench.

If Mary was right, it looked like she could expect a visit from a Russian team before too long.

—————— • ◆ • ——————

CHAPTER 9

The West Wing
The White House
1600 Pennsylvania Avenue
Washington DC
The United States of America

RICHARD EASTON HAD occupied the large comfortable corner office for more years than he could remember. In that time, he had made it entirely his, bringing in his own furniture, and filling the dark mahogany bookcases with treasures from his personal library.

If he was honest with himself, most of it was for show – the Harvard yearbooks, constitutional histories of the US, and bound volumes of Supreme Court judgements. There was even a small section on biographies of the sporting greats. People who came to his office liked seeing that sort of thing.

But the only area that really interested him was tucked away in the corner, where few people looked. It featured volumes on the political histories of the world's great nations – the United States, the United Kingdom, France, Germany, Russia, Spain, Portugal. He had recently added a shelf on China and India: the two economic areas to watch. But the books that really fascinated him – that he pulled down when it was late and no one was around – were on the shelf about Israel. They covered everything from the Hebrews' earliest wanderings, all the way up to the modern military geopolitics of the Near East.

His interest was not in Judaism as a religion. He was of pure Anglo-Saxon descent, and his family had been pillars of the Presbyterian Church for generations. What enthralled him were the prophecies in the Book, and how they were all turning out to be true.

He walked over to the deep Chesterfield armchair, and picked up the crystal carafe from the elegant side table. He poured himself a glass of chilled water, savouring the sound of the ice crackling in the heavy leaded glass.

Loosening his tie, he took up a large leather-bound book from the shelf beside the table, and eased himself into the heavily padded chair.

It had been a long day overseeing National Security Council committees. Relaxing now, he opened the book's thick covers on his knees, and returned to the page he had marked with the purple ribbon.

The archaic print would have been challenging for most people to read, but he had long ago taught himself to understand its cramped spiky columns.

It was, he knew, an immensely valuable volume – one of the earliest, of which there were only a few hundred left. Not an original from 1611, or one of the blasphemous 1631 reprints with the outrageous commandment, 'Thou shalt commit adultery'. No. This one was the pure and uncorrupted word of God.

The ancient book had come down through the male line in his family, solemnly entrusted from father to son, having been brought from England by a direct ancestor – one of the earliest settlers aboard the Mayflower.

He did not draw attention to the treasure publicly. In fact, no one had ever even noticed it on his shelves. The White House was a busy place, and few people had time for his old books.

That suited him just fine. He had no desire to share his innermost thoughts with them anyway.

They would know soon enough.

He looked down at the dense columns of text, seeking the line that always filled his heart with joy.

𝔄𝔫𝔡 𝔍 𝔰𝔞𝔴 𝔞 𝔫𝔢𝔴 𝔥𝔢𝔞𝔲𝔢𝔫, 𝔞𝔫𝔡 𝔞 𝔫𝔢𝔴 𝔢𝔞𝔯𝔱𝔥 : 𝔣𝔬𝔯 𝔱𝔥𝔢 𝔣𝔦𝔯𝔰𝔱 𝔥𝔢𝔞𝔲𝔢𝔫, 𝔞𝔫𝔡 𝔱𝔥𝔢 𝔣𝔦𝔯𝔰𝔱 𝔢𝔞𝔯𝔱𝔥 𝔴𝔢𝔯𝔢 𝔭𝔞𝔰𝔰𝔢𝔡 𝔞𝔴𝔞𝔶.

It was all here, he knew, in the Apocalypse.

It had all been foretold by John, two thousand years ago, on the Greek island of Patmos.

His eyes ran down the page.

𝔄𝔫𝔡 𝔍 𝔰𝔞𝔴 𝔞𝔫𝔬𝔱𝔥𝔢𝔯 𝔄𝔫𝔤𝔢𝔩 𝔞𝔰𝔠𝔢𝔫𝔡𝔦𝔫𝔤 𝔣𝔯𝔬𝔪 𝔱𝔥𝔢 𝔈𝔞𝔰𝔱, 𝔥𝔞𝔲𝔦𝔫𝔤 𝔱𝔥𝔢 𝔰𝔢𝔞𝔩𝔢 𝔬𝔣 𝔱𝔥𝔢 𝔩𝔦𝔲𝔦𝔫𝔤 𝔊𝔬𝔡 : 𝔞𝔫𝔡 𝔥𝔢 𝔠𝔯𝔦𝔢𝔡 𝔴𝔦𝔱𝔥 𝔞 𝔩𝔬𝔲𝔡 𝔳𝔬𝔦𝔠𝔢 𝔱𝔬 𝔱𝔥𝔢 𝔣𝔬𝔲𝔯𝔢 𝔄𝔫𝔤𝔢𝔩𝔰 𝔱𝔬 𝔴𝔥𝔬𝔪 𝔦𝔱 𝔴𝔞𝔰 𝔤𝔦𝔲𝔢𝔫 𝔱𝔬 𝔥𝔲𝔯𝔱 𝔱𝔥𝔢 𝔢𝔞𝔯𝔱𝔥 𝔞𝔫𝔡 𝔱𝔥𝔢 𝔰𝔢𝔞, 𝔖𝔞𝔶𝔦𝔫𝔤, 𝔥𝔲𝔯𝔱 𝔫𝔬𝔱 𝔱𝔥𝔢 𝔢𝔞𝔯𝔱𝔥, 𝔫𝔢𝔦𝔱𝔥𝔢𝔯 𝔱𝔥𝔢 𝔰𝔢𝔞, 𝔫𝔬𝔯 𝔱𝔥𝔢 𝔱𝔯𝔢𝔢𝔰, 𝔱𝔦𝔩𝔩 𝔴𝔢𝔢 𝔥𝔞𝔲𝔢 𝔰𝔢𝔞𝔩𝔢𝔡 𝔱𝔥𝔢 𝔰𝔢𝔯𝔲𝔞𝔫𝔱𝔰 𝔬𝔣 𝔬𝔲𝔯 𝔊𝔬𝔡 𝔦𝔫 𝔱𝔥𝔢𝔦𝔯 𝔣𝔬𝔯𝔢𝔥𝔢𝔞𝔡𝔰. 𝔄𝔫𝔡 𝔍 𝔥𝔢𝔞𝔯𝔡 𝔱𝔥𝔢 𝔫𝔲𝔪𝔟𝔢𝔯 𝔬𝔣 𝔱𝔥𝔢𝔪 𝔴𝔥𝔦𝔠𝔥 𝔴𝔢𝔯𝔢 𝔰𝔢𝔞𝔩𝔢𝔡 : 𝔞𝔫𝔡 𝔱𝔥𝔢𝔯𝔢 𝔴𝔢𝔯𝔢 𝔰𝔢𝔞𝔩𝔢𝔡 𝔞𝔫 𝔥𝔲𝔫𝔡𝔯𝔢𝔱𝔥 𝔞𝔫𝔡 𝔣𝔬𝔲𝔯𝔱𝔶 𝔞𝔫𝔡 𝔣𝔬𝔲𝔯𝔢 𝔱𝔥𝔬𝔲𝔰𝔞𝔫𝔡.

He stared at the ancient words, hope and excitement surging.

He knew what was to come.

He read on.

The moon became as blood ; and the stars of heauen fell unto the earth.

He smiled.

It would not be long before it came to pass.

Things had already begun.

The offices around him were buzzing with outrage and alarm about the jihadi video that had been uploaded onto the front page of the White House's website.

Questions were already being asked at the highest level about how this could have happened. There was talk of coordinating a military response to the unprecedented attack on the dignity of the President. Meanwhile, on social media, a slew of jihadist videos was going viral around the world, inspiring groups and individuals to acts that were once unthinkable.

Something was definitely happening.

It was not as shocking as all that, Easton smiled to himself. Anyone who had read the Bible knew that there had to be the war of the Antichrist before there could be the Rapture and salvation.

DAY TWO

—————————— ⋅ ◆ ⋅ ——————————

CHAPTER 10

British Museum
Bloomsbury
London WC1
England
The United Kingdom

"THE GRU ARE nasty," he grimaced. "You don't want to get mixed up with them."

Ava looked over at the man standing on the other side of the most famous piece of granite in the world. He had not changed in the three years since they had first met at the US Central Command military base in Qatar.

As Swinton had mentioned in her kitchen, the US Army and Defence Intelligence Agency had called her in, and asked her to assist with an African militia holding what they claimed was the Ark of the Covenant. In no time, she had ended up in a vortex of extremism and violence – a world beyond anything she had previously experienced.

Ferguson had been an MI6 odd-job man – an ex-soldier, helping out the intelligence services. Throughout the operation, he had stayed by her side. He had not been obliged to. But he did. And despite her inclination to work alone, she had been surprised to find his help – and his companionship – very welcome.

When it was all over, he had returned to his former profession and got a job in Baghdad as an architect, where they had become close friends. But, before she knew it, the deteriorating security situation in Iraq had ended her museum contract in Baghdad, and she had been summoned back to London.

Ferguson had eventually made his way home to London, too. But whatever might have happened between them never did. She sensed he was disappointed and still slightly hopeful, but the moment had passed.

"Honestly," he was looking serious. "The GRU are trouble you can do without."

"Any idea why they might be interested in antiquities?" she asked.

He shook his head. "Assassinations and unpleasant interrogations are more their line."

She sank back into thought, staring down at the angled slab of pink-streaked granite.

"We've got over eight million objects here in the Museum, but not a single one about Jesus that dates from his lifetime."

"Does any museum?" He peered low over the three scripts incised into the ancient stone, comparing the Egyptian hieroglyphics, Egyptian demotic, and Greek.

She shook her head. "Not unless we're all mistaken about the piece of ancient linen I've got in the lab downstairs."

He glanced up, a dubious expression on his face. "I hadn't put you down as a Shroudie?"

"That's not quite what I mean." She tapped the Rosetta Stone, tracing the Greek writing with her finger. "Take this. It's a proclamation about a child king called Ptolemy V Epiphanes. He was Cleopatra's great-great-grandfather. Like other pharaohs, he was worshipped as a living god. This stone is one of the most famous objects in the world. And yet, Ptolemy V is hardly a household name. Jesus, on the other hand – another living god – was born only a few hundred years after Ptolemy, and currently has over two billion living followers. But he left no stones like this. In fact, there's no archaeological proof he ever even existed."

"Unless the Shroud is real."

The voice came from behind Ava.

She turned around, surprised by the sudden intrusion.

It was Swinton.

He nodded a tired greeting. "So did our Russian friends have the Shroud from the cathedral?"

"It looks like it, from what I can tell." Ava nodded. "Mary's taking it back to Turin tonight."

Swinton grunted, then pulled a large smartphone from his pocket. He swiped it, bringing up a photograph, which he held out for Ava to see.

"This is the Russian oligarch, Oleg Antonevich Durov." He was speaking more quietly now. "We verified the information Mary got off Lunev's phone. It all checks out."

Ava gazed down at the screen.

The man looked in his mid-forties. Intelligent blue eyes shone out from a broad face with high Slavic cheekbones and long brown hair swept back in a ponytail. There was something keenly knowing about his gaze. Charismatic, even.

"From what little we know," Swinton continued, "even by the low standards of Kremlin gangsters, he's in a league of his own. Not a friendly fellow. After the farce in Nuremberg, it's possible he knows who you are. So if you see him or his men, take the threat seriously."

"Where is he now?" She stared at the face, burning it into her memory. "His dacha on the Black Sea?"

Swinton shook his head. "Closer to home. He's here, opening an exhibition on cultural art this evening at the Russian Embassy."

Ava's jaw tightened.

Ever since Swinton had first shown her the footage from Turin cathedral, she had been wrestling with the same thought, returning to it again and again.

What on earth did the Russians want with the Turin Shroud?

Now she knew the Kremlin was involved, the question bothered her even more.

It was exactly the sort of problem that got under her skin – a collision of intelligence work and archaeology.

And now Durov was in London.

"Send me," she announced.

Swinton clicked the phone off, shaking his head. "Handling a man like Durov needs detailed regional expertise. Kremlinology is a minefield. We're putting our Russia desk onto it."

Ava thought she detected a note of hostility in his voice.

Or was it fear?

She continued. "Whatever this is about," a new hardness entered her voice, "it's clearly not regular Kremlin intrigue. The highest circles in Moscow now embrace Orthodox Christianity as a badge of social elitism. Whoever runs with this assignment needs to understand ancient Christianity, the Orthodox Church, and the Shroud – I do."

Swinton put the phone back in his pocket. "I'm sorry, Dr Curzon. This follow up is not for you. But we'll call if we need anything." His tone left no doubt that this was the end of the conversation. "Meanwhile, be vigilant."

With that, he turned and was gone.

Ava looked back down at the inscription on the Rosetta Stone. Its elusive secret had not been unlocked until Thomas Young realized that the hieroglyphs run in the direction the animals face, and the pictures are not words, but a mixture of letters and sounds. With those two small revelations, the whole world of ancient Egyptian writing had been cracked open, and the carvings on hundreds of temples and sculptures became readable for the first time in a millennium and a half.

Things could seem so inexplicable, she reflected. But then, with the smallest insight, all could suddenly become clear.

"Come on then." She shot a glance over at Ferguson. "No time like the present. We need to do some homework."

"Here we go." He shook his head and smiled as he followed her out of the Museum and into the staff carpark. "I must've misheard when he said 'case closed'."

Ava passed a row of cars, and stopped in front of a long low vintage motorcycle.

She climbed onto the old-fashioned brown leather triangular seat – more like one for an old bicycle than a motorbike – and kicked the starter.

Ferguson sat down on the passenger cushion mounted on the glossy black mudguard.

"We need to make a few calls to brush up on Russian art," she shouted over the noise of the engine. "First up: Pushkin House. Then we've got an important exhibition to get to tonight."

CHAPTER II

Camp Filon
The Golan Heights
Israeli-Occupied Syria

THE DUST-CAKED *ACHZARIT* heavy armoured personnel carrier rumbled back towards base. From its top hatch, the gunner surveyed the surroundings through the sights on its machine gun.

Built on a modified Soviet T-54/T-55 tank chassis, and armed with a state-of-the-art remote-control weapons system, its name, 'Cruel', was not an idle boast.

In the back, Private Danny Aronov sat on the hard metal seat, barely noticing the vehicle's lumbering progress. It was sweltering inside the metal hulk, and he was dripping with sweat under the heavy Kevlar body armour and helmet.

He stared from behind his cheap knockoff Raybans at his three platoon mates.

He had known this would be a difficult two and a half years. His friends had warned him that military service was going to be physically tough. He had not minded that. He had got into shape, and looked forward to serving his country.

What he had not been prepared for was the other guys in his artillery section.

They were rich kids with places at top universities, endlessly rubbing his less privileged background in his face. They weren't subtle about it either. They made him feel small. Like dirt.

He grimaced.

They had a surprise coming.

He might not be going on to a flash education abroad, but he did know the history of his people. Where they had come from. Their struggles. The hostility. He knew how hard they had fought.

And he knew what was written.

What did Israel even mean for them, he wondered? Was it just another club to get the badge from, before heading off to boardroom tables?

Well, they were soon going to wish they had read the Scriptures, like he had.

Then they would see who was laughing.

The First Sergeant in charge of them, Gilad, was a good guy. Normal. But he could not see everything that happened. And there was no way Danny was going to grass up the others.

He was not afraid of them though.

In fact, he had nothing but contempt for them.

And today would be a big day.

There was a reckoning coming.

Anyone who looked around knew it. Even the Christians. Not that he was one of those Messianic Jews who followed Jesus. He pitied them. Jesus was obviously not the *Moshiach*. He had not unified the tribes, or ushered in a Messianic age of peace. Nevertheless, the early Christians had listened to the wise ones, and they had heard the warnings.

As had he.

There were many ancient prophecies of the End Times in the *Nevi'im* and *Ketuvim*, if you knew where to look. The seers like Isaiah, Jeremiah, Ezekiel, Joel, and Zechariah had spoken plainly. And the mighty Daniel – after whom Danny had been named – had been gifted the greatest vision of all: of a reckoning, justice, and salvation.

Danny knew the verses off by heart:

As I looked on, Thrones were set in place, And the Ancient of Days took His seat. His garment was white like snow, and the hair of His head was like lamb's wool. His throne was tongues of flame; Its wheels were blazing fire. A river of fire streamed forth before Him; Thousands upon thousands served him; Myriads upon myriads attended Him; The court sat and the books were opened.

The armoured personnel carrier's eight hundred and fifty horsepower engine grunted, bringing Danny back to the present as the vehicle began mounting the steep incline up to the blast walls of the barracks.

He blinked slowly, focusing himself.

He knew exactly what he was going to do.

When the thick rear door finally popped open, he climbed out of its sweaty soupy air, hauling his M4A1 and backpack into the dusty Israeli sunshine, pulling off his helmet, and feeling the mountain wind cool his head.

In the distance, he could see Mount Hermon, where the Watcher angels had descended to Earth in the book of Enoch. Its snow-capped peak shone brightly in the summer sun, filling him with confidence. He breathed in the cool air, and headed directly for the Quartermaster's cage, leaving the others joking by the vehicle.

The Master Sergeant grunted as Danny placed the carbine, magazines, and pair of fragmentation grenades onto the counter.

"Flashbang?" the older man muttered, pulling the items through a hatch in the grille, then placing them on a shelf behind him.

"Discharged," Danny lied. "Training."

"Then bring me the form." The quartermaster shot him a stern look. "Before I have to remind you."

"No problem." Danny nodded, then headed back out into the sunshine with his backpack slung over his shoulder.

Inside it, the M84 stun grenade nestled snugly beside his field dressings – ready to play its role in history.

--- ◆ ---

CHAPTER 12

Embassy of the Russian Federation
6–7 Kensington Palace Gardens
Holland Park
London W8
England
The United Kingdom

EVEN WITHOUT THE flags outside, Ava had no problem identifying the Russian Embassy.

A line of limousines was pulling up in front of numbers six to seven, dropping off a succession of expensively attired men accompanied by their jewel-draped wives and mistresses.

Ava had seen from the embassy's website that the art exhibition was going to be a grand occasion, so had dressed accordingly – swapping her usual casual clothes for a long dark dress, adding some discreet gold jewellery which picked up the colour in her eyes, and doing her best to pile up her hair. Ferguson had put on a suit and tie.

They followed the crowds up the red-carpeted steps, past the two heavily armed officers from the Metropolitan Police's SO6 diplomatic protection squad, and into the building.

"I hear the number of Russian spies operating out of the embassy is up at Cold War levels," Ferguson whispered to Ava as they entered the grand main doorway. "Forty or fifty of them monitoring the UK, while keeping an eye on the expat oligarchs who want to get as far away as possible from the Kremlin."

They approached the desk, where three formally dressed members of embassy staff were ticking off guests and handing out goodie bags with catalogues and gifts.

Ava slipped Ferguson a cream business card, and gave her own to the lady nearest her.

"We had to turn down your kind invitation because we were in New York," Ava explained, as Ferguson passed over his card. "But we got home today, earlier than expected, and thought … "

"Of course, madam," the lady answered, reading the details printed beside a large imperial eagle on Ava's business card:

MAGDALENA QUINAULT
Volkonsky Fine Arts

Ava had printed out the business cards at home before leaving, using the address and telephone number of a Berkeley Square gallery she had noticed was currently closed for refurbishments.

The lady noted down Ava's and Ferguson's assumed names, and returned the cards. "Delighted you could make it." She smiled, nodding to indicate that all was well.

As Ava and Ferguson passed through the open double doors into the main reception room, they each took a flute of champagne from the white-gloved butler tendering a silver salver of drinks to each guest.

The doors led them into a lavishly furnished reception space decorated in the style of a grand eighteenth-century drawing room. It was almost French, with rich silks and damasks, and finely carved Rococo ornamentation adorning the chairs, tables, fireplaces, and lamps.

As she looked around the room, Ava could not suppress a small intake of breath.

Large black velvet display panels had been placed at various points around the floor and against the walls. On them were hundreds of priceless treasures of Russian art. It was mesmerizing.

Discreet spotlights glinted on dozens of lavishly gilded picture frames, and a dazzling variety of precious stones shone from an array of sacred objects.

Over in the far corner, a collection of imperial Fabergé eggs glittered in a tiered display case. Ava's eyes widened – not so much at their sparkling opulence, but because she knew that only forty-three of the fifty original Fabergé eggs survived. And she was looking at half a dozen of them.

This was quite obviously a major exhibition.

At the far end of the room, a microphone stand was set up on a red-draped podium, and a striking man with long brown hair in a ponytail was moving into place behind it.

Ava did not need to wait for the introduction.

It was unmistakably Oleg Durov.

He was tall, with broad shoulders and an athletic physique: fit rather than muscular. He was dressed in the uniform of the super rich – a hand-made black suit and crisp white open-necked shirt, complemented by highly polished black shoes and an oversized leather-strapped watch.

Simple, expensive, and effective.

Ava surveyed the rest of the people in the room, and immediately spotted his bodyguards. She counted four of them – all with bulges under their left arms, and matching wires in their ears. From the way their eyes kept returning to Durov, it was clear who they were protecting.

Dotted among the crowd, she also noted other security details close by their bosses. But Durov's men were in a different league. While the others sported shaved heads and steroid-enhanced physiques, Durov's had been chosen to blend in rather than stand out. Not that they looked any less effective. She would not have classified them as friendly.

Up at the podium, Durov was now standing behind the microphone, gazing about calmly as the room fell silent.

"When the glory of ancient Rome was threatened by barbarians," he began, his voice authoritative, with a slow, slightly detached delivery, "the great emperor Constantine built a Second Rome, to the north. He named it Constantinople, and it was the most spectacular city in the empire. When it fell to Muslim jihadists a thousand years later, civilization again relocated north, creating a Third Rome – this time in Moscow. It was a natural choice. Just like Rome and Constantinople, it also had seven sacred hills. The word Caesar became Tsar in our language, and Christendom was safe once more."

There was a murmur of approval in the room.

Ferguson leaned across and whispered into Ava's ear. "How did religion become so big in Russia again so quickly, after seventy years of Soviet persecution?"

"Fashion," she replied quietly. "The top people at the Kremlin are flocking to the Church. They're seduced by its flamboyant Russianness."

She focused back on Durov's speech.

"Most of you in the West know little about my country. But you should. For many reasons. We are by far the largest nation in the world – covering around a ninth of the planet's landmass. Mother Russia spans eleven time zones, and is almost as big as the United States of America and China combined. At twelve million people, Moscow is the largest city in Europe, and half as big again as London or even New York."

There were more nods of approval.

"Russia is the biggest Christian country on the planet, with a heritage stretching back, unbroken, to Constantinople and Rome. We are the guardians of the faith – and the living soul of the West."

There were more mumblings of assent.

"Not a view you'll hear too often," Ferguson whispered again. "Tell that to the Christians sent to the Siberian gulags."

"Russia saved Christianity," Durov continued. "And in the twentieth century it saved Europe. In World War Two, Britain and the US each sacrificed around four hundred thousand people in the fight against Nazism." He paused, scanning the room. "These are big numbers. Until you learn that *Matushka Rossiya*, Mother Russia, sacrificed twenty-seven million of her children in the same struggle. That's thirty-four times more than Britons and Americans combined." His voice dropped, becoming quieter. "So don't ever tell a Russian that the Yanks and Tommies won the war. And don't ever doubt that Russians understand blood and country."

Ava shuddered. The casualty figures were numbing. And there was something else, in the way he was talking. It was as if it was about the present, not the past.

"Russia stands for stability, continuity, and tradition. We savour our precious way of life. While others lose the strength and soul that once made them great, we fight to protect ourselves against the ills of the rest of the world."

"Swinton's people will love this," Ava muttered to Ferguson. "Communism fell twenty-five years ago, and the Kremlin agenda has already moved seamlessly on to fascism."

"Then Durov's right." Ferguson nodded. "They're proper Romans.

They just need to carry around the ancient *fasces* bundles with whipping sticks and executioners' axes and all that. It's quite trendy these days. Last time I was in the US I noticed two huge *fasces* on the main wall in the House of Representatives, and on the seal of the Senate, too."

Ava leaned closer to avoid being overheard. "This isn't about old symbols as far as the Kremlin is concerned. This is real. When anyone starts preaching about the superiority of their race, country, and traditions, and at the same time sees existential threats to their way of life from outside – that's textbook fascism. Their days as communists are long gone. You've got to … "

Ava trailed off as she caught sight of a familiar figure out of the corner of her eye. She turned discreetly to check, and then looked again, not quite believing her eyes.

Mary had just entered the room.

Ava leant closer to Ferguson. "You see the woman in blue, over by the door?"

He glanced across.

"That's Mary, from Vatican Liaison."

He looked bemused. "Vatican what?"

A plan was quickly forming in Ava's mind.

Swinton had said there were not many rules in MI13, and she intended to find out if he meant it. "Look, I need to talk to Durov once he's wrapped up. Can you find out what she's doing here?"

He nodded. "It's a tough call, but I'll do my best." He smiled, straightening his tie.

Ava turned back to listen to Durov's closing words as he commended the cultural artefacts to the audience.

When the applause had died down, he stepped away from the microphone and back into the crowd, moving towards a large canvas of a featureless river meandering through bleak empty snow-covered wilds.

Ava seized her chance, walking slowly over to the painting, arriving a few moments before Durov.

As he stopped next to her, she suddenly became aware of quite how large he was – around six foot three, she guessed.

"Do you like Russian landscapes?" he asked, his voice rich with confidence.

"Not especially." She smiled, looking at the large painted icon of Mary next to it. "Sacred art is more my thing."

She carried on gazing at the icon, feeling his eyes on her.

"Sorry, your name was?"

She had his attention now.

"Quinault," she answered, turning to face him and holding out her hand. "Magdalena."

He shook it perfunctorily. His hand was large, with the texture of paper, and his eyes never left hers. They were intelligent and engaging – but there was something more there. Something chaotic. She could not quite put her finger on it.

"I'm a dealer," she continued. "Christian, Jewish, Islamic – it's all good as far as I'm concerned."

Durov frowned. It was gone in an instant, but she had seen it.

"Orthodox art is, of course, the most skilled." He announced it as a fact, rather than an opinion. There was no hint of humour in his voice.

"Well, doesn't that depend?" Ava had no idea how long he would stay talking to her before someone else approached. She needed to make her point quickly. "Some of these icons are exquisite, but they're not very well known outside Russia. Not like, for example, Michelangelo's Sistine Chapel ceiling, Hieronymus Bosch's Last Judgement, or the enigmatic Turin Shroud, which have inspired millions of people down the centuries. Wouldn't you say they're also skilful artwork?"

She smiled and took a sip of her champagne, noting that Durov's eyes narrowed a fraction.

"Although," she raised her eyebrows questioningly, "in the case of the Shroud, some people say that it once belonged to the Orthodox Church, don't they?"

He was now looking at her intently.

She pressed on, enjoying herself. "Something to do with a French crusader, I think, who saw it during the Fourth Crusade, in Constantinople, in the Orthodox Church of Our Lady Saint Mary at Blachernae."

A flicker of surprise crossed his face, then it was gone.

She had his total attention now.

She paused, waiting for his reply.

"I heard something of the sort," he answered carefully.

She forced herself to wait longer.

He was starting to engage.

She needed to take it slowly – make it feel natural. "Wasn't it known in the Orthodox East as the Mandylion, or the holy image of Edessa, or something like that?"

She could see he was unsure how to take her questioning.

"Holy images are very sacred in our tradition," he replied slowly, his eyes searching hers for any clues that the conversation had some ulterior purpose.

Was that it? Ava wondered.

Was it as simple as that?

Had he merely taken the Shroud because it was holy to his Church?

She tried another angle.

"But who knows?" She smiled. "I've also heard that the Knights Templar painted it as an image of their last Grand Master, Jacques de Molay, suffering like Jesus."

His eyes darkened. "Then they are confused, Miss Quinault." His expression was now altogether more menacing. "The *Plashchanitsa* is unique. The Templars brought it back from Constantinople after they and the barbarian crusaders sacked the city in the Fourth Crusade. When the Shroud appeared in Europe, it was owned by the de Charney family, and it is no coincidence that, fifty years earlier, the Templar knight burned alongside Grand Master Jacques de Molay was his most faithful companion, Geoffroi de Charney."

Ava pulled back.

Gone was Durov's mask of the affable businessman. His eyes were gleaming now. The hint of chaos she had noticed earlier was now plain to see.

It was a rigid fanatical belief in the unassailable correctness of his opinions.

What he was saying was wrong in almost every detail, but she had found out what she wanted to know. She had no difficulty believing he was the kind of man who thought himself justified in killing to get what he wanted.

And he knew a lot more about the Shroud than most people.

She sensed the conversation was at a tipping point. If she went in too hard now, she would lose him. But if she got it right, she might just be able to work out what his real interest in the Shroud was.

"You say the Shroud's unique," she ventured. "But it isn't really, is it? There are others – the *acheiropoieta*, or images not made by hand – like Veronica's Veil, or the cloth on which Jesus printed his face before sending it to King Abgar of Edessa. Many people don't realize, but there are maybe a dozen ancient relics around the world said to be miraculous images of Jesus."

Durov's face hardened. "These are common misconceptions, Miss Quinault."

Ava could see that he clearly did not like being contradicted. Nor did he like having the Shroud questioned.

His eyes bored into her. Then, just as suddenly as his mood had turned dark, it changed again. The menace lifted, and he reverted to the urbane cosmopolitan.

"Magdalena, if I may?" He smiled genially. "Would you care to join me for a tour of my private collection? I would be honoured to show you the error of your views."

Despite the lightness of his tone, there was an unmistakable chill in the challenge.

Her pulse quickened.

"It's just around the corner," he added. "We could slip away. No one would know."

She took a deep breath, trying to calm a rising sense of anxiety.

Was he setting a trap? A rather unsubtle one?

It was one thing fencing with him in a crowded room. But being alone with him in his home would be something else entirely.

Did he know who she was?

She was unarmed, and would be entirely at his mercy – or that of his bodyguards.

Was he perfectly aware that she had taken the Shroud?

She could hear Swinton's words echoing in her head as the adrenaline started to race in her system.

"From what little we know, even by the low standards of Kremlin gangsters, he's in a league of his own. Not a friendly fellow. After the farce in Nuremberg, it's possible he knows who you are. So if you see him or his men, take the threat seriously."

She forced herself to focus.

The fact was that none of Swinton's people were going to get as close to Durov as she was right now. No amount of expertise in Kremlinology was going to get any of his officers into a direct conversation with Durov about the Shroud. And, as things stood, Durov was their only lead in establishing why the Kremlin wanted the Shroud badly enough to have murdered for it.

Slowly, she nodded. "I would like that very much."

＊ ◆ ＊

CHAPTER 13

Kensington Palace Gardens
Holland Park
London W8
The United Kingdom

AVA STOPPED IN front of Durov's house – a large detached Italianate mansion set well back from the road.

As he had said, it was just around the corner from the embassy, on a leafy private street protected by armed police checkpoints at either end.

She had never been to the road before, but knew it by reputation.

Most famously, in World War Two, the building at numbers six to eight was 'the London Cage' – a secret facility where MI19 held and questioned Nazi prisoners. Among the most famous inmates were the twenty-one *Gestapo* men responsible for executing the fifty RAF officers who had broken out of Stalag Luft III in 'The Great Escape'.

Now, the street had become one of the most expensive and exclusive addresses in London, and behind its trees and gas lamps were the private residences of the new mega-elite.

She looked ahead, noting that the mansion's front garden was neatly landscaped, and through the upstairs windows there were chandeliers twinkling in the first floor rooms.

Even for a Russian oligarch, she mused, Durov was doing well for himself.

She had noticed Ferguson spot her leaving the embassy. He had been deeply engaged in an animated conversation with Mary, but had nevertheless seen her and Durov moving to the door.

She figured he would put two and two together.

Durov ushered her up the house's white steps, through the front door, and into a spacious marble entrance hall.

Looking about casually, she checked for surveillance cameras, but there were no signs of any. Presumably the two bodyguards who had entered before them, and the two still out on the street, were all the security he needed.

Durov was walking ahead of her, past an elegant long table, down the opulent hallway. He passed under a large ornamental archway, before arriving at a closed door. Ava followed, stopping beside him as he gently turned the brass handle and pushed the door open.

The room behind it was utterly bizarre.

It had no furniture, but was draped in thick scarlet damask silk covering the walls, windows, and ceiling. The only light inside came from a dozen or so candles fixed to the walls in a variety of assorted antique candleholders.

Durov motioned for Ava to enter.

It was hotter inside than in the hallway, but she barely noticed.

Her attention was fully locked on what was inside.

She had never seen anything like it.

Religious icons filled every square inch of wall space. But unlike an iconostasis screen in an Orthodox church – where the icons were usually arranged in neat groups – here they were hung wherever there was a space, creating a seamless mosaic of floor-to-ceiling sacred imagery.

She had never seen so many icons in one place.

Her eyes scanned the artworks, taking in the wide variety in size and age – the large almond eyes, the faded reds and golds, and the ancient warped boards on which most of them were painted.

It was an unnerving collection – far too intense to be aesthetic.

As she started processing the individual images, an alarm bell began ringing in her head – quietly at first, but getting louder in the second or two it took her to survey the whole room.

Unlike most Orthodox shrines, there were no images of Mary, George, Basil, Nicholas, Christopher, or any of the other best-known eastern saints.

And that was for one simple, but very troubling, reason.

All the icons were of the same man.

The same almond eyes, gaunt face, and long hair greeted her, but with an incalculable number of variations.

She was already feeling uneasy about being alone with Durov – what she saw in front of her was not helping.

The room was an obsessional shrine to the face of Jesus.

Even without the earlier warning from Swinton, her instinct was now telling her unambiguously that she was in dangerous territory.

The bizarre room was just one further indication that inside Durov's mind ordinary rules simply did not apply.

She looked across at her host, who was indicating for her to walk over to the far wall.

After a moment's hesitation, she complied, and he pushed the door firmly closed behind him.

As the latch clicked loudly in the silence, she was aware of the tension in the room heightening instantly.

And she knew exactly where it was coming from.

She could feel his excitement.

This was clearly one of his pleasures.

He was enjoying closing her in.

She focused on his eyes as the candlelight played on his features – casting dramatic shadows across his face.

She was aware that the situation was moving quickly, and had just become significantly more dangerous.

He was clearly playing games. But she refused to give in to her natural instinct to leave the room as fast as she could.

He had information, and she wanted it.

"This," he indicated a large icon in front of him, "is an ancient copy of the Image of Edessa, the cloth you mentioned, which tradition says Jesus sent to King Abgar."

Ava turned to look at the centuries-old image, wondering how he came to have it in a private residence in London. She was not an expert in icons, but her best guess was that it was early Byzantine.

"As you see, the face has a delicate teardrop shape, unlike the Turin Shroud, where the face is rugged and rectangular, with deep eyes under a prominent brow." Durov was now pointing to a replica image of the Shroud on the adjoining wall. She had not noticed it before, hidden among the dozens of facial images.

He moved a little to the left. "And this is a copy of the *Plat Veroniki*, the veil that Veronica pressed to His face."

Ava's gaze shifted to the icon. It was also extremely ancient – older than the Image of Edessa. The face on it was almost invisible under the black patina left by centuries of oil and candle smoke.

"It's almost identical to the Image of Edessa." Durov indicated the lower portion of the icon. "They both have three distinctive V-shaped clusters of hair – a beard in the middle, and long hair falling from either shoulder."

She compared the paintings.

He was right. They were strikingly similar.

"By contrast," he moved to the replica Shroud image, "the Turin man has a forked Viking-style beard, and his hair is gathered into a ponytail."

She stood back and watched him peering fixedly at the picture.

What was his point?

She was finding the lecture baffling.

Of course the images were different.

Back at the embassy, when she said the Shroud was not unique, she meant that cloth relics like the Image of Edessa and the Veronica were also believed to be miraculous imprints of Jesus's features onto material. She had not meant that the images were visually identical.

What did he think – that they were photographs?

All three images were the work of different artists, divided by country and separated by many centuries.

She took a deep breath to clear her mind.

Was it the Shroud that fascinated him, she wondered, or – as the dozens of other icons in the room suggested – was it a general obsession with pictures of Jesus?

Taking a step forward, she decided to push him a little further. "On the other hand," she ventured, "none of these pictures are anything like the historical Jesus."

He turned his head sharply and glared at her.

She had expected he would not like the idea, but she was unprepared for the depth of resentment she could see etched into his face.

He was annoyed now.

It was an emotion whose positive uses her instructors at MI6 had drummed into her. Durov's feelings now had the better of him. He would not be thinking entirely rationally, and he was more likely to say something unguarded.

The fine judgement she had to balance was how far she could go before she sent him over the edge, into the violence he was clearly no stranger to.

Years spent in MI6 and then living in the Middle East had left her with no concerns about defending herself in a fight. But she would need speed and surprise to match Durov's strength, and the small hot room offered no opportunity for either.

She therefore had to be very careful.

"Written descriptions of Jesus give a different picture," she explained. "And they're much older than these icons."

Durov snorted derisively. "There are no descriptions in the Bible."

"Who mentioned the Bible?" It never ceased to amaze her how little some people strayed beyond the Biblical texts, despite the mass of other writings from the period.

"There are many other books that circulated widely in the earliest decades of the Church. Some were pagan. But others were Christian – although eventually discarded from the canon of official Church literature."

He was glaring at her now.

This was no time to stop.

"In the first century, the pagan philosopher Celsus said Jesus was ugly and small. Around the same time, the Jewish-turned-Roman writer Flavius Josephus said Jesus was short, hunchbacked, with scanty hair, a thin beard, and eyebrows that met in the middle."

She knew that the Josephus manuscript in question was no longer thought to be genuine, but for centuries people had considered it to be accurate, and it had been widely influential.

"A little later," she continued, "the second-century Acts of Paul and Thecla say Jesus was small, bald, hook-nosed, with crooked legs, and eyebrows that met in the middle."

Durov was breathing harder now, not even attempting to disguise his anger.

"I thought you might have been a believer," he spoke slowly, his voice low. "I was clearly mistaken." He seemed to be struggling to control his feelings of rage.

It was a striking contrast to the serene images of Jesus around them.

As his internal struggle to control himself became more apparent, she began to wonder if she had made a terrible miscalculation.

The skin across his temple tightened, then suddenly the atmosphere was broken by the sound of a mobile phone vibrating.

He let it continue several times, not taking his eyes off Ava. Then he slowly reached into his pocket and took out a slim handset. He continued to glare at Ava, leaving it to buzz in his hand several more times, before pressing the button to answer it, and placing it to his ear.

He listened for a few moments, then replied curtly in Russian.

Ava knew she was not going to get another chance.

She pointed to the door, then headed for it.

Once in the hallway, she breathed deeply, relishing the cooler air.

She checked the front entranceway to make sure the coast was clear, then turned and headed in the opposite direction, deeper into Durov's house.

She had no idea how long she would have before his call ended, so walked quickly down the elegant corridor.

Almost immediately, she saw a door down at the end of the wide hallway. It was set a little apart from the others, and was almost certainly the lavatory.

Despite the impression she had given Durov, it was not what she was looking for.

She passed silently on down the hall.

The first door she came to on her right was ajar. She stopped and peered through the crack into a darkened sitting room.

She moved on.

Further down, across the hall, there was another partially open door. But this time her heart started beating faster at the sight of light spilling out from behind it.

Crossing the shiny-floor, she peered through the gap and found herself looking into a book-lined room with a circular dark wooden desk at its far end. On its surface, a brass lamp was casting a narrow pool of light onto a selection of papers and books.

Durov's study.

Gently pushing the door open a little wider, she peered around it to check there was no one in the room.

It was empty.

She was alone.

Once inside, she made straight for the desk.

On it, spot lit by the lamp, was an A3-sized photograph of the Turin Shroud.

She peered at it, bewildered, trying to make sense of the lines in ver-
million ink that Durov had drawn onto it.

He had marked a circle around the body, like some macabre homage
to Leonardo da Vinci's Vitruvian Man. Then he had added an array of
squares, triangles, and interconnecting straight lines, as if working out
the underlying geometry of the body depicted on the Shroud.

She frowned.

What on earth was he doing?

There did not seem to be any logic to the bizarre geometric shapes he
had created.

What did he think the Shroud contained?

Something coded into it?

A map?

Perplexed, her eyes flicked to the small open book lying on the table
next to the photograph.

It was cased in a soft dark grainy Moroccan leather binding, coarse
and worn. It looked old, like a World War One pocket book.

But instead of the diary or journal entries she was expecting to see, its
open page revealed a curious picture.

It was drawn with a scratchy fountain pen, and showed a cross resting on a skull, with faded Russian writing around it in an old-fashioned
hand. The characters were poorly formed, and there were unpredictable
and clumsy size differences in the letters.

It was utterly bizarre.

It certainly did not match her expectation of Durov's writing. He was concerned with appearances, and she expected his writing would be neat and slightly flamboyant.

She gently flicked through a couple more of the pages, and found they were all covered with the same chaotic scrawl. Sometimes it filled the whole page, other times just a few lines.

She lifted the book's front cover to check for any information there or on the spine, but they were blank.

Turning to the first page, there were just three simple hand-written words in large letters.

She read them slowly, trying to make out the individual letters.

Although jerky, the writing was legible.

ГРИГОРИЙ ЕФИМОВИЧ РАСПУТИН

She worked through the first word methodically.

G R EE G O R EE

She had hoped the three words might be a title. But it was clearly a name: Gregory.

That made sense. The three words were most likely a full Russian name.

She tried the second.

Y E F EE M O V EE TCH

That was definitely a patronymic, which always came second in a Russian name. It was YEFIMOVICH, or son of Yefim.

So it was definitely not Durov's name.

She turned to the third word, which would be the surname.

R A SS P OO T EE N

She whispered the word out loud, and as she did, felt a charge of electricity run straight through her.

She stopped dead, and stared at the paper.

That was surely not possible?

She must have made a mistake.

She deciphered each letter again carefully, going over the whole word once more.

As she came to the last letter, the blood drained from her face.

There was no mistake.

She said the word again quietly, as if not believing it until she heard it aloud.

"Rasputin."

She stared in disbelief at the little notebook – taking in its age and the faded handwriting and ink.

Was it possible?

Her training as an archaeologist and in museums had long ago taught her that what at first seemed to be blindingly exciting often turned out to be much more mundane.

She flicked through the book, fighting back her mounting excitement.

There would be definitive tests that could establish its date and content.

Experts would be able to tell.

In all likelihood, it would turn out to be a fake – like the infamous discovery in the 1980s of sixty volumes of Hitler's diaries, which a leading German newspaper had purchased for nearly four million dollars before the hoax was uncovered.

She laid her hands on the pages of the book.

The chances of this being Rasputin's pocketbook were virtually non-existent. It was much more likely that some Russian conman had found an old notebook and pen, then thought of an excellent scam. He no doubt had a good laugh inventing the innermost thoughts of one of the twentieth century's most infamous mystics. It was probably a great project, recreating the personal jottings of the rough country monk who charmed his way into the tsar of Russia's household as healer to the young Tsesarevich, then personal counsellor and political adviser to the distraught and lonely Tsaritsa Alexandra.

On the other hand, if it genuinely was Rasputin's pocketbook, and if it had been hidden in one or more private collections all these years before coming onto the market, then she had no doubt believing that Durov was exactly the kind of person who would acquire it.

Thinking fast, she pulled the phone from her small formal handbag.

Holding it eight inches above the desk, she rapidly took half a dozen shots of the Shroud photograph with Durov's superimposed geometric patterns, the front page of the notebook, and the page with the bizarre cross.

As she took the photographs, she tried to order her thoughts, which were beginning to run away with her.

How was the notebook linked to the Shroud?

Had Rasputin known something about it?

She doubted it. Epic drunken binges and debauching the women of Saint Petersburg were far more his style.

She took a more detailed close-up of the cross and skull, making sure she had captured all the writing.

With a jolt, her concentration was broken by the sound of the front door closing at the other end of the hallway.

Startled, she was suddenly acutely aware that time was ticking.

She had been gone too long already.

She slipped the camera back into her bag, and made sure the objects on the desk were in exactly the same position as when she had arrived.

Satisfied that she had left no traces of her visit, she moved silently to the doorway, and listened carefully, her heart hammering.

Was anyone heading this way?

She could not hear anything.

She counted to five, then left the room quietly, making quickly for the lavatory at the end of the hallway, praying she had not been spotted.

Once the door was safely closed behind her, she leant up against it, breathing deeply.

At least she now had an answer to one of her questions.

Durov had a personal obsession with the Shroud.

And with Jesus.

And possibly with Rasputin.

What she still did not know, though, was whether it was a fixation shared by other people he was connected to.

When her pulse had returned to normal, she flushed the loo and washed her hands.

Opening the door, she stepped confidently out into the hallway.

Retracing her steps, she passed the sitting room, which was now lit, and saw Durov leaning against the carved chimneypiece of the large period fireplace.

She entered, and as she did so, realized too late that they were not alone.

There was another man in the room, who had just stepped midway between her and Durov, and was looking right at her.

Ava's insides knotted as she recognized the slim bearded face.

It was Lunev – the Spetsnaz soldier who had escaped from the road-block at Nuremberg the previous morning.

Her hand was already closing around the nearest heavy object on the side table next to her. It was a miniature bronze bust of some historical figure.

"It's her," Lunev snarled, his eyes widening in surprise. "The one who took it."

Ava saw Durov's face collapse into a mask of rage.

Without waiting a second longer, she hurled the metal bust with all her strength at Lunev's head, before spinning and sprinting out of the door, pulling it tightly shut behind her.

Running faster than she knew she could, she held out her arm as she passed the long hall table, swiping the lamp and vases off it, spraying them onto the floor behind her.

The obstacles would not detain Durov and Lunev for long, but every second counted.

Arriving at the front door, she hit the golden light switches with the heel of her palm, plunging the hallway into darkness. At the same time, her other hand was on the door's heavy latch, tearing it open.

Her heart was pounding so loudly it all but drowned out the bellowing voices of Durov and Lunev, who were roaring out of the sitting room behind her.

She was already running down the mansion's wide steps, scanning the road ahead frantically for any cover.

With rising panic, she saw there was nothing close.

A little way further up the street, on the left, a darkened taxi was parked with the driver's 'FOR HIRE' light unilluminated.

It would have to do.

She prayed she would make it.

She increased her speed, feeling her balance going, destabilized by the unexpected burst of panic and danger. She willed her legs to carry her to the cab, where she could dive behind it, out of range.

She was aware of pounding footsteps getting closer behind her as the scene rushed by in a blur and she drew level with the car.

She barely had time to register that the taxi's engine was running, when its rear passenger door opened and a hand reached out, grabbing her upper arm in an iron grip, dragging her with unexpected strength towards the cab's dark interior.

She clenched her teeth and pulled away for all she was worth, wincing from the pain in her shoulder as she tried to wrench herself free.

A suppressed gunshot behind her swamped her body with more adrenaline, giving her an extra boost of strength as she saw the taxi door buckle around the bullet's entry hole.

The grip on her arm tightened and pulled her again with immense force. This time there was nothing she could do, and she flew crashing into the interior of the cab.

Then she remembered.

The other two bodyguards.

She was feeling sick.

She had not seen them enter the house.

Maybe they were waiting in the cab to take Durov to his next meeting?

The taxi was already accelerating as the hand released its hold on her, and she was able to sit up and look into her captor's face.

"Disappointing first date, was it?" Ferguson asked.

———————— • ◆ • ————————

Chapter 14

Kensington Palace Gardens
Holland Park
London W8
The United Kingdom

DUROV FELT CALM as he walked back up the steps of his house and through the front door.

The Holy Mother had sent him a test – like the Lord did with Job and Jeremiah – and he would not fail her.

The path was clear now.

He felt no anger.

The woman's intervention meant nothing. The Holy Mother had led the woman to him for a reason – so he could take care of her, before she became a problem.

It was the Mother's will.

But first he had to help Lunev. He had to show him how the all-holy *Panagia* could forgive those who failed her.

He stooped to pick up a foot-long column of cut crystal, which had broken off from a table lamp when the woman had swiped it off the hall table onto the floor.

Quickening his pace along the corridor, he drew level with Lunev, and the soldier barely had a moment to register that all was not well.

Durov swung hard, relishing the sensation as the weighty shaft of lead glass connected with the back of Lunev's head.

The Spetsnaz major dropped heavily to the floor, his legs folding under him instantly.

Durov put down the glass club and grabbed Lunev's left arm, dragging him along the hallway, through the open door of the icon room, and into the centre, where he laid him on his back.

He looked down with a smile at the soldier's bearded face, the gash on his forehead still bleeding from where the Quinault woman – if that was even her real name – had hit him with the bronze bust.

The candlelight flickered over the soldier's prone form, and Durov felt himself filling with the Spirit.

"Failure, Dmitri, is an abomination in the eyes of the Holy Mother," he admonished quietly. "It is a terrible sin. There can be forgiveness. But first there must be contrition – an act of sacrifice: a sign of sorrow and submission to her love."

He locked his eyes on Lunev's unconscious face. "I failed, once, and the Holy Mother took something very precious from me. But she gave me a far more special gift in return – an intimate covenant."

He paused, breathing in the scent of the wax – the sensual smell of divine light.

When he spoke again, it was quieter, more reverential. "The gift of sight is sacred. When Samson had fallen from the path, the Lord spared him, and only allowed the Philistines to put out his eyes, for He loved him well. Centuries later, in memory, the emperors of Byzantium offered the same grace to their enemies, only blinding those they could have executed in a noble display of charity and compassion."

He leant lower over Lunev, whose eyelids and lips were beginning to twitch as consciousness returned.

"The Holy Mother is going to take your eyes, Dmitri. Afterwards, when you see clearly with the eyes of your heart, you will know that it was her grace that brought you this holy gift of forgiveness. And, one day, when you have sinned no more, she may restore your sight, just as the Lord did to the blind man of Jerusalem."

Durov's voice dropped even lower. "She will decide when you are ready, and when you are failing her no more."

As Lunev's eyes fluttered open, Durov sat astride his chest, noting the distant look of incomprehension in the soldier's bleary eyes.

Durov laid his large powerful hands over the face beneath him, and his strong thumbs quickly found their quarry.

With a smile of benign compassion, he began his sacred work.

As the blood, aqueous, and vitreous humours spurted from the eye sockets and down Lunev's face, Durov heard the screams coming from under him. But he was focused on the calm holy images of Jesus around him – the Blessed Mother's most sacred treasure – and his heart swelled in gratitude at saving another soul.

DAY THREE

· ◆ ·

CHAPTER 15

Marylebone
London W1
The United Kingdom

AVA SAW SWINTON first, hurrying out of the main doors of BBC Broadcasting House.

"He doesn't look very happy," Ferguson muttered.

Ava had pulled her bike off the road, and parked it beside the 'candle snuffer' church in Langham Place – a local landmark thanks to its two column-circled drums topped off by a long sharp spire.

Swinton had told her and Ferguson to meet him there so he could introduce them to someone.

Ava watched as Swinton crossed the road quickly and drew level with them.

"I thought I was very clear that we would handle Durov." He looked drawn. His tone was abrupt.

"The opportunity just sort of came up," Ava answered honestly. "He invited me to his house."

Swinton glowered at her. "You shouldn't have been at the embassy in the first place." He rubbed a hand across his jaw.

"Let's not mess around if we're going to get to the bottom of why Durov took the Shroud," Ava countered. "Last night I found out more about what he's up to than your Moscow political desk would've learnt in a week of shuffling papers."

She paused to let the point sink in. "We now know that he's obsessed with images of Jesus, he believes the Turin Shroud contains some kind of clue, that Lunev and the team in Turin and Nuremberg are closely connected to him, and that he takes all of this seriously enough to have tried to kill me, in the open, in a London street."

He glared at her.

She changed the subject, onto what was foremost in her mind. "Did you manage to get anything from the photographs I texted you of the notebook on Durov's desk?"

He shook his head, and hailed a passing taxi. "They're still working on it. Follow me," he announced, getting into the cab and closing its door hard.

Ava climbed onto her bike, and Ferguson got on behind her. She pulled away, and joined the cab in the traffic, following it west into London's medical district.

It was an area of elegant four-storey townhouses that had been home to the country's most exclusive medical practices for over a century.

The cab turned into Harley Street, where it stopped outside a grey stone building.

Despite knowing the street well, Ava had not noticed the particular house before. She could now see that it was decidedly eccentric, mixing square and circular elements in striking ways, and sporting a riot of small carvings on the stonework – lions, beads, wreaths. It was an extraordinary jumble, yet it blended effortlessly into the hotchpotch of houses lining both sides of the wide old street. Her eyes travelled up the building, and behind the balustrade crowning the fourth floor she caught just a hint of a concealed fifth storey with a range of communication dishes on top.

She parked up, and joined Swinton on the building's steps, where he flipped open the lid of what she had assumed to be an old electrical junction box, and peered into a hi-tech retinal scanner.

After a moment, the elegant art nouveau door clicked open.

Intrigued, Ava followed him inside.

Instead of the usual smart reception desk under a large panel listing the names of the building's doctors and dentists, there were merely two glass timed-delay security pods of the sort she was familiar with from MI6's building at Vauxhall Cross.

Swinton indicated for her and Ferguson to take one each, while he entered a code in a keypad between them. He followed, then led them along a nondescript hallway and into a lift.

When its doors opened two floors down, Ava was surprised to see a modern operations room, significantly larger than the building she had entered above ground.

The walls were lined with screens of varying sizes stretching from waist-height up to the low ceiling. On them, she could see live feeds coming from a wide range of locations. The main panel in the middle was showing the interior of a Middle Eastern café. From the Arabic on the signs by the counter, Ava guessed it was Egypt.

Operators wearing a mixture of military and civilian clothing – most with headsets – were sitting at computers and other electronic equipment set into consoles and desks built into the lower sections of wall.

It was all bathed in a cool blue light, and looked more like the control room of a warship than the usual drab committee rooms she was used to in governmental buildings.

It was a far cry from the earliest days of British intelligence, in 1909, when MI5 and MI6 were set up together in a simple office in Victoria Street, Westminster. Then the teams had been able to work in daylight, long before they discovered that Russian eavesdroppers were monitoring conversations by firing laser beams at closed windows to listen in by analysing the micro-vibrations in the glass.

"Did you find out anything about Mary?" Ava asked Ferguson quietly as they followed Swinton.

"Like, what's a nice girl like her doing at the Vatican?" he asked.

"I was hoping you could tell me. You two seemed to be getting on very well."

Ferguson looked pleased with himself.

"Over here." Swinton ushered them towards an inch-thick sheet of glass protruding horizontally from the far wall under a panel of recording equipment.

A tall man in a suit emerged from a lift on the other side of the room, and headed across the floor towards them.

Ava guessed he was in his late fifties. He looked like he might have been a sportsman when younger. There was still some black left in his hair, and the neat coloured handkerchief tucked into his suit's outer breast pocket gave him an old-fashioned look.

He nodded an affable greeting to Swinton, before introducing himself to Ava and Ferguson.

"Mark Jennings," he announced, with a confident and deep voice that sounded as if he had enjoyed several decades of port and cigars. "So, you're interested in Durov?"

"Sir Mark was with the Diplomatic Service," Swinton explained.

"US mainly," Jennings clarified. "Looking after the special relationship, and all that."

"Then he was British ambassador to Russia. And now he's one of our most helpful Foreign Office friends." Swinton looked at him expectantly. "He's been doing some digging into Durov for us."

Jennings took a credit-card sized piece of silver metal from his jacket pocket, and slipped it into an unobtrusive slot in the top surface of the glass table. "Well, you'll be very aware that he's not a pleasant man."

Ava had already come firmly to that conclusion.

"There are two things you need to know about Durov," he continued. "He's a religious fanatic, and he's extremely well connected in the Kremlin."

The screen filled with the image of an official-looking Russian document. It had two columns of printed and hand-written information. Near the top, Ava made out the words: 'Олег Антонович Дуров'. Oleg Antonevich Durov.

"Birth certificate," Jennings continued. "Born in Communist Russia, 1970. It was a happy twenty-first birthday for him when the USSR collapsed."

Jennings touched the screen, and the birth certificate dissolved, to be replaced by a map overlaid with gridlines. "Home was a small village in Oryol Oblast." The grid zoomed into a spot halfway between Moscow and Kiev. "In the middle, you could say, of nowhere."

He tapped the image, which melted into a vista of forests and lakes. "And that's a very important part of his story."

He looked up at Ava. "Have you ever heard of the Skoptsy?"

She shook her head.

Swinton and Ferguson looked equally blank.

"The dazzling lights of Moscow and Saint Petersburg often make us forget that Russia still has thousands of villages where life remains an unforgiving struggle to live off the land. In a country so vast, it should come as no surprise that there are still pockets where peasant life hasn't changed for centuries – where timeless rhythms of life go hand in hand with old ways."

"Pagan beliefs?" Ferguson asked.

"That's certainly part of it." Jennings paused. "But the Orthodox Church has been there for over a thousand years so, at least on the surface, the country people are nominally Christian."

"Syncretists," Ava clarified. "Like Louisiana Voodoo or Caribbean Santería, mixing pagan beliefs and Christianity."

Jennings nodded. "Out in the countryside, the ancient Slavic beliefs have persisted for millennia."

The image on the screen changed to a statue of a bearded man wearing a conical crown and holding a Russian cross. "Vladimir the Great of Kiev brought Christianity to Russia in 988. The peasants embraced the new religion, but in their own way. They viewed it as an addition to their traditional beliefs, not a replacement. It's called *dvoyeveriy*, double faith."

"Common in many cultures," Ava nodded. "Especially when Christianity was replacing an existing religion that was very deep-rooted."

"But this is a bit different," Jennings continued. "A lot of their Slavic country beliefs were fertility-based."

Ava had heard something about Russian cults linked to celebrations of the sensual.

"The Skoptsy were first heard of in the late 1700s," he continued. "They brewed up a powerful mix of Slavic and Christian dogmas and, in the process, decided that the greatest sins – the biggest barriers to the afterlife – were sexual urges."

"So what did they do?" Swinton asked.

"You're not going to like this," Jennings replied, tapping the screen again.

The photograph of Vladimir the Great disappeared, to be replaced by an old black-and-white image of a man and woman. Their unsmiling faces were staring suspiciously at the camera, but what was making Ava feel nauseous was what had been done to their bodies. Where their genitals should have been, and where the woman once had breasts, there were only deep scars. They had all been surgically removed – and not especially skilfully.

"Something to do with the forbidden fruit being stuck onto Adam and Eve's bodies after they were expelled from the Garden of Eden," Jennings continued. "That's what they think testicles and breasts are. Cutting them off makes them innocent again."

"Jesus," Ferguson whispered.

Ava went cold. "And what's Durov got to do with the Skoptsy? Don't tell me they still do this?"

Jennings swiped back to the map he had brought up earlier. "The Skoptsy originated in Durov's home region, around Oryol. As a child, he was deeply spiritual, and although by the 1970s the number of Skoptsy had dropped to only a few thousand, the young Durov became obsessed with their traditions.

"To get him away from the influence of the Skoptsy, his parents handed him over to an Orthodox monastery down south, near Kursk. The monks found the boy to be a handful, but they also recognized his spiritual gifts, as well as his strong piety, and his way with people. They thought hard about his future, and eventually settled on a course of action. When he was old enough, they passed him from the novitiate to the first monastic degree of Rassophore. He tried to settle into the quiet routines of monastic life, but suffered some sort of relapse, and again became obsessed with the Skoptsy. One day the abbot entered Durov's cell to find him lying on a blood-drenched bed after performing the Skoptsy ritual on himself."

Ava was feeling lightheaded.

She could not believe she had been rifling through his study the previous evening.

"The monks cared for him while he convalesced, but once his body had healed, the abbot ruled he had no place in their community, and the monks turfed him out. For a while he was seen hanging around the area begging, but then he disappeared. Several years later, he reappeared in Moscow, where he had found a new life – as a successful but ruthless businessman, and also as a spiritual adviser to a number of senior Kremlin officials."

"Riches through friends in high places?" Swinton asked.

Jennings punched up a series of photographs, showing Durov at a range of gatherings in the company of a number of very recognizable senior Russian political and industrial figures.

"His friends certainly helped with contracts and privileges. But by all accounts he's highly astute and ruthless in his own right."

An image of Durov stepping out of a limousine by the Kremlin faded, and the screen went black.

"So what does he believe?" Ava asked. "What spiritual advice does he give?"

Jennings shook his head. "We don't know. These days the Kremlin is a hotbed of religious intrigue, but Durov is altogether more radical than most of the staid Moscow clerics."

Ava was lost in thought.

What did government officials want with someone like Durov?

"We do know, however," Jennings continued, "that he's the guide and guru of a modern international group of the Skoptsy. His core supporters are in Russia, but he has votaries all over the world."

"And do they still, you know … " Ferguson's voice trailed off.

Jennings looked grim-faced. "From what we hear, Durov insists on it. Under his personal supervision, every adult – male and female – is fully mutilated with the Great Seal."

Ava shuddered.

"His followers are deeply faithful to him. As you can imagine, not many leave the group after enduring such a ceremony."

"That's not a religious movement," Ava murmured. "It's depraved."

"Let me know if I can be any further help," Jennings concluded. "Although the best advice I can give is to stay well away from Durov. He lives in a different world to the rest of us, and it's not a pleasant one."

Swinton ejected the silver disk from the reader and handed it back to Jennings, who pocketed it, wished them all good day, and headed for the bank of lifts.

When he had gone, Ava glanced across at Swinton, who was staring into the middle distance, pre-occupied.

He seemed miles away.

"That's all we need." Ferguson was tapping a finger softly on the glass. "As if being a trigger-happy Kremlinite wasn't enough, Durov's also a religious nutjob."

Swinton's phone pinged in his pocket. He pulled it out and swiped open the message, scrolling through it.

"Well," he glanced up at Ava. "It seems we've got a result on the photographs you took last night. The handwriting is an exact match for … " His voice trailed off.

Ava looked at him expectantly.

He looked at her, then back down at his phone. "It says here that the handwriting appears to be a match for the Russian monk, Grigory Rasputin – healer and adviser to the last ruling Romanovs of Russia."

Ava's heart started to beat faster.

So she had been right.

It was almost too extraordinary to be true.

Rasputin had left a notebook that no one had ever heard of.

And now Durov had it.

"There's more," Swinton continued. "The experts say that given Rasputin's highly idiosyncratic handwriting style – as he only learned to write later in life – they have compared it with all other known examples of his writing, and are unanimous that it's genuine."

Ava had not wanted to allow herself time to speculate about what-ifs. But now that she had the confirmation, the mental barriers she had erected disappeared, and her mind kicked fully into gear.

Two Russians: Rasputin and Durov.

Both country people.

Both monks.

Both close to the levers of power.

Swinton tapped on his phone, and the SMS he was reading appeared on the large glass screen.

"They've translated the writing," he continued.

Ava looked down at the image, which was glowing white on a smoky black background.

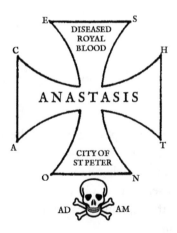

Swinton tapped an icon on the side of the screen and a printout emerged from behind him.

"What on earth does all that mean?" Ferguson asked, peering down at it.

"It means," Ava answered slowly, "that whatever Durov is into, I'm betting it goes way, way beyond the Turin Shroud."

---- ◆ ----

CHAPTER 16

The West Wing
The White House
1600 Pennsylvania Avenue
Washington DC
The United States of America

IN HIS PRIVATE office, Richard Easton looked down at the list of dates, times, and grid references.

Apart from the traditional Bouillotte lamp on his desk, the piece of white paper was the only object on the shiny mahogany, and it had his full attention.

The volume of information passing through the White House on any given day was immense. And, in his position, he had access to almost all of it. No one questioned what he wanted it for. He had served five administrations. As a senior figure in the National Security Council it was his job to know things, and to pass them on up to the Executive Office of the President.

In strict intelligence terms, the paper in front of him was not that singular.

It was a list of scheduled airstrikes by the Russian Air Force stationed at Khmeimim airbase in Syria.

The targets were, as expected, moderate Syrian opposition groups

who might one day form a government. It was not new news to anyone – especially not those on the ground who felt the Tupolev TU-160s
thundering overhead – that Russia was muscularly assisting the existing
governmental regime.

Easton had no idea whether the document came from good old-fashioned human intelligence sources, or whether it had been picked up or
hacked by one of the US government's many signals capabilities. Either
way, the most important thing was that the sensitive combat data had
been coming into the White House for over a month, and it had always
proved accurate.

In the ordinary course of events, there was no problem with him having this category of information. He had the highest security clearance
possible, as well as an unblemished record of thirty-two years' service to
the US government.

In any event, he was always careful. He had not signed for the document, but had taken it from his Chief of Staff's office earlier, hidden in a
folder of other materials. He was in and out of there all the time, and he
would soon put it back again. The CCTV footage of him in the corridors
carrying folders was commonplace and meaningless.

He looked down at the dates and grid references embedded in the
paragraphs of military jargon.

It was a shame the US government could never really use intelligence
data like this. Any deployment of it militarily would immediately dis-
close to the Russians that the US had it.

Still, the information could be very valuable in other ways.

Like for the current plan.

He received his orders in a number of ways.

On this occasion it had been via his ten-year-old first generation Kindle.

He and the contact he knew only as '489' shared log-on details for
the anonymous Amazon account that the Kindle was synced to. Using a
VPN routed into Washington, 489 had sideloaded Fyodor Dostoyevsky's
War and Peace to the account, then highlighted individual words in the
correct sequential order to spell out a message. Once Easton had opened
the ebook, read the message, and highlighted the words 'The End', 489
deleted the book from the Amazon account.

Easton's Kindle was so old that it contained no on-board memory
capable of being analysed if it was ever seized.

In a month's time, Easton would destroy the Kindle, and 489 would delete the Amazon account. They would then move on to a different system for communicating.

Easton turned back to the sheet in front of him. If he was ever caught, it would mean a lifetime in a Federal facility. But he brushed the idea aside. It was not going to happen. He knew the system far too well to make rookie errors.

He pulled out a cheap plastic digital camera he had picked up for cash that morning from a street seller. It was a basic point-and-shoot, without the hundreds of filtering options becoming so popular on higher-end models, but at sixteen megapixels, it would do everything he needed.

Slipping in an unused SD card, he focused through the viewfinder down onto the piece of paper, and took three shots of it from different heights and angles. After checking they had all come out, he shut the camera off and popped out the SD card, slipping it into the knot of his tie.

He would stop off at an internet café on his way home – one he knew did not have internal camera surveillance – and upload the photographs into the Drafts folder of an anonymous webmail account.

A short while later, in Moscow, the Russian would log into the same account, and print off the photographs.

No one would be any the wiser.

The Russian would then do what needed to be done. He would be able to doctor the document suitably, find someone with an Israeli passport, set up the meet, and make it happen.

Easton smiled.

When he got home, he'd run his car over the flimsy camera and SD card, then dump the bits in different trash bins around town at the weekend.

There would be zero trail back to him.

There never was.

Chapter 17

Harley Street
Marylebone
London W1
The United Kingdom

AVA'S MIND WAS buzzing as Swinton clicked off his phone and the glass screen cleared.

Religious cults had always been her father's speciality. He had created a dedicated section at MI6 specifically focused on the dangers they posed when they turned political.

In the last few years, it seemed it was now becoming her speciality, too.

She would have loved to talk this case through with him. She was sure he would have excellent ideas on what might link the Turin Shroud, the Skoptsy, and Rasputin.

But that conversation was never going to happen. He had been killed years ago – On Her Majesty's Service – and she was on her own with her questions.

She pushed thoughts of her father out of her mind, and went back to what Jennings had been saying about the Skoptsy.

She was still in shock at what the photograph of the man and woman had shown.

How could people do that to themselves?

Or to others?

She could not imagine what sort of torturous ideology could lead people to mutilate themselves that severely.

As an archaeologist with expertise in the Middle East, she was well aware that male circumcision had been common in ancient Egypt, Arabia, and the wider Middle East thousands of years before Judaism, Christianity, and Islam had made it a religious rite. Female circumcision also dated back to ancient Egypt, before becoming common across large swathes of Africa, and eventually further afield – even being adopted by European and American surgeons in the 1800s as a treatment for women's sexual 'hysteria'.

But the Skoptsy's uniform removal of their entire external sexual organs was in a league all of its own. From what Jennings had been saying, it sounded like it was tied up with a bizarre cocktail of ancient fertility rites and a fundamentalist interpretation of Christian sin and salvation.

She shuddered.

It was as if the Skoptsy believed that their god had made human bodies with such irredeemable design flaws they had to perfect themselves with workmen's knives – running a very real risk of death from shock, bleeding, and infection, not to mention a lifetime of disfigurement and medical complications.

It was monstrous.

And Durov was one of its chief advocates.

"Let me show you to your desk," Swinton announced, interrupting Ava's thoughts.

She pulled herself back to the present, and followed him across the floor and back into the lift. He pressed the button for the fifth floor, and the polished cabin started to rise silently.

When the doors slid open, they revealed an airy open-plan space, with a pair of four-person workstations in the middle of the floor, and two offices behind glass walls down the side.

"If MI13 is off the radar and does covert work for the other intelligence agencies," she asked, "who pays for all this?" She pointed around the room.

"We've gone back to our roots." Swinton smiled. "The MI sections were originally part of the War Office. MI13 was the Special Operations wing. That's why we chose the Ministry of Defence as home. When you think about the budget for aircraft carriers, submarines, tanks, heavy bombers, and the rest of it, our tiny cost gets swallowed up – just another obscure civilian-military research and development partnership. We work hard not to be noticed, and the expense disappears when the headline numbers get rounded for the bean counters."

Ava moved into the centre of the room, where a flat screen television suspended from the ceiling was showing a news story about an oil spill from a Saudi tanker in the Arabian Gulf.

She looked at the images with dismay, reading the captions announcing that a Saudi tanker heading for the US had developed a fatal fault and was now haemorrhaging millions of tonnes of crude oil into the Gulf.

She looked away. It was only going to make her angry.

How did these things still happen?

The ecological disaster would be immense. The clean-up operation would take years. The toll on marine life would be catastrophic.

"Here are your log-on credentials," Swinton announced, handing Ava a small piece of white card. "You can use any of the desks. As I said, there's always space for you here."

His expression suddenly turned graver. "Just so there's no misunderstanding, our Russia desk will handle Durov. You stay away from him. I need you to work on the cryptograph in Rasputin's book, and how it might connect to the Turin Shroud. But you steer clear of Durov. Are we clear?"

Ava glanced quickly at Ferguson.

This did not feel right.

Was she being shut out of the case?

"I could help," she suggested, trying to sound casual. "I got close to Durov last night. Very close — "

Swinton interrupted her. "Don't do it again. I'm sorry. That's the way it is. Now, let me know if you need anything."

She nodded, and he turned and let himself into one of the glass offices, where he sat down at the desk and flicked on his computer.

"What on earth was that about?" Ferguson asked, stepping over to Ava. "Touchy, isn't he?"

She sat down in the nearest chair and peered into the middle distance.

Her vague feelings of unease about Swinton were beginning to coalesce into something more solid.

Was he protecting something?

Or someone?

She flicked on the computer in front of her, and was greeted by a screen with the letters 'MI13' above a large globe. Superimposed onto it were two snakes entwined and facing each other around a winged staff.

Very fitting.

The motto in a ring around the globe read: *Ars armis validior.*

Ava smiled to herself.

Craft is stronger than weaponry.

She was beginning to like MI13.

"That's the symbol of the US Army Medical Corps." Ferguson frowned, tapping the snakes. "What's it got to do with MI13?"

"It's a caduceus." Ava nodded. "Lots of US hospitals use it, too. But it's an error. Two snakes around a winged staff is the symbol of the god Hermes – an emblem of peace and balance. Hermes used the caduceus to send the wakeful to sleep, and to awaken the sleeping. It's got nothing to do with medicine. Doctors should be using the sign of Asclepius, who was a Greek healer god. His sign is just one snake wound around a plain staff. The mix up comes from an English printer in the 1800s. He specialized in medical books, but his printer's mark was the caduceus – so people came to use it as a medical symbol. The two are now irretrievably muddled."

"They should put it on a plaque outside the door," Ferguson grinned. "It fits right in around here in Harley Street."

Ava turned back to the computer and entered the login details Swinton had given her.

Laying the printout of the translated Rasputin cross on the desk, she pulled up a blank document on the computer and quickly typed in the phrases:

> DISEASED ROYAL BLOOD
> ANASTASIS
> CITY OF SAINT PETER
> AD
> AM
> ESHTNOAC

"Do you know what any of it means?" Ferguson asked. "This stuff is usually right up your street."

She peered at the letters. "Well, I'm guessing it's what got Durov thinking about the Turin Shroud."

"Go on." Ferguson glanced at the sheet.

"ANASTASIS is Greek for resurrection. According to the Bible, the burial cloth or cloths that Jesus was wrapped in were found in the tomb after he was resurrected. Many people believe that the Turin Shroud was one of those cloths. The cross and skull would also tie in with the idea of Jesus's death."

Ferguson nodded. "What about CITY OF SAINT PETER?"

She peered at the cryptograph. "Believers say that the Shroud is proof of the Church's claims about Jesus. Peter was the first pope. So you could say that Rome – and by extension its religion built around Jesus – is the city of Saint Peter."

"And DISEASED ROYAL BLOOD?" Ferguson was looking pensive.

Ava paused before answering, not entirely sure what to make of the line. "According to the Bible, Jesus was of royal blood. The Gospel of Matthew starts with his family tree, showing Joseph's descent from King David and King Solomon. And the Gospel of Luke has the story of Mary and Joseph going south to Bethlehem for the census, because that was the royal town of King David and therefore Joseph's ancestral home."

"How does that actually work?" Ferguson pulled up a chair and sat down beside her. "I've always wondered about that. If Mary was a virgin and conceived miraculously, then Joseph wasn't Jesus's biological father. So even if Joseph had royal blood, he didn't pass it on to Jesus."

"It's even more confused than that," Ava acknowledged. "The Bible's birth story is muddled in other ways, too. For example, the Gospel of Luke says that Joseph had to go south to Bethlehem for the census of Caesar Augustus, which is why Jesus was born there, seventy miles from his home in Nazareth. As it happens, the only known Roman census at that time was the one ordered by the new Roman governor of Syria, named Quirinius, who annexed Judea in AD 6 and ordered a census of all his new lands. The problem is that Roman censuses did not require people to go back to their ancestral homes. What would be the point? The census was an economic snapshot to see how many people lived in each town and village. It helped the Romans plan their tax revenues. If everyone moved around the country to register, the result would be worthless."

Ferguson nodded. "Makes sense."

"And then there's the problem with the date. Quirinius's census was in AD 6. But the Gospel of Luke also says that the census took place during the reign of King Herod the Great – who was the king who tried to have all first-born children killed to remove the threat of Jesus becoming a rival king of the Jews. Now, problematically, Herod died in 4 BC, nine years before the census. So Luke has made a mistake with one of these facts. Jesus cannot have been born before 4 BC and after AD 6."

Ferguson pushed his chair back. "If you were alive five hundred years ago, you'd have been ducked in a village pond."

"If I was alive five hundred years ago, I wouldn't have been able to read or write, so it wouldn't have been an issue," she smiled, looking back at Rasputin's cross. "Anyway, coming back to DISEASED ROYAL BLOOD, it's probably something to do with Jesus's genealogy, but I'll need to think about it more. I don't know about the letters AD and AM. Maybe they're part of a reference to a date and time? *Anno domini* and *ante meridiem*? ESHTNOAC isn't clear, either."

"An anagram?" he suggested.

She looked at it again, shuffling the letters around in her mind. "It might be a warning to stay away. It spells out, CHASE NOT."

"Which would tie in with the skull and crossbones," Ferguson agreed.

They both peered at the enigmatic drawing.

"The outline shape is a Templar cross," she observed, breaking the silence. "It could be another reference to the Shroud, as for centuries there have been rumours that the Templars brought the Shroud back from Constantinople during the Fourth Crusade. And there have been other ones that the Shroud image is, in fact, the last Templar Grand Master, Jacques de Molay. Either way, it's another potential connection with the Shroud."

She sat back and pushed the hair out of her face. "But I think Durov was wrong about the Turin Shroud. I don't believe Rasputin's cryptograph has anything to do with it. All of these are just coincidences. Durov is obsessed with the Shroud, and was just seeing what he wanted to see. I've got a strong feeling the answer to Rasputin's cryptograph lies elsewhere."

Swinton popped his head out of the door of his office. "Major Ferguson, if you fancy joining the team, I've got a little job for you this afternoon?"

Ferguson shot Ava a glance.

"You don't have to stay here for me," she answered. "I'm going to be reading."

"Right," Swinton concluded, throwing Ferguson a set of keys. "There's a black Audi outside. Mary – the Vatican lady – is at the Shangri-La Hotel in the Shard, and getting a flight from Heathrow to Rome tonight. I want to know everywhere she goes today, and anyone she talks to. Do not make contact."

Ferguson pocketed the keys. "Understood. Apart from dinner for two, obviously." He smiled, jabbed the button to open the lift, and was gone.

Swinton went back into his office, and Ava returned to the computer.

She had a lot of work to do.

In the top right-hand corner of the screen was a small icon saying 'LOGGED IN: CURZONA'. She clicked it, and the link brought up her profile page.

Her name had been filled out, as had her home address and telephone number.

She raised her eyebrows in surprise: not so much that they had the information – she was aware they knew most things about her – but that they had got it onto the system so quickly.

Next to the box headed 'LINE MANAGER' it said 'ALAN SWINTON'. She clicked the name, and the computer took her through to his page.

Disappointingly, there was not much there – just some departmental acronyms and numbers, and his contact details.

She pulled out her phone, hit the mute button, and took a photo of the entry.

Navigating back to the main page, she wanted to read more about the Skoptsy and Rasputin – to find out anything she could that might begin to make sense of what was going on.

Scrolling through the menus, she was pleased to see her profile had been set up with access to a number of classified governmental databases. She navigated to the Foreign Office, and pulled up the section on Eastern Europe. From there, it did not take long to locate the detailed archives on Tsarist Russia, then Communist Russia from 1917–1991.

She wandered over to the kettle in the corner of the room and made herself a cup of tea.

She had a long day ahead of her.

Settling down, she started going through the files one by one, hunting out information about the Skoptsy, Rasputin, and their alien worlds.

As she flipped between the confidential archives, digitized books, and academic and governmental papers, she began to learn more about the dreadful world of the Skoptsy, and to fill in the gaps in her knowledge of Rasputin's life.

She barely noticed as the evening drew in, the windows darkened, and the sound of rain started to drum on the glass.

When she was done, she went back to the Foreign Office's archive on Communist Russia, and ran a search for Oleg Antonevich Durov.

The result came back instantly.

One file.

She looked over her shoulder to check Swinton was not watching, and clicked on it.

The system asked for her personnel number, so she reached for her Ministry of Defence identity card and typed in the long code stamped across the bottom.

To her relief, Durov's file opened.

Most of the material was in Russian. But the English chronology at the start gave the same history Jennings had shared with them, and a number of reports filed by UK personnel in Russia over the years backed up the conclusion that Durov currently moved in the highest Kremlin circles.

Hearing a noise behind her, Ava toggled onto a different page, before turning to see Swinton standing outside his office, leaning against the glass and watching her.

"Time to call it a night," he announced.

She nodded.

It had been a long day.

She quickly logged out of all applications, and signed herself off the computer.

Swinton wandered across to her. "Leave me your identity card tonight." He held out his hand. "I'll have access rights for the building added onto it for you."

Ava pulled the card from her pocket. "Sure." She passed it to him.

"You might need this." He handed her a flimsy-looking green umbrella, his eyes moving to the rain-spattered window. "Don't worry about giving it back. It was an unwanted corporate gift."

Ava smiled, and took it gratefully.

She had somewhere to be.

———————— ◆ ————————

CHAPTER 18

Bucephalus Gallery
Old Bond Street
London
The United Kingdom

AVA WALKED OUT of the MI13 building into the rain.

As consuming as Rasputin's cryptograph was, she had Museum business she needed to take care of.

She got on her bike, and headed south, savouring the fresh air after spending the day indoors. The feeling of independence she got from the motorbike had never stopped being a thrill. A friend had looked after it while she was in the Middle East, and being reunited with it had been one of the biggest joys of coming home.

It was a vintage Brough Superior, and she had been captivated by the old make ever since, as a teenager, she had seen one in the Imperial War Museum. The sign beside it said that it had belonged to Lawrence of Arabia, one of her heroes, and she had instantly fallen for its sleek elegance. She had done some research, and discovered that Lawrence had owned eight of them, and would regularly disappear for long rides of seven hundred miles or more around the English countryside.

Something about the romance of the old motorcycle had gripped her – not least its gleaming exoticism and raw power. Back in the 1930s, each one had been fully customized for its buyer, and sold with a guarantee that it had been tested to a speed of over one hundred miles per hour.

When she had finally been able to afford a vintage bike, and when a Brough Superior had come on the market, the decision was a foregone conclusion, and it had made her smile ever since. As Lawrence of Arabia had said, the old machine had 'a touch of blood in it'.

She crossed Oxford Street, down to Berkeley Square, and was quickly lost among the exclusive designer jewellery shops, tailors, and art dealers of the area around Old Bond Street.

It was raining heavily when she pulled up outside the particular business she was looking for. Etched into its glass frontage in gold was the name: 'Bucephalus Gallery'.

She parked up, then pressed the silent buzzer, and a moment later the security system clicked loudly.

Pushing open the heavy glass door, she entered an airy whitewashed room furnished with a dark tan leather sofa, a glass table with brochures, and three tall rectangular cream-coloured plinths, each displaying a spot-lit fragment of ancient sculpture.

She walked over to the nearest one.

It was a life-size torso of a Greek hoplite. The spotlight above it threw the sculpture's carved breastplate into sharp relief, highlighting the heavily stylized abdominal muscles and the exquisitely detailed lion's head crest.

"It's spectacular, isn't it?" The voice came from an elegant blonde-haired woman in her early fifties, who moved across the room and joined Ava beside the torso.

Ava pointed to a slightly open doorway at the rear of the gallery. "I want to talk to whoever sits in there."

"I'd be more than happy to help with — " the woman began.

"I'd say Roman, second century," Ava cut her off and nodded at the statue. "Copy of a Greek original. Maybe Athens, school of Pheidias? With the right paperwork, it's an immensely valuable piece. Without documentation, well, it could be worth as much as a lengthy prison sentence."

The assistant's lips compressed slightly with resignation. She nodded curtly, and led Ava to the office door, which she knocked and opened.

Inside, the room was busily decorated with prints and sketches of classical art. Two antique upholstered chairs faced a heavy dark wooden desk, behind which sat a man in a smart pale-blue open-necked shirt, the sleeves rolled up above the wrists. He had a prominent brow, and thinning grey hair.

The room smelled heavily of cigar smoke.

"Can I help you?" He looked surprised at the interruption. His accent had a trace of South America.

Ava's eyes flicked to the stack of business cards in a silver pen holder on the desk:

JOSÉ RAMOS
Director
Bucephalus Gallery

"That depends." She pushed the door to behind her, but was careful not to close it. "Do you buy?"

Ramos shook his head. "Not from the public. I work with select suppliers." He emphasized the last two words.

Ava could well believe that.

When she had been based in Baghdad, her work had focused on the aftermath of the war. Now, back at the British Museum, her department was swamped with a different crisis.

Law and order had broken down in vast swathes of the Middle East, creating an open season for the systematic looting of the region's unparalleled archaeological heritage. There had always been money to be made from smuggling antiquities, but lawless armed factions were now cashing in on the anarchy on an unprecedented scale.

The free-for-all had shocked her deeply.

She had despaired at the television images of irreplaceable artefacts bring carved up with angle-grinders, and bludgeoned to powder and rubble with jackhammers. And then she had seen with horror the footage of the ultimate desecration of the past, as some of the world's greatest archaeological sites disappeared in hundred-foot plumes of high explosives and dust.

Shocked, she had made some enquiries, and quickly learned that the destruction was only half the story. At the same time as the vandalism, artefacts from the destroyed museums and sites were being funnelled onto the black market to fund the wars, and there was a cynical mathematical calculation underpinning the destruction – the fewer artefacts there were in existence, the higher the price for those being sold.

As her feelings of shock turned to anger, she had decided to do something. She knew that the Metropolitan Police's Art and Antiquities Unit was on the case, but she was also very aware that it was chronically overstretched. So she had started working on uncovering what she could of the networks behind the illegal imports into London.

By monitoring the market and keeping her ear close to the ground, she had established that there were several principal routes into the UK. And, after months of painstaking analysis, she was confident that the Bucephalus Gallery was a key coordinator in the illegal trade.

She looked across at Ramos, doing all she could to conceal her loathing. It was bastards like him who propped up this criminal racket, happy to make dirty money for himself, no matter what the cost to the Middle East's people or heritage.

In the van the night before last, when Swinton had offered her the role with MI13, one of the reasons she had jumped at it was his mention of working on operations of her choosing. If she had the resources of MI13 behind her, then a good deal of the work she was now doing by herself would get a lot easier.

"Mr Ramos, your suppliers are amateurs," Ava ventured. "For instance, the chryselephantine Nike you sold last week had no papers." She pulled a photograph of the statuette out of her pocket and dropped it onto the desk in front of him. "We all know what the authorities would think about that, if they found out."

It had been sheer luck that the proud purchaser had brought the three-inch ivory and gold statuette to the Museum to have its date verified. Although the man had been cagey about how he got it, he had not been able to stop himself mentioning Old Bond Street.

Ramos's expression darkened. "Thank you for your trouble. But I believe you've outstayed your welcome."

"You know how things are these days," Ava continued. "All those dreadful images of antiquities being destroyed, while others are sold onto the black market. There's not much sympathy any more for dealers who do business with the wrong people."

Ramos did not flinch.

"I'm sure you have many suppliers around the world," she continued. "Italy, Greece, the Aegean, Anatolia, North Africa. That's all your business. I'm happy for you. I just need you to hook me up with your contacts for Iraq and Syria."

Ramos studied Ava closely. "And why, exactly, would I do that?" His tone was mocking.

"Because I can help them," Ava injected a breezy confidence into her voice. "Stock. Sourcing. Validating. Papering. All the things that can make their business flow smoothly and stay under the radar."

Ramos picked up a partially smoked cigar from the large crystal ashtray in front of him. He lit it with a match, puffing thick clouds of pungent smoke into the air. "So, you think I'd be helping them?" he clarified.

She nodded, watching the tip of his cigar flare bright orange in successive crackling bursts. "I'm a specialist. I have expertise that would be useful to them." She leant across his desk and picked up a heavy silver pen, then wrote down on his blotter the number of a pay-as-you-go mobile phone she had bought earlier that week, together with the name 'Sophie Vosper'.

She had selected the name a few weeks ago, and set up a LinkedIn page showing Sophie Vosper had graduated from the University of Durham with a Masters in Classics, had worked at a number of the big auction houses in London and New York, and now ran an independent art dealership out of the British Virgin Islands from an address in Tortola. Creating the company had taken forty-eight hours and cost a few hundred pounds. Its register was not public, so no one would see that it had done no business. The cover would not hold up to deep investigation, but it would be good enough for this.

Ramos sat back in his chair smoking, studying Ava closely. After a few moments he leant forward, spreading both his hands on the desk.

As he stretched his arms forward, the shirt sleeve on his right arm rode slightly higher, and Ava caught sight of part of a tattoo.

It was the lower half of a skeleton, wearing a black robe, with a long rope of rosary beads hanging from its belt.

He noticed she had seen it, and quickly shrugged his shoulder so the shirt sleeve fell lower, covering the tattoo again.

Ava was surprised he was sensitive about it. But she was even more taken aback by the fact that the feet and legs of the figure had no flesh. They were just bones, treading on roses.

He leant back again, balancing the cigar on the side of the ashtray. "I don't know anything about a statuette of Nike," he declared slowly, waving his hand dismissively over the photograph. "We've never had one. In any event, all our artefacts are sold with full provenance and paperwork." He paused. "Nevertheless, I'd be happy to put in a call to our main Syrian suppliers and pass on your interest. Then it's up to you." He paused, glaring solemnly at Ava. "I presume that after doing you this favour, I will never see you again?"

Ava nodded.

"Then we understand each other," he concluded, standing up. "Someone will call you."

Ramos walked over to the door and opened it. "In Mexico, we say that flies don't enter a closed mouth." He indicated for her to leave. "One can ask too many questions." His expression was cold. "You should be careful what you wish for."

It was still raining heavily as she left the gallery and headed south and west, through the quieter roads of Mayfair.

Her mind was still buzzing from the meeting with Ramos.

It had gone well.

It felt good to be getting somewhere.

Once south of Piccadilly, she turned into St James's Gardens, and parked the bike in a small garage in the mews a few doors down from her house.

She ran the last few yards to get out of the downpour, enjoying the fresh smell of the rain. But as she approached her front door, noticed a figure on the step beside it. She tensed, then saw it was only a neighbour, Julia, sheltering under the porchway, clearly waiting for the rain to ease.

"Here." Ava handed her the umbrella, and Julia took it with gratitude.

Ava hurriedly opened her front door and stepped into the dry hallway.

As she shook out her hair, the calm was shattered by two distinct gun shots.

Stunned, she ran to the door's spyhole and peered out.

She could see nothing through the rain droplets obscuring the view on the bubble of glass, so she opened the door carefully, and gazed out through the driving rain into the street.

Julia was lying on the pavement immediately outside Ava's door, the green umbrella still in her hand, a pool of blood oozing from her neck into the puddles of water around her body. At the end of the street, a racing bicycle was disappearing around the corner at speed.

"Oh my God, Julia!" Ava shouted, running out and crouching beside her, placing her first two fingers on the radial artery of Julia's outstretched left wrist.

The flesh was warm and dripping with rainwater, but there was no pulse.

It was hardly a surprise.

The majority of Julia's neck and one side of her face had been ripped out by two expanding bullets.

Her dead eyes stared up glassily.

Ava heard another neighbour coming out of his front door onto the pavement. He was shouting hysterically into his mobile phone for the emergency services.

Ava stood up slowly, her heart hammering hard, the horror at the situation now compounded by a sickening realization.

Those bullets had not been intended for Julia.

They had been meant for her.

DAY FOUR

$\cdot \blacklozenge \cdot$

CHAPTER 19

Oryol Oblast
Russian Federation

TWO HUNDRED AND fifty miles south-west of Moscow, Durov replaced the grey Soviet-era telephone's handset onto its cradle, cutting the line dead.

He smiled to himself.

A world away, in northern Israel, the boy had done well.

He now had the means to do what had to be done.

Durov felt a flush of excitement at the knowledge the plan was coming together.

It would not be long now.

He crossed the room's old tea-coloured floorboards, and reached for the rectangle of undyed cream wool hanging on the back of the door. Lifting it off the hook, he moved his long hair aside as he draped the heavy tasselled shawl around his shoulders and over his simple rustic clothing.

Feeling buoyed up, he strode through the simple wooden house, into the hallway, then out into the morning sunshine.

As he shut the door, two bodyguards fell in step either side of him.

Around him, a sprawling settlement of rustic wooden houses and barns gave way to fertile open green countryside. Nearby, the River Oka meandered north, where it would eventually be joined by the Moskva, before ploughing into the vastness of the Volga at ancient Nishny Novgorod.

He stared down at the track's rich black *chernozyom* earth, its fertility famous throughout the country.

His eyes lingered on it appreciatively.

This was where he had grown up.

Wild Russia.

Home.

This is where the Holy Mother had first visited him, years ago, marking him out as special.

Here his house was simple. He could live among his people as one of them. They knew of his other life, in Moscow, but they understood that it was necessary for him to have fine things and mix with the elite. How else was he going to gain the trust of the men in the Kremlin and guide them? Look at what had happened to Rasputin – another country boy who had walked in the corridors of power, and who had paid with his life for not being one of them.

Durov was not going to make the same mistake.

There was a wooded area off to his left, where several dozen cars nestled in a clearing, the number plates indicating some had travelled many miles to be there.

Turning off the track, he headed up among the oaks, ash, and elms towards a large semicircular building built out of the same forest woods as the other houses, although with visibly more care and attention. It was an unusual structure, with only one storey, and its smooth walls unmarked by windows or any other feature.

Pushing open the *Knista*'s heavy main door, he breathed in the smell that always made him feel so alive.[1]

The smell of his people.

The Elect. The White Doves. Those who had been chosen.

The ancient chamber was set up as an amphitheatre, and the only light came from standing candelabra casting a theatrical glow.

The Skoptsy were sitting silently on solid wooden benches arranged

---

1 See the Aramaic appendix for a translation of the Aramaic words used in this chapter. *Knista* means 'assembly place'. *Urha* means 'the Way'. *Meshiha* means 'Messiah'. *Sheliahin* means 'Apostles'. *Rabbuni* means 'teacher'.

in concentric semicircles, all focusing on a large empty chair mounted on a raised dais at the far end of the hall. Behind it, carved into the wood high on the wall and burnished with gold leaf, was one vast word:

URHA

Durov gazed around the familiar chamber as he made his way up to the dais.

Arriving at the imposing chair, he faced the audience, and waited until all eyes had settled on him.

"Today we remember the very earliest times," he began, his delivery slow and slightly detached, mildly hypnotic. "We recall the days immediately following the *Meshiha*'s glorious journey beyond the sacrifice of the Cross, to rule in triumph beside his heavenly Father."

It was a subject he knew well.

It had been his life's study.

"His eleven faithful *Sheliahin*, who had remained in Jerusalem and not gone home to Galilee, soon elected another to replace Judas Iscariot. According to the Scriptures, they also chose James, the brother of the *Meshiha*, to be their leader. In turn, he was assisted by the fisherman, Simon Kepha, and by John, the disciple whom the *Meshiha* loved the most. Together, this triumvirate formed the Three Pillars of the new community."

He surveyed the room, taking in the attentive faces all around, soaking up their adulation.

"The *Meshiha* said: 'I am the way'. In remembrance, his earliest followers in Jerusalem named themselves *Urha*, the Way – a name we, their direct descendants, bear with honour. We reject the later labels imposed by the pagans. The Way was our name in Jerusalem long before the word 'Christian' was invented in the pestilential filth of Antioch."

Durov felt the words flowing freely.

He knew he was being guided from above.

"Names are power. Therefore, never forget: the *Meshiha*'s given name was Yeshua – Joshua. The Romans hid it, twisting it into their barbarous Latin name: Jesus."

Durov watched the flickering candles, feeling their calming effect.

It was important that the Elect truly understood all these things, if they were to be ready.

"We must honour our ancient heritage. The birth of a redeeming *Meshiha* was foretold by the Hebrew prophets. The *Meshiha* and his followers were Jews. The Way was Jewish, and worshipped in the synagogues, keeping the laws of Moses – circumcision, kosher, Passover."

He lowered his voice, feeling the audience hanging on his every word. "But then, Satan came in the form of Saul the Pharisee. Saul knew nothing of the *Meshiha*, being from far-off Tarsus. He persecuted the Way, ravaging its numbers, hurling its men and women into prison, gleefully participating in the stoning of Stephen, our first martyr."

Durov sensed the power in the room. Redemption was present in the holy Russian Orthodox Church, of course, in the gilded domes of the Kremlin. But that was just the outside layer of the Mystery. Here, in this room, among the Elect – this was where salvation dwelt in fullness.

"Then came the lie. Saul the Persecutor says he was visited by the *Meshiha* on the road to Damascus, and he claimed that he had been chosen. He changed his name to Paul, and joined the Way. But, deceitful snake that he was, he sowed dissent, tempting the *Sheliahin* to abandon their ancient ways. He turned them from the path, and moulded them into a religion fit for the pagan Hellenes and Romans."

He felt his blood running hot.

"We alone remember the true faith of the Way. We alone observe the order, 'Prepare ye the Way of the Lord'. Therefore, this is a day for joy – as two among us are preparing to join those blessed by our holy covenant. The Great Seals they receive today will number them among the Elect, and they shall be saved at the Rapture and the great Tribulation. For in — "

Durov broke off at the sound of a commotion outside the door.

It burst open, and four men entered, dragging a man and a woman between them.

Durov stared at the intruders, anger flaring at the unprecedented interruption in his teaching.

The prisoners were in their early twenties. They looked dishevelled, dejected, and beaten.

The emaciated man leading the party addressed Durov. "*Rabbuni,* these two have brought shame onto this community."

Durov liked Yegor, the guard who had spoken. He was not a subtle man, and had come to the Skoptsy late. But forty-five years in the KGB – then its successor the FSB – had given him a good instinct.

Behind Yegor, the captured man glared at Durov with hostility.

The woman's eyes were cast down.

Durov inhaled deeply. "It has been our custom since the earliest days to confess our sins before the whole community." He spoke softly. "The confessional is a place of forgiveness, freely given to all who desire it with their hearts."

Yegor continued. "We found their white vigil gowns smouldering in the furnace. They had discarded them after abandoning the prayers of preparation in the little oratory. We tracked them down on the road to Trosna, already six miles from here."

Durov stared at the couple with disbelief.

These were the two preparing for the Sealing?

The blood started to pump harder in his veins as he looked more closely at the woman's baggy clothing, and noticed the tell-tale shape of her chest.

"Your names?" he demanded, fighting down the rage surging within him.

"Brother Nicolay and Sister Nataliya," Yegor answered.

Durov stared at each of them in turn, his eyes black with indignation. "Is what Brother Yegor says true?"

An oppressive silence filled the room, becoming heavier as the seconds passed by.

"Sister Nataliya," Durov addressed the woman. "What is your explanation for this?"

Her head was hung in shame, her flaxen-blonde hair falling messily over her face. Durov could just make out tears gathering on her eyelashes.

She did not look up.

He turned to the congregation. "The Gospel of Matthew is clear." He raised his voice, letting it fill the chamber. "He said unto them: For there are some eunuchs which were so born from their mother's womb: and there are some eunuchs which were made eunuchs of men: and there be eunuchs which have made themselves eunuchs for the kingdom of heaven's sake. He that is able to receive it, let him receive it."

He gazed around the room again, his expression stony as the ominous words settled on the crowd.

"From the beginning, the righteous have always heeded this commandment. Even in the early Church, the great theologian Origen of

Alexandria understood, and castrated himself to live more fully in the *Meshiha*."

He stared at Nicolay, his voice dropping in volume. "So, my brother, why do you think you know better?"

Durov could see the emotional struggle on the young man's face, and after a long pause he raised his eyes up to Durov on the dais.

"Some of them were married." Nicolay's expression was smouldering with resentment. "The gospels say the *Meshiha* cured Simon Kepha's mother-in-law of a fever. Paul even wrote that Simon Kepha's wife used to travel with them. Simon Kepha was the rock on which the *Meshiha* said he would build his Church, and he became first pope of the Romans. Being married didn't stop — "

"And yet," Durov cut him off, his eyes narrowing. He spoke slowly, and with mounting venom. "Can you tell me where the Scriptures say that Simon Kepha and his wife had carnal knowledge of each other?"

Durov smiled, confident in his argument.

Of course he couldn't.

Durov had studied it for years.

He knew he was right.

All lust was odious – repulsive and bestial. It was hateful in the eyes of the *Meshiha*. Only abstinence marked out the Chosen, setting them aside for God.

"They were all chaste, just as the Holy Mother was a vessel of purity, so was the *Meshiha*."

He was angry now.

"Yet you come in here and besmirch their names with your filth?"

He glared at them. He had offered this couple the most precious gift of eternal life. And they had thrown it back at him.

"Haven't you been taught that Abraham made a covenant with the Lord, binding his people to show their devotion by circumcision? Yet the *Meshiha* explicitly gave us the new covenant of the Seal – 'let him receive it' – he enjoined. Accordingly, as related in the Scriptures, was not one of the first men baptized into the Way a eunuch from Ethiopia?"

Durov felt the Spirit strongly now.

And it was swelling with rage.

Divine love was not always merciful. At times it was hot enough to combust and consume.

He turned to the woman. "Sister Nataliya, did you lead our brother astray? Did you lure him into temptation? Did you corrupt him?"

He stared closely at her for a reaction. But she remained with her head hanging, immobile.

There was a pounding in Durov's head.

"Very well," he strode towards her. "As our brother, Nicolay, chose to place his trust in you rather than in the Way, we will honour that confidence."

He searched for a reaction beneath the hair falling loose over her face. There was none.

He stopped a few feet from her. "Who better than you, Sister Nataliya, to decide his fate? As the Lord gave Abraham a choice over Isaac, I give you one. Brother Nicolay can be Sealed, or he can be stoned for his blasphemy. He trusts you, Sister Nataliya. So you choose. What will be his fate?"

Durov watched with satisfaction as she crumpled against Yegor. Her face drained of all colour, and her frail body began to tremble at the enormity of the responsibility thrust upon her.

He watched as she raised her face and her lips moved, but no words came out.

"Very well," he moved closer. "I can choose for you."

Now he could see real fear in her eyes.

Her lips moved again, but her voice was inaudible.

Yegor leant in closer as she repeated the word almost soundlessly.

"Sealed," he announced to the room.

Durov turned on his heel and strode back to the chair.

He felt a wave of revulsion.

She was a coward.

His lips tightened in disgust.

She was not one of the Elect.

Neither of them were worthy.

He sat down heavily in the chair, the anger receding, to be replaced with a small smile of satisfaction.

At least he had found them in time.

He inhaled again deeply, feeling the wisdom running through him.

"The sentence of the *Knista* is that you shall both be taken from here and Sealed." He paused, allowing the words to sink in. "But for you it will be a harsh punishment, not a blessing of redemption. Neither of you will be among us on the coming day of glory. Instead, the wounds you receive today will be your end. By your deeds, you have relinquished the right to be numbered among us, now and always."

They would not pollute the ranks of the Chosen Ones.

He would not allow it.

He turned to the congregation. "It is for you to confirm or reject my sentence."

Durov knew they would not go against him. They had learnt years ago that he was guided from above.

He was a prophet.

Without hesitation, they nodded solemnly, their heads the only discernible movement in the flickering candlelight.

CHAPTER 20

10b St James's Gardens
Piccadilly
London SW1
England
The United Kingdom

"IT WAS A professional job," Ava confirmed, sitting down at the kitchen table and tying her hair back. "No question."

"Did you get a look at him?" Ferguson's face was grim.

She shook her head. "Dark clothing, Helmet. Could've been anyone. We can pull the CCTV footage from the area, but we won't get anything. He'll have dumped the bike somewhere out of sight. And he knew not to use a car or motorbike to avoid the number plate being logged and tracked real-time on the ANPR camera feeds."

Within fifteen minutes of the shooting, the police and scene-of-crime team had turned out in force, and the noise of voices and engines had gone on late into the night.

Ava had told them everything she could recall, but there were always small details that came back later.

One of them could be important.

She had lain awake for hours, replaying the scene in her mind over and over again, trying to remember every aspect of what had happened.

It made her sick thinking about it.

Julia was not involved in any of this. She was something senior in a trendy fruit juice company, and should still be very much alive.

Ava had been unable to sleep, and in the small hours of the morning had got up and padded through to the book-lined study, where she had sat awake in an armchair, staring through the window at the blue-black night sky.

Who had tried to kill her?

On her own doorstep?

It brought back memories of her father's death. He had not been a violent man. Yet he had died a brutal death. And now there was Julia.

Why was death always part of the story? And why was it so often the wrong people who lay cold on the mortuary slab?

Her eyes had settled on one of the photographs on her shelves. It showed her with the local team of archaeologists and conservators at Palmyra in Syria. They were all smiling in the picture, excited to be working on one of the world's richest archaeological sites – a national heritage of which they were immensely proud. And now they were all dead – butchered in their own country in the war of ideologies tearing the region apart.

When growing up, she had never dreamed that she would be surrounded by so much bloodshed. She knew it was occasionally a feature in the world of intelligence. But it had never occurred to her that in some parts of the world archaeology would move onto the front line.

She had finally fallen asleep shortly after daybreak, and she was now sitting in her kitchen while Ferguson prepared breakfast. He had rung for an update on her afternoon at MI13, but when she told him what had happened, he had come round immediately.

She took a sip from the cup of fresh tea in front of her, instantly feeling more alive.

"Any idea who ordered it?" His voice was full of concern.

"A few." She had been turning the options over in her mind ever since it happened. "For starters, after the other day, I don't think I'm on Durov's Christmas card list. And then there's Ramos."

Ferguson frowned.

"I went into an Old Bond Street gallery yesterday," she explained, "and leant on a dealer who's importing antiquities from Syria." She took another sip of the tea. "It's just Museum stuff."

"Right." Ferguson grinned. "I'm sure you asked very nicely."

"I need to know who he's buying from," she explained. "There are only a few routes for Syrian antiquities into London, and they urgently need to be closed down. To do that, I have to get higher up the supply chain."

She watched Ferguson as he unpacked the bacon, sausages, eggs, mushrooms, and tomatoes from the thick brown paper bag he had brought in with him.

He turned and noticed her gaze. "Any soldier will tell you the same." He took the thick slices of bacon from their waxed paper wrapping. "There aren't many mornings that can't be improved by a good breakfast."

"Then there's Swinton," she added.

Ferguson stopped unpacking the ingredients and looked back at her over his shoulder. "Seriously?"

She had given it a lot of thought. "Just before I left MI13 yesterday, he took my pass. That means I was carrying nothing to link me to him. He also gave me a green umbrella, which Julia was carrying, right by my doorstep, when she was hit."

He rubbed his hand across his chin. "Christ. That's all we need." He stared out of the window for a moment. "Why would Swinton want you dead?"

She could not put her finger on it. "Maybe I've done something to upset him in the past? Or perhaps it's not even about me. Maybe Swinton wants to frame Durov – stitch him up for murdering one of the team, but without losing anyone valuable?"

Ferguson chewed his lip. "That's pretty off the scale. You really think he'd do that?"

"I don't know," she answered truthfully. "Maybe he's working for Durov? I mean, what do we really know about him?"

Ferguson checked the temperature in the frying pan, then carefully laid in the rashers of bacon. "The sound money has to be on Durov. We know for sure that he's not your biggest fan."

"But how does he know where I live?" Ava was finding it hard to believe. "Can he really have traced me that quickly?" She stood up and walked over to the window.

Peering through the blinds, she looked out onto the pavement, at the spot where Julia had been lying. The police had already taken away the small white tent they had put up, and the road looked just as it always did.

It was as if Julia had never existed.

"Well, we're going to have to wait and see who comes out of the woodwork," Ava concluded quietly. "They tried and failed. So the chances are they'll come again."

Ferguson turned on the grill, and slid the tomatoes under it.

"Anyway," she changed the subject, "I've been thinking about Rasputin's cryptograph, and I reckon I'm getting somewhere with it."

She returned to the table, and Ferguson pulled up a chair and sat down opposite her.

She put Swinton's printout of the bizarre cross onto the table between them.

"I'm assuming that this was written in Russia by Rasputin in the last decade of his life. At that time he was heavily connected with the Russian royal family, as he was treating the young Tsesarevich Alexei for haemophilia. In other words, the prince's blood had a dangerous clotting disorder."

"DISEASED ROYAL BLOOD," Ferguson agreed.

He looked down at the cryptograph and put his finger on the words: CITY OF SAINT PETER. "Don't tell me, the Russian royal family spent a lot of time in Saint Petersburg?"

Ava nodded. "In Rasputin's day, Saint Petersburg had been the capital of the Russian Empire for two hundred years. It was the home of the Russian government. And the royal family had their court there."

"The only problem is this." Ava pointed to the word in the middle: ANASTASIS.

"Anastasia was the prince's sister." Ferguson frowned. "It fits nicely, doesn't it?"

Ava twisted the sheet so he could see it more clearly.

"It might be a reference to her," Ava conceded. "But it clearly says ANASTASIS, which is the Greek word at the root of her name. Why not just write Anastasia?"

"It's part of a concealed message." Ferguson walked back over to the cooker. "So it's been slightly disguised. Anastasia would make complete sense. After all, Rasputin was very friendly with the whole family, wasn't he?"

Ava took another sip of her tea. "True. He got to know her mother, the Tsarina Alexandra, when he began treating the prince. The doctors could do nothing, and Rasputin was the only one who seemed to be able to help. Inevitably, Alexandra became his greatest fan, and their friendship lasted for a decade, becoming ever closer.

"But, when the Revolution came in 1917, the Communist revolutionaries herded the whole imperial Romanov family off to a secret location. They crammed them into a basement, where a group answering to Lenin shot and bayoneted them. Then they doused the bodies in sulphuric acid to obliterate all traces of the murders. Alexei was thirteen at the time. Anastasia was seventeen. There were three other sisters, too: all executed."

"Christ." Ferguson's face fell. "Child murder. One hell of a basis for a new political system." He cut two thick slices of bread. "But weren't there rumours Anastasia survived?"

Ava nodded. "There was speculation for decades. But all their graves have now been found near Yekaterinburg, a thousand miles east of Moscow in the Urals, and DNA tests have confirmed their identities."

Ava tapped the drawing, lost in thought. "However, Rasputin was killed a year and a half before the Romanovs were murdered, so this clue isn't going to be about rumours of Anastasia's survival."

"You said *Anastasis* meant resurrection in Greek. Rasputin was a seriously hard man to kill, I seem to remember. Could that be a connection? Is it about Rasputin coming back?" Ferguson cracked an egg into the frying pan.

"He was a walking scandal." Ava had read up on the story with fascination the previous afternoon at MI13. "His clothes were filthy. He didn't wash. He was almost permanently on an epic drunken binge. And he maintained that it was important to sin as much as possible in order to be truly forgiven by God. So the endless spiritual counselling sessions he offered his many female devotees usually involved having sex with them so they could all repent together afterwards. He was quite the charmer, it seems."

"Eventually, a group of ultra-conservatives decided that he had to go before he dragged the Romanovs down with him. They gave him poisoned wine and teacakes, but he shrugged it off. Then they shot him, but he kept going. So they shot him again. He was still alive, so finally they tied him up and dropped him through a hole in the ice on the river, where he finally drowned."

"With all that going on, I'm amazed he had time to keep a notebook," Ferguson muttered.

Ava watched as he scooped the bacon out of the pan and put it on two plates, carefully adding the rest of the food.

It had been a long time since anyone had cooked breakfast for her.

He was a good friend, she mused, casting her mind back to Baghdad, and the time when he had wanted to be more than a friend. They had become very close then. But she had never let it happen.

"So you think there may be a Russian royal link, rather than a connection to the Turin Shroud?" He brought the two plates to the table.

As Ava took a mouthful, she realized she was starving. After the events of the previous evening, she had been too wired to eat.

She nodded. "I haven't found anything to suggest that Rasputin had ever heard of the Turin Shroud. The only link in all this that I've been able to discover is between Rasputin and Durov."

"Really?" He looked up. "Rasputin's spiritual exercises seem at the opposite end of the scale from the Skoptsy's rituals."

Ava had been delighted when she had found the connection while looking through the Foreign Office files.

She shook her head. "It seems that, for a while, Rasputin was a member of the Khlysty – a rural cult that went in for religious ecstasies, tempered with doses of flagellation and self-mortification. After a while, Rasputin broke away from them, and focused more intensely on the ecstatic side of Khlysty life. At the same time, others went in the opposite direction, becoming more puritanical. One group became the Skoptsy."

Ferguson looked pensive as he topped up Ava's tea. "So the Khlysty and Rasputin are both in the ancestral DNA of the Skoptsy, which explains why Durov might see Rasputin as some sort of guru?"

Ava could feel the warming food bringing her strength back. "Exactly. Anyway," she changed the subject, "how was the stake out yesterday? Did Mary get to the airport?"

"As it happens, she called me," he answered. "So it was more of an escort service than a stake out."

Ava looked across at him. "She must like you if she's tracked down your number."

He shook his head. "I gave it to her that night at the embassy."

Ava felt a pang of something she could not quite define.

She glanced down at her mug of tea, avoiding his gaze.

Where had that come from?

"I ended up driving her to the airport," he continued. "She didn't say too much. She's been at the Vatican a few years. She used to be with the Los Angeles police department, and there was some story about something to do with a gang in LA killing a child. It left her feeling responsible, so she wanted to get away and make a clean break. A local priest connected her to the Vatican. That's all I got, so I still don't know exactly what she does there."

Ava was stumped too. She had dealt with various parts of the Vatican when borrowing items from their collections for exhibitions. There was the Swiss Guard, who looked after the pope and the Apostolic Palace. But it was unlikely Mary was connected to them, as they were an all-male unit. Then there was the Gendarmerie Corps, which managed all policing and security for the Vatican and its properties. But that was also all male, and anyway, Mary said she was a "liaison".

Ferguson interrupted her thoughts. "What about the other letters in Rasputin's drawing? The eight around the cross?" He looked down and pointed to them. "ESHTNOAC, or CHASE NOT."

Ava finished a final mouthful of the breakfast, and stared into the middle distance. "Right now, I have absolutely no idea."

Her phone vibrated. Glancing down, she read the message, and her heart started to beat a little faster.

"Come on," she announced, getting up. "We may get answers to at least one of our questions. Swinton wants to see us. Now."

CHAPTER 21

The Cavalry and Guards Club
127 Piccadilly
London W1
The United Kingdom

SWINTON'S SMS TOLD them to come to 127 Piccadilly.

It was a short ride away, and when they got there, the large navy-blue flag flapping over the entrance announced it was the Cavalry and Guards Club.

"Seriously?" Ferguson looked bemused. "Swinton didn't strike me as the sort to hang around playing billiards all day."

They headed up the stone steps between the four-columned portico, and through the grand double doors.

Inside, the polished marble, cream, and mahogany atrium was hushed – a world away from the traffic thundering along outside between Piccadilly Circus and Hyde Park Corner.

There was a reception desk, a painting of a Georgian monarch on the wall, and an elderly man in a pinstripe suit sitting in a black leather armchair reading a broadsheet newspaper.

With no formalities, they were shown through into a comfortable drawing room, where Ava immediately spotted Swinton and Sir Mark Jennings.

"This is alright," Ferguson indicated the opulent surroundings.

"Reminds me of my misspent youth." Jennings smiled. "Coldstream Guards. You?"

Ferguson shook his head. "Infantry. Green Jackets, originally."

Jennings motioned for them to sit, and Swinton leant forward to speak.

"So what the hell happened last night?" He was not looking friendly.

Ava struggled to keep her composure.

He was angry with her?

She was the one with the assassination on her doorstep.

"How did you hear about it?" she asked quietly, keen to see his reaction.

"The whole town knows," he erupted. "It's not every day someone's gunned down in St James's."

"Not someone. Her name was Julia," Ava replied, barely able to conceal her emotions. "And what's everyone saying?"

"They're all mystified," he answered brusquely. "They're all wondering why anyone would want to take out a minor businesswoman in a drive-by shooting." He peered at Ava. "Fortunately, the police don't know who you are, yet, but they'll work it out sooner or later." He slumped back in his chair. "Is there anything you're not telling me?"

She shook her head.

He did not need to know about Ramos.

She had been thinking about it further on the ride over, and had come to the conclusion that if Ramos had wanted to get rid of her, he would have done it discreetly, to avoid questions. What had happened the previous evening in her street may as well have had spotlights and a band playing. It did, in fact, have all the hallmarks of a bold attention-seeking Russian hit.

Or someone wanted it to look that way.

"Anyway," Swinton continued, "I'm glad you're here. We've picked up reports that Durov is putting noses out of joint in the Russian military, and that he's somehow connected to the Saudi oil spill that's all over the news. I haven't changed my view that you're to stay away from him, but for the moment we need to build the best picture of the man we can."

"What does satellite intel say?" Ferguson chipped in. "Did we have anything in the sky?"

Swinton nodded. "There's always something watching the Saudi ports. Our friends in the Ministry of Defence have ruled out an accident. They think it was sabotage."

"Frogmen could have attached limpet mines with timers to the hull while the vessel was in the harbour, or later, when it was in open waters," Ferguson suggested. "It's going to be very hard to pinpoint. Were there Russians in the areas?"

"The Middle East is swarming with Russians." Swinton pursed his lips. "Half the Red Army and Air Force are in Syria. And I hear that restaurant menus in Dubai now list the food in Russian first."

"Why Durov?" Ferguson asked. "What's the connection?"

"His business interests are in petrochemicals," Jennings answered, joining the conversation. "There's been a full-on economic oil war for several years now. The Saudis are depressing the price to hurt the Iranians, whom they want to cripple before Iran can reassert itself too fully in the region. Meanwhile, the Americans are sitting by happily, as the low oil price is whipping Russia, which does Washington all sorts of favours."

"And reducing the Saudi oversupply of oil helps push prices back up." Ava finished the train of thought for him. "And an increased oil price helps Durov."

"It could've been Iran, of course, attacking the tanker," Jennings continued. "It's just as much in their interest to see Saudi's oil industry hurt, while getting the price back up."

Ferguson looked uncertain. "That'd be a big step for Tehran, though, wouldn't it? They're doing well in Iraq and Syria at the moment, and the lifting of sanctions is bringing them back into the mainstream. Why would they take on Saudi now? They've got more to lose than gain."

Ava nodded. "The Persian Empire under Cyrus the Great stretched from Eastern Europe to China. Their monarchy lasted for almost five thousand years until 1979. They have a highly educated population, developed industry, deep financial markets, and a lot of oil. And they're well aware that they're a natural regional superpower, regardless of who has, or doesn't have, oil at any moment. With the US withdrawal, they're gradually and successfully coming out as the region's dominant power, so I agree. I can't see them starting a full-on war with Saudi now."

"If not Iran, there's always Israel," Swinton added. "Just like Iran, their interest in hurting Saudi is about the regional balance of power."

One of the club's staff approached Swinton, handing him a large navy-blue wallet embossed in gold with the club's crest.

Swinton nodded an acknowledgement and opened the folder, pulling out a thin sheaf of A4-sized photographs. "Ah. Good. They were able to print these." He handed Ava one of them. "We've had a team of watchers on Durov. They've sent through some interesting photographs. What do you make of that?"

Ava looked down to see a white limousine parked outside Durov's house in Kensington Palace Gardens. The shot was from a high angle – a neighbouring property, she guessed.

Durov was in the backseat, peering down at something.

Swinton handed her another photograph, this time shot through Durov's car window.

It clearly showed that he was looking intently at two books – one resting on each leg.

The right one was open at an instantly recognizable page. It was Rasputin's notebook, and Ava could plainly see the cross, drawn in Rasputin's shaky hand, with the coded phrases inside.

DISEASED ROYAL BLOOD
ANASTASIS
CITY OF SAINT PETER
AD
AM
ESHTNOAC

As her eyes tracked left across the photograph, the breath caught in her throat on seeing that on Durov's other knee was a second notebook, identical to the first, and he was studying its open page closely.

Her pulse started to quicken as she saw it was also a drawing.

Swinton handed her another A4 photograph. "We've enlarged it."

She took it, and stared in amazement at the image.

"And here's the translation," he added, handing her a fourth sheet.

MELITA

SEDROH · HORMIA

CHILD OF THE THEOTOKOS
PHILERIMOS
ZZ
♍

"The experts have confirmed that it's definitely also by Rasputin. They say it's in the identical hand to the first drawing you sent us."

Ava exhaled slowly.

This was unbelievable.

Rasputin had left a pair of matching cryptographs.

"What do you think?" Swinton leaned forward in his chair. "Do they go together? Is this a code in two parts?"

Ava's eyes were flicking from one photo to the other, her mind whirring as she tried to fit the pieces together.

"On the face of it," she answered, her thoughts coalescing, "there's nothing to link the two. Except," she looked up at Swinton and Jennings, "they're both by Rasputin. They're both in his notebooks. And Durov very much wants to know what they both mean. So yes," she concluded, "until we know differently, we should assume that they're very much connected."

◆

CHAPTER 22

Borough Market
Southwark
London SE1
England
The United Kingdom

AVA WALKED QUICKLY up Bedale Street, under the industrial-looking railway bridges, and into the vast glass brick and metal expanse of Borough Market.

Forty-five minutes earlier, she had received a call on the pay-as-you-go phone number she had given Ramos.

The voice had instructed her to go to *Los Tres Toros* restaurant in Southwark.

She had punched the name into Google to get the exact address, then ridden south, crossing the Thames over London Bridge – enjoying the flash of blue in the morning sunshine – before speeding down to the towering glass pinnacle of the Shard, and parking up just off Borough High Street.

The moment she entered the covered space of the ancient market, the first thing to hit her was the smell.

It was an intense punch of exotic herbs, spices, breads, cheeses, and dozens of other foods laid out on immaculately presented stalls. Around them, street-food vendors tended trays of sizzling roast meats, skillets of fresh shellfish, and immense karahis of curry.

A sign told passers-by that the market had been at the southern end of London Bridge since at least AD 1014, before the Battle of Hastings, and it was proud to have served London for over a thousand years.

Walking north, she headed further into the huge market, the unique atmosphere bringing back happy memories of her student years.

From the mid-1100s until the Reformation, the bishops of Winchester had run the area from their nearby palace, licensing it as London's pleasure district – filling it with hundreds of squalid stews and brothels, bull- and bear-baiting pits, theatres, and the infamous Clink Prison. Much of the money they raised from these seedy trades was then used to build the spectacular cathedral seventy miles away in Winchester. Ava had spent one university holiday here in Southwark as part of a team surveying the abandoned Cross Bones cemetery, long believed to contain the remains of the Winchester Geese, as the bishops' prostitutes had been called.

Pushing deeper into the labyrinth of alleyways, Ava finally found the sign she was looking for – three black bulls' heads above the words: *Los Tres Toros*.

It was a small restaurant with a green and red front. Outside, a couple were drinking coffee at a battered round metal table. Through the window, she could see the interior was decorated with arches, greenery, patterned tiles, and large garish paintings.

She pushed open the door to find that the breakfast crowd had already moved on and the restaurant was mostly empty.

As she neared the counter, a surly-looking man approached. "Vosper?" he grunted.

She nodded, and without speaking, he began to pat her down.

When he was done, he led her through a set of battered swing doors into the kitchen. It was a small and shabby space, with a sweaty-looking man loading grubby beige tubs full of steaks into a large fridge.

She made a mental note never to eat here.

At the far end of the kitchen was another door. The man knocked on it once. Without waiting for a response, he pushed it open, and ushered Ava into a windowless back room.

Inside, the air was thick with cigarette smoke swirling around a grimy table littered with beer bottles and overflowing ashtrays.

She took in the scene in an instant.

There were three men sitting at the table. One had his back to her. The other two were facing each other. There was no other exit.

The man to her left indicated for her to take the empty chair furthest from the door.

Great.

They were leaving her no way out. If things kicked off, she would have to get past them.

Confidence is everything, she reminded herself.

She walked around the table, pulled out the remaining chair, and sat down.

She had come this far.

She would see it through.

"You think you can help us." It was the same man, now on her right. His voice was sandpapery from decades of cheap tobacco. The accent was Mexican, like Ramos's, but far thicker.

She nodded.

His face was shaped like a hatchet, with small eyes, and a droopy moustache blending into several days' worth of stubble. It was not a friendly face. But even more startling were the tattoos covering his arms and what she could see of his chest through the largely unbuttoned short-sleeved shirt.

At first she thought the tattoos were just a mesmerizing swirl of colours, but looking more closely, the designs were actually an intricate web of flowers, knives, and crosses. More arresting still, his neck was also tattooed – with a broad necklace of rose- and cross-patterned skulls.

She had thought Ramos's tattoo was unusual. But the ones she was looking at now made his look tame. They were like a psychedelic mix of South American Catholic kitsch and an Aztec death cult. If it was meant to intimidate, then it worked.

She pulled her eyes away, not wanting to be caught staring, and quickly sized up the other two men. They were younger and, judging by the bulges under the arms of their jackets, well-armed.

The tattooed man reached down under his chair, and lifted a brown leather satchel onto his lap. He held it open and delved into it, grabbing what looked like a piece of pottery. As he lifted it out, his hand brushed against a notebook inside the bag, fanning out several of its pages.

Ava had been prepared for many things.

But not this.

Her blood ran cold.

"Where did you get that?" she blurted out, hearing the shock in her voice, and instantly regretting having asked.

She could not let them see that she knew anything about it.

The man ignored the question, and passed her the shard of pottery.

"What is this?" he asked, his eyes narrowing to little more than hostile slits.

Ava's mind was still on the page of the notebook she had just seen, which had been open long enough for her to see the jottings in both French and flowing Arabic.

Her heart was beating hard.

She knew that handwriting anywhere.

The previous year, Professor Amine Hamidou from the Sorbonne in Paris had contributed an article to a collection on cylinder seals published by the British Museum, and Ava had helped edit the book, dealing directly with the authors for their corrections.

She had spent hours reading his handwriting and notes, including his Arabic.

It seemed completely incongruous.

What was a gangster in Borough Market doing with Professor Hamidou's notebook?

The man across the table was staring at her expectantly.

Registering his question, she looked down at the piece of smooth pottery in her hand.

It was a flat rectangular shard of earthenware the size of a small dinner plate. On it was a clearly etched Chi-Rho monogram, around which were grouped three clusters of text in the unmistakable jagged slashes of ancient Aramaic.

She scanned it quickly, reading the words from right to left.

The carving was clear, neatly executed, and she could make out the words with ease.

She stared numbly at the writing, a wave of light-headedness washing through her.

Was this a joke?

She felt the blood rushing to her head as she tried to focus again on the small piece of earthenware, forcing herself to read it all again.

When she finished the short text for the second time, she went into a form of mild shock.

Without thinking, she pulled a small double-barrelled magnifying loupe from her pocket. Flicking on the LED light in the side barrel, she peered at the writing through the sixty-times magnification lens.

She focused carefully on the carved words, studying the letter forms and their edges in minute detail. If it was a modern fake, there would be tell-tale signs.

She angled it under the light, and examined the first cluster of letters meticulously.

As she moved to the second group, and then the third, she saw no signs of machine tooling, later additions, or re-cutting.

She closed the loupe and put it back in her pocket.

Holding the pottery in both hands, she took in its dozens of distinct features – size, colour, texture, temperature, wear, depth of carving, shape and size of writing, vocabulary, spelling – and knew beyond a shadow of a doubt that it was genuine.

She would bet her career on it,

Overwhelmed, she put the pottery gently down onto the table, terrified that she might drop it.

Never in her wildest dreams had she imagined she would one day hold an object of its significance.

It wasn't just another antique.

It would change everything.

Dozens of questions tore through her mind.

Dazed, she looked back at the man sitting opposite her.

"Well?" His tone was impatient. Belligerent.

She was sure he must have noticed her reaction.

She forced herself to calm down, to focus.

If they did not know what it was, there was no way she was going to tell them.

She prayed her voice would not betray her.

"It's Aramaic," she answered, focusing on bland generalities, "one of the most widespread language of the ancient Middle East, spread by the Assyrians, Babylonians, and Persians. When King Nebuchadnezzar of Babylon carried the Hebrews into captivity in 597 BC, they abandoned Hebrew as their day-to-day language and started speaking Aramaic. This piece could therefore come from anywhere in the Middle East, and it's not really possible to be more specific about culture, time, and place."

She held her breath.

If the men in the room knew even the first thing about the object, they would laugh her out of the room.

There could be absolutely no doubt where the piece of pottery came from.

The words on it were unmistakable.

The tattooed man grunted.

She held his gaze, praying her face gave nothing away.

He lit a cigarette, and slowly blew out a cloud of smoke. "Read it."

Her palms were starting to sweat.

This was not good.

Was it a trap?

Did he know what the writing said?

If she read it out in English, all hell would break loose.

She stared into the middle distance for a moment, wrestling with the options.

"*Ta bien*," he grunted, "not an expert after all," He smirked, turning to his companions, inviting them to share in the joke.

Ava took a deep breath.

"*Ya'qov bar halpai thadai bartalmai yehuda sicari'*," she began, "*Ya'qov bar zabedai yohanan philippos tauma —* "

A silence descended over the room as the ancient language filled the air – its sounds alien and guttural.

"*Shim'on kepha matai andreas shim'on qan'ana'.*" She finished and looked up, terrified she had given too much away.

"So, what is it?" he growled, his face wreathed in cigarette smoke.

She blinked slowly, fumbling to get her thoughts in order.

That was the question she had been fearing, hurriedly preparing an answer while she had been reading out the list.

If he knew what the pottery was, and if this was a test, the wrong answer would destroy her credibility in an instant. Given the weapons and atmosphere in the room, that was not an attractive option.

Yet if they did not know what it was, she could not risk giving them even the first clue.

The consequences were unthinkable.

She was aware of sweat on her brow.

"It's names," she answered, summoning a confidence she did not feel. "Probably commemorating notable individuals involved in a significant event – paying for a building, concluding a trade or peace treaty, dying in battle. Some occasion the community wanted to mark with a permanent record."

She struggled to keep her voice level.

That was a lie.

She knew exactly what the names were, and what they commemorated.

The man stubbed out his cigarette slowly, then leaned forward and took the pottery from the table in front of her, returning it to the satchel.

She stared at the bag, numbed by the sudden sense of loss, quickly followed by a rising panic.

What was he going to do with it?

It was, without doubt, one of the most important artefacts ever to have been discovered.

Maybe the man knew exactly what it was. She had learned long ago that people were rarely what they seemed. Deep pools of skill lay everywhere. Snap judgments were often wrong. And dangerous.

There was one quick way to find out.

She leaned forward in her chair. "It reminds me of a well-known piece from Palmyra in Syria." She did not let her eyes leave the man.

He stared back at her, expressionless.

"Do you know the Mongol period at Palmyra?" she asked, her stomach tightening.

He grunted an acknowledgement, and gave a shallow nod. But not before she had seen the almost imperceptible widening of his eyes as he struggled with the question.

She had her answer.

He was bluffing.

He was not the Syrian end of Ramos's operation.

He knew nothing about the region's archaeology.

Even a schoolchild in Syria could have told her that Palmyra was a Roman city, not Mongol.

Whoever these people were, they were middle men. Which meant their speciality was almost certainly crime and violence, not antiquities.

She suddenly felt ill.

They had absolutely no clue what it was.

What if they just threw it away?

"You can go," he announced perfunctorily.

Her heart was thumping.

Was that it?

He nodded towards the door dismissively.

She stared at him, rooted to the spot, unable to tear her mind away from the piece of pottery in the bag he was placing back down into the floor.

"What are you going to do with it?" she asked, her voice coming out slightly strangled.

The man smirked. "You want it? How much?"

For a moment she thought he was serious, then realized he was mocking her.

"We know where to find you." He stood up, nodding in the direction of the door.

Ava moved towards it mechanically.

This was not happening.

She had to do something.

As she took hold of the handle, she turned back to face him. "It's valuable." She prayed her excitement and anxiety did not show. "Good condition. Undamaged. Clear writing. I can get it placed with a buyer, and provide all the appropriate paperwork to deflect any questions. I know what it's worth. I can make sure no one pulls a fast one on you." She tried to sound breezy, as if this was all in a day's work. "Do you want me to take it?"

The question hung in the room.

Had she gone too far?

He took another cigarette from the soft packet in his shirt's top pocket, and shook his head. *"Adios."*

Ava felt herself starting to panic.

What if it was never seen again?

She looked down at the floor, praying for inspiration. But there was nothing more to be said. Unlike the two men guarding their leader, Ava was unarmed, so taking it by force was not an option.

With nothing left to say, she turned the handle of the door, and stepped out into the kitchen.

The man who had shown her in was waiting at the far end, over by the swing doors. He opened them for her, followed her through into the restaurant, and showed her out.

As she stepped onto the tarmac, she spotted Ferguson at a stall about twenty yards ahead.

She did not acknowledge him. They had agreed he would make his own way to the restaurant, and keep an eye on it from a discreet distance. If he became concerned for any reason, he would investigate.

Ava walked in the opposite direction, breathing hard, not believing what had just happened.

What she had just left behind.

She made herself walk slowly. Whatever impression she had left with the Mexicans, she knew someone from the restaurant would still be watching her. Regardless of whether they bought her story – or whether they had concluded she was an imposter – they would now be taking a keen interest in who she was.

And that suited her just fine.

Whatever she had wanted when she entered the restaurant had just fallen way down her priority list.

The only thought in her mind now was that the names on the small piece of pottery – the nineteen short words – were enough to change the world.

---- • ◆ • ----

CHAPTER 23

10b St James's Gardens
Piccadilly
London SW1
England
The United Kingdom

"THE CHI-RHO is one of Christianity's oldest symbols."

Ava was sitting next to Ferguson on the sofa in her flat, re-drawing the shard of pottery she had seen at Borough Market onto a large piece of paper.

She was still trembling slightly, finding it hard to believe what she had seen.

"It's called a Chi-Rho because it's made up of the first two letters of the ancient Greek word *Christos*. The first is a *chi*," she wrote the letter down:

$$\chi$$

"And the second is a *rho*." She wrote it underneath the first:

$$\rho$$

147

"If you superimpose them, you get the Chi-Rho monogram, which the early Christians adopted as a symbol. People often think they're an X and a P, but they're not." She wrote another word:

χmas

"We say 'Xmas' for Christmas, but it's actually a Greek *chi*, short for *Christos*. In other words, Christ's mass."

"The Chi-Rho is often linked to the pagan Roman Emperor Constantine." She was starting to relax as the adrenaline from the restaurant ebbed away. It was good to talk it through. "It's said that in AD 312 he saw it in the sky, along with the words '*en touto nika*', or 'in this, conquer'. So he had the sign painted on his men's shields before going out to win the crucial battle of the Milvian Bridge. In gratitude, he converted to Christianity, became the first Christian Roman emperor, and allowed Christians to practice their religion without persecution across the Empire. As a result, the Chi-Rho became a symbol of imperial Roman Christianity. You still see it all over churches."

Ferguson nodded.

"But actually," she continued, "it's far older than Constantine. Long before Jesus, Greek scholars used it in the borders of manuscripts to mark passages they liked. For them, the *chi* and *rho* were the first letters of the very similar word *chrestos*, meaning 'good'."

"And how old was the pottery you saw it on today?" Ferguson pointed to the drawing Ava had completed while talking.

She had not yet told him what she thought the pottery shard actually was.

It seemed so implausible.

She still could not quite believe it.

"These things are notoriously difficult to place," she hedged. "You have to look at the shape of the letters and the spellings, because they all change over time."

"And what do you reckon?" He tapped the spiky letters she had drawn in Aramaic around the Chi-Rho, just as she had seen them at *Los Tres Toros*.

"It dates to the first century," she answered softly. "Which means it's the language of Jesus, his disciples, and his earliest followers."

Ferguson looked impressed. "I assume that means it's pretty rare?"

"Not just rare." She paused. "Totally unique. One of the most important biblical artefacts ever found."

She stood up and walked to the window, feeling a fresh wave of excitement. "If it's what I think it is, it's the earliest known reference to the story of Jesus."

"But what about the Bible?" Ferguson looked unconvinced. "That's pretty early, isn't it?"

Ava smiled. This was always a fun topic. "That depends. If you want physical manuscripts of the books in the Bible, the oldest surviving fragment of the New Testament is a tiny scrap of the Gospel of Saint John, about as big as a credit card, kept a couple of hours from here, up in Manchester. It dates from AD 100 to 200, which is a long time after the traditional date of the crucifixion in AD 33. The earliest whole gospels date from the AD 200s. And the first full New Testaments start around the AD 300s. So they're all pretty late, and all of them were written in Greek, which was the language of educated people in the Roman Empire." She paused. "Not only is the pottery I saw today from the century Jesus lived, it's also in Aramaic, his own language."

Ferguson's eyes widened. "Go on."

She was almost afraid to say the words. "It's a list of the twelve apostles."

Ferguson frowned. "What's so special about that? Everyone knows who they are."

Ava walked back to the sofa and sat down next to him. "They don't tell you this in religious studies lessons at school, but the different books in the Bible don't actually agree on the names of the twelve apostles. There are differences, and there are more than twelve."

"Seriously?" He looked incredulous. "How come people don't know this stuff?"

She shrugged. "It's all there for anyone who looks. If you count them up, you'll quickly find the problem."

She leant over to the shelves behind her and pulled down a large white hardback book. She flicked through it for a moment, running her finger down the pages. "Here we are. One: Simon Peter, the first pope. Two: Andrew, who some say was his brother. Three and four: James and John, the sons of Zebedee – John being the beloved disciple who may or may not have written the Gospel of John, the Letters of John, and the

Apocalypse. Five: Philip. Six: Bartholomew. Seven: Nathaniel, who some people say was the same as Bartholomew, but there's no real evidence for that. Eight: Thomas the twin, also called Doubting Thomas. Nine: Matthew the tax collector. Ten: James, son of Alphaeus. Eleven: Judas – often called Jude – son of James. Twelve: Thaddeus, who some say was the same as Jude, but again there's no real evidence for that, apart from wanting to trim down the number of apostles to twelve. Thirteen: Simon the Canaanite. Fourteen: Judas Iscariot." She closed the book. "If you add in Matthias, who was chosen to replace Judas Iscariot after the crucifixion, you get fifteen."

Ferguson sat back in his chair. "Well that rather messes up the numerology, doesn't it? I thought there were twelve apostles for the twelve tribes, signs of the zodiac, hours of the day and night, and so on?"

She nodded, feeling a burst of excitement again. "But the pottery has something else, far bigger than a definitive list of the twelve. And it's going to create a serious storm."

"Don't tell me, one of them was a woman?" Ferguson smiled.

Ava shook her head. "More radical than that – we already know there were women in his group." She pointed to one of the names. "This apostle is traditionally called Simon the Canaanite. But there's always been a problem, because the Greek word people translate as Canaanite is actually nothing to do with the place called Canaan, which is spelled differently and had ceased to exist centuries earlier. It's long been thought that the word might be linked to the Aramaic word for Zealot. In fact, elsewhere in the Bible, he's explicitly called *Zelotes* in Greek, which is pretty unambiguous. The theory goes that some early Christians didn't like the idea he was a Zealot, so played with the words and implied he was from Canaan instead. As nothing about the Bible is ever agreed by everyone, the debate has never been resolved."

She tapped the name on the drawing, and looked at Ferguson, her eyes shining. "But one reason why that pottery is going to change the world is that we've now got the name – for the first time ever – written in the original Aramaic. And it gives a clear answer."

Ferguson looked down at the word Ava was pointing at.

"It's *Qan'ana'*," she announced, "which means – beyond a shadow of a doubt – that Simon was not from Canaan, but was a full-blooded Zealot, with a capital Z."

"So he was a bit keen." Ferguson shrugged. "Why's that such a big deal?"

"Well, obviously … " she began, but then stopped herself. She forgot sometimes that other people did not live and breathe the ancient societies of the Middle East. There was no reason why he should have the first clue about its significance.

She leaned forward. "It doesn't mean keen. The Zealots were an armed Jewish rebel group, rabidly opposed to the Roman military occupation of their country. When Jesus was a child, they became a serious problem in Judaea, especially around Jerusalem, where they had a reputation for violent insurgency."

"Terrorism?" He looked surprised. "Back then?"

She shrugged. "Terrorism's a modern word. It's hard to apply it to ancient societies. But they killed and intimidated in order to change the politics of the region and force the Romans out."

"I'd call that terrorism." Ferguson sat back. "Textbook definition. And you're telling me that one of Jesus's followers was a member of this insurgency?"

Ava took a red marker pen and circled Simon the Zealot's name. Then she moved to the next group of names, and circled another one.

"Not quite," she smiled. "There were two."

Ferguson stared at her in disbelief.

She tapped the name she had just circled. "Judas Iscariot as well."

"But Iscariot sounds nothing like *qan'ana'*," he protested.

"No," she conceded, "but his name also has a disputed meaning. The Biblical Greek says *Iscariotes* or *Iscarioth*. It's said to come from *Ish Kerioth*, meaning man from Kerioth. But for a long time there's been a theory that it's a veiled reference to a Jewish group known as the *Siqarin* in Aramaic or the *Sicarii* in Latin. The name comes from the Latin word *sicae*, meaning dagger."

"Go on." Ferguson was listening eagerly.

"The whole Zealot movement was into violence," she continued. "But there was an inner group called the dagger-men. They had a reputation for mingling in crowds, especially at festivals, and for pulling daggers from under their cloaks to assassinate Romans and Jewish collaborators."

"Occupation's never pretty," Ferguson muttered.

"The point is," Ava continued, "people have claimed that Iscariot means dagger-man. Words in Arabic, Hebrew and Aramaic are all based on three-consonant patterns, and they say that Iscariot is derived from SCR, as is *siqari'*."

Ferguson leant in. "So what does the original Aramaic on the pottery say?"

"*Yehuda Siqari'*," she answered quietly. "Which means," she paused, "it would appear that Judas was a political assassin."

The doorbell rang.

Ava frowned as the interruption broke her train of thought.

Standing up, she walked into the hall, and looked through the front door's small circular spyhole.

There was a white courier delivery van parked outside, and a large man in a worn blue FedEx uniform on the doorstep.

On her guard now, her eyes swept the road for other vehicles or activity. *Would they try again so soon?*

The man put his hand slowly into his jacket pocket. She tensed immediately, straining to make out the shape of the object he was reaching for.

As she watched, he brought out a battered packet of chewing gum, and placed a small piece into his mouth, all the while trying not to drop the cardboard package and grey electronic tracking unit he was holding.

She watched him closely, noting that he looked severely out of breath from the simple effort of getting a sugar fix. If this was a hit, then he was the most out-of-shape and unlikely-looking assassin she had ever seen.

She relaxed, pulled the door open, signed for the package, and brought it indoors.

"Anything interesting?" Ferguson looked up.

"From Israel," she read the label out. "Tel Aviv."

She turned the package over in her hands, uncertain about it. "Museum mail always goes to the Museum. I don't use this address."

"Aren't you going to open it?" He walked over to join her at the table.

She weighed the parcel in her hands. "It's too heavy for papers."

"I doubt a letter bomber is going to use FedEx." He reached for the large envelope. "I'll do it if you want."

She shook her head and grabbed the slim perforated cardboard tab. She pulled, tearing off the detachable strip.

Putting her hand into the envelope, she felt something cold and smooth. Tipping it out, a brand new black touchscreen tablet slid out onto the table.

"Israeli electronics?" He looked over her shoulder, shaking his head. "Late night internet shopping? Unmissable deal?"

She turned it over for any indication who had sent it. Or why. But there was nothing. Just a small maker's mark in Hebrew.

Holding down the power button, she watched for a few moments as the screen came to life, glowing a lighter shade of black. An instant later, one small word appeared starkly in bright green:

PASSWORD

"Go on, then," Ferguson encouraged. "MASTER, LORD, 123456, QWERTY, STARWARS – try all the usual ones."

She shook her head. "We're not guessing someone else's password. This was sent to me. For me." She paused. "It's going to be something they think I'll use."

She looked down at the screen and began typing:

BAGHDAD

Nothing. The screen remained unchanged.

"How well do they know me?" she muttered, trying again:

GILGAMESH

Still nothing.

She paused, then typed again:

IRON MAIDEN

"Seriously?" Ferguson raised an eyebrow. "I'd never have guessed."

"Well, now you know." She pushed the hair out of her face as she started typing again.

"Here," Ferguson leaned over, "let me have a go". He typed three letters:

AVA

Immediately, the screen dissolved, and a new instruction appeared.

WESTPHALIAN CASTLE YOU VISITED RECENTLY

Ava glanced up sharply at Ferguson.

No one knew about that.

Well. Very few people. And two of them were standing looking at the screen.

"Is this from you?" she asked.

Ferguson shook his head.

She had only been to one German castle recently. It had been with Ferguson, and it was not something she wanted to remember in a hurry.

She quickly typed a single word:

WEWELSBURG

The screen changed again to display a black home page with just one icon – the familiar stylized white and blue 'S' logo of Skype.

She tapped it, and the app quickly opened into an address book, disclosing just one contact:

CALEB

As she processed the name, the pieces of the puzzle clicked neatly into place.

There were a limited number of people who knew what had happened at Wewelsburg. And as far as she knew, only one of them had any connection to Tel Aviv.

Besides that, the name Caleb was not exactly subtle.

There were many Calebs in the world, but they were all named after a man in the Bible, in the ancient Hebrew book originally called In the Wilderness, but better known as Numbers, from its numbering of the twelve tribes of Israel. In it, Caleb was a Hebrew spy sent by Moses to reconnoitre the Promised Land, to report on how many Canaanites lived there, and to assess how best they could be conquered.

"What does he want?" she asked Ferguson.

"Caleb?" He frowned.

She shook her head. "Uri."

After a moment's hesitation, she tapped the Video Call button.

A VPN connection flashed up, then it switched to video camera mode as the call opened and the screen filled with the real-time image of a man in a slate-grey t-shirt sitting at a desk in a hotel room. He was athletic, with short dirty-blond hair. Beside him, she could see a wire trailing from a large grey satellite telephone towards what she imagined was his laptop.

She breathed in deeply.

Uri was an assassin. That was his job. The only reason he was not in a prison somewhere was that he killed for the State of Israel as part of Mossad's elite *Metsada* division.

"You've hit the radar of some senior people here at the Institute," he began.

"Nice to see you, too," she replied, with no warmth in her voice.

"The file on you here is growing." His tone was business-like.

"Haven't you got anything better to do?" She did not have time for games. If he was trying to intimidate her, it was not working.

There was nothing new in intelligence agencies collecting data on the staff of other agencies. She assumed her time in MI6, and her subsequent extensive work in the Middle East, meant she featured on any number of classified databases in the region.

"Whatever you're doing," he answered blankly, "is not my area. I don't do desk work." He paused. "But I've been tasked to deal with you."

She was starting to get angry now.

He had a nerve.

"Deal with me?" She was not some schoolchild.

He shrugged dismissively. "The point is – you're upsetting senior people."

She thought back to the ancient Aramaic shard of pottery she had been holding several hours earlier.

Is that what he was saying?

Was Mossad involved?

Uri's face was impassive. "The Russian. Oleg Durov."

She was not quite sure she had heard right.

He continued. "Stay away from him."

Ava's mind was whirring. "Durov?" She struggled to keep the surprise out of her voice. "He's one of yours?"

Uri ignored her. "People here are surprised you even have clearance to engage with him."

She could not believe what she was hearing. "Let me get this straight. You're protecting Durov?"

The electronic face on the tablet remained expressionless. "As I said, this is not my file."

She was thinking fast. "That makes no sense. Russia is fighting to keep the current Syrian regime in power. Moscow is dropping heavy ordnance all over the opposition. That makes Durov and his Kremlin friends your number one enemy at the moment. It simply — "

He cut her off. "You need to understand something," his tone was sharp. "Your name has come to me only because I know you. But it's seriously not a good sign. You're being given one warning. So take it, and stay away from Durov."

"Or what?" Ava felt anger getting the better of her. "You're going to get on a plane and pay me a visit?"

Uri ignored the question. "I understand there was an incident at your house last night."

Ava reeled, as if someone had knocked the wind out of her.

What was he implying?

"That wasn't you." Her cheeks were getting hot. "You're not that sloppy. If you had — "

He cut her off again, his expression cold. "You're not listening. Do not interfere with the security of the State of Israel."

"That's absurd — " she began. But his image had disappeared, and she was looking at the Skype address book once more.

She stood staring at the black glass, momentarily speechless, before turning to Ferguson in disbelief. "What on earth was that all about?"

He looked back at her warily. "I've got no idea," he answered slowly. "Uri's just a foot soldier. But you've seriously annoyed someone very high up the food chain in Mossad."

CHAPTER 24

Oryol Oblast
Russian Federation

DUROV WAS KEENLY aware of his responsibility to instruct the younger members of his flock.

It was a task he undertook fervently.

The afternoon was mellow, and he had gathered the children around him, under a spreading ash tree, shimmering green beneath the blue sky.

He was sitting cross-legged, his simple linen prayer shawl draped around his shoulders.

He had chosen them specifically – exactly fourteen of them – selecting the ones aged between six and eleven. He had found it was the ideal age range. Old enough to have opinions. Young enough to be guided. Independent enough to go out afterwards and influence their peers with what they had learnt.

He pulled a bundle of soft richly decorated red cloth from his jacket pocket, and slowly unwrapped it to reveal an old book.

He knew the children would be impressed by the worn shiny black leather and the gold-tooled decoration. He let the sunlight play on it, picking out the single word embossed in large faded gold letters on the front.

It read simply: Библия. Bible.

He placed the red cloth onto the ground in front of him, and laid the Bible on it, facing the children.

"Who can tell me what is special about this book?" he asked the group.

They looked at it, nervously.

"Who wrote it?" he probed.

One of the boys closest to him made as if to speak.

Durov nodded his permission.

"God?" the boy asked.

"Good." Durov laid his hand lightly on the edge of the leather cover. "It's the word of God."

He let silence descend to allow the words to sink in.

"And should we obey the word of God?" He glanced around the group, from one to the next. "Do you think God expects us to do what he told us to do?"

They nodded in unison.

"And after trusting us with all the best gifts in life – our families, friends, and all the things that make us happy – do you think he has a right to be upset if we don't do what he asks?"

Again, the children nodded, before being distracted by a squirrel, which had emerged from a nearby tree.

Durov let them watch.

They would understand soon enough.

"Now," he resumed, when the squirrel had disappeared. "Here's a more difficult question. How do we know that God loves us?"

"Because his son died for us?" a girl at the back answered, her confidence bolstered.

Durov's anger flared suddenly, but he suppressed it.

Now was not the time.

"Your parents are Brother Artyom and Sister Galina, aren't they?" he asked.

The girl's lip started to tremble as she slowly nodded – uncertain whether to be proud that he knew who she was, or worried that she had done something wrong.

"Good." Durov made a mental note of the names.

He turned back to the group. "The *Meshiha* is not God's son." He was watching closely for any dissent. "He is God, in the form of God-the-Son. He is of the mystical Trinity – three-in-one."

He could see the girl was still confused.

It was no matter.

She would understand after her parents were disciplined. She would not make the mistake again.

"God allowed himself to be killed to save us," he continued, "because he knew we'd understand. He knew we'd see that a good death is the gateway to eternal life."

He gently picked up the book, and opened it at an old ribbon marking a page.

He reverently handed the volume to a girl in the front row. "Read," he commanded, "where I have marked the text."

In a halting voice, the girl began to read aloud.

"For if we believe that Jesus died and rose again, even so them also which sleep in Jesus will God bring with him. For the Lord himself shall descend from heaven with a shout, with the voice of the archangel, and with the trump of God: and the dead in Christ shall rise first: Then we which are alive and remain shall be caught up together with them in the clouds, to meet the Lord in the air: and so shall we ever be with the Lord."

"Wherefore comfort one another with these words," Durov completed the passage from memory. He breathed in deeply, feeling the power of the Spirit moving within him.

"So what is God telling us?" he asked, after a pause. "Who does he say goes to heaven with the *Meshiha*?"

A boy at the front spoke. "Those who get lifted up to heaven with him."

Durov nodded. "Good. And who else?"

There was silence.

"Who else did he say" Durov pressed them. "Didn't he say, 'Them also which sleep with Jesus'?"

The children nodded solemnly.

"So the living and the dead rise with him." He dropped his voice reverentially. "Now, this is important. Who did he say rises first?"

He nodded towards the girl. "Read it again, just to yourself."

The girl put her finger on the page, and began tracing out the words, her lips moving as she read. Then she looked up. "The dead in Christ."

"Good," he answered quietly. "And after them, which living people will be saved, do you think?"

The group was silent at first. Then a boy to his side answered. "The good ones."

Durov paused, then nodded. "But what if God isn't sure who among the living has kept his rules?" He took the Bible from the girl. "Or what if we had once done something bad, and it counted against us? It would be a shame to miss out on heaven, wouldn't it?" Durov suggested quietly but firmly.

The children looked sombre.

"But, you're clever children. And I know you listened carefully to the Bible. I know you heard God's word telling us that the dead will definitely rise and be Raptured in the air. And they will rise first."

"So the dead people will all go to heaven?" the boy responded.

"Clever boy." Durov smiled.

Now the children understood.

"Those who die for the *Meshiha* definitely go to heaven."

--- · ◆ · ---

Chapter 25

The Eurostar
The United Kingdom | The Republic of France

AFTER THE CONVERSATION with Uri, Ava had returned to thinking about the earthenware artefact she had seen at *Los Tres Toros*, along with Professor Amine Hamidou's notebook and what she assumed was his satchel.

She was still stunned by what had been carved onto the pottery.

It had left her overwhelmed – and furious she had not found a way of taking it with her.

Her number one priority now was to try and find a way to get it back.

The idea that the gang at Borough Market might break it – or worse, lose it – was plaguing her, partly for reasons that were not wholly self-less. She would love to bring the piece to the British Museum and be part of all the excitement that would surround the announcement of such an amazing find. But she also knew that an artefact of that importance unequivocally belonged in a world museum, where scholars would pore over it and rewrite the history of the Bible. The thought that it might languish unnoticed in some personal collection of black market antiquities was almost unbearable.

She had quickly concluded that there was only one person who could fill her in on the background, and help her to get it back.

Professor Hamidou.

When she had tried calling the Sorbonne, where he worked, he had not answered his phone. The departmental secretary had eventually picked up, and explained to Ava that Professor Hamidou had not been in for a couple of days, and had missed a number of classes.

Alarmed, Ava had looked up his home address, then made two reservations on the next Eurostar train to Paris.

Once on the train, there had been nothing further to be done about the pottery, so Ava had spread the two printouts from Rasputin's notebooks on the table in front of her, and focused on the one Swinton had given her that afternoon at the Cavalry and Guards Club.

———— • ◆ • ————

CHAPTER 26

Gare du Nord
112 Rue de Maubeuge
10ᵉ arrondissement
Paris
The Republic of France

THE UNDERGROUND PLATFORM at the Gare du Nord was crowded.

Moments earlier, Ava and Ferguson had clambered off the Eurostar train, passed through the barriers into the heaving station's main concourse, then descended the central stairwell into Paris's vast Métro system.

Once on the underground platform, there was no sign of the subterranean network's famous art nouveau architectural panache. Instead, the space was hot, smelled of drains, and the decoration was limited to some unappealing grubby grey tiles.

The platform started to fill quickly.

As she waited for the next train, Ava began thinking through what she might discover from Professor Hamidou about the Aramaic pottery.

She fervently hoped he would be able to help – to shed some light on where the shard was from, how he came to have it, why he had not told anyone about it, and how the Mexicans had acquired it. Most of all, she hoped he would be able to tell her how they could get it back again.

The more she thought about it, the more worrying it was that Professor Hamidou had not been to the university for a couple of days. She hoped it was simply that he had been temporarily out of town. After all, he was a researcher, and could be in any of a hundred and one places. But something did not feel right. If he was simply away on a study-trip, his assistant at the university should have been well aware of his movements.

Even though Ava did not want to think about it, she had to face the possibility that something far more final might have befallen him. Many artefacts from the Middle East were currently passing through hands with blood on them. And the gang at *Los Tres Toros* was plainly not involved in the antiquities trade on the basis of their technical archaeological skills.

She saw a flash of grey on the tracks.

Rats.

At least that accounted for some of the smell.

Around her, the crowd was beginning to turn into a crush. It was at least four people deep.

As she thought through how she would approach Professor Hamidou, she realized that although she knew what he looked like from his photograph in the British Museum book, he would probably not recognize her. She made a mental note to fish out her Museum identity card when arriving at his flat.

She glanced at her watch. It was still the rush hour.

Unlike most London underground platforms, which only catered for one train at a time, this was a double tunnel, with space for trains going in both directions. She could see right across the two rows of wide black tracks to the opposite side, where a similarly large throng of people was gathering to go south.

Finally hearing her train approach, she glanced along to the end of the platform, and watched as the brightly lit large-windowed carriages emerged from the tunnel and began rattling their way loudly towards her.

As the train neared, she sensed a fast movement beside her.

Surprised, she turned, just in time to see a man emerging quickly from the crush. He was wearing a brown hoodie, with the hood pulled over a wide-peaked baseball cap. From the way he was looking at the floor, keeping his face almost completely obscured, she immediately knew there was something very wrong.

He darted in behind her, with the front of his left shoulder pressed up against her back.

Instinctively, she glanced down at his hands, and a wave of horror flooded through her.

He was holding a short hypodermic needle – in a small syringe.

The crowd of commuters, oblivious, was crushing her from all sides.

She felt her muscles flood with adrenaline.

He was about to attack.

She could not get away. There was nowhere to go. The crowd was too thick.

She jinked hard to the side, watching as his fist passed less than an inch from her hip.

Her brain was flooding with questions.

Who was he?

Who had sent him?

Her eye never left the thin spike of sharpened steel.

She was barely aware of what was happening, but as she saw him prepare to strike again, she knew she had to counterattack, or he would keep coming.

He only needed to hit her once, and it would be over.

She swivelled to face him as he turned towards her, punching the needle forwards again, directly at her abdomen.

But this time she was ready.

She swerved out of the way, wrenching herself out of range, knocking hard into the passengers beside her.

As the needle sliced through empty air, she grabbed his other arm, yanking him forwards as she stepped around and behind him. In a split second, she swung her right fist into the back of his head, then followed through with her elbow, driving him down onto the concrete floor. As he fell, she stamped hard on the back of his knee joint.

She was on autopilot.

It was all happening so fast.

Ignoring the horrified faces around her, she bent down to hit him again, but he was too quick, and rolled away.

Before she could do anything, his arm and shoulder disappeared over the edge of the platform. She saw his other hand scrabbling to hold onto the platform, then his head went over the edge, followed by rest of his body.

Time froze, and there was a pause of what seemed an age. Then suddenly everything began again, and she heard the inevitable sickening thump of several tons of steel train slamming into the man's body, smashing him down onto the tracks, then powering over him.

A moment later, the noise of the train squealing was joined by screaming, sobbing, and people shouting in horror and panic.

Her blood pounding, Ava straightened against the person immediately behind her. Wheeling around with a clenched fist, she registered just in time that it was Ferguson.

"Walk fast," he ordered, grabbing her elbow firmly, his voice low. He propelled her towards the exit behind them, which was already filling with hysterical commuters. "He won't have been alone."

———— • ◆ • ————

CHAPTER 27

Gare du Nord
112 Rue de Maubeuge
10ᵉ arrondissement
Paris
The Republic of France

EMERGING ONTO THE street, Ava gulped in deep lungfuls of air.

Ferguson took her shoulder, steadying her. "Are you okay?"

She nodded. The adrenaline was still coursing around her system. "He just … " She left the sentence unfinished, still in shock.

She had no idea what had been in the syringe. Air? Ricin, like in London in the 1970s? Mercury like in Germany in 2012?

But one thing she was absolutely sure of – someone had unequivocally and very deliberately tried to kill her.

"In here." Ferguson directed her through the glass door of a small *bar-tabac*.

Inside the low-lit café, a row of men sat at the shiny high metal bar, variously drinking a range of coffees, beers, and liqueurs.

Ferguson pulled up two chairs at a small table near the back.

"*Deux cafés cognacs,*" he ordered as the waiter approached.

When the waiter returned a few moments later and put the tall thick glasses down on the table, Ava took a large mouthful of the scalding hot drink, feeling the bite of the cognac on the back of her throat, and the relaxing warmth of the sweet coffee.

Her mind was racing.

Who the hell was trying to kill her?

Again?

Who knew she would be in Paris?

One thing was now totally clear.

The shooting outside her house in London the previous evening had not been a coincidence.

Someone definitely wanted her dead.

And they were not amateurs. They knew she would be in Paris.

Or else they had followed her there.

Either way, they were organized.

Swinton almost certainly had access to all border information. He could have found her details on the manifests from the Eurostar. But then so could anyone from the right departments of the Kremlin. Or Mossad.

About the only people who probably had no official idea of her movements were Ramos and his Mexican friends, but they could easily have tailed her there, or seen her board the Eurostar and got onto their associates in Paris. Their operation was certainly international.

She took another mouthful of the hot drink.

Her senses were firing on all cylinders now. "Did you get a look at him?" She looked up at Ferguson. "English? Russian? Mexican?" She had not managed to get a clear view of his face. Maybe Ferguson had noticed something.

He shook his head. "Just his back." His voice dropped. "He could've been anyone. Very professional, though. CCTV won't have picked up his face, or the needle."

Her phone buzzed.

"Ava?" It was Swinton.

She froze for a moment.

What on earth did he want?

"Yes," she answered after a pause.

"Your pass is ready," he announced. "It's had all the necessary access rights put onto it."

She had forgotten about her pass.

"I've left it at reception at HQ for you to collect."

Was he checking up on her?

To see if she was still alive?

"Thanks," she answered carefully.

"Anyway, what do you make of the second cryptograph from Rasputin's notebooks?" he continued. "Have you had any thoughts yet?"

She frowned.

He had not asked for progress reports before.

"I've got a few ideas," she answered cautiously. "I just need a bit longer to knock them into shape."

"Okay." He paused. "Keep in touch."

The line went dead.

Ava put the phone slowly back down onto the table, lost in thought.

What was that all about?

Ferguson was stirring the inch of cream sitting at the top of his cup into the coffee. "I can't believe that just happened down there. I should've —"

"You're not my minder," Ava cut off his sentence. "We established that a long time ago."

As she said the words, Ferguson flinched, and she immediately regretted them. "I mean, I don't expect any favours," she added. "I know what kind of people we're dealing with. If I drop the ball, it's my fault."

"I'm not talking about favours," Ferguson countered. "I wasn't paying attention back there. I should've been alert."

"You got me out of there." Ava smiled, finishing the last mouthful of her coffee, savouring the mix of heat, sugar, and bitterness. "Thanks."

She put a ten Euro note down onto the table. "Drink up. We need to get to Professor Hamidou's flat. We can walk from here. It'll take a bit longer, but I've gone right off the Métro."

---◆---

CHAPTER 28

Private aircraft
Latvian airspace

THE GULFSTREAM V sliced through the night, forty-five thousand feet above the earth's surface.

Inside its luxurious darkened cabin, Durov was sitting on a plump cream leather sofa, his eyes closed in concentration.

He had tuned out the noise of the twin Rolls Royce engines, and was aware only of the hiss of the compressed air circulating in the cabin.

It was almost time.

He just needed the sign.

The last few weeks had given him immense strength.

And hope.

The Rasputin notebooks he had been sent were filled with wisdom, and he was sure he now understood what the wandering mystic had been at pains to record.

He breathed deeply.

He was on the right track, and the Holy Mother was with him.

His success was clearly predestined.

The sender of the notebooks had not identified himself, nor explained the purpose of the gift. There had simply been a slip of paper with the hand-written number '489' on it. Nothing else.

It was no matter.

The Holy Mother moved in purposeful ways.

And he was sure that her hand was in this.

Her breath filled his lungs.

Inspiration.

It was what the word meant. *In-spirare*, to blow into. The All-Holy suffusing him with wisdom.

He looked out of the small window at the night sky, and down onto the lights of Riga.

He thought of all the souls wandering about their meaningless lives, wrapped in confusion.

They were lost.

But he knew the ultimate truth – the secret to all life's mysteries.

The only way to be sure of redemption was to embrace the ultimate self-sacrifice of death.

The time was at hand. The proof was everywhere. International tensions were running high. Fear was increasing. Instability was spreading.

The Holy Mother had not deceived him.

These were her works, for all who had eyes to see.

And he was her instrument.

When he gave the word, the Skoptsy would be ready.

Even the children.

He was their saviour, and they loved him for it.

They loved him so much, they would follow him into eternal glory.

All he needed was the sign.

—————— ◆ ——————

CHAPTER 29

Rue Myrha
La Goutte d'Or
18ᵉ arrondissement
Paris
The Republic of France

ONCE BEYOND THE Gare du Nord, Ava and Ferguson were into the Goutte d'Or – the Drop of Gold. It was a simmering slice of Africa in the heart of northern Paris, filled with a bustling population from the Maghreb and the sub-Sahara.

The famous outdoor markets of spices and fabrics – or drugs and weapons, if you knew where to look – had long since closed for the night, and the streets were now the fiefdoms of gangs of drifting youths.

As Ava and Ferguson passed, a group of men was loitering beside a burnt-out car, the pungent sweet smell of marijuana hanging heavily in the air.

"Nice neighbourhood," Ferguson muttered as they eased past them, pushing further north into the *quartier*.

"It's fine." Ava dug her hands into her pockets. "Unless we're unlucky, no one's going to bother us. They've got enough of their own problems."

She had memorized the simple map of the area while on the Eurostar.

As they headed further from the centre and into the more residential zones, the streets became quieter. Eventually they turned left into the Rue Myrha, making their way unobtrusively down the narrow road, keeping to the shadows of the buildings.

Ava was grateful for her black jeans and battered black corduroy jacket, which blended perfectly into the darkness.

Two thirds of the way down, she stopped and tucked herself into an unlit concrete doorway. "That's it," she announced softly, nodding at a building on the other side of the road. "Fifty-two."

It was a tired-looking beige four-storey apartment block. Inside, she could see a dimly illuminated staircase behind a wide strip of grimy glass bricks running the full height of the building.

They waited for five minutes, scanning the area, but the street was deserted, and no cars passed.

Approaching the front door, Ava pulled her British Museum identity card from her pocket, and readied herself to explain to Professor Hamidou exactly what she was doing there.

She reached out to the intercom panel, looking for his flat number, but to her surprise the dull steel unit had only one button. Peering more closely, she saw the single word *Concièrge* faintly visible under it.

She pressed it, and a moment later the lock buzzed loudly.

Ferguson pushed the scruffy black door, and it swung open to reveal a bare concrete lobby, whose only feature was a wall-mounted unit of scuffed metal mailboxes.

Ava walked over to them, and gently lifted the postal flap for the one marked 'App 304'.

She peered inside, and her heart sank as she counted the six envelopes nestling there.

This was not good.

If Professor Hamidou got as little postal mail as she did these days, it looked like he had not been home for a while.

She followed Ferguson in silence to the stairs, and climbed quickly up to the third floor.

Emerging from the stairwell, she could see ahead of her into a long bare corridor with six doors on either side – the whole space dimly illuminated by the streetlights shining through the partially obscured glass bricks of the stairwell. Ferguson ignored the timer light switch by his shoulder, and moved swiftly down the hallway, stopping outside number 304.

Ava joined him a moment later. He held up his hand for her to be silent, and pointed to the left of the lock, where the door met the frame.

There was a gap.

Her stomach tightened.

The door was open.

She listened carefully, but could hear nothing from inside.

Glancing at Ferguson, she pushed gently on the door, which swung open, revealing fresh damage to the jamb where the lock had been forced, splintering the wood.

"Christ," Ferguson muttered, as the light from the hallway spilled into the room. Together with the glow coming through the slats in the windows' shutters, it was enough to see the full extent of the interior clearly.

The flat was a large bedsit. There was a table under the window, a bed along the right wall, and a small kitchenette area facing it on the left, next to which a door opened into a small tiled shower room.

"I guess the last visitors didn't like the coffee and dates," Ferguson murmured, following her inside and closing the door behind them. "Don't touch the lights."

The flat had once been comfortably furnished and decorated, with a distinctly Maghrebi feel. The carpets were vibrant. There was an upholstered North African divan. And beside it was an attractive pair of intricately carved hexagonal side tables with long-spouted silver tea and coffee pots beside them.

But it was not a scene of oriental comfort.

All the furniture lay upturned and smashed. The contents of the cupboards and drawers were scattered across the floor. The side lamps had been knocked over and broken. Hundreds of the books on the shelves lining the four walls had been pulled from their places and lay strewn about, many of them with their covers ripped off. Even the bed had been overturned, and the mattress and linen slashed.

"We can safely assume it wasn't the DGSI." Ferguson peered into the washroom. "Not exactly a covert search."

Ava gazed around, feeling a wave of anger surge through her. "Either they didn't care," she stooped to pick up a quarter-bound book that had caught her eye, "or they knew Professor Hamidou wasn't coming back."

She turned the book over in her hand.

It was a close-printed hardback, in English. She guessed from the look of the print that it was probably from the mid-1700s. The frontispiece was beautifully engraved, with an archway, ornamental foliage, and flamboyant type. The title read: *Ecclesia Anglica Veterior Exspoliata: A Gazetteer of the Dissolution of the Monasteries, 1536–1541.*

"Isn't Tudor religion a bit modern for his tastes?" Ferguson was peering over her shoulder.

She thumbed through the fragile pages.

There was no reason why Professor Hamidou should not have wide interests. But the ransack of the monasteries in the mid-1500s did seem slightly unlikely reading material for an Algerian scholar of the ancient Middle East.

She scanned the scattered papers and books lying around the floor by the upturned table. As her eyes continued to sweep the room, she suddenly saw a movement.

It was an old-fashioned telephone answering machine, and its red light was slowly flashing.

"Over here," she called to Ferguson, bending down and pressing the Play button.

Almost immediately, the room filled with a mechanical female voice. *"Vous avez un message,"* it announced, before emitting a long beep, then continuing. *"Aujourd'hui, à treize heures trente-quatre."*

Ava and Ferguson exchanged looks.

The message had been left today, at 1:34 PM.

"Allô, Monsieur le professeur?" It was a woman's voice. Formal. Strained. *"C'est Isabelle à l'appareil. Ça fait trois jours que vous n'êtes pas à la faculté."* There was a pause. *"Il y avait des gens ici pour vous. Ça avait l'air urgent. On aurait dit des musulmans conservateurs, avec des barbes, de longues chemises noires, et des bouchons de prière. Est-ce que tout va bien, monsieur le professeur?"*

The machine clicked.

"Did you get that?" Ava turned to Ferguson.

He shook his head.

"Isabelle from the university. She asked if everything was okay. Said Professor Hamidou hadn't been in for three days. Said some strict Muslims had been looking for him. Beards. Long black shirts. Prayer caps."

The machine beeped again. There were no other messages.

"Sounds like *mujahideen* uniform." Ferguson bent down to look through a pile of papers on the floor. "Friends of his?"

She shook her head. "Not his style at all." She pressed the Erase button. "He's Christian."

"Do you think what they were looking for is still here?" Ferguson was carefully examining the reverse of a large print of the Roman remains at Timgad. It had been pulled off the wall, and torn from its frame, leaving a mess of old Arabic newspaper and mounting card exposed.

"I don't know." She was looking round with more urgency. "We can't stay here much longer."

She stepped carefully over the mounds of books and personal effects, and moved over to the window.

The louvres of the shutters were half-open, and as she passed, she distinctly saw the unmistakeable flare of a lighter flame across the street in the doorway she and Ferguson had been standing in.

Her heart missed a beat.

"We're being watched." She turned quickly to survey the room. "There may be someone on their way up already."

At least this time she would be ready.

"We need to be out of here," she announced, stepping over a pile of books and away from the window.

It did not matter who it was outside – the people from her house the previous evening, the men from the Métro station, or even the group who had done this to Professor Hamidou's flat. Whoever it was, she assumed they were hostile.

"Let's look at this from another angle." He straightened up. "If you had to hide something in here, where would you put it?"

She stared around the room.

It was small, with minimal furniture. There were not many options.

"Everyone avoids other people's loos, don't they?" She walked over to the washroom. Ferguson followed.

Inside, there was just a lavatory and a small ceramic shower tray and hose attachment. It was gloomy in the cramped room, but she could clearly see it was largely empty, with nothing on the walls apart from a small mirror and a narrow shelf, and nothing on the floor except a mess of broken toiletries and a scrunched up mat.

Ferguson pulled the plastic lid off the lavatory's tank.

There was nothing in it except water and pipes.

Ava stamped down hard on the floor, starting at one end and moving to the other. As she expected, it was solid concrete.

There was nothing there.

"Whatever it was, it looks like they found it," Ferguson concluded.

Ava turned to leave, but as she did, something caught her eye.

"Pass me that knife," she indicated a heavy bread knife on the kitchen counter.

Ferguson handed it to her, and she knelt down by the lavatory, reaching for the small wooden housing she had just spotted, where the porcelain waste pipe disappeared into the wall.

Feeling with her fingers in the dark behind the bowl, she found a small gap between the wood and the wall.

Jamming the knife deep into the crack, she pulled the handle back hard, using it as a jemmy. After a second tug, the wooden case came away in her hands.

"Well, I'll be … " Ferguson was staring at Ava as she lifted out a small clear ziplock bag that had been sitting on the pipe, concealed by the nondescript small wooden casing.

She undid the plastic zip of the clear bag, and pulled out a waterproof pouch. Opening it, she found a smaller one inside.

It weighed next to nothing.

Ferguson was standing by her as she undid the Velcro and unrolled the bag's closure.

Putting her hand inside the pocket, she was surprised to feel the familiar texture of old paper.

She pulled it out, and gazed down at a small rectangle of folded parchment. It was a light leathery colour, and about the length of a packet of cigarettes.

Written on it, in a bold italic handwriting, were three words:

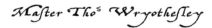

The ancient writing was arresting enough. But what drew her eyes more urgently was the large dark red seal next to the name, with sprays of frayed and faded yellowing silk sticking out from under it.

She turned it over, a sense of excitement mounting.

The underside of the folded parchment was blank, apart from an identical seal over another frayed layer of threads.

"What on earth is that?" Ferguson peered at the arrangement of wax and threads.

"Anti-tamper device," she replied. "You wind silk around the folded letter," she pointed to the fine strands of blue, "then you stamp a wax seal over the threads on either side. Anyone who wants to open the letter has to cut the silk, which leaves the frayed ends embedded into the seal."

"So the reader knows if it's been opened." Ferguson nodded.

"Exactly." Ava turned it over again to look at the name. "The only thing is, nobody's sealed letters like this for a very long time."

He raised his eyebrows. "Just how long, exactly."

She peered at the seal and handwriting more closely. "I'd say this letter's about five hundred years old."

He exhaled sharply and stared at her. "So it really could be, then?"

"Could be what?"

"A letter to Thomas Wriothesley," he answered. "Well, open it."

Ava could hear the excitement in his voice.

Turning it over again, she slowly unfolded the parchment, section by section, until she was left holding a quarto-sized sheet covered with a firm bold handwriting.

She and Ferguson read it together.[2]

> *Master Wryothesley,*
>
> *Be aduis'd that the true Master of the cunning Monke, like all of his poxe-ridden breede, is indeed the Diuell. Yet, hauing been put to the rack, the unholy whore-son shew'd contrite teares, and open'd his heart to Our will. He sayes that the Tablet was once keep'd with a signe, and a Booke or Gospell.*

---

2 'Master Wriothesley, be advised that the true master of the cunning monk, like all of his pox-ridden breed, is indeed the Devil. Yet, having been put to the rack, the unholy whoreson showed contrite tears, and opened his heart to our will. He says that the tablet was once kept with a sign, and a book or gospel. I do, therefore, pray you, please you to pursue with haste this sign, and book or gospel, and secure them for our favour. From London, this 12 of May 1539, your very assured and loving friend, Thomas Cromwell.'

J doe, therefore, pray you, pleaſe you

to purſue with haſte this ſigne, and Booke or

Goſpell, and ſecure them for Our favour.

From London, this xii of May 15 39,

your very aſſur'd and loving friend,

Thoˢ Cromwell

"Looks like we found it then." Ferguson strode towards the door.

Ava was staring down at it. "Who's Thomas Wriothesley, I wonder?"

"You know Thomas Cromwell?" Ferguson was clearly enjoying telling her something for a change.

She nodded. "King Henry VIII's lawyer and fixer."

"Way more than that." He was speaking more excitedly. "Cromwell was the brains behind England breaking away from the Catholic Church. He also masterminded the programme to shut down all the monasteries and line his and Henry's pockets with their money."

"Since when did you become a Tudor fan?" She put the old letter carefully back into its bag.

"Architects don't just do glass and chrome." He smiled. "I told you, I've got a thing about English medieval buildings – most of which were pulled down by Cromwell, and Wriothesley was one of his enforcers. Cromwell sat in London, coordinating it all, while Wriothesley toured the monasteries with his henchmen, smashing the old buildings to bits and walking off with anything valuable that wasn't nailed down."

Ava carefully put the letter back into its protective bags and slipped the bundle into her jacket pocket.

"If the letter's genuine," Ferguson looked at her, "then whatever the professor was mixed up in was something that Cromwell and Wriothesley were prepared to torture and kill for over five centuries ago. And, by the looks of it, some people still are."

Ava bent to pick up the book on Henry VIII's destruction of the monasteries, then moved to the door. "We need to get out of here."

CHAPTER 30

Rue Myrha
La Goutte d'Or
18ᵉ arrondissement
Paris
The Republic of France

PULLING THE APARTMENT door closed behind her, Ava turned and
ran towards the far end of the corridor.

Whoever was watching would not be far away.

When she got to the last door, she saw what she was looking for – a
sign marked *Sortie de Secours*.

She pushed the thin black horizontal bar, and the door swung open to
reveal a metal fire escape.

Taking the steps two at a time, she landed in a narrow concrete yard
filled with bins. Beside them was a shoulder-high metal gate, which she
hauled herself over.

Ferguson was immediately behind her.

Up on the fire escape, a door slammed shut and someone ran out onto
the external stairs.

Pulling into the shadows on the near side of the small street, Ava
began sprinting back down towards the main road.

There was a good chance that whoever had been watching them also had the rear of the building under surveillance, too.

She powered down the street, unable to hear anything over the noise of her own footfalls and her heart hammering in her chest.

Now on the main road, she saw a taxi parked up at a rank around a hundred and twenty yards ahead.

Looking over her shoulder, she could clearly make out two men running after them. She could not tell whether they were armed, but she had no intention of hanging around to find out.

Ferguson had seen them, too, and together they sprinted for the taxi.

Up ahead, a couple was stooping to speak to the taxi driver through the open passenger window.

Arriving breathlessly at the car, Ava shouted an apologetic *"Désolée!"* at the couple as she yanked open the door and threw herself into the back seat at the same time as Ferguson piled into the front.

She breathlessly ordered the driver to get going, and the taxi moved off, leaving the bewildered couple staring at the disappearing car.

As they accelerated, the taxi passed the two men running on the pavement directly towards them. Ava ducked down, but not before she had seen the one in the lead spot her, and put a telephone up to his ear.

Once the car rounded the corner, she sat upright again.

"They saw us," Ferguson announced, his voice deflated.

"They'll have the number of the cab," Ava acknowledged. "We need to get out of this one as soon as we can."

At the next rank they changed taxis, and soon joined the great Boulevard de Sébastopol, heading south.

The name turned her mind to Durov, and whatever he – and the Kremlin – were up to.

It seemed fitting that they were speeding down a street named after one of the most decisive military actions against Russia. How many people passing up and down it, she wondered, knew of the ghastly siege of the great Crimean port of Sevastopol, when the English, French, and Ottoman forces fought for control of the home of Russia's Black Sea Fleet? After eleven months of dreadful conditions on both sides, the Russians scuttled the fleet and blew the city up, then abandoned it. And now, as if history was incapable of learning from itself, the great powers were again fighting over the Crimean Peninsula and its famous port.

She wondered if anyone had ever drawn a map of the several dozen most strategic places on earth, showing how many centuries of repetitive conflict they had each seen.

She was keeping an eye out of the back window, but to her relief there was no sign of anyone following.

Pulling onto the Pont au Change – former home of the medieval moneychangers – they sped across Paris's main island, passing the great east end and spire of the Sainte-Chapelle, her favourite building in the city. Although the tourists flocked to the imposing cathedral of Notre-Dame, whose twin towers she could see illuminated out of the car's left windows, she had always held a soft spot for the lesser-known Sainte-Chapelle – a jewel box of delicate tall Gothic stone tendrils woven between what looked like whole walls of rainbow-coloured stained glass.

Finally, they arrived at the left bank, and entered the Quartier Latin – Paris's medieval university district. The taxi dropped them off, and Ava led Ferguson into the rabbit warren of narrow streets.

CHAPTER 31

Quartier Latin
5ᵉ arrondissement
Paris
The Republic of France

AVA AND FERGUSON had checked into their rooms near the ancient and impossibly narrow Rue du Chat-qui-Pêche.

Now they were sitting in a darkened dining room, illuminated only by the glow from a thick red candle in an antique candlestick on each of the dozen small round wooden tables.

They were already tucking into steaming bowls of thick onion soup and melted cheese, washed down with a solid red wine.

Since getting out of the taxi, they had been discussing the letter from Thomas Cromwell to Thomas Wriothesley, and had come to the conclusion that there was nothing more to be done about it until they had found out exactly what Professor Hamidou had been working on, which they would not be able to do until the university opened in the morning.

Ava reached into her pocket, and removed the printout Swinton had given her of Rasputin's second cryptograph.

With everything that had happened since meeting Swinton and Jennings at the Cavalry and Guards Club, she had not found time to look at it in detail beyond some initial thoughts on the Eurostar.

She laid it on the table between her and Ferguson.

Taking a pen from her pocket, she wrote out the first word on the large paper napkin by her side:

MELITA

Then the ~~group of two words either side of the head:~~

SEDROH
HORMIA

And finally the remainder, down at the bottom:

CHILD OF THE THEOTOKOS
PHILERIMOS
ZZ

"The only famous head on a plate I know is John the Baptist," Ferguson offered.

Ava nodded. "And MELITA means honeyed, which ties in with the Bible's description of him eating only honey and locusts."

She tapped PHILERIMOS. "John lived by himself in the desert. *Philerimos* is Greek, meaning a lover of solitude, so that fits as well."

She looked down at the rest.

SEDROH could be rearranged to make shored, hordes, or horsed, but neither of those seemed very promising. Equally, HORMIA was an anagram of mohair, but that did not help much, either.

Ferguson was watching what she was writing. "What's THEOTOKOS?"

"It's a central element in Orthodox Christianity," she answered. "It's the Greek word for God-bearer, which is the name they usually use for the Virgin Mary."

He drummed his fingers on the table. "So why write CHILD OF THE THEOTOKOS? Isn't that a bit convoluted if everyone in Russia knows who the *Theotokos* is? Why not just write Jesus?"

"True." She had been wondering the same. "Unless it's referring to one of Jesus's brothers or sisters."

"His what?" Ferguson looked surprised.

"Brothers and sisters," she repeated. "They're mentioned in the gospels."

"You're joking, right?" He looked at her warily. "I've sat through my share of chapel services at school and in the Army. No one ever discussed Jesus's brothers and sisters."

"That doesn't mean they didn't exist," she replied. "In the Gospels of Matthew and Mark, it says that some people from Galilee spotted Jesus speaking in a synagogue, and couldn't quite believe their eyes. They asked if he was really Jesus, the carpenter, son of Mary, and brother of James, Joseph, Judas, Simon, and a number of sisters. And after Jesus's death, the Acts of the Apostles says that his brother, James, stepped up to lead the band of bereaved apostles in Jerusalem."

Ferguson looked unsure. "But doesn't the Church say that Mary was a perpetual virgin? Surely they can't have it both ways?"

Ava took a piece of baguette from the basket in front of her. "People have come up with all sorts of theories over the centuries. Some say they were Joseph's children from a previous marriage. Others are happy with the idea Mary had them after Jesus. And some even dispute the translation, preferring the idea that the Bible writers meant cousins, or perhaps even spiritual brothers and sisters."

"As always, time spent with you is never dull." Ferguson refilled their glasses with wine from the carafe. "The Virgin Mary reference could explain the Virgo sign as well."

"I'd forgotten you knew tarot cards." She tapped the Virgo glyph under the writing absent-mindedly, deep in thought. "Actually, that sign could mean a lot of things. A person. A place. A time of year. A navigational direction. Or it could even stand for the Greek letters *pi*, *alpha*, *rho*, which the Virgo symbol is probably a stylized form of."

He peered at the symbol. "How do you get that?"

She wrote out two more words on the napkin, and spun them around for him to see.

παρθένος
Parthenos

"*Parthenos* just means maid or virgin, and in ancient Greece it was a title of the goddess Athena, who was sometimes called Athena Parthenos. That's why her most famous temple in Athens is the Parthenon, although the name is way older. Originally, Parthenos was a daughter of Apollo. When she died young, Apollo immortalized her as a constellation – the one we now call Virgo. The constellation was always associated with Parthenos's virginity, which is how it later came to be connected with the Virgin Mary. So the symbol for the constellation Virgo is probably a jumbled up version of the Greek letters παρ. You can sort of see it if you look closely. The M-shape is a mixture of the π and α. And the loop at the end is the ρ."

Ava took another mouthful of the soup, and put the code out of her mind for a moment, allowing herself to enjoy the taste, and the feeling of being back in Paris.

It was not her all-time favourite city in Europe – she felt more at home in the south, by the Mediterranean. But it was still pretty good. Especially the food. And she liked to visit the Louvre when she got the chance.

She had taken the Channel Tunnel many times since it had been built. It was incredible that Paris was now only just over two hours away from London. It made life so much easier. As a child, it had been a whole performance with cars and ferries to get from one capital to the other, and taken the best part of a day.

The tunnel still amazed her – a series of concrete tubes dug under the floor of the English Channel, like large drainpipes, through which cars and trains could speedily avoid the twenty-one miles of cold water between the two countries.

She remembered how, at the time it was opened, she had been surprised to learn from the television news that the earliest plans for the

Channel Tunnel had been drawn up in 1802 at the insistence of the inde-fatigable Napoleon Bonaparte. Not content with conquering large parts of the Mediterranean, he had dreamed of annexing England and —

She froze as an idea suddenly hit her.

Surely not?

She stared down at the photograph of Rasputin's notebook.

Her eyes locked onto the image, her excitement rising.

There it was.

It had been staring her in the face all along.

"The Knights of Saint John," she announced breathlessly, barely able to keep the triumph from her voice. "The crusader knights. That's what this clue is about."

"Crusaders, like the Knights Templar?" Ferguson sat forward. "Feels like old times again."

Ava thought back to their recent experience at Wewelsburg Castle, where they had come face-to-face with the modern-day descendants of the Knights Templar.

It had been quite an eye-opening experience.

She nodded. "The Knights of Saint John and the Knights Templar were the backbone of the crusader armies. They were both orders of crack troops, with a fierce rivalry. When Saladin captured the crusader army after the disastrous battle at Hattin, he spared everyone except the Templars and Knights of Saint John, whom he ordered to be beheaded so his men would never have to face them again."

"Here," she pointed excitedly to the first word. "MELITA means hon-eyed in Latin. But it's also the name the Romans gave to the island of honey – a name which has come down the centuries to us as Malta." She paused. "These days they are known as the Order of Malta."

She was kicking herself.

She moved her finger to SEDROH. "I wasn't thinking about place names before." She tapped the letters. "It's an anagram of Rhodes, the largest of the Dodecanese islands."

She looked up at him expectantly. "And you know what the two islands have in common?"

He shook his head.

"The Knights of Saint John had their headquarters on Rhodes, then on Malta," she continued. "And do you know where else they had head-quarters?"

"Go on." He was staring at the picture.

She pointed to HORMIA. "There."

He squinted at the word. "Is that a place?"

"It's an anagram," she answered. "For Moriah."

He looked blank. "Doesn't mean anything to me."

"Jerusalem," she answered, "is built around Mount Moriah." She felt a growing sense of certainty that she was absolutely right. "It's the sacred hill at the city's centre, where tradition says Abraham prepared to sacrifice Isaac, before God appeared to him as a burning bush. The tip of Mount Moriah is still visible inside the Dome of the Rock mosque at the centre of Temple Mount. It's also where David and Solomon built the great Jewish Temple, now under the al-Aqsa mosque just to the east, where the Knights Templar had their headquarters."

She beamed at him. "And Rasputin drew Saint John the Baptist because the Order of Malta started life as the Knights of Saint John, in crusader Jerusalem."

Ferguson was staring at her. "How on earth do you know all this?"

Ava took the last mouthful of her soup. "When I was at Amman, I used to visit Jerusalem regularly. You'd see regular reports of the Order of Malta – they're still closely involved in the work relating to the region's Christian people. I was just thinking about Napoleon's battles in the Mediterranean, and remembered how he expelled the Knights from Malta."

Ferguson was looking pensive. "How does that tie in with everything else on the clue? CHILD OF THE THEOTOKOS, PHILERIMOS, and ZZ?"

Ava glanced down at them. "I don't know yet," she answered honestly. "But whatever they are, I'll bet you any money they're linked to the Knights of Saint John."

Her thoughts were interrupted by her phone buzzing.

She pulled it out of her pocket, and saw it was displaying an anonymous number.

"Hello?" the woman's voice asked as soon as Ava answered it. "Is that Dr Curzon?"

"Who is this?" Ava asked, immediately on her guard.

"Ava, it's Mary," the voice answered hurriedly. "You need to get to Rome."

DAY FIVE

———— • ◆ • ————

CHAPTER 32

Piazza di Spagna
Rione IV (Campo Marzio)
Rome
The Republic of Italy

AVA WAS ON the Spanish Steps at 9:45 AM.

It was a perfect place to meet, already bathed in early morning July sunshine, and awash with busloads of tourists, even at this hour.

Mary had told her to be at the south-eastern end of the landmark by 10:00 AM, so she had arrived early to make sure she had not been followed.

Looking at the grand sweep of pale stone steps leading up to the twin-towered church at the top, she smiled at the irony of history.

The church, the Trinità dei Monti, had been built by the French, and was still maintained by them. The world-famous steps plunging down from its parvis to the square below had also been designed and paid for by the French. But the Spanish embassy at the bottom had resulted in everyone calling them the Spanish Steps.

Sometimes life was just not fair.

At 9:55 AM Ava spotted Mary approaching.

"Nice touch to meet here." Ava nodded at the building behind them – a museum to the English romantic poet, John Keats, who had died there aged twenty-five.

"Is your colleague here?" Mary asked, looking around.

Ava was lost for an instant, unsure who she meant.

"The Army officer?" she prompted.

"Oh, Ferguson?" Ava was surprised to hear him described as a colleague. She shook her head. "He'll join us later."

She saw a hint of disappointment on Mary's face. Then it was gone.

Mary turned and walked down the few remaining steps. "You left the reception at the Russian embassy early." Her tone was breezy, but it was clearly a question. "With Oleg Durov." She paused. "Did you find out anything worthwhile?"

Ava smiled to herself.

So the Vatican had not just been concerned with getting the Shroud back, and Mary's appearance at the Russian embassy had not merely been to catch sight of Durov – or even to keep an eye on her and Ferguson.

The Vatican was actively following up on Durov.

Ava had no intention of telling Mary the details about her trip to Durov's house – not until she knew exactly what the Vatican's interest was. "I was surprised to see you there," she countered.

Once off the steps, Mary kept walking across the Piazza di Spagna. "When we were back in London, at the Museum, you asked whether I really got the information on Lunev and Durov from the Vatican. You seemed surprised that Rome would have access to that kind of data."

Ava nodded. "Well, you have to admit, it's not widely known that the Vatican has a hi-tech security and intelligence capability."

Mary stopped at a fountain, lost in thought. "That's true, but put it this way." She pointed to the sculpture. "This water comes from an ancient aqueduct that feeds over a dozen fountains. Many claim it's still the finest water in Rome. When the engineers built this fountain in the early 1600s, the water pressure wasn't strong enough to make huge jets, so instead they opted for a sculpture of a battered boat struggling on a pond."

Her expression was deadly serious. "You may think the Vatican has similarly lost the energy and vigour it once had, and that it's now no more than a battered ship. But you'd be wrong. Its spiritual waters are still highly rated by billions, and as the single largest religious organization on the planet, the Holy See has a vast global empire to protect. It's never been afraid of technology, and nowadays it uses every means available to secure and protect its operations."

When Mary had first introduced herself as 'Vatican Liaison', Ava had wondered if she had been joking – although there had been nothing funny about her marksmanship at Nuremberg.

"Who exactly do you work for?" Ava probed. "Does your department have a name?"

"The *Dipartimento delle Intellegenzia Vaticana*." Mary exited the piazza into the Via del Condotti, the heart of Rome's high-end fashion district. "DIV for short, affectionately known as Five-O-Four, from reading it as Roman numerals."

Ava smiled. It was a nice touch.

"And what does Five-O-Four look after?" Ava was keen to know more now that Mary was talking.

"The Swiss guard are the military. The Gendarmerie Corps is the police. As you can imagine, that leaves a lot of other areas: terrorism, espionage, sabotage, cyber – internally and externally."

Ava watched as two nuns passed them.

Maybe it was not so difficult to believe.

The Church had always been high on the hit lists of a variety of hostile organizations. It was not that long ago that the pope had been shot in Saint Peter's Square.

So, from what Mary was telling her, the Vatican now had a full intelligence service, like MI5, MI6, and GCHQ in the UK, or the FBI, CIA, and NSA in the US.

Or maybe it always had?

"What about you?" Mary asked Ava. "Nobody's told me who you lot are. The initial call came through to us from the UK's Ministry of Defence. But you work for the British Museum?"

"I'm just part-time with the MoD," Ava replied, feeling a small thrill at realizing it was the first time she had told anyone of her new role. "It's a specialist unit. To be honest, I'm still finding my way around."

"Don't worry," Mary smiled. "I'm pretty used to departments no one has ever heard of."

Ava was grateful for being cut some slack. "Anyway, what brought you to Rome?" she asked, changing the subject. "You're a long way from home."

"Los Angeles." Mary stopped to let a couple pass her. "I was a cop. LAPD. A neighbour's child was taken hostage by a gang trying to intimidate me into closing down a narco-investigation. They told me they'd kill him if I carried on. I didn't think they'd do it … " Her voice trailed off.

"I'm sorry," Ava replied, when it was clear Mary had finished the story. "Did they get the gang?"

Mary shook her head. "They're way too connected. No one touches *La Santa Muerte*."

Ava wondered if she had heard right. *"La Santa Muerte?* Saint Death?"

"Mexicans," Mary confirmed. "Really, really bad news. Creepy religious tattoos, too."

Ava's pulse quickened. "Skeletons, skulls, rosaries, flowers – that sort of thing?"

"Oh, you've heard of them." Mary nodded. "It's a very particular look – kind of Catholic tat meets voodoo. You know it when you see it."

Ava had.

"Where does the name come from?" Ava was intrigued. "Is it a Church thing?"

"Nuestra Señora de la Santa Muerte is a popular folk saint in Mexico and the southern US. She's death – a female grim reaper – but she also takes care of people: protects them, heals them, and guides them to the afterlife. If you see a skeleton saint in a shroud with a scythe, flowers, owl, hourglass, or scales, that'll be her. The Church and government are pretty unimpressed, although millions of people love her for her miracles. This particular gang has adopted her, and you don't want to get mixed up with them."

So now she had a name for the antiquities gang she was dealing with.

Saint Death.

She dug her hands into her pockets and started following Mary again. "Why did you choose the Vatican?"

"I needed to get away," Mary replied, "do something completely different. I'd always fancied coming to Europe. At the interview I fell in love with Rome. I felt that if I looked hard enough, everything was here. I still do. And the best bit's the ice cream."

Ava smiled. "Anyway, you've got the Shroud back, so what's your ongoing interest in Durov?"

"His men murdered a Church employee in Turin." Mary's expression was grim. "Until I'm certain he won't do it again, he's staying firmly on my radar."

Ava walked a few paces in silence, mulling over what she had learned from Mary. "Why did you call me here?" she asked after a few moments. "Has something happened?"

Mary nodded. "Durov's in Rome."

She set off walking again. "After seeing you leave the embassy with him in London – and then hearing about that nastiness outside your house the other night – I figured he might still be of interest to you."

Did everyone know about Julia, and the fact she was killed on her doorstep?

Ava stopped at the window of an old-fashioned café. It looked like a throwback to a previous century, with its richly papered walls, oil paintings, tinted mirrors, elegantly upholstered sofas, and marble-topped tables.

First Mossad were protecting Durov.

Now he was at the Vatican?

What was going on?

"Don't tell me he's friendly with some senior cardinal?" Ava asked, remembering what Jennings had told her about the Skoptsy and their bizarre religious rituals. "Not really his scene, is it?"

Mary shook her head. "He's not at the Vatican. I could deal with the situation if he was. I'm afraid he's in there."

They had drawn level with a large arched gateway sandwiched between Jimmy Choo and Hermès. Mary nodded towards it as they passed.

"He flew in on a private jet overnight. We spotted his name on the paperwork and discovered he was going to be a guest here, at 68 Via del Condotti. That's when I called you. He entered the building in the early hours of the morning, and hasn't come out yet."

Ava looked up at the high stone wall, and a tingle of electricity ran through her as she saw a large Maltese cross carved into the stone above the doorway, and two flags either side of it emblazoned with Maltese crosses.

"What's inside?" Her excitement was mounting.

"The palace of His Most Eminent Highness the Prince and Grand Master of the Order of Malta."

Ava felt a flush of satisfaction as she gazed up at the imposing entranceway.

Just like in Rasputin's cryptograph.

She had been right.

"What's he doing in there?" she asked as they passed, and the large wooden gates began to open. "Have you got Five-O-Four people on the inside?"

Mary turned right, steering Ava into the narrower Via Bocca di Leone.

"I'm afraid it's not that easy." She shook her head. "The Order of Malta are part of the Church. And they accept the leadership of the pope … "

"Then what's the problem?" Ava was unsure why Mary was being so hesitant.

Mary looked tense. "They're not like any other organization on earth. They're a country, with their own passports, number plates, stamps, and coins. Their property is independent sovereign territory. When you step through their doors, you leave Italy. There'd be all hell to pay if I walked in unannounced."

Ava was momentarily flummoxed that a religious order of the Catholic Church was also an independent country. "Then what's the plan?"

"I was rather hoping," Mary answered slowly, "that you'd have one."

• ◆ •

CHAPTER 33

Majdal Shams
The Golan Heights
Israeli Occupied Syria

THE MOBILE M270 multiple launch rocket system was the pride of
the Israeli Defence Force's artillery. It could discharge a salvo of twelve
high-explosive warheads in forty seconds, scorching and pulverizing an
entire half-mile grid square back to the Stone Age.

It was *Menatetz*: the Smasher.

From inside its heavily armoured cabin, Danny Aronov looked out
through the sturdy blast grilles at the mountains of the Golan.

He had volunteered for training as the M270's gunner, and had
quickly learned that it was not a difficult role. The job required only
that he sit between the driver and the section chief, with the computer
fire control panel in front of him. Apart from that, there was not much
to do, except ensure the targeting and guidance system was properly
hooked into the data feed from the Command Post. When the time was
right, he merely had to close the external grilles on the cabin windows,
punch the button to initiate the launch sequence, and let the computer
do the rest.

Industrial killing had never been so easy.

The driver steadied the two steering handles and jabbed the heavy accelerator, coaxing the twenty-eight tons of steel and armour up the ancient incline.

Around them, the northern Golan was tranquil.

Oaks, junipers, black mulberry and olive trees clung to the brightly sunlit volcanic mountainsides. The scene was majestic and pure, but Danny had stopped seeing it long ago. He was aware only of how it had all been defiled by mankind. How, over the millennia, with slingshots, spears, swords, guns, and bombs, man had soured what the Lord had offered as a priceless gift. Greed, jealousy, and violence had turned Paradise into Hell.

He looked down at the launch control panel in front of him.

Well, not for much longer.

He had read the ancient writings, and knew that the end would bring a new beginning.

But first, there had to be a descent into the abyss.

He checked his watch. They were still a long way from the plateau where they would park and stand guard over the hostile frontier – surveying the area where the Golan dropped away to the desert of western Syria, and the lawlessness that lay out there.

Once parked, they would train the rockets on the jihadi-controlled badlands, arm the system, and wait for instructions – just like men from their battalion did every day.

Almost nothing ever happened.

A few years ago, another battery had brought down a Syrian Sukhoi SU-24 bomber straying over Israeli airspace. But that had been the most exciting thing to occur in a long time.

The job was the textbook definition of monotony.

He looked at the unending terrain, allowing himself a small smile.

Stretching his gloved hand down to the hip pocket of his dark green combat jacket, he felt for the reassuring bulge of the stun grenade he had failed to return to the Quartermaster three days earlier.

The *Menatetz* powered on.

As they climbed, he looked down into Syria, onto the abandoned United Nations observation post far below. International peacekeepers had monitored the area since 1974, but for the last few years it had been too dangerous for them, and the camp lay derelict and dilapidated.

It was the perfect spot.

He had no idea what the M270 was worth. A couple of million dollars, he had heard. It was state-of-the-art artillery technology – a stretched Bradley fighting vehicle chassis, fitted with a bombproof cab at the front and a large rectangular multiple rocket launcher on the back that could be swivelled, raised, angled, and aimed to direct its lethal payload to targets up to a hundred and eighty miles away. It was a crushing amount of firepower – as much as an entire traditional artillery battery. And even though standard operating procedures were to run it with a crew of three, it only needed one man to drive it and unleash the biblical Armageddon it carried.

Danny gazed up ahead at the three peaks of Mount Hermon, where the melting snow mixed with the natural springs and ran south as the mighty River Jordan.

It was a place that was blessed.

The call to action lay in the ancient Song of Songs. He knew it by heart:

From Lebanon come with me; From Lebanon, my bride, with me! Trip down from Amana's peak, From the peak of Senir and Hermon, From the dens of lions, From the hills of leopards.
This was where it would begin.

Behind him was the Sea of Galilee. In Roman times – when Jesus had lived there – it had been at the heart of the Decapolis, a network of ten cities connected by Graeco-Roman culture rather than the local Jewish, Nabatean, or Aramean, yet now it was a hinterland. It was funny how things changed, he mused. Back then, Damascus, too, had been one of the leading cities of the Decapolis, but now it was a world away, at the bloody heart of a brutal war.

He shifted on the metal seat's thin plastic-covered padding.

He had only fully understood when he had first started reading the *Nevi'im*, the prophets of the Tanakh. Then he knew he had a destiny.

And it was also the destiny of the world.

He thanked the Lord for the Brothers of the Seven Seals, who he had found deep in the dark web, preparing to do what needed to be done. It had been a revelation to know there were others who saw the signs and understood what needed to happen.

And he also gave thanks for the day he had received the first approach from the prophet. In the encrypted pulses of clandestine cyberspace, the Russian had sought him out. And he had known immediately that this charismatic stranger was the man he had been waiting for – the one he had been put on this earth to follow.

Danny was watching carefully out of the cab's front grille, and when he finally saw the four large boulders pushed up around the base of the roadside telegraph pole – one with a Star of David spray-painted onto it in blue – he started to sweat with excitement.

It was all going to happen. Just like he said it would.

"Stop," he ordered the driver next to him. "I have to take a leak."

The driver ignored him.

"Seriously," he insisted. "Unless you want the cabin to stink all day."

"*Ma nisgar*," the driver cursed, braking hard and bringing the vehicle to a shuddering halt. "You're pathetic."

Danny ignored the jibe.

He had been suffering them throughout his military service.

But not for much longer.

Feeling wired, and with his senses on full alert, he scrambled over the section chief next to him, and pushed open the heavy armoured door.

The cold mountain wind slapped him in the face, but he welcomed it – the low temperature meant there were less likely to be walkers about.

Hitting the ground, he pulled the grenade from his pocket. Gripping the safety lever to the body of the slim canister, he rapidly pulled out the pin. Without pausing, he spun and hurled the grenade back into the cab, slammed the door shut, dropped to the floor, and clamped his hands over his ears.

Despite the thick material of his gloves and the dense armour-plating on the vehicle, two seconds after he had released the lever, he heard the grenade detonating.

It was a deep pressure wave of disorientating sound that must have been devastating in the small confines of the metallic cab. He had been looking at the ground, so was spared the simultaneous lightning flash of magnesium that accompanied the explosion, but knew that his two compatriots in the vehicle would be blinded for at least five seconds, and blinking away coloured lights and optical interference for half an hour or more as their seared retinas tried to recalibrate.

He picked himself up just in time to see the two black-clad and balaclavad figures swarm the vehicle's cab.

The muffled sound of the six suppressed shots came instantly, three for each of them.

Danny smiled.

This was the time of the prophecy, the start of the final heavenly battle – the one the Russian had promised.

And he was going to be part of it.

His heart swelled with pride as he watched the black-clad men jumping down from the M270's cab. But his joy turned to incomprehension as one of them strode towards him, his OTs-38 Stechkin silent revolver raised and aimed straight at Danny's head.

Danny opened his mouth to demand an explanation, but saw the briefest hint of a flare at the end of the gun's muzzle, then nothing.

By the time he hit the dust he was dead, as one more round entered his skull and another ripped his heart apart.

The men then moved swiftly, disabling the vehicle's GPS system, then loading Danny's body into the cab alongside the other two.

They started it up, and headed off again. But instead of keeping to the tracks leading to the designated observation post, they turned and crunched over the scrub, heading down the mountain towards the Syrian border.

When they got to the bottom, they rumbled up to the flimsy fence that marked the limits of Israel. Another team had already removed a section of the fence, and staked out a path through the mines left from the wars of the 1960s and 1970s.

The M270 passed across the narrow strip, then the non-existent Syrian border.

With a determined burst of speed, the mobile missile system disappeared over the dunes, and into the heartlands of one of the most vicious civil wars in history.

⋄ ◆ ⋄

CHAPTER 34

Palazzo Malta
68 Via del Condotti
Rione IV (Campo Marzio)
Rome
The Republic of Italy

MARY PULLED OUT her phone, and checked the surveillance logs.

"Durov's still inside," she updated Ava. "He hasn't left the building once."

That was exactly what Ava had been hoping to hear.

If Durov was in the Order of Malta's palace, then it was something to do with Rasputin's cryptographs.

She was sure of it, and had reached a decision. "If he's not coming out, then one of us has to go in. And I'm guessing it can't be you."

Looking around, she spotted a luggage shop a little way down a side street.

"Wait here," she told Mary, as she crossed the narrow road and headed down towards the boutique. A few moments later, she emerged with a small black rectangular bag.

Mary was waiting for her outside. "What are you going to do?"

"I'll think of something," Ava replied, pulling the price tag off one of the handles and dropping it in a bin.

"Be careful," Mary warned. "The Order is not like anything else in Rome."

Ava nodded.

Approaching the front of the building, she saw that the heavy wooden gates were now hooked back, revealing a large internal courtyard.

High on the right hand wooden door was a large polished brass plaque. She quickly translated it:

*SOVEREIGN MILITARY HOSPITALLER ORDER OF ST JOHN OF
JERUSALEM OF RHODES AND OF MALTA
MAGISTRAL PALACE
EXTRATERRITORIAL SEAT*

She pulled a pair of sunglasses out of her jacket and put them into her hair, Italian style. Then she walked through the gateway.

Looking straight ahead, she ignored a small reception room to her left, and strode through the inner gateway, into an elegantly arcaded private courtyard.

At its centre, inlaid into the tarmac, was a large white eight-pointed Maltese cross. Around it, parked against the walls, were a number of cars with non-standard licence numbers. She spotted a Diplomatic CD plate with an XA code, which she assumed was the Order's specific diplomatic identifier, as well as several bearing the acronym SMOM and a number.

The courtyard was overlooked by four storeys of shuttered windows and, directly ahead, her eyes were drawn from a fountain springing out of a satyr's mouth up to a large sculpture of the eight-pointed cross of Malta on the courtyard wall.

There was no doubt who the building belonged to.

In front of her, standing by the open door at the far end of the courtyard, was a soldier in camouflage battledress cradling an assault rifle.

She worked hard to keep the surprise from her face.

What was the Italian army doing here?

As she approached and could see his uniform in more detail, she was astonished to notice on his arm, under the small Italian flag, a tactical recognition flash displaying the Order of Malta's cross.

She could barely believe her eyes.

The Order of Malta had an army?

With weapons?

"I'm a doctor," she announced brusquely, drawing level with the soldier. "The chaplain called me."

She prayed there was a chaplain in the building.

Without waiting for a reply, she kept her eyes fixed straight ahead, and carried on walking. In life, she had discovered, being self-assured was everything.

The soldier did not react.

Continuing through the door, she found herself passing under an archway of large battle banners. She spotted white Latin crosses and Maltese crosses on a range of black flags and red flags. Although the distinctive banners had many meanings now – care for the poor, hospitals, pilgrimage – the display was a blunt reminder that the Order was once an elite military unit, and its standards had fluttered on the battlefield, where they inspired fear and awe.

And she was now trespassing in their headquarters.

Once through the arch, she entered a richly decorated hallway, whose walls were covered in a collection of large oil paintings. She glanced around, noting saints, nobles in silk and armour, Mediterranean castles, and battle galleys in full sail.

Ahead of her was a larger-than-life-size crucifix with an enormous wooden Jesus nailed to it in agony. To its left was a cannon stamped with the Order's cross, and mounted in a pair of display cases were a double handed broadsword and two chain flails with viciously spiked balls. With what she knew about the Order's history in the crusades and great battles in the Mediterranean, she had no doubt that the weapons had not always been decorative.

The corridors and rooms branching off the hallway looked largely administrative, so she headed to the grand stone staircase dominating the hall at the far end, and began taking the steps two at a time.

As she did, she passed an immense oil painting of an epic naval battle, with galleys bearing the crescent moon of Islam ranged against an alliance sailing under the flags of the Papal States, the Knights of Saint John, Venice, Spain, and other Christian countries. The scene was wreathed in cannon smoke, and looked like the mother of all engagements. The plaque underneath read simply, 'Glorious Lepanto, 1571'.

Arriving at the top of the stairs, she stopped at a doorway immediately to her left. She listened carefully outside it for a moment, then stole a glance into the room.

It was a library, with dark bookcases running from floor to ceiling. The centre was dominated by a large table, on which was a carefully built reconstruction of a city.

There was no one about, so she stepped quietly over to the model, and peered carefully at it, instantly recognizing the topography of the Old Town in Jerusalem.

She had been to the ancient city many times, and could easily visualize its distinctive hills and topography – with the Temple Mount on the apex of Mount Moriah, rising out of the valleys between Mount Zion and the Mount of Olives.

Over the years, she had studied hundreds of plans of the city, from the original pagan Jebusite settlement of Salem, where King Melchizadek had anointed Abram, to the modern-day urban sprawl.

The maquette in front of her was unmistakably medieval Jerusalem, divided into its four different quadrants.

The area modelled in most detail was the north-western sector – the Muristan in the Christian Quarter. She knew its narrow alleys and unending *souqs* well, all largely unchanged since medieval times. At its centre was the distinctive form of the Church of the Holy Sepulchre. And just to its south was a large area comprising three churches, a hospital, and other smaller buildings – all flying the white-on-black cross of the original Knights of Saint John.

It was a map of the Order's birthplace in Jerusalem.

Behind the large model, also on the table, were smaller maquettes of the Order's fortifications on the Mediterranean islands of Rhodes and Malta, which the knights had conquered and made their home after the Christians lost the crusades. On the wall beside the models was a display charting the evolution of the Order's patronage – from Saint John the Almoner in the beginning, to the more prestigious Saint John the Baptist.

Listening intently for any movements out in the hallway, Ava waited in the library for a few minutes, then slipped quietly out of the room and back into the corridor.

There was a corner ahead, and turning, she froze at the sight of the back of a man entering a room ahead and to her right.

And behind him, to her horror, staring straight at her, was Oleg Durov.

She dropped her face instinctively to shield it, but he had recognized her.

He hissed something to the bodyguards following a step behind him, then turned, following the other man into the room.

Ava spun and started back down the corridor.

She was fast. But not fast enough.

The bodyguard in front was already running. Launching himself forward, he grabbed her upper arm before she could get any further.

She twisted hard to wrench free, lashing out with her arm and shoulder, knocking him off balance, and sending him crashing into the wall. But the other bodyguard was already on her, smothering her in a body lock.

Before she knew it, she was being bundled back into the library, and there was a hand over her mouth.

   ◆

CHAPTER 35

The West Wing
The White House
1600 Pennsylvania Avenue
Washington DC
The United States of America

IN THE WHITE House, Richard Easton reached for his telephone, and punched in the number he knew by heart.

He had been in politics long enough to know that getting things done often required alliances with the strangest bedfellows.

He looked over to his shelf, to his treasured King James Bible.

The Lord really did work in mysterious ways.

At the other end of the line, the man picked up.

"It has begun," Easton announced simply, then hung up.

◆

CHAPTER 36

Palazzo Malta
68 Via del Condotti
Rione IV (Campo Marzio)
Rome
The Republic of Italy

AVA WAS STRUGGLING as violently as she could, but the guard had one hand over her mouth, gripping her jaw tightly, with his other arm wrapped around her body, immobilizing her.

Beside him, the second guard was typing something into his phone.

She tried to wrench herself clear, but the guard was far too strong, and she quickly realized that her attempts to break free were futile.

Redirecting her efforts, she felt with her teeth for any flesh on the hand covering her face. Finding some, she bit down hard.

The guard bellowed, and pulled his hand away. Seizing the chance, she twisted her shoulders violently to throw off his grip, but was stilled by a blow to the back of her head.

As nausea washed through her, the guard tightened his hold, and again placed his hand over her mouth – this time holding her jaw painfully hard.

She watched helplessly as the door ahead of her opened, and Durov strode in.

"You." He was approaching her quickly. "Are persistent." Arriving in front of her, and with no warning, he slapped her viciously across the face.

"Still interested in icons, I see?" He stepped back, watching her carefully.

She stared defiantly at him, her ear ringing from the blow.

The guard behind her changed his hold, putting one arm around her neck, and pinning her upper arms behind her back with the other.

It was excruciatingly painful.

"You have something belonging to me." Durov declared. It was a statement, not a question.

Ava remained silent.

He pulled back the cuff of his jacket to reveal a large old-fashioned-looking watch. From behind it, he released a small triangular blade of blackened steel. "Developed by the British SOE in World War Two," he explained, holding it up in front of Ava's face. "This is an original."

She stared at it.

This was not good.

"Saint Peter was a noble man." His tone was business-like. "In the Garden of Gethsemane, when Jesus was being betrayed to the Roman soldiers, do you know what he did?"

She looked again at the blade, which he was still holding up in front of her face.

She knew exactly what the Bible said happened in the Garden of Gethsemane.

Durov rested the blade on her neck, against her jaw.

"To protect Jesus, he cut off the ear of the high priest's servant."

She held his gaze.

"Violence," he murmured, "in the name of the Lord, can be the most holy of acts." As he spoke, she felt him angle the blade so its edge was touching the underside of the soft skin below her ear.

"Where is my Shroud?"

She gazed at him in astonishment.

His Shroud?

She did not answer.

"Why are you here?" His tone was becoming more urgent, and she felt him increase the pressure of the blade under her ear.

"Research," she spat out the answer, trying to shut off the pain in her shoulders. "Thought I'd go to Malta this year for my summer holidays."

Durov widened his eyes with pleasure for a half-second as he flicked his wrist, and Ava felt a sharp sting to the back of her ear, followed by the sensation of blood on her skin.

He held the blade in place. "Unlike you, I am a guest in this palace. The continued operation of the heretical Order of Malta in Orthodox Russia is a matter of great diplomatic delicacy."

"I didn't have you down as the peacenik type," Ava answered.

Anger flashed across his face. "The time for reconciliation between the Churches is long past. We are now approaching the *eessatton*."

Ava did not understand what he had just said.

The eessatton?

What was that?

"How did you know about the icon?" He slid the blade into the cut, and Ava pushed back the tears of pain gathering behind her eyelids.

What icon?

He removed the blade, wiped the blood off on a cloth from his pocket, and slid the weapon back behind his watch.

"Have it your way. It's no matter." His expression was brimming with arrogance. "You'll never see it."

Ava frowned.

Was he still talking about the icon?

"Take her to the embassy," Durov instructed the guards. "By the time I get back, I don't care if she can still walk, but she needs to be able to talk."

Ava was now beginning to feel real fear.

They would not dare really harm her in the palace, she assumed. There was every chance she could attract the attention of others if things got really nasty. But once in the basement of the Russian embassy, there was every likelihood she would not come out again.

Without waiting for any further instructions, the two bodyguards bundled her towards the door, and out into the corridor. Behind them, Durov headed off in the other direction.

With a hand again clamped firmly over her mouth, and her arm twisted up behind her back, there was nothing she could do as they frog-marched her down the corridor.

They passed an ornate doorway on the right, and through it Ava caught a glimpse of a richly decorated baroque chapel. It was a long rectangular room, with pews running the length of the nave, collegiate-style, facing each other across the central aisle. Around the walls, there were holy pictures of men and women wearing the habit of the Order.

Up at the far end, at the altar, a priest in traditional clothing – a full chasuble, stole and maniple – was standing and quietly praying.

The guards drove her forward, and in no time they were approaching a closed door at the end of the corridor. Ava assumed it must lead to a lift, and realized that the three of them would not be able to get through it walking abreast.

As they drew up before the door, the guard on her left released his grip, and stepped forward to open it.

She knew she would not have another chance.

And she had only one shot.

She planted her right leg firmly, placed all her weight on it, dropped down, then spun round, low and hard, swinging her left fist up into the groin of the guard on her right, focusing all her strength into a brutal uppercut.

He bellowed, gagging, and dropped to the floor, instantly releasing his hold on her.

She sprang backwards, dodging his flailing arm, and sprinted back down the corridor in the direction they had just come.

Despite having broken free, she was acutely aware that she had almost no chance of making it out of the building. The guard she had punched would only be down for a while, and the other was already starting towards her.

She needed somewhere safe.

And fast.

As she accelerated down the corridor, she drew level with the open door of the chapel.

She could hear that the guard was now only a fraction behind her.

Seeing no other option, she threw herself through the chapel's doorway, and slammed into a row of dark mahogany pews.

The priest at the altar spun round at the commotion, gazing at her sprawling over the benches. His initial look of incomprehension turned to anger at the sight of the bodyguard crashing through the doorway after her.

"Sanctuary," Ava yelled at the priest.

In England, the ancient medieval law of Church sanctuary had been repealed centuries earlier. She prayed it still meant something to a traditional religious order in Rome.

The priest eyed her in bewilderment.

"I'm demanding the Church's protection," Ava shouted across to him, scrambling to her feet and running towards the altar.

"I know what sanctuary is," the priest answered tartly in a heavy Italian accent. "I'm — "

He broke off and stared as the Russian bodyguard headed for Ava.

Whatever the modern Church's position on sanctuary was, Ava did not have time to find out. She looked around for anything to protect herself with. Nearby were two reliquaries: one of the Blessed Gerard – the Order's founder – the other of Saint John the Baptist.

She doubted very much she would win any friends if she used either of those.

Turning, she saw a long wooden processional staff slotted into a brass hoop on the end of a nearby pew.

If there was going to be a fight, she was not going to wait for the guard to attack her first. Taking control of the situation had been lesson number one in combat training.

In a fluid movement, she ripped the pole from the slender bracket holding it to the pew, and swung it at the bodyguard's head.

He raised an arm to protect himself, and the wood crashed hard into his shoulder, sending him sprawling into a table piled high with leather-bound prayer books.

His face contorted into a grimace of pain as he reached into his underarm holster and pulled out a small black PSM pistol.

"That's enough!"

The authoritative command came from the doorway.

Ava recognized the voice instantly, and turned to see Durov entering the chapel, glaring at her with an expression of intense hatred.

"Not in God's house," he ordered the guard, never taking his eyes off Ava.

"Get out." The priest was stalking towards the two men. "How dare you bring violence into this sacred place."

Durov nodded slowly at the guard, who re-holstered his gun, and walked back to the door.

Durov's eyes were still locked on Ava, radiating rage.

He turned to the priest. "Good day, father," he spat, before striding out and down the corridor, followed by the guard.

The priest was now level with Ava, equally angry. "You'd better explain yourself." He glared at her.

She opened her mouth to protest, but he cut her off. "Not to me."

◆ ◆ ◆

CHAPTER 37

Palazzo Malta
68 Via del Condotti
Rione IV (Campo Marzio)
Rome
The Republic of Italy

THE PRIEST LED Ava to the door she had earlier seen Durov and the other man enter. Behind her, an armed soldier in camouflage moved into the doorway, shutting off her exit.

She was in a large Italianate salon, which stretched the full width of the building. The decoration was intense, with thick red damasked wallpaper and gilding on every piece of detailing – from the intricate coving on the ceiling to the finials ornamenting the extravagant fireplace. The whole space was illuminated by a gentle light coming through the thin cream silk coverings over the tall graceful windows.

The sign on the main entrance door had said the building was a *palazzo*, and she could now clearly see that it was.

The man Durov had followed earlier was sitting in a heavily upholstered chair.

As she stepped forward, Grand Master Joaquín de Torquemada put down the sheaf of papers he had been reading, and looked across at her, giving her a full view of his face for the first time. It was long, with large hooded eyes, overly full lips, and a heavy jaw. It was crowned by a thick mane of white hair, swept back from a sharp widow's peak.

He was looking at Ava coldly. "My Russian guest told me that his men captured a thief in the building."

Ava winced.

It was not a good start to a meeting.

"You understand where you are, don't you?" His tone was not friendly.

Even if Mary had not told her what the building was, the banners and objects she had seen downstairs had left her in no doubt, and nor had the room she was now in. It was hung with three rows of portraits running around the walls, and she quickly calculated that there must be around eighty individual pictures.

Each painting was of a man wearing the cross of the Order. Some bore it emblazoned on a tunic, others on a cape, and most also wore it as a jewel around their necks, or pinned to their breasts.

Under each portrait was a name and a date. The collection was arranged chronologically, and her eyes alighted on the oldest canvas at the far end of the room. The plaque under it read: BLESSED FRA' GERARD. The painting was distinctly Renaissance, but the date inscribed under it was centuries earlier: AD 1040–1120.

She swallowed hard.

That meant the Order dated from a time when the Anglo-Saxons were still running England – a period closer to the Roman Empire than the modern world, and long before any of the countries of Europe had assumed their current borders and systems of government.

As she took in the portraits, she realized that the gallery of Grand Masters before her represented a slice of European nobility spanning a millennium – from France, England, the Crusader States, Portugal, Aragon, Italy, Malta, and Germany. There was even a Borgia.

"You are trespassing," he continued. "You left Italy the moment you illegally entered this building, and you are now subject to my jurisdiction and justice." Torquemada was eying her with suspicion. "I would like to hear your explanation." He looked at her expectantly.

Ava returned his gaze, and that is when she saw it.

The picture was in the centre of the wall behind him, in pride of place. It was smaller than the others.

And it was a woman.

As Ava focused on it, she began to feel a tingling running up her spine.

At the centre of the picture was a woman's face. It was long and mournful, although the details were almost impossible to make out from the years of smoke, oil, grease, and dirt obscuring it. She had a long Greek nose, sad yearning eyes, and her head was tilted slightly to the left, as if she was looking at something in front of the frame.

"You'll never see the icon," Durov had taunted her, back in the library.

And yet here was an icon.

A Greek Madonna.

A Theotokos.

Ava peered at it more closely, and saw that the icon was actually made up of several layers. A thin covering had been placed over the painted wood, with a hole cut to reveal just the Madonna's face underneath. The covering was decorated with a Maltese cross, making the eight points look like a sunburst around her head. On top of the covering was a jewel-studded border of gold, which encircled the Madonna's face like a scarf, and the whole ensemble was encased in an ornate golden frame.

She stared at it, transfixed.

Rasputin's second cryptograph.

Was this what he was referring to?

The head of John the Baptist, and the anagrams of Jerusalem, Rhodes, and Malta all pointed to the Knights of Saint John.

CHILD OF THE THEOTOKOS and the Virgo symbol referred to the Virgin Mary.

Was the cryptograph supposed to lead to this icon?

Is that what Durov had worked out?

It was an odd-looking icon, but there was something vital missing.

Rasputin's clue said: CHILD OF THE THEOTOKOS. Yet on the icon in front of her, there was no infant Jesus in Mary's arms.

The picture was just her face.

Ava frowned.

Maybe this icon was not what Durov was after.

"Did your Russian guest show any interest in the holy icon?" Ava asked the Grand Master, indicating the image behind him.

Torquemada remained silent for a moment. "Now, why would you enquire about that?" His voice was pensive. "As it happens, he did."

"What did he want to know?" Ava asked, trying to keep her voice from trembling.

The Grand Master fixed her with a penetrating glance. "Its history."

"Is it unusual?" Her insides were beginning to knot.

"It's the Order's most holy relic," the Grand Master answered. "Our Lady of Philermos … "

Ava could not believe her ears.

"Philermos?" she repeated.

Torquemada nodded. "It's been in the Order's possession since at least the 1300s, when we held Rhodes. It was kept in our chapel on the island, at Philermos, now called Filerimos. Legend has it that the image was painted by Saint Luke himself."

Ava's heart was hammering.

That definitely was part of the clue.

PHILERIMOS.

So now she knew. Rasputin had not meant the Greek word *philerimos*, a lover of solitude. He meant the place on the island of Rhodes.

She was too far away to see the details of the icon.

"Is that the original?" She struggled to stifle her excitement.

The Grand Master's manner changed. "I have answered your questions. Now you owe me the courtesy of answering mine. I repeat: what are you doing here?"

"I'm not a thief," she replied. "Your guest – Oleg Durov – is a very dangerous man."

Torquemada pulled a white cotton handkerchief from his jacket's breast pocket and stepped forward, handing it to her. "You appear to be injured." He pointed at her neck.

Ava had forgotten about the cut.

She took the soft laundered cotton and held it under her ear. When she pulled it away, she was surprised by the amount of blood.

"If you're not a thief, then what are you?" Torquemada sat back down in his chair.

Ava did not want to lie to him, but doubted he would believe the real story. "I'm keeping an eye on Durov," she answered simply.

He gazed thoughtfully at the window. "But for whom, I wonder."

"He's not what he seems," Ava persisted.

After a few moments, Torquemada turned back to face her. For the first time, she noticed the tired look in his eyes.

"I can assure you that he's not the first of his kind to enter this palace," he answered in a matter-of-fact way. "The centuries have been kind to us. These days we carry out our work on many different continents.

But you cannot suppose we do that – from the corridors of Washington to the most violent shanty town in Brazil, not to mention hundreds of warzones from Somalia to Indonesia – without having to deal with men like him?"

Ava was not listening.

Something he said had sparked an old memory.

"What was the name of your Order's first monastery in Jerusalem, before the crusades?" She pictured it on the model she had seen earlier in the library. It was the large church, just to the south of the Church of the Holy Sepulchre.

He eyed her closely. "Saint Mary. Known as Saint Mary of the Latins, to distinguish us from the Eastern Greek Church that had historically run the city."

A shudder passed through her as the pieces of the puzzle finally slotted into place.

Durov had been right.

This icon was the answer to Rasputin's clue.

She took a short step closer towards it, elation washing through her.

The child in Rasputin's notebook was not the infant Jesus.

That was why he was not in the icon.

The child was the Order of Malta itself, which had been born of Saint Mary's, in Jerusalem.

The Order was Mary's offspring.

"Grand Master, please may I see the icon?" Ava asked, taking another step forward.

He shook his head slowly. "Whatever you are both up to, you are wasting your time. There's nothing for you here." He nodded at the soldier by the door. "Escort her from the building."

As the guard approached to lead her away, Torquemada gave her a parting look. "If you're found on the property of the Order again without permission, there'll be consequences. I don't know what you're involved in, but do it somewhere else."

———————— • ◆ • ————————

CHAPTER 38

Saint Hilarion Castle
Kyrenia Mountains
The Republic of Cyprus (Occupied)

THE TAXI FROM Ercan International Airport had taken José Ramos north out of Nicosia, and towards the ancient city of Kyrenia, traditionally said to have been founded by the victorious Greeks returning from the Trojan war.

In less than thirty minutes, the car had crossed the Mesaoria plain, and headed up into the limestone and marble mountains that fell away the other side to the northern coast.

Nearing an enormous moutaintop statue of a soldier in full battledress, they turned left, and onto a narrower winding road. It led them past a military base with two armed guard posts and a smaller statue of a soldier in action, before ending in a dusty car park, where a sign in Turkish announced:

ST HİLARİON KALESİ

Ramos told the driver to wait for him, then got out of the car, purchased a ticket in cash, and entered the castle's monumental curtain wall at the barbican.

Once through, he was in the lower ward, which had formerly swarmed with the garrison's men-at-arms. Hundreds of yards above him, high on the craggy mountaintop, he could see the castle's upper buildings clinging to the jagged rocks – still fiercely dominant and aggressive after centuries.

As he climbed, he caught snatches of a monologue from a tour guide, whose small group was ascending the ancient steps just behind him. The guide was excitedly explaining the building's extraordinary past, from its earliest days as a hermitage in the tenth century, down to its key role in the scarring royal battles for medieval Cyprus.

Ramos had no interest in the history of the island and the old fortification. Who cared that Richard the Lionheart bound the island's tyrannical ruler in silver chains because he promised not to clap him in iron ones? He was far more focused on the business to be done with the man he was about to meet.

Arriving at the middle ward, he ignored the Byzantine chapel and assorted chambers and towers. He passed through, following signs to a rougher and steeper series of worn stone steps cut into the mountainside. He began to ascend them confidently, oblivious to the fact that a slender metal handrail was the only thing between him and a vertiginous drop.

After a hard climb, he arrived at the mountain's peak, and the castle's third ward – the area formerly reserved for the Lusignan royal family.

After taking a moment to catch his breath, he headed across to the northern side, and spotted a sign declaring that he was now seven hundred and thirty-two metres up. He peered down the dizzying masonry walls and cliffs falling away beneath him, before looking out to the azure blue of the Mediterranean.

He turned away quickly.

He was not here for the sightseeing.

Looking about, he spotted the man he had come for, standing by a dramatic fragment of wall encasing a large gothic traceried window.

The man was dressed all in black – combat trousers, a long loosely buttoned shirt, and a matching *shemagh* wrapped around his neck.

Ramos knew him only as al-Irlandi, which he had been told was Arabic for 'the man from Ireland'.

Al-Irlandi was average height, muscular, and in his early forties. His face was long and angular, with fleshy lips and several days' beard growth. His long dark greasy hair was pushed back, reaching down over his collar. A healed injury to his right eye socket had left his eye-lid slanted and frozen.

Ramos was no expert, but he would hazard a guess al-Irlandi was originally Pakistani.

"You're late." Al-Irlandi's accent was a mix of Asian and the strong sound of Northern Irish.

Ramos had no idea where al-Irlandi had flown in from. It could have been anywhere – Iraq, Syria, Egypt, Libya, Tunisia, Algeria. They were all only a short flight away. A lot closer than London.

The jihadi paused to look out over the Mediterranean. "Once, the *Khilafah* encircled this ocean: Spain, North Africa, Palestine, Turkey, Sicily. The crescent of Islam ruled the shores, and billowed from the corsairs cutting the waves." He paused. *"Insh'allah* it will be so again."

Ramos had no interest in his contact's agenda. He had no idea who the Irishman's allegiance lay with, and he did not especially care. He was only interested in looted conflict antiquities, and was happy to work with whoever could supply him.

"Where's the statue?" Ramos demanded.

"Bonded, in Rotterdam," al-Irlandi answered. There was no apology for the three-month delay.

Ramos heard the arrogance in the jihadi's voice.

If they had been back in Mexico, he would have thrown the arrogant *cabrón* over the railings. But they were not. And Ramos needed him. There was a hierarchy. Al-Irlandi supplied the artefacts, and Ramos off-loaded them through his shop in Old Bond Street. They were tied by a chain of interdependence. Besides, he knew al-Irlandi's reputation, and did not want a gang war upsetting the lucrative arrangement they had going.

"How long?" Ramos insisted.

The jihadi did not answer. He was gazing out over the mountain peaks. "Did you give the woman the test, like I said?"

Ramos nodded.

"What did she say when she saw the object?"

Ramos shrugged. "I don't know. She saw something." His men had not been able to put her reaction into words. "She wanted it badly."

Al-Irlandi's eyes narrowed. "How can you be sure?"

Ramos snorted. "My men grew up on the streets of Ciudad Juárez.

They know when someone wants something."

Al-Irlandi turned to look directly at Ramos. "Did she tell you what it was?"

He nodded. "A list. Some kind of commemoration."

The jihadi was attentive now. "Anything else? What did it say?"

He shrugged. "Names."

"What names?"

Ramos had no idea. "Just names." He passed al-Irlandi a piece of paper with a handwritten Liechtenstein address. "Send someone to here. The owner has your cut of the last deal."

The jihadi took it and lapsed into thought. "She might be able to help us." He paused. "Find out who she is. Do some digging."

Ramos was reaching breaking point. He could not care less about the woman. "I've done you the favour you asked. Now I need the statue."

"Soon," al-Irlandi replied. He pulled out his phone and opened a photograph, which he held out for Ramos to see.

It showed a large stone sculpture of a regally-dressed man with earrings and a corkscrew beard. Around it, a band of militiamen were waving AK–47s. "You'll get this one, too, at the same time. Meanwhile, stay close to the woman. Ask around. Find out what you can."

Al-Irlandi pressed a number on speed dial, then looked up at Ramos, indicating the meeting was over.

Ramos did not fancy the woman's chances with al-Irlandi if it turned out she had been lying. But that was none of his business. It should be easy enough to check her out. And if that was what it was going to take to keep the jihadi happy, then so be it.

Ramos turned and headed back to the steps down to the lower wards.

Bien.

They had a deal.

· ◆ ·

CHAPTER 39

The Vatican Apostolic Library
The Vatican Palace
Cortile del Belvedere
Vatican City

EXITING THE PALAZZO Malta, Ava looked for Mary, but could not see her anywhere.

She hailed a cab, then opened up her phone and found the number Mary had called from the previous evening.

It took Mary a while to pick up. "Did you find anything?" she asked Ava. "What was Durov doing there?"

"He's after an icon," Ava answered. "The Order of Malta's holiest and most famous relic." Ava checked her watch. "I need to check a few things. Can you get me into the Vatican Library?"

"The Secret Library?"

"Just the regular one," Ava replied. "I need general materials, not the private affairs of the popes."

"No problem," Mary confirmed. "There'll be a pass ready for you at Reception."

"Great." Ava gazed out of the car's window at Rome passing by. "Let's meet outside the library at five o'clock."

The taxi took her over the Ponte Cavour, around the great Roman fortress of the Castel Sant'Angelo, and dropped her at the top of the Via della Conciliazone. From there, she entered Vatican City on foot.

It was as breathtaking as ever.

The piazza's quadruple rows of Tuscan columns encircled her like welcoming arms, drawing her toward the immensity of Saint Peter's Basilica. Above the colonnades, one hundred and forty stone saints looked benignly down.

She headed through Saint Peter's Square, then across into the Belvedere Courtyard, where she picked up her reader's pass, and entered the Vatican Apostolic Library.

Once in its grand reading room, the air heavy with the smell of book leather and wood polish, she headed straight for the catalogues. As she found her way around the indexing system, she began searching for anything she could find on the icon of Our Lady of Philermos and the history of the Knights of Saint John.

She was not disappointed.

There were hundreds of works on the enigmatic crusaders.

Once she had placed her orders, there was nothing to do but wait for the books to be delivered.

With time to kill, she looked about the extraordinary reading room, with its long rows of desks and ornately frescoed vaulted ceiling. It was dazzling – emblazoned with golden paintings bathing the whole space in a warm glow.

She found it hard to imagine that there had been a papal manuscript collection since the 300s, making it probably the world's oldest continuously functioning archive. It was enormous, with millions of ancient manuscripts and printed books, covering every subject imaginable, from the dawn of time up to the modern day. All the manuscripts and books were there to be consulted, although – as a result of centuries of thefts – there was only one reader in the world actually allowed to take books out.

Behind her, on display stands, was a temporary exhibition on the library's seventeen love letters from King Henry VIII of England to his mistress, Anne Boleyn.

While she was waiting, Ava read a couple of the panels.

Apparently no one knew how the Vatican Library came to have the letters, but the suspicion was that they had been acquired as ammunition in the battle over England's religion in the 1500s.

Large facsimiles of Henry's *billets-doux* were pinned to the exhibition boards, and as Ava skimmed them, she learned to her amusement that part of his royal seduction technique had involved assuring Anne that he hoped he would soon be able to 'kysse' her 'pretty Duckys'.

Ava shook her head at the pointlessness of it all, recalling that within three years of finally marrying Anne, Henry had grown bored of her, and arranged for her to be beheaded on trumped-up charges of adultery and conspiring to have him killed.

She wandered over to one of the reference stacks lining the long wall. She had a dozen questions about the letter from Thomas Cromwell to Thomas Wriothesley she had found at Professor Hamidou's flat, and hoped she could use the time to fill in some of the background.

Without too much difficulty, she found a handful of reference books on the dissolution of the English monasteries, and took them back to her desk, where she started to go through them.

After an hour or so, one of the librarians wheeled over a trolley, and delivered a dozen volumes to Ava's desk.

She began leafing through them, becoming increasingly absorbed by the history of the Knights of Saint John, and how the Order had survived for almost a thousand years. The books set out in amazing detail how a group of monks tending the sick in Jerusalem had evolved into an Order of crusading knights, finally becoming the modern world's only 'sovereign military and hospitaller' country. As she leafed through the ancient and modern volumes, she failed to notice lunchtime coming and going, until she was disturbed by a cough beside her, and looked up to see Mary.

To her surprise, Ferguson was standing beside her.

"Have you found anything?" Mary asked, looking at the large pile of open books on the desk.

Ava turned from Mary to Ferguson, her mind going blank for a moment.

"The icon ... " she began, momentarily lost for words. "It's ... "

"It's what?" Mary was frowning.

"It's ... " Ava started again, the sentence dying in her throat.

Ferguson shifted from one foot to the other.

Mary looked across at him, then laid her hand lightly on his arm.

The moment of disorientation Ava was feeling suddenly passed, as the confusion lifted.

She stared at them in disbelief.

They were sleeping together.

Her stomach lurched.

That's where they had been all day.

Ferguson jumped in to fill the lengthening silence. "Five-O-Four saw Durov enter the Russian embassy after he left the Palazzo Malta. He's still there."

Ava was vaguely aware of Mary confirming that some of her team were staking out the embassy.

She found herself just nodding, not really hearing a word Mary was saying.

She suddenly felt alone – for the first time in a long time – and also confused that what Ferguson did was having such an effect on her. She had no claim on him. She had turned down his advances in the past.

"So, shall we get the Vatican Gendarmerie Corps to invite Torquemada in for questioning?" Mary continued.

"Yes." Ava nodded mechanically.

"Seriously?" Mary's eyebrows lifted in surprise. "You think we'll get away with it?"

"What?" Ava realized she had answered without listening to the question.

"Shall we have Grand Master Torquemada brought in and interviewed?" Mary repeated.

Ava blinked hard, and looked down at the image of the icon, her thoughts coming into focus once more.

She did not have time to indulge herself emotionally.

She needed to concentrate.

Durov was one step ahead of her. He had made the connection to the Knights of Saint John – and to their icon – before she had. She had no idea what lay at the end of the trail, but from the way Durov was pursuing it, she felt sure something highly significant depended on it.

"No," she answered, snapping back into the moment. "Torquemada won't tell us anything, and we'll only antagonize him. It's Durov we need to watch now. And we need to find the original icon of Our Lady of Philermos before he does."

"Doesn't the Order know where it is?" Ferguson asked.

She shook her head. "The Knights of Saint John have moved their HQ frequently. From Jerusalem to Acre, Cyprus, Rhodes, Malta, and Rome – with short stints in Messina, Catania, and Ferrara, too. There have been times when their lives were chaos, especially after Napoleon conquered Malta. A lot of things have gone missing over the years."

"That sounds pretty hopeless." Mary looked dismayed. "The icon could be anywhere, then."

Ava shook her head. "Actually, I know exactly where it went."

Mary and Ferguson both stared at her.

"Before settling back in Rome, the Order briefly set up somewhere rather unusual."

Ava flicked to a page of the book showing a man wearing an ermine cloak over a red tunic emblazed with the Maltese cross. He was holding a royal sceptre, and wearing a bulbous golden crown on his head.

"Russia," she announced, pointing to the picture. "It turns out that after Napoleon conquered Malta, the Romanovs and another noble family ran the Order from Saint Petersburg for five years. And afterwards they kept hold of the knights' most sacred relics, including Our Lady of Philermos."

"But weren't the tsars Russian Orthodox?" Mary chipped in. "How did that work?"

"Bizarrely, it didn't seem to be an issue." Ava had also been surprised. It did sound highly improbable. "The knights hoped the tsar's prestige would help them get back on their feet again, but it didn't work out." She flicked to a picture of the icon. "By then, the Romanovs had care of the relics, and they stayed in Russia. Now scroll forward a hundred years, and things become messy again when St Petersburg went up in flames in the 1917 Bolshevik revolution."

"Religion was banned." Ferguson nodded.

"The official record says that the Dowager Empress Maria Feodorovna smuggled the knights' relics out of Saint Petersburg and back to her native Denmark. They were then apparently moved to Berlin and Belgrade, where they were entrusted to Alexander I of Yugoslavia. However, when the threat of a Nazi invasion became too strong, the relics were sent to safety in the countryside, to the monastery of Ostrog in Montenegro."

"Quite a trip." Mary looked impressed.

"And then they were lost." Ava paused. "Until the icon was found in 1997 in the National Museum of Montenegro."

Ava pulled another book from the pile, and opened it where she had marked a page with a slip of paper.

It showed a photograph of an icon, hanging alone on a wall, lit by a strong blue light in an all-blue room. The caption underneath the image stated that the photograph was from the National Museum of Montenegro, in Cetinje.

"So is that the real one?" Mary asked with a hint of excitement.

Ava shook her head. "Tsar Paul I had many copies made. One is in Assisi. The version I saw today in the Palazzo Malta is almost certainly another."

"How can you be so sure the Cetinje one is a copy?" Ferguson was peering at the image.

Ava began closing the books and stacking them into a pile on the desk. "If you were Grand Master of the Order of Malta, would you leave your most precious relic in an out-of-the-way museum? And besides, Rasputin died in 1916, and I bet any money he saw the original icon in Russia, then left clues in his notebook to indicate where it was taken."

"Well, go on then." Ferguson was hanging on her words.

Ava looked up at him, feeling a mounting sense of triumph. "Jerusalem," she smiled. "Where else?"

---------- • ◆ • ----------

CHAPTER 40

Russian Embassy
Via Gaeta 5
Rione XVIII (Castro Pretorio)
Rome
The Republic of Italy

TWO AND A half miles away, Durov was finding it hard to breathe.

He clenched the slender crystal glass tightly in his hand, feeling the anger surging in him.

What was that woman doing in the Order of Malta's palace?

He stared at the meticulously furnished ambassadorial room around him.

What did she know?

The glass shattered, cutting the skin of his hand.

He continued staring at the floor, the anger raw.

And she had escaped again.

He tried to think of something else.

Something soothing.

Aside from her, everything was perfect.

He now knew where the icon was.

When he had been inside the Order of Malta's palace, he had worked it all out. He had been through all the options, and he was certain he now had the answer.

He would find the icon, and it would give him the sign.

He was sure of it.

But now there was the problem of the woman.

He felt his anger rising again, and forced himself to calm down.

It would be fine.

The Holy Mother was merely testing him.

His mind again moved to his flock, and to his epiphany at how they would find eternal glory and their place in the Kingdom.

His breathing slowed as he let his mind rove over the scene, playing out all the details.

It would be traditional – the way that throughout history sinners had prepared themselves for the next world. Sometimes voluntarily. Sometimes with the guidance of others.

It would be clean and pure.

He allowed himself to feel tantalized by the idea.

The solution was clear.

It was unavoidable.

They had to burn.

The idea filled him with joy.

The fire would be like the flames of Pentecost that came down and blessed the apostles. In the tongues of golden fire, the martyrs would be joined with the Holy Spirit, who would become one with their very beings, sanctifying them.

There, in the white-hot brazier, they would encounter I-am-who-I-am, the God of Moses, who had appeared as a burning bush, cloaking his searing splendour.

In the blessing of the fiery furnace, they would meet their God.

◆

CHAPTER 41

Cortile del Belvedere
Vatican City

AVA WAS STANDING outside the library, in the Belvedere courtyard.

Her recent thoughts of Jerusalem took her back to the call she had received the previous day from Uri.

She was still not clear how he had known exactly what she was doing.

Which department in Mossad had handed her file to him?

Why were they taking an interest in her?

She had not been back to the Middle East in a while, and struggled to see why the Institute would have an active file on her.

Uri had warned her to stay away from Durov. That sounded like Mossad were protecting him.

But why?

There was clearly an element to all this that she was unaware of.

Uri had even known about the hit outside her house.

Was it a coincidence that both Swinton and Uri were warning her to steer clear of Durov?

The similarity made her uncomfortable.

Was there a connection?

She pulled out her phone, opened the RedPhone encryption app, and called Swinton.

He answered almost immediately. "Where are you?"

"Rome," she answered. There was no harm telling him. He would be able to trace her phone anyway. "But not for much longer."

"How can I help?" he asked.

"There's someone I know who works for Mossad," she began, keen not to give too much away.

"Go on."

"He called me yesterday," she continued, "and seemed to know a lot about what I'm doing. He explicitly warned me to steer clear of Durov."

"As did I." Swinton's tone was suddenly harder. "I hope you're following instructions."

"I'm not especially keen to meet Durov again, either." She sidestepped the question, putting her hand up to her ear, feeling the tender skin where the knife had cut. "But I've got a good lead on why he was after the Shroud, and what the Rasputin cryptographs represent." She paused. "I need to visit Jerusalem."

There was silence on the other end of the line before Swinton answered. "And I presume you're not keen on your Israeli friend finding out you'll be visiting?"

If it was not for her reservations about Swinton, Ava realized, she would enjoy working with him. He had good intuition.

"I'd rather steer clear of him," she confirmed. "It's only going to complicate things if the Institute gets involved."

There was more silence on the other end of the line.

"My passport's got more Arab stamps in it than the Cairo post office," Ava added. "There's a real chance they won't let me in."

"I'm sure they're going to regret every minute you're there," Swinton responded. "Fine. I can't guarantee that the Institute won't find you, but I'll have clean passports and travel documents couriered round for you and Major Ferguson immediately. Give the courier your real ones. We'll keep them safe for you. Husband and wife?"

For a second, Ava's mind flashed to the memory of Mary's hand on Ferguson's arm, and the pang of resentment she had felt.

"No," she answered quickly. "Business colleagues is fine."

"Done," Swinton replied, and the line went dead.

DAY SIX

— • ◆ • —

CHAPTER 42

Commercial aircraft
Greek airspace

ON THE PLANE, Ava and Ferguson had been sitting side by side in silence.

Mary had taken an earlier flight, while they waited for Swinton's people to deliver the fresh travel documents.

"Everything okay?" Ferguson asked, breaking the silence.

She nodded absent-mindedly. This was not a conversation she particularly wanted to have. She needed to be thinking about Rasputin's cryptographs and the icon of Our Lady of Philermos.

"You've been very quiet." He frowned slightly.

"I'm fine," she answered, feeling a flash of irritation.

Why wouldn't she be okay?

"Has something happened?" he persisted.

Before she could stop herself, it started to come out. "I met Durov and his bodyguards yesterday. It wasn't a particularly friendly chat."

He frowned. "You didn't mention anything."

"It's really not that important," she answered flatly.

"What did Durov want?" There was genuine concern in his voice now.

"Seriously?" She looked at him directly. "If what I get up to is important to you, then you could've been at the Palazzo Malta with me yesterday, instead of ... " She allowed the thought to trail off. It did not need saying.

He sat back in his seat and looked away.

Ava stared out of the window, instantly aware that she had to pull herself together. She did not like the way she was reacting. It was out of character, and she needed to get a grip on herself. If she had wanted Ferguson, she should have done something about it years ago. This was not his fault. It was not Mary's either. In fact, she liked Mary – she was an impressive operator.

She watched the bright white clouds gleaming below them, and knew she needed to sort this out in her head.

She allowed her mind to wander to Ferguson, and to what exactly it was that was bothering her.

She had thought about letting something happen between them – more times than she wanted to admit.

But it never seemed straightforward.

Years earlier, at university, an earnest – and, in hindsight, somewhat tedious – boyfriend had told her that she was cold. He laid out a whole theory about the invisible damage her mother had done by walking out while she was so young, and how not having a mother around had affected Ava's emotional makeup.

Ava had told him bluntly that he did not know what he was talking about, and the relationship had quietly died. But what he said had stung her – because he had been half right. She did not suffer from deep-seated abandonment issues. But what she had carried into adulthood was a profound sense of quite how much the break-up of her parents' relationship had hurt her father. And that was not something she ever wanted to do to anyone.

She watched the vapour trail of another plane in the distance, and realized that the situation was ridiculous. If she had not begun a relationship with Ferguson years ago because she was uneasy about the prospect of one day causing unhappiness, then being short with him now was absurd.

She needed to reassess her thinking – and that now meant moving on. If Ferguson and Mary were an item, she had no right to get in the way.

And anyway, after all this time, she could not blame him for having moved on.

"Why Jerusalem?" Ferguson's voice interrupted her thoughts. "How do you know the icon's there?"

Ava pulled herself out of her reverie, relieved to be able to focus on the job in hand again.

She had stumbled across the missing piece of the puzzle while in the Vatican Library.

"I saw a map of crusader Jerusalem in one of the books. On the map, the Church of the Holy Sepulchre was called the Anastasis – the resurrection. I looked it up, and apparently that's always been its name in the Orthodox tradition, ever since it was built in the fourth century."

"Makes sense," he nodded. "So Rasputin would've known it as the Anastasis."

"And also, CITY OF SAINT PETER now fits, because it also means Jerusalem."

"Not Saint Petersburg?" He frowned.

She shook her head. "I don't think so. Not in this case. After Jesus's death, Saint Peter became bishop of Antioch, then pope of Rome. But before then, in the dark days immediately after the crucifixion, Peter had a special status in Jerusalem. The Bible says that James – who was Jesus's brother – led the group, assisted by Peter and John. But it also indicates that Peter was the real power behind the scenes. It says people deferred to him. He was even arrested by the Jewish religious police and dragged before the Sanhedrin to answer for the early Christians and their schismatic split from mainstream Judaism."

"So, the clues are nothing to do with Russia, then," Ferguson replied.

Ava shook her head. "What we're looking for is down there." She pointed out of the window at the approaching Israeli shoreline. "I'm certain of it."

$\bullet\ \blacklozenge\ \bullet$

CHAPTER 43

Ben Gurion Airport
Near Tel Aviv
The State of Israel

WHEN THE PLANE eventually landed just outside Tel Aviv, Ava and Ferguson disembarked quickly, and headed into the most secure airport terminal in the world. As usual, it was awash with some of the heaviest security Ava had encountered anywhere on the planet.

At passport control, she answered the repetitive questions patiently and politely, fully aware that the profiling of each passenger passing through was a key element of the infamous and intensive security procedures.

In the past, she would have requested to have the Israeli immigration stamp put onto a separate piece of paper so she could travel freely around the Middle East afterwards. But seeing as it was not her passport, she simply smiled as the guard inked the arrival stamp next to a random assortment of phoney holiday visas.

Once through customs, the final set of doors slid back, and they emerged onto the arrivals concourse.

It was bedlam.

There were groups of adults and teenagers holding up signs in Hebrew, while others were waving blue-and-white Israeli flags as they welcomed arrivals off the plane. Scattered among them were groups of heavily armed soldiers and airport security teams with Malinois attack dogs.

The scene was an incongruous mixture of joy and lethal force.

As Ava headed into the crowds, she was suddenly aware of a woman approaching fast from the side.

She tensed, before realizing it was Mary, who called out a hello to Ferguson.

He waved back.

Ava nodded amicably.

Once out through the main doors and into the fresh air, Ava instinctively sensed her spirits rise as she felt the hot Middle Eastern sun on her face. After so many years in the region, anywhere from Israel to Iraq felt like her second home.

"Keep smiling," Mary instructed, as they headed towards the car park. "There's surveillance everywhere here – cameras, plainclothes officers, and even unmanned combat vehicles.

"Still," she continued, as they passed through a patch of shade cast by overhanging metal sunscreens, "you'll be grateful for these." She unobtrusively handed them each a diminutive handgun. "Lots of people carry here, and it's getting easier by the day while local tensions ramp up. Just keep them low-key. They're not registered."

Ferguson glanced down at the distinctive weapon in his hand. "Taurus Curve." He nodded appreciatively. "You're spoiling us."

Ava was staring at Mary in amazement. "You've only been here a few hours. How on earth —"

"It's better you don't ask," Mary cut Ava off and shrugged. "The Church has had a presence on this soil for around two thousand years. A lot of regimes have come and gone. We've learned to look after ourselves."

Ava looked about at the high-security features all around them.

She imagined the sense of siege had been similar for the Knights of Saint John and other medieval crusaders arriving from Europe. The only difference was, back then, the territory was a Christian country called Outremer – the Land Beyond the Sea.

As she turned the corner of the building, someone collided with her, hard.

She was suddenly back in the Paris Métro station – but this time she was ready.

She spun round to confront the person, who had stopped dead in their tracks and was staring at her.

To her shock, she recognized the face instantly.

Uri.

"You must have a death wish." His voice was hard and aggressive.

"Friend of yours?" Mary moved in beside Ava.

"What a coincidence." Ava glared at Uri. She had thought there was an outside chance he would be waiting for her. But it had still taken her by surprise.

"Entering Israel on false papers is a serious offence." He glanced from Ava to Mary. "You want to be more careful who you travel with." He indicated Ava and Ferguson. "These two are dangerous."

"Time will tell." Ferguson was smiling at Uri amiably, but Ava could see he was poised, absolutely still, ready, watching Uri's every move. "Good to see you again."

The Mossad *katsa* focused back on Ava. "I thought I had been very clear. My organization is not happy with you." He glanced at the passport and tickets in her hand. "Did you think that fake papers were going to keep you off the radar? There are facial recognition cameras all over this country." He glared at her. "You'd better not be in Israel for anything to do with our Russian friend."

"I wouldn't describe him as a friend, exactly," Ava answered. "More of an acquaintance."

She did not buy his facial recognition camera story. Why would he have been looking out for her? Why today? On this flight?

It was far more likely that someone had tipped him off.

Before she could say anything else, he grabbed her by the arm. His grip was hard. "This time I won't save your life."

She felt a surge of indignation.

How dare he?

"You've never saved my life." Her voice was low and threatening. "And you need to take your hand off me."

It was not an idle threat.

The tension with Ferguson, coupled with Uri's sheer arrogance on the video call yesterday – and again now – was surfacing as hot anger.

Uri was far stronger than her, and judging by his physique, he clearly kept in good condition. But she was furious enough to risk getting hurt if it meant she would have the satisfaction of taking him down a notch or two.

He continued to stare at her coldly, then slowly released her arm, and stepped away. "I'm going to be keeping an eye on you."

"I look forward to it," she retorted, the anger still simmering. She nodded at Ferguson, and set off in the direction of the car park, turning her back on Uri.

His arrogance was insufferable.

Keep his eye on her?

She had no intention of leaving a trail for anyone to follow.

Mary guided them to a black Hyundai Sonata, which beeped twice as she squeezed the key. "You two have history, or something?" she asked after a few moments' silence as she steered the car out of the car park.

Ava shook her head. "Our paths crossed once. And that was once too often for me."

Mary pointed at an open-backed United Nations truck up ahead. "Look – they get everywhere." Inside were a dozen soldiers wearing Italian army uniforms and the blue berets of UN peacekeepers.

Ava looked more closely, and – sure enough – under the Italian flags on the soldiers' sleeves was the white eight-pointed cross of Malta on a red badge.

"ACISMOM," Mary explained. "The Army Corps of the Order of Malta. They serve alongside the regular Italian army. And here they are, in Israel, over a thousand years after they were founded in Jerusalem."

Mary slowed and filtered into the queue for the car park's exit barrier.

"Airport surveillance will have registered our licence plate." Ava was looking about for cameras. "We'll need to ditch this car."

•◆•

CHAPTER 44

Donetsk
Donetsk People's Republic (unrecognized)
Ukraine

BY THE BANKS of the Kalmius river, in a run-down northern quarter of Donetsk, Sergei Glinin looked down at the body in the car.

The unbroken ring of livid bruising around the man's neck did not leave much doubt about the cause of death.

As chief of the city's Security Department, Glinin had seen a lot of corpses.

Ever since the regional unrest had kicked off a few years earlier, the city had been a warzone. Emotions ran high over the breakaway region's rejection of Ukrainian identity and its new collaboration with Russia. Things were quieter now than at the height of the tension, but tanks and troops were still on the streets.

Glinin had no interest in run-of-the-mill homicides. There were plenty of other people to deal with those. What mattered to him was the security of the fledgling republic – and that especially included the activity of any foreign intelligence agencies.

He glanced at the nervous sergeant standing beside him. From what he had passed on to Glinin over the telephone an hour earlier, the corpse in the car was someone Glinin needed to know about.

The victim was Zayd Jamoussi – a Tunisian national.

The car was parked in an area well known for the after dark availability of sex and drugs, and Jamoussi was not the first – and would not be the last – to fall victim to the city's vice trade.

Glinin looked down at the body.

Maybe it was an opportunistic robbery gone wrong? Perhaps Jamoussi was connected with drug gangs? Maybe he had upset a prostitute, and her pimp had intervened? Who knew? These things happened.

But whatever it was, Jamoussi was not just another tourist.

Before calling Glinin, the sergeant had run a check on the grey Renault Logan's number plate, and quickly learned that Jamoussi was staying at the Radisson in the centre of town. He had gone round to the hotel, but there had been nothing interesting in Jamoussi's light luggage. He had a few clothes, a tourist map, and a return ticket to Istanbul for that evening.

It was only when the hotel staff had opened the safe in Jamoussi's room that the sergeant had decided to call Glinin. He knew when something was above his pay grade. In this case, a murdered man whose safe contained a Russian military document headed ОСОБОЙ ВАЖНОСТИ – Top Secret (Special Importance) – followed by a list of dates and grid references, and marked in the top right corner with some kind of stamp in Hebrew.

He had reached for the telephone immediately.

While Glinin had made his way to the murder scene, one of the sergeant's junior colleagues had been in the hotel manager's overheated office, going through the split screens of CCTV footage. It had only taken him around twenty minutes to find something interesting.

The video feed showed that Jamoussi had only left his room twice since checking in. Once to visit a minimarket next door. Then later to go down to the hotel's gym.

As the young policeman stared at the grainy footage of the hotel's fitness facilities, he noted that, in the gentlemen's changing rooms, Jamoussi unhesitatingly took the third towel from the bottom of the fluffy pile on the bench. Intrigued, the policeman had scrubbed backwards in the footage. Sure enough, five minutes earlier, a wiry dark man could clearly be seen entering and placing something into that exact towel.

A quick search of the hotel records had revealed that the dark man had checked in on an Israeli passport as Yehuda Hitzig. He had only stayed one night, and was now gone.

Before leaving his office for the crime scene, Glinin had run Zayd Jamoussi and Yehuda Hitzig through the FSB mainframe database, and the results had been telephoned through to him as he was en route.

Jamoussi was indeed Tunisian, and had flown in from Istanbul. He was firmly involved in the Syrian civil war as a known courier for one of the moderate groups in opposition to the government regime. Yehuda Hitzig, on the other hand, drew a blank. There was no one of that name reported anywhere. Not even on the airport or border control records entering or leaving the country.

Glinin looked down at the dead body again, and then at the piece of paper from the hotel safe, now in his hand, safely sealed in a clear evidence bag.

He exhaled slowly.

He recognized a Russian military target list when he saw one. A quick grid reference check on his smartphone revealed that they were all in Syria.

It was really going to hit the fan when he passed this up the line to Moscow.

Worse, he was going to take some serious heat over it happening on his patch.

He tucked the paper carefully into the pocket of his mac, and lit a cigarette.

The whole business had Mossad's fingerprints all over it.

He inhaled the tobacco smoke deeply.

At least he was not the only one who was going to get carpeted over this.

With the mood Moscow was in at the moment, he would not be surprised if this tipped the Kremlin over the edge into picking a fight with Israel, too.

---・◆・---

Chapter 45

Route 1 (westbound)
The State of Israel

AS MARY DROVE out of the airport complex, Ferguson was sitting in the back seat.

He spotted the blue Volvo first, four cars behind. He would not ordinarily have noticed it, except that it was one of the few cars leaving the airport with no passengers.

"Uri's tailing us," Ferguson announced, once they had taken two turnings and the Volvo was still behind them.

Ava's heart sank.

This was something she could do without. The last thing she needed was to wind up in a Mossad basement somewhere before she had even got to Jerusalem.

"You would have thought he had better things to do," Mary said distractedly, turning off the slip road and onto the highway. "Rumour has it the IDF have lost an M270 multiple launch rocket system."

"How do you lose an MLRS?" Ferguson sounded incredulous.

"God knows." Mary eased back into her seat as the car hit cruising speed on the highway. "Somewhere up in the Golan Heights, apparently. It's the Wild West up there these days."

Ava was looking out of the window. The scenery around them was flat and grassy, with occasional fir trees and houses breaking up the identical view on either side of the road.

"Where can we get another car?" Ava asked. "This one's going to be in every law enforcement database in the country by nightfall."

"Nazareth," Mary answered. "It's about an hour and twenty minutes north of here, with friendly people who can help us."

Ava was looking at the map she had found in the glove compartment. "Meanwhile, let's lose our tail. Head west on Route 1, direction Tel Aviv."

"Isn't that the wrong way for Nazareth?" Mary sounded uncertain.

"Exactly." Ava turned the page to check all options.

"Why Nazareth?" Ferguson asked from the back seat.

"Home to Israel's largest community of Christians," Ava answered, unfolding the next section of the map. "The Christian communities here are ancient. After the Romans banished all Jews in AD 135, this country was effectively Roman, and its citizens converted to Christianity when it became the state religion of the Roman Empire. Despite the Muslim conquest in AD 638, there have been pockets of Christians here ever since."

"They're some of the last Christians in the Middle East now," Mary added. "But they're fading fast. After World War Two they made up a quarter of the Palestinian population. Now they're a small fraction of that. In the rest of the region they're going, too – victims of genocide in sectarian wars."

Ava was watching the traffic behind them in the wing mirror, and could see that Uri was keeping a steady distance behind them.

Had he radioed for another car to cut them off ahead?

Was he planning something?

She had no way of knowing.

But she could not take any chances.

The three of them in the car were armed, but any kind of confrontation with Uri was out of the question. She did not know what the Israeli Penal Code said, but was pretty sure that anyone opening fire on a serving member of Mossad, in Israel, would probably never breathe fresh air again.

Up ahead, there was a sign for a turning off the highway.

It was exactly what she had been hoping for.

"We need to get in front of that." She indicated a large 'Maccabee Beer' haulage lorry three places in front of them. "Do it quickly, and once you're ahead of it, don't let anyone tuck in behind us."

Mary nodded, and jabbed down hard on the accelerator, speeding ahead of the car immediately in front.

Barely pausing, she did it again, so they were now immediately behind the lorry.

Ava eyes were fixed on the large blue and white overhead signs and the road up ahead.

They passed a farm of greenhouses on the right.

"Do it now," she urged Mary.

Mary floored the pedal again, and they sped ahead, before tucking neatly in front of the lorry.

"Now, slow a little," Ava urged.

She was clenching the map tightly. "And turn off..." She watched the surrounding traffic intently, waiting until the last possible moment. "Now!"

Without indicating, Mary yanked the wheel over, and the car screeched right, onto the slip road.

Behind them, Ava knew, Uri's view would have been blocked by the lorry until the last minute, and he would not have seen them turn off until it was too late.

He would shoot right past the turning.

As they sped off along the slip road, Ava breathed out slowly and slumped back into the seat. "Okay. Let's get to Nazareth, find a clean car, then head south to Jerusalem. We haven't got time to waste."

---------- ◆ ----------

CHAPTER 46

Old Town
Jerusalem
The State of Israel

AVA'S EXCITEMENT MOUNTED as they neared Jerusalem.

Over the millennia, countless armies had approached the great city from the west, across the Hinnom Valley. In medieval times, the hill at the north end of the valley had been the *Mont Joie* – the Hill of Joy – which gladdened the hearts of pilgrims as they gained their first sight of the sacred city.

Ava directed Mary through the traffic towards the centre of the city's northern wall and up to the ancient Damascus Gate, where they parked the replacement car Mary had sourced for them in Nazareth.

Once on foot and through the immense ancient stone tower, they headed into the Old Town's warren of medieval streets.

Voices and music filled the air.

Ava was moving quickly, but it was not easy in the narrow streets, which were only a few people wide in places, with a ragbag of ancient buildings either side creating narrow tunnels for the pedestrians.

Cluttering the narrow passageways were hundreds of shops and stalls. Goods were laid out everywhere – on barrows, handcarts, tables, counters, hanging on bars, suspended from the hotchpotch of low balconies, and just piled in the street.

It was a chaotic Aladdin's Cave of almost everything imaginable. At the first few stalls alone Ava spotted strawberries, nuts, sweet pastries, phones, jewellery, fabrics, bags, and lamps. The list was endless.

She rushed on quickly down the hill, with Ferguson and Mary behind her.

The mix of bright light, colours, and smells was heady, pulling Ava back to days when she had worked at the Amman museum in neighbouring Jordan, and had visited Jerusalem regularly.

The ancient city was an exhilarating cocktail of cultures, with the buzz of Hebrew and Arabic all around, men in skullcaps, Orthodox Jews in their distinctive black coats and hats, men and women in traditional Palestinian dress, Christian priests, monks and nuns, and heavily armed young men and women in the dark green of the IDF.

It was like nowhere else on earth, and its energy was addictive.

There was so much history – in the stones and in the air. The city had seen a vast succession of conquerors and cultures, and few places had hosted and fervently worshipped so many different gods within their walls – Canaanite, Hebrew-Israelite-Jewish, Babylonian, Persian, Greek, Roman, Christian, Muslim. It was a heady mix of the histories of all the peoples who had ever called it sacred.

Turning right, she entered the Christian quarter, and headed for the Muristan.

Although the voices about her were still a mishmash of Arabic, Hebrew, and English, an increasing number of stalls were now hawking Christian souvenirs – crosses, icons, and other sacred mementos.

She ducked under an ancient stone arch, and as she emerged into a small open square, a muezzin began the call to prayer.

She listened to the words ringing out across the stones. The syllables had a mesmerizing alliteration and rhythm, made all the more arresting by the haunting eastern tones.

She waited until it was over, then moved further into the square, finding herself in front of the mighty Church of the Holy Sepulchre, with its distinctive honey-coloured crusader architecture and twin domes, all glowing softly in the sunlight.

It was a spectacular building.

Ahead of her, Mary was explaining its significance to Ferguson. "It's the most important church in Christendom. Originally built by the

Roman Emperor Constantine, it houses the mound where Christians believe Jesus was crucified, as well as enclosing the rock tomb where he was buried."

"So close together?" He sounded dubious. "Bit convenient isn't it?"

Mary shrugged. "This area used to be outside the ancient Roman city walls, on the site of an old olive grove – so who knows? Maybe it truly is where people were buried."

Ava bit back a desire to correct Mary. It had been a disused stone quarry in Jesus's day, not an olive grove, so was, in fact, exactly the sort of place where the Romans crucified people.

"The building is shared by a range of Churches – Greek, Armenian, Syriac, Coptic, Ethiopian, and Roman," Mary continued. "Running it is a nightmare." She pointed to a window overlooking the courtyard. "See that, on the balcony?" She was indicating a rickety wooden ladder perched on a ledge just above the main entrance. "It's been there for at least two hundred years because no one can agree what to do with it."

Ferguson shook his head in bemusement. "Better than the United Nations."

"Oh, far better," she continued. "There are some mini-monasteries up on the roof. A few years ago, a Coptic monk guarding a section moved his chair eight inches into the Ethiopians' territory. Eleven people were hospitalized in the punch-up that followed."

"None of them turned the other cheek?" Ferguson smiled.

"They even fight over who opens the front doors," Mary added. "To defuse the tensions, since the time of the crusades, two neutral Muslim families have been in charge of the keys. They open up at dawn and lock it up again at dusk."

Ava was now right behind them.

"We need to split up," she instructed as the three of them reached the main doorway. "We have to find the icon, and we need to assume that Durov is close by."

Or has already been and gone, she thought, but pushed the idea out of her head.

She knew it was here.

It had to be.

--- ◆ ---

CHAPTER 47

Church of the Holy Sepulchre
Shuk ha-Tsaba'aim Street
Old Town
Jerusalem
The State of Israel

FERGUSON AND MARY entered the arched crusader doorway first, and immediately peeled right.

Ava followed close behind.

As her eyes grew accustomed to the cavernous gloom, she spotted an old wooden bench to her left, just inside the door. There was a pile of leaflets stacked messily on it. She picked one up, and flipped through it, delighted to find a floor plan in the centre spread.

As she scanned it, her heart sank at the realization that her search was going to be significantly more complicated than she had thought.

The map revealed that the building contained a jumble of more than thirty separate chapels, altars, crypts, and tombs – all divided up between the assortment of religious denominations that shared the building.

Looking for one icon in so many shrines was going to be like trying to find a bolt in a factory.

On entering, Ferguson and Mary had gone right, towards the east end, so Ava turned left, directly into the Chapel of the Three Marys – built over the spot where tradition said the women had stood and watched the crucifixion.

As she headed deeper into the ancient church, she scanned the low-lit interior for the icon of Our Lady of Philermos, but saw nothing resembling it among the wide-eyed saints hanging on every wall and decorating the innumerable altars.

Checking her watch, she headed swiftly on, through an arcade of enormous pillars, and found herself in a colossal rotunda. Directly under the centre of the high dome, and encircled by crowds, she could see the Edicule – a tall, ornate, and balustraded Orthodox shrine. It was the centrepiece of the church, housing the rock tomb that Constantine believed Jesus was laid in after the crucifixion.

To those who believed the Turin Shroud was real, it was the place where the linen was wrapped around Jesus's mutilated body before he rose from the dead, from that very tomb.

It was the epicentre of the miraculous *anastasis* – the resurrection.

Next to Ava, a short bearded man with glasses was shuffling pieces of paper with diagrams on, trying to identify the different parts of the building.

She glanced over his shoulder at the diagrams and saw that the Romans had originally built a temple of Venus over the two separate sites of Jesus's execution and his subsequent burial. Then the Emperor Constantine had put up the Anastasis rotunda over the tomb, and built a separate structure, off to the east, around the place of the crucifixion.

From the brief descriptions she could see on the man's charts, they had both been pulled down by a mad caliph in 1009, before being rebuilt by the crusaders, who brought them both into the same building under one roof.

The result was a confused but awe-inspiring journey through over a millennium and a half of sacred Middle-Eastern Christian architecture.

Approaching the Edicule, which was incongruously buttressed with ageing steel girders, she started to scan the dozens of icons and images covering the shrine's walls. But as she got closer and jostled her way around it – straining her eyes to take in all the busy details – she could clearly see that the icon she was looking for was not there.

Turning towards the western end of the rotunda, she passed a Coptic chapel leaning up against the end wall of the Edicule. It was hung with yet more icons, but again there was no sign of Our Lady of Philermos.

In the centre of the western wall, a narrow archway set into the ancient stone blocks opened into a run-down Syrian chapel. From there she ducked through a crack in the rock, then into a passageway and an area marked as the Tomb of Joseph of Arimathea, which contained a number of ancient rock-cut *kokhim* burial ledges.

Ava peered around in the gloom, but there was no sign of the icon.

Heading back out into the main body of the church, she skirted the north side of the rotunda, passed through the Archway of the Virgin, and started towards the central nave.

Everywhere she looked, she was confronted with displays of icons and images on walls, screens, altars, and shelves. The visual assault of saints and biblical scenes was becoming overwhelming.

She blinked hard, trying to stay focused.

As she approached the main nave and *Katholikon*, her hopes mounted on seeing that the church's principal altar was shielded by a traditional Orthodox iconostasis screen.

Before entering the church, she had already decided that – as the Romanovs and Rasputin were Orthodox – the icon was probably going to be in one of the Orthodox areas. That meant she had ruled out the sizeable number of Roman Catholic chapels.

It also meant that this central iconostasis was exactly the sort of place the icon might be.

She approached, increasingly aware of the screen's height and grandeur. But as she neared it, she could plainly see that the ceremonial screen was decorated with large painted panels rather than being hung with individual icons.

Disappointed, she turned and headed back down the nave, past a stone basin set into the middle of the exquisite mosaic floor.

She recognized it immediately as an *omphalos* – an ancient Greek marker to show the centre of the world.

The most famous one was at Delphi, but she noted from the sign that Christian tradition claimed this exact spot in Jerusalem was the one true centre – the *umbilicus mundi* –where earth was connected directly to heaven. However, the *omphalos* was alone in the centre of the nave, and there were no icons anywhere nearby.

The more she took in the differing sections of the building, the more baffling it all became, and the more uncertain she was about finding the icon.

Where would it be?

She was sure it was here.

Had she missed a clue?

She looked around, spotting an area of low columns that almost certainly dated back to Constantine's original structures.

She ran over Rasputin's first cryptograph in her mind again, anxious to ensure she had not overlooked anything.

CITY OF ST PETER was Jerusalem.

ANASTASIS had to mean the Church of the Holy Sepulchre. And so did the skull, which represented Golgotha.

Then there was Rasputin's second cryptograph, which she was sure alluded to the Virgin Mary and the Knights of Saint John.

Most of what she could see around her was undoubtedly crusader architecture.

The Knights of Saint John had been here, as crusaders.

Was that the connection?

She forced herself to concentrate.

Think!

With a growing sense of desperation, she looked down at the leaflet, and saw that the church's other main Orthodox area was at the opposite end of the building, at the Crucifixion altar – built over the site where Jesus's cross was supposed to have been driven into the rock.

Keenly aware of time passing, she abandoned all sense of propriety and jogged back to the main entrance door, then headed up the curved honey-coloured stone stairwell leading to the hill of Calvary.

At the top, the smooth worn steps opened out into a room with three altars. The central one was an elaborate Orthodox shrine, festooned with lamps and icons. Around it, a large throng of people was crushing for the chance to crawl under the altar and insert an arm through a metal covering laid into the floor, through which they could touch the tip of the rock of Golgotha.

Ava jostled her way into the crowd, and made it to the front more quickly than she had anticipated.

Now she had a clear view of the altar, she scanned its icons, taking them in quickly one by one, running her eyes up the left side and down the right of the extravagantly ornate shrine.

When she reached the last image, she was almost ready to shout with frustration.

It was not here.

None of the icons resembled Our Lady of Philermos.

Exhausted, she threaded her way out of the crowd and stared down at the leaflet's floor plan again, scanning through the seemingly endless list of chapels and altars.

It was overwhelming.

The icon could be in any one of them.

And then, suddenly, one of the lines caught her eye.

CHAPEL OF ADAM
(GREEK ORTHODOX)

She frowned.

A chapel to Adam?

That did not make sense.

Why would a church have a chapel to him?

Adam was not a saint or martyr.

He was not even a Christian.

It was one thing having a statue or painting of him in a church. Like Abraham, Moses, or any of the other towering figures of the Old Testament, Adam had his role in the history of the Hebrew people. But a chapel where he could be venerated?

She had never heard of such a thing. Chapels were to honour Jesus and those who believed in him.

She flicked to the page with details about the chapel.

CHAPEL OF ADAM

Early Christian traditions relate that Adam was buried at 'Golgotha', the Place of the Skull, where Jesus was crucified. They recount that the Cross of the Crucifixion was driven into the ground over Adam's grave, with the base of the cross resting on Adam's skull. In this chapel, the crack in the rock from the earthquake at the time of Jesus's death is still visible. Some traditions maintain that Jesus's blood flowed through the crack and filled Adam's skull, redeeming him.

Ava froze.

Oh God.

Rasputin's first cryptograph had a cross resting on a skull.

More than that, she now realized that the letters either side of the skull – AD and AM – were not abbreviations for *anno domini* and *ante meridiem*.

They were a name.

ADAM.

She sprinted across the room, pushing her way through the crowd, before flinging herself down the stairs at the far end.

As she descended, she heard a small bell ringing to summon the Orthodox to a service in the Golgotha chapel.

The icon must be in the Chapel of Adam.

Hitting the ground floor hard, she swung right, and was immediately in front of the doorway into the chapel.

With her heart hammering, she ran forward, and found herself in a small room directly underneath the crucifixion altar above.

She gazed around intently.

It was an intimate space, with smooth stone flags on the floor, and ancient low arches overhead. All the edges and right angles had worn off the walls' aged blocks, giving the windowless chapel a mellow feeling of the passing centuries. At the east end, behind a low gate, there was a semi-circular apse with a simple undecorated altar. Behind it, a glass panel in the brickwork revealed the natural rock, said to be Golgotha, with a crack visibly running through it.

She looked back down at the leaflet's description of the chapel.

All medieval crusader kings of Jerusalem were buried in the Church of the Holy Sepulchre. The tombs have been lost, although two survived in the Chapel of Adam until 1808, and their designs are known from drawings.

Ava felt a frisson of anticipation.

Was that why Rasputin had drawn a Templar cross?

Was it an oblique reference to the crusader tombs?

Off to her right, at the end of a barrel-vaulted tunnel, there was a low narrow doorway connecting the chapel back to the church's main entrance area where she had first entered.

And there – either side of the narrow doorway – were two long stone slabs.

Her heart was beating harder now.

The low plinths were exactly the sort of place where sarcophagi would once have been placed.

Her mind was racing ahead, and suddenly another piece of Rasputin's cryptograph slotted into place.

She already knew that none of the clues had a Russian link. They were not about Anastasia or Saint Petersburg, and DISEASED ROYAL BLOOD was not an allusion to the haemophiliac Tsesarevich Prince Alexei Nicolaevich Romanov.

She now knew exactly who it referred to.

She could not believe that she had not made the connection earlier.

Alongside Prince Alexei, the most famous diseased royal in history was a king – a very powerful one.

A king of Jerusalem.

His crippling disease formed the basis of the Arthurian myths of the wounded fisher king, whose illness brought blight to the land.

He was Baldwin IV – the leper king of Jerusalem, and his demise was forever linked to the twilight of the once indomitable Crusader Kingdom of Jerusalem.

It all made sense.

She ran to the two stone plinths, and looked about feverishly.

As her eyes scanned the rows of icons hanging in the vault above the slabs, she registered a succession of traditional Orthodox images of patriarchs and saints.

And there, in a darkened recess by the narrow entranceway, was the icon of Our Lady of Philermos.

A wave of elation ripped through her.

She had been right!

Although blackened by age almost beyond recognition, the image of the Virgin Mary had exactly the same long mournful face and sad eyes as the one she had seen at the Palazzo Malta. And, almost imperceptible in the gloom, she could just make out some of the eight points of the Maltese Cross radiating from behind her head.

Grand Master Torquemada had mentioned a legend that the icon had been painted by Saint Luke. Looking at it now, she doubted that. But it was definitely medieval – from at least the 1200s. The frame was a later addition, maybe from the 1500s. And the golden jewelled riza mounted on the front was the most recent part of all, but still centuries old.

She checked there was no one about, then leant forwards and put her fingers behind the icon, lifting gently to pull it away from the wall.

To her frustration, it did not move.

She probed behind the icon more thoroughly with her fingers, and discovered that it was firmly bolted into place by metal pins sunk into the vault's stone ashlars.

The icon was not going anywhere, and there was no way she was going to be able to force it off the wall. The wood was old, and if she exerted any more pressure it would splinter or crack.

She was just going to have to examine it in place.

Leaning in close, she began to study it in detail.

The image itself was identical to the one in the Palazzo Malta and the various copies she had seen in books in the Vatican Library.

There did not appear to be anything unusual about the icon – and she doubted that whatever it was hiding was in plain sight, anyway.

It was far more likely to be concealing something.

She ran her fingers around the smooth wooden edges of the frame.

It was hiding a secret.

She was sure of it.

She laid her hand lightly on the riza, and tried sliding it.

The covering stayed firm.

What was she missing?

She pictured the second cryptograph in her mind's eye again, and then suddenly it hit her.

There were the two letters at the bottom.

ZZ

She had not paid much attention to them so far.

Did they tell her what to do now she had found the icon?

She concentrated on them.

Did ZZ mean something in Russian?

If it did, then she was stuck.

She did not speak Russian.

There were probably Russian tourists in the building, but the last thing she wanted was to draw attention to what she was doing.

She thought back to the meeting in the Cavalry and Guards Club, when Swinton had shown her the photograph of Durov, in his car, looking at Rasputin's notebooks.

She concentrated hard, recalling the original image in the notebook.

She had clearly seen the two Russian letters: *ze* and *ze*.

What on earth began with Z and Z in Russian?

She could not think of anything. She simply did not know enough Russian.

As she pictured the letters in her head, she suddenly felt a wave of doubt, followed by excitement.

What if they weren't Russian letters at all?

The Russian letter for Z was 3.

What if didn't say ZZ at all?

What if they were numbers?

What if it said thirty-three?

She let the idea sink in for a moment.

It was certainly possible that Swinton's translator had assumed they were Cyrillic letters and overlooked the possibility they were just ordinary numbers.

Three and three. Or thirty-three.

In handwriting – especially Rasputin's scrawl – it would be easy to confuse them.

But what would that mean?

What was the significance of 33?

Jesus was thirty-three years old when he was executed.

Was that it?

She dismissed the idea.

No.

The clue had to tell her what to do with the icon.

She stared at the sorrowful image of the Virgin Mary, and noticed that the riza was surrounded by pearls. Hundreds of them.

Was it a reference to those?

Was she supposed to count the pearls somehow?

She doubted it. They were in a continuous loop, with no obvious start or end.

Inside the outer band of pearls were larger rubies and clusters of pearls.

Did it refer to those?

She started at Mary's left shoulder, and counted the third ruby up from the left.

She pressed it, and felt a surge of exhilaration run through her as it sank gently into the frame, then popped back to its original position.

That was it!

On the other side of the icon, she counted up three rubies from Mary's right shoulder, and pressed it.

The precious stone did exactly the same as the first, sinking softly into the frame, then popping out.

She frowned.

Nothing had changed.

Frustrated, she pressed both stones simultaneously.

As the gleaming red jewels entered the wood, there was the soft but distinct sound of a metallic mechanism operating, then the bottom edge of the frame unclicked a fraction from the rest of the frame.

She stared in disbelief.

Reaching gingerly for the bottom bar of the frame, she pulled it down slowly.

To her amazement, it slid freely, opening like a drawer.

As she continued to pull, the breath caught in her throat at the sight of a recess carved into the drawer – and at what it contained.

A small rectangle of vellum.

With trembling hands, she carefully lifted the ancient piece of skin out of the concealed hiding place.

The side facing her was blank.

Momentarily overwhelmed by the enormity of what she had discovered, she slowly turned it over, and gasped at the medieval script covering the other side.

It was bold and black, in a crisp neat hand.

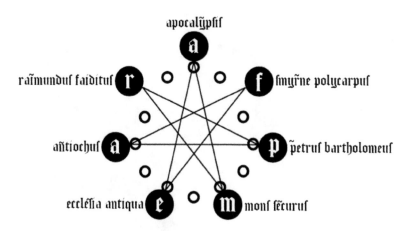

She gaped at the seven-pointed star, lost for words.

Around it were twelve smaller circles, and at each of its tips was a black circle with a letter in it. Beside each black circle was a word.

She read them:

APOCALYPSIS

SMYRNE POLYCARPUS

PETRUS BARTHOLOMEUS

MONS SECURUS

ECCLESIA ANTIQUA

ANTIOCHUS

RAIMUNDUS FAIDITUS

She goggled at the star blankly, translating the words from the medieval Latin.

It meant absolutely nothing to her.

It seemed meaningless. Incoherent.

Pulling out her smartphone, she took several photos of the bizarre drawing, then pushed the concealed drawer closed again, and clicked the bottom bar of the icon's frame back into place.

She was about to place the piece of vellum between the pages of a book in her jacket pocket, when, with no warning, she felt a blow to the back of her head.

It was fast and savage, and as the pain exploded across her skull, she went hot then ice cold, and started to black out.

—————— ◆ ——————

CHAPTER 48

Church of the Holy Sepulchre
Shuk ha-Tsaba'aim Street
Jerusalem
The State of Israel

FIGHTING TO STAY conscious, she was aware only of an overpowering nausea, then a pain in her knees as they crashed into the stone slab in front of her, and she was sent sprawling over it.

At the same time, there was a burning pain in the back of her hand as something was jabbed into it hard, breaking the skin.

She instinctively opened her palm, and the piece of vellum was snatched away.

Through a daze, she realized she was still holding the smartphone in her tight hand. Without pausing, she swung her arm round hard and fast, angling the corner of the phone into the head of her attacker.

He grunted as it connected, and she got her first glimpse of who it was.

He had a broad face with high cheekbones and brown hair swept back in a ponytail.

Durov.

Her mind immediately filled with images of him slicing her ear the previous day, and she felt her rage rising.

He was not going to get the better of her this time.

And he was absolutely not going to take the vellum.

Without pausing, she kicked him savagely in the kneecap.

He might be strong, but she was better trained.

Now off balance, he swung a vicious backhand at her, but she saw it coming, and ducked. Before he knew what was happening, she hammered her elbow into the back of his shoulder, and he grunted as he crashed to the floor.

The vellum was still in his hand and, without pausing, she stooped to grab it back.

But before she reached it, her left arm was yanked backwards so hard her shoulder burned, then she was smothered in a crushing hold from behind.

Completely trapped, she twisted to look backwards, but the person was behind her, and she could not see his face.

"Don't struggle, and it won't hurt," a voice commanded her.

She knew that voice anywhere.

Uri.

Something inside her snapped, and she began to lash out with her head and legs.

But Uri was far too strong. He was restraining her so hard she could not breathe.

She fought for air, watching helplessly as Durov picked himself up and walked briskly out through the chapel's doors, tucking the vellum into his jacket pocket as he left.

Uri loosened his grip on her slightly.

"What the hell are you doing?" Ava shouted as her coughing subsided. "He's got the … "

With an iron effort of will, she stopped herself just in time. Things were complicated enough, without Uri knowing about the icon and the vellum.

She was apoplectic with rage, and started struggling again, converting all her frustration into aggression. "You bastard. You have no idea what you've just done," she spat.

"I warned you," he answered coolly, with no trace of emotion. "I told you clearly to leave Durov alone. But you didn't listen."

"Nice friends, you keep." Ava hurled the accusation at him. "What is it? Money? Favours? Dirty laundry?"

Uri did not reply. He checked that Durov had disappeared, then released her.

Her blood was still pumping hard, and without hesitating she grabbed the diminutive gun from her pocket, raised it, and pointed it directly at Uri.

He was at point blank range.

"Come with me," he ordered, ignoring the weapon.

For a split second she found herself squeezing the trigger a little tighter, taking aim.

"If I put a hole in you," she was breathing hard, still struggling to control her anger, "no one in London would blame me – not after what you just did."

Uri looked dismissively at her. "But you're not in London. This is Jerusalem."

As she absorbed his words, the reality of the situation sank in.

He was right.

She was in Israel. On his territory.

She gradually released the pressure on the trigger and lowered the gun.

Slumping against the cold wall in defeat, she took several deep breaths to calm herself.

Praying that her phone was still working, she swiped it on, and heaved a sigh of relief when the camera app appeared with a little square in the corner showing the last photo she had taken.

It was a miniature image of the piece of vellum. She tapped it, and the photograph filled the screen. The focus was sharp, and she could make out all the words clearly.

At least it was something.

"Now what?" She pushed the hair out of her face and glared at Uri.

"Follow me," he answered, reaching down and taking the gun from her hand.

He turned and started walking back out of the chapel into the entrance area, then out of the building and onto the parvis in front.

Drained, Ava followed.

As they approached the archway back into the *souq*, he took her arm – more gently this time – and steered her through it.

She pulled away in irritation.

Without stopping, he turned left at the end of the square, and made for the labyrinth of stalls lining the narrow streets of the Muristan.

Looking around, Ava figured she could easily make a run for it. There were alleyways branching off the narrow street in all directions, and there were so many stalls and goods cluttering the area that she would have a hundred places to hide.

She was confident she could lose him pretty quickly.

But logic told her that if Durov had the piece of vellum, then she was more likely to get it back if Mossad was not on her case as well.

Right now, that meant going to the station with Uri, and answering whatever questions he had.

She was reassured by the fact he would not be able to pin anything on her. She had not followed Durov to Israel, and Uri knew nothing about the icon. So when it was over, he would let her go, and she could carry on.

Except this time, she promised herself, she would make sure Uri was nowhere near her.

———— • ◆ • ————

CHAPTER 49

The Muristan
Jerusalem
The State of Israel

URI WAS SILENT as he led Ava through the narrow streets of the Muristan's spreading *souq*.

That was fine by her. She did not want to say anything more than she had to. Her head still hurt from where Durov had tried to knock her out, and she was grateful for the silence.

Uri turned up a stall-cluttered side street, and then again into another narrower street which led up a slight hill. The goods on display here were altogether less shiny – thin bunches of tired and unwashed vegetables, and limp sprigs of yellowing herbs.

He stopped at a small wooden door – its worn geometric carvings battered and chipped by the decades – and tapped a code into a panel mounted beside it.

The mechanism clicked noisily open, and he ushered her into a bare tiled hallway, up a narrow stone staircase, then through another locked doorway, and into a small sitting room.

A mellow light filtered in from the warped wooden shutters, through which she could see slices of the Muristan's chaotic roofs and alleyways.

There was a low carved wooden table in the middle of the room, with a sofa, two armchairs, and a television arranged around it. A door opened into a small kitchen, and another to a room with a bed, a desk, and a window with bars and solid wooden shutters.

"Safe house," Uri said, locking the door behind them. "Sit down," he said, indicating the sofa. "You've got a lot of explaining to do."

"As have you," Ava retorted. "What the hell were you doing back there? And why are you following me?"

"I told you," he answered, taking out her Curve gun. "Some senior people in the Institute want you to leave Durov alone."

"Why?" Ava fired back. "What's the connection between Mossad and an insane petro-oligarch?"

Ava sank into the sofa, glaring at him as he moved over to the window.

"I'm not holding you here," he answered, unclipping the magazine. "You're free to go. But if you keep harassing Durov, someone from the Institute – and it will probably be me – will be tasked to put you permanently out of action. You can't say you haven't been warned."

He leant up against the window and began meticulously removing the rounds from the Curve's magazine one by one. "So, are you going to tell me?" he asked quietly, focusing on the weapon.

She was watching his movements. They were neat and efficient. Dextrous.

He did not look up, but continued with the magazine.

A wave of fatigue washed over her as the adrenaline of the fight with Durov wore off.

She glanced across at Uri, angered by his air of superiority, and increasingly irritated by the sound of the gun's metal parts clicking.

As she struggled to understand why Uri was protecting Durov, she was overcome by an urge to stop him fiddling with the gun. He had finished with the magazine, and was now stripping the chassis.

It was driving her mad.

Agitated, she stood up, and walked over to him. She grasped his hand, pressing it around the gun.

He tensed – aggressive – eyeing her coldly.

She held his gaze for a moment, then kissed him hard on the mouth.

Gratifyingly, she could feel him waver.

Taking advantage of his surprise, she slid her hands down his back, under the material of his waistband, and pulled him firmly towards her.

She could sense him calculating whether or not this was a ruse.

Still kissing, she steered him towards the bedroom. Unbuttoning her shirt, she pushed him down onto the bed.

He was excited now, reaching to undo his trousers.

She was gratified to see that he was not always in control. He was not an automaton.

She stepped out of her jeans, and sat astride him, pulling off his t-shirt.

He reached up to undo her bra, but she moved his hand away, then took it off herself.

She looked down at him, stroking her hand across his chest. His body was toned and beautiful, as she knew it would be.

She drank in the sight.

Feeling an urgency now, she allowed him to enter her with no conscious thought, sensing only a wave of satisfaction.

Closing her eyes, she abandoned herself to a blur of unconnected images – abstract clouds of emotion from the last few days. The last few years.

As the intensity built, Uri rolled her over, and she was on her back, looking up at him. He was focused and incessant. He wanted her approval. But she had no interest in giving it.

This was for her.

She wanted the release, and as it came she felt a flood of pleasure wash down through her.

Lying next to him later, she stared blankly at the bars on the window as he got up and went to the kitchen, where she heard him flick on the kettle.

She got dressed, and walked through into the sitting room. He looked at her quizzically, but she did not say anything as she let herself out of the building.

She walked away quickly, and did not look back.

——— • ◆ • ———

CHAPTER 50

Jerusalem Helipad
Mount Scopus
Jerusalem
The State of Israel

TO THE EAST of the Old City, Durov looked down at Jerusalem's helipad disappearing rapidly beneath him.

The view from Mount Scopus was spectacular – even better now that he was swiftly rising above it.

The mountain's name came from the Greek word *skopos* – meaning watchman – as for millennia it had been the lookout post for the city's vigilant sentinels.

But it had been used by enemies, too.

Invaders had climbed the rocky outcrop to survey the ancient capital before launching cataclysmic attacks. The Roman XII Thunderbolt and XV Apollo's legions had used it as their base to destroy Jerusalem in AD 70, as had the crusaders in 1099. And as recently as 1917, General Allenby had encamped the British army there before smashing four centuries of Ottoman Turkish control.

The helicopter banked west, flying low over the Temple Mount – above the golden cupolas of the Dome of the Rock and the al-Aqsa mosque.

Durov turned his attention to the small square of vellum in his hand, and smiled.

It all made sense.

He knew exactly what it meant.

Everything on it was where it should be.

Rasputin had not lied.

The many references Durov had found dotted throughout the mystic's notebooks had prepared him for this. The only clues he had been waiting for were now in his hand, and they completed the picture.

Clever.

He congratulated himself.

Finally, he had the missing pieces.

Now he knew where he would find the roll, and where to light the pyre.

The helicopter climbed, and he looked down over the receding domes of the Church of the Holy Sepulchre – covering the exact spot where the *Theotokos* had stood and watched her son's final victory over death.

She had not intervened, but had let the prophecies take their course.

Now, nearly two thousand years later, everything was set for the next phase of His glory.

The Holy Mother had been right to trust him.

CHAPTER 51

The Regent's Park
London
England
The United Kingdom

AVA HAD TAKEN a taxi to Ben Gurion airport, then booked a seat on the first flight back to London.

There had been nothing further for her in Jerusalem.

Durov would be on his way to Moscow, London, or somewhere else.

She had no idea where Ferguson and Mary were. She had texted him to say she had found the icon and was heading home, and figured he would call her when he was ready.

It was early evening by the time she arrived at her flat. She showered and changed, then set out on the Brough, heading up through Piccadilly and Marylebone to Regent's Park.

Chaining the bike up in the Outer Circle, she walked across into the park, and made for its south-west corner, grateful for the fresh air and solitude after being stuck in an aeroplane.

The boating lake was one of her favourite spots.

She bought a cider from the café, and took it to one of the battered wooden tables and chairs that had been set out on the grass overlooking the lake.

Sitting down, she watched as the boat keeper settled a succession of people into brightly painted rowing boats and pedalos, before pushing them out onto the sparkling evening water.

Standing under the shower earlier, feeling the hot water drain away the tensions of the previous few days, she had found herself wondering what on earth she was doing. So far, there had been three serious attempts on her life – the shooting on her doorstep, the attempt to inject her with something in Paris, and Durov attacking her in the Holy Sepulchre. As she felt herself relaxing in the steam, she had suddenly felt acutely aware that she was not immortal, and wondered whether it was all worth it.

But then she had seen Durov's face again in her mind's eye – his insanity radiating from it – and knew that he needed to be stopped. Whatever he was up to, no one was in a better position than her to bring him down, and prevent whatever it was that he was bent on doing.

Looking around the park, she took a gulp of the cold cider, pulled out her smartphone, and opened the image gallery to bring up the photograph of the piece of vellum from the Church of the Holy Sepulchre.

As the ancient seven-pointed star filled the screen, she fought to repress a sense of failure at having allowed Durov to take the original. He had been one step ahead of her all the way, and now – following Uri's intervention – he had the prize.

She could not blame Uri completely. She should have been faster to solve Rasputin's cryptographs. In the Holy Sepulchre, she should have been more careful – more aware of who was nearby. If she had pocketed the fragment and left more quickly, things might have been different.

Instead, Durov now had the manuscript.

She pushed the thoughts away. There was nothing to be done about it. All that mattered now was which one of them would solve the writing on the vellum first.

And she was still in with a chance of that.

She stared at the mysterious message, conscious that she had never seen anything quite like it before.

If she was going to understand it, the first two priorities were to work out who had written it, and why.

She had been mulling it over on the plane.

The handwriting looked fourteenth-century, but she knew from experience that did not prove anything. There were plenty of good forgers out there who could reproduce dozens of different medieval scripts well enough to fool even the most experienced experts.

On the other hand, she did know that Rasputin had almost certainly seen the cryptic fragment of vellum before 1916, so it was at least a century old. And if someone had spent the time and effort forging it a hundred years ago, then there had to be a reason why.

She tried to look at the question from all sides.

Why, if the vellum had been created by a conman at the turn of the nineteenth century, would it have been placed in an old icon rather than used to generate publicity or money?

Why would a forger have hidden it so securely?

As she worked through the options, it seemed far more likely that the fragment was exactly what it seemed to be – a medieval message, most likely written by a Knight of Saint John.

She took another sip of the cider, enjoying the hit of aromatic apples.

The next question was what the words meant.

Some were more straightforward than others.

APOCALYPSIS was the apocalypse, although it was not clear from the context whether it meant the biblical book of that name, or the final cataclysmic end of the world.

SMYRNE POLYCARPUS was Saint Polycarp, one of the Church's first bishops. He was a thinker and writer, based in the ancient city of Smyrna – now İzmir in Turkey – where he had been a pillar of the early Church.

PETRUS BARTHOLOMEUS was someone called Peter Bartholomew. The name meant nothing to her.

MONS SECURUS was safe hill.

ECCLESIA ANTIQUA just meant ancient church.

ANTIOCHUS was Antioch, although it was not clear which one. It could mean Antioch-on-the-Orontes, one of the main cities in the Roman Empire, and among the earliest centres of Christianity. It lay in a spur of southern Turkey that stuck down into Syria, about fifty miles west of Aleppo, and was now known as Antakya. The other possibility was the far less important city of Antioch-in-Pisidia, which was in the middle of Turkish Anatolia.

RAIMUNDUS FAIDITUS was a name: Raymond Faiditus or Faidit. Again, it meant nothing to her.

As she surveyed the words, she realized that she had almost nothing to go on.

And from what little she could work out, the list of words and names seemed meaningless.

She glanced up, looking out over the boating lake, and at the scattering of Londoners and visitors enjoying a carefree moment.

It was a lovely mellow summer evening, and in other circumstances she would have been quite happy to take a boat out herself and enjoy the calm sound of the oars and the water washing against the hull.

She often did, but this evening she had work to do.

She looked back at the star diagram.

The only possible connection she could see between the words was that four of them were suggestive of ancient Christianity. The APOCA-LYPSE was an obsession of the ANCIENT CHURCH. ANTIOCH was an early Christian city. And POLYCARP OF SMYRNA was a famous early Church leader.

But even if the words were connected in that way, it still did not tell her very much.

She took another sip of the cider, and wondered if she needed to approach the puzzle in another way.

It was clear that the author of the text was purposefully playing with the reader. That was plain from the small lines over some of the letters. She had spotted the irregularity immediately.

In medieval Latin, a small macron line above a letter indicated that certain letters were missing. For example, $\bar{p}$ always meant *pre*, and $\bar{q}$ always meant *quae*. There were other symbols, too, like a big curly apostrophe meant the letters *us*. There were also some set abbreviations for entire words – like *dn̄s* meant *dominus*. So a scribe could simply write:

$$d\bar{n}s \; \bar{p}fect^9$$

and the reader would know to expand the words as *dominus prefectus*, or Lord Prefect.

But she had immediately noticed that this was not how the macrons in the vellum fragment were being used. The words on the vellum were all written out in full, as whole words – with nothing missing – so the macrons were not indicating that anything needed to be added.

They were plainly being used in some other way.

She pulled a scrap of paper and a pen from her pocket, and wrote out each letter of the manuscript that had a macron over it:

YRPEENI

She peered at the seven letters, reshuffling them in her mind to find any anagrams.

There were none in medieval English, but she was not expecting that there would be.

She tried medieval Latin then medieval French, which seemed the most likely languages for a fourteenth-century Knight of Saint John. But she could not see any seven-letter anagrams.

She crossed the word through and tried again, this time ordering the words on the vellum sequentially, placing the one with the macron over the first letter first, the one with the macron over the second letter second, and so on for the rest.

She looked down at the result:

PETRUS BARTHOLOMEUS
ANTIOCHUS
RAIMUNDUS FAIDITUS
SMYRNE POLYCARPUS
ECCLESIA ANTIQUA
MONS SECURUS
APOCALYPSIS

She peered at them, wondering if the words were now in any kind of intelligible order.

She could not see anything obvious.

It was still all meaningless.

She was tired. It had been a long day.

She took another swig of the cider, and stared at the list, allowing her mind to go blank, letting the shapes rearrange themselves in random ways. She slipped her eyes slightly out of focus, watching as the letters become blurred at the edges.

Then suddenly she saw it:

PARSEMA

It was an acrostic, from the initial letter of each word.

She sat bolt upright, alert now.

Most of the Knights of Saint John had been French. And *parsema* was a French word. It meant 'he scattered'.

She peered at it, feeling her energy returning.

Who had scattered?

Polycarp? Peter Bartholomew? Raymond Faiditus?

And what exactly had been scattered?

She swirled the cider in the bottle, mesmerized by the clouds of rising bubbles.

Perhaps the remaining words would tell her what had been scattered. But to find that out, she would need to make sense of them first.

Her eyes moved to the seven-pointed star at the centre of the diagram.

Why a star?

Was it a clue to the order of the words?

Starting at the top, she ran her finger along the lines of the star, clockwise, not lifting it from the image. That gave her:

APOCALYPSE

SAFE HILL

RAYMOND FAIDITUS

It did not seem to reveal anything.

She started again at the top, and this time traced the star anticlockwise:

APOCALYPSE

ANCIENT CHURCH

POLYCARP OF SMYRNA

She stopped dead at the realization that the words were in a chronological order.

Saint John had written the APOCALYPSE. He had then sent copies of it to the seven churches of the ANCIENT CHURCH. And one of the bishops who had received it was POLYCARP OF SMYRNA.

So was it John who had scattered the manuscripts of the Apocalypse?

To the seven churches?

She looked back over the list and continued tracing the star pattern anticlockwise with her finger.

The next word it gave was ANTIOCH. But that was not one of the seven churches.

Ava frowned.

She opened the map app on her phone, and pulled up Turkey.

The ancient journey from Smyrna to Antioch would translate on modern roads to a trip from İzmir to Antakya.

It looked about seven hundred miles.

It was a feasible journey in the ancient world.

Maybe it wasn't John. Maybe Polycarp took his copy of the Apocalypse to Antioch.

She continued tracing the star anticlockwise to complete the pattern with all the words:

ANTIOCH
PETER BARTHOLOMEW
RAYMOND FAIDITUS
SAFE HILL

An idea was forming in her mind, which was now starting to buzz with possibilities.

She quickly drained the rest of the cider, and stood up to leave. She needed to get home, where she had books that would help.

Her excitement was mounting as she rode hurriedly back to Piccadilly, eager to test her hypothesis.

Once indoors, she headed straight for the study.

If ANTIOCH was followed by PETER BARTHOLOMEW, then she needed to find a connection between the two.

Peter Bartholomew struck her as a medieval European name, and the only medieval connection she knew between Europe and Antioch was the crusades, when western armies fought over the ancient city.

She reached up to the bookshelves and pulled down her battered three-volume history of the crusades.

Turning to the back, she flicked through the index, then started scanning the section headed P.

With a flush of exhilaration, she saw that the name PETER BARTHOLOMEW was listed.

He had been a real person.

Excitedly, she carried the three books through to the sitting room, and settled herself down on the sofa to read.

Half an hour later, she put the books down and stood up.

She had been right.

Two more clues on the vellum fragment were beginning to make sense.

She could tick off ANTIOCH and PETER BARTHOLOMEW, who she now knew was a Provençal pilgrim – the leading character in an extraordinary drama that had taken place in crusader Antioch. The event had involved Peter Bartholomew and the most powerful crusader of his day – Count Raymond of Saint-Gilles.

A wider theory about the meaning of the vellum fragment was beginning to take shape in her mind.

Heading back to the study, she spotted out of the corner of her eye that the small light on the side of her landline handset was flashing red.

She picked it up and connected to her voicemail.

A message had been left earlier that afternoon.

As it began to play, she recognized the raspy Scottish voice immediately.

It was Swinton. And he was not happy.

She listened to the whole message, then put the receiver down, the blood rising to her face.

Swinton had received a call from a Mossad officer complaining about Ava harassing Oleg Durov and getting into a public brawl in the Church of the Holy Sepulchre. Mossad informed Swinton that they had already taken steps to warn Ava off Durov, and now they were formally complaining about her visit to Israel.

Ava leaned up against the wall, her mind spinning.

Was this Uri's doing?

And how, if MI13 was so ultra-secret, had Mossad known to call Swinton?

She started to go cold.

Or had Swinton made contact with Mossad?

Is that how Uri had known she was on the flight to Israel?

She took a deep breath.

She had never been able to shake off the feeling that Swinton was hiding something from her.

Why had he warned her off Durov in the first place? Why had Julia been shot outside her house when she was carrying the green umbrella Swinton had given Ava? Why had Swinton called her in Paris only minutes after she had been attacked?

Ava strode into the hallway and put on her jacket.

It was time to see Swinton.

He had a lot of questions to answer.

_____ • ◆ • _____

CHAPTER 52

Belsize Park
London
England
The United Kingdom

AVA CHECKED HER watch.

It was too late for Swinton to still be in the office, so she pulled out her phone and brought up the photo she had taken of his profile page on the MI13 computer.

It showed his personal address was in Belsize Park.

She got back on the Brough and headed north. The rush hour was over, and the ride took less than twenty minutes.

When she arrived at the address, she parked up around the corner, then approached on foot.

The street was quiet, and Swinton's house was set back from the road. A screen of carefully tended hedges blocked out any view of the ground floor and provided privacy.

She approached the narrow gate, and caught a glimpse through a gap in the hedge of a small front garden. Behind it was a detached three-storey Victorian red-brick house. A small flight of white steps led up to a portico and doorway set between two bay windows.

It was plainly not a cheap house, and she realized how little she actually knew of Swinton.

Easing open the gate, she covered the few yards of flagged paving stones and steps up to the front door.

The bay to her right was in complete darkness.

The slatted blinds on the inside of the window to her left prevented her seeing into the room, but there was light glowing behind the wooden louvres, and also through the patterned transom glass over the front door.

She spotted a small brass bell ringer in the brickwork beside the door, but as she reached out to press it, the silence was broken by the muffled report of a suppressed gunshot, followed a moment later by a second.

Her adrenaline fired instantly, and she darted to her right, out of the doorway.

What the hell was happening in there?

Who was shooting?

Her pulse was racing as she hauled herself over the wooden side gate, and dropped down into the back garden, where the moon and streetlamps provided ample light for her to see her way along the path.

Moving swiftly alongside the neatly tended lawn and shrubs, she rounded the corner of the building and quickly assessed the back of the house. It was unfussy, with a large window next to a pair of patio doors opening off a kitchen-dining room.

She approached softly, and peered through the glass.

The lights in the back room were off, but there was enough illumination filtering through from the front of the house and the windows to reveal a long room with a large kitchen table.

There was no outside handle on the patio doors, so she hooked her fingers around the end of the outer sliding pane and tried moving it.

It was firmly locked.

Reaching into her pocket, she pulled out her ring of keys, and selected one which had six teeth of equal height, separated by five valleys of equal depth. She knew she should not really carry the key, but it was very handy for the endless storerooms and cupboards at the Museum, and old habits died hard.

She stopped to pick up a fist-sized ornamental pebble from the edge of the patio, then returned to the doors and jiggled the bump key into the lock, pushing it all the way home. She then withdrew it a fraction, and turned it lightly, avoiding any excess pressure on the pins that might inadvertently restrict their free movement.

Holding the pebble firmly, she tapped it on the end of the key several times, forcing the lock's pins to jump from the shock. On the third tap, the lower set of pins fell back into the barrel at the same time, and the light pressure she was exerting on the key turned it.

It was as easy as that.

She gently slid the patio door open, stepped inside the building, then closed the door quietly behind her.

Now she could see the room more clearly, it was plain that everything about the décor was masculine and had not been updated for decades. Even more revealingly, the absence of any family clutter and the pile of identical takeaway food boxes by the cooker suggested strongly that Swinton lived alone.

Her heart was racing, and she had no way of knowing whether whoever had fired the gunshots was still inside the house. He or she could have left by the front door while she was round the back. Or they might still be there.

Grabbing an old metal poker from beside the fireplace, she moved silently through the kitchen and up a short flight of steps into the hallway.

The wide passageway was hung with large maps of Scotland on one wall, and a collection of antique prints of policemen on the other.

That made sense. She could believe Swinton had been a detective before entering the intelligence services.

The doors off the hall to the left were closed, but the ones to the right were ajar.

Her feet made no noise on the soft carpet as she moved forward and peered cautiously into the first room.

It was dark and empty.

She tried the second, but as she leant round the corner, she sensed a rapid movement behind her, and spun round just as a gun was being raised to her face.

Without hesitating, she brought the poker crashing down on the collarbone above the arm holding the weapon.

There was a loud crack of bone, followed by the sound of the gun falling to the ground. Whoever had surprised her thudded back against the hallway wall with a whimper.

His face was a mask of pain, and as Ava caught sight of his features, she was astonished to find herself looking directly at Sir Mark Jennings.

She had the poker raised again, but Jennings was leaning up against the wall, pale and sweating heavily. The noise of his panting was filling the silence, and from the ashen colour of his skin, it was evident he was in no condition to fight any more.

With one hand he was clutching his stomach, and she did not need medical training to appreciate the severity of the ragged wound bleeding out heavily over his ripped shirt. As she lowered the poker, he began ineffectually trying to clamp the fabric of his jacket over the injury to staunch the loss of blood.

"Where's Swinton?" Ava asked, looking about for any sign of a struggle.

When it became clear Jennings was not going to answer, she grabbed hold of his good arm, pinned it roughly behind his back in a shoulder lock, and pushed him through into the front sitting room.

As she entered, her eyes swept the room, and she felt a rising wave of nausea.

Swinton was sprawled on the floor, with a bloodied kitchen knife by his right hand. There was a bullet entry wound in his chest, and another – unmistakeably an execution shot – in the centre of his forehead.

He was lying completely still, his eyes staring glassily at the ceiling.

Ava pushed Jennings down into an armchair beside the bay window.

Piecing together what had happened in the room, she stepped back into the hallway, picked up Jennings's gun, then re-entered the room, training the weapon on him.

Walking over to a telephone on a side-table, she pulled her sleeve over her hand, and telephoned for an ambulance, giving the address and explaining there was a victim of a serious stabbing at the property. She gave no other details, and hung up.

When she was done, she turned her attention back to Jennings. "Why?" she asked, looking down at Swinton's body.

"Because he picked the wrong side," Jennings rasped.

Ava was staring at Jennings closely.

"Nice of you to come and protect him," he continued. "Although you should've been quicker."

"So it was you," Ava murmured, as the pieces of the puzzle snapped together. "You're the one helping Durov."

"And Swinton was protecting you." He nodded. "He was thrilled to have got you into MI13. He reckoned you were going to be the rising star of his team. But he was always anxious you were getting too far out of your depth with Durov."

"Protecting me?" Ava repeated. "But then how … " she began, then stopped as she realized that it did, in fact, make complete sense.

She just had not seen it.

"You shouldn't blame yourself entirely," he added. "When he called and asked for my help, I knew it was a sign. I was waiting outside the building that night, and it was me who gave your address to Durov and told him you were carrying a green umbrella. It was also me who saw from the passenger manifests that you were on the Eurostar, so I gave Durov another chance at taking you down. When Swinton called you immediately afterwards, that was because I asked him to. I wanted to know whether you were still around. And, if you were, whether you had made any progress with the Rasputin cryptographs. As you can imagine, I wasn't happy that Swinton had given you the second one, although there was nothing I could do about it. Swinton was obliging enough to make the call at my suggestion. He didn't suspect anything – and definitely not that he was making you increasingly more suspicious of him."

Ava looked down at Swinton's body, feeling an intense wave of regret that she had misjudged him.

And now she knew who it was that had been trying to kill her.

"It turns out he was onto me," he wheezed. "Like you, he had figured out that Durov was getting help with your movements. He confronted me with my 'treachery'. But, then, I don't see it that way. I'm not betraying my country. This isn't still the Cold War. This is about the redemption of mankind – about saving us all."

"You're one of them – the Skoptsy?" Ava stared at him in disbelief.

"Lord, no," Jennings grunted. Then his voice changed as he began reciting. "There was war in heaven. Michael and his angels fought against the dragon; and the dragon fought and his angels, and prevailed not; neither was their place found any more in heaven. And the great dragon was cast out, that old serpent, called the Devil, and Satan, which deceiveth the whole world: he was cast out into the earth, and his angels were cast out with him. And I heard a loud voice saying in heaven, Now is come salvation, and strength, and the kingdom of our God, and the power of his Christ: for the accuser of our brethren is cast down, which accused them before our God day and night. And they overcame him by the blood of the Lamb, and by the word of their testimony; and they loved not their lives unto the death."

"The Apocalypse." Ava did not take her eyes off him. "What's that got to do with it?"

"Everything." Jennings's breathing was coming with more difficulty. "Durov's far cleverer than you." He paused. "Then again, he knows what he's looking for. You see, he knows that the prize is one of the original letters of the Apocalypse."

"Written by Saint John," Ava confirmed.

Just as the vellum manuscript said.

Jennings was now holding a cushion in front of his stomach in an effort to contain the bleeding.

"The Bible tells us," he panted, "that when Saint John had his divine vision of the Apocalypse, he wrote it out seven times, and sent a copy to each of the seven churches of Asia."

Ava nodded. "So what?"

"Each was a scroll, closed with a seal," he wheezed. "Don't you see?"

She did not. He sounded delusional.

"In John's vision, there's a scroll with seven seals, and only the Lamb has the power to open them. But if you read on, you'll know that only once the seals have been opened can the climax of the End Times begin. The first seal lets loose a white horse with a conquering rider. The second unleashes a red horse with a rider bringing war. The third conjures up a black horse with a rider holding scales. The fourth summons a pale horse whose rider is Death. The fifth gives a vision of the souls of all the dead in the Word of God. The sixth brings an earthquake, the sun turns black, the moon becomes blood, and the stars fall to earth. And the seventh calls forth seven angels with seven trumpets."

Ava was lost. "In every age there have been madmen prophesying the arrival of the end times. Is that what Durov is doing?"

Jennings coughed and turned paler. "Saint John sent out seven physical scrolls of his apocalyptic vision. And in that revelation there were seven seals on a scroll. Don't you see the connection?"

Ava stared at him, the gun she had aimed at him not wavering.

"Legend has always said that the seal on John's seventh letter was never opened."

"That's deranged." Her eyes widened. "You're saying that the seven imaginary seals in the Apocalypse vision are the same as the physical seals on the seven letters John sent out?"

It was ludicrous.

He nodded. "The Devil has been loose for two millennia, and hence the world has been in chaos. Only by opening the seventh seal can we enter upon the time of the angels and trumpets and the final Rapture and Tribulation."

Ava tightened her grip on the gun.

He was certifiably insane.

"Durov is guided by the Blessed Virgin," Jennings's voice was coming in gasps. "He knows where the seventh seal is – the one that has yet to be opened. It's on the unread letter John sent to the church of — "

"Smyrna," Ava finished his sentence for him. "To Bishop Polycarp."

Jennings smiled weakly. "Maybe you are as clever as he is – in which case you know that Saint Polycarp was like Saint John's son. They lived together on Patmos as master and pupil. But once John revealed the Apocalypse, Polycarp could not bring himself to open the seal. Perhaps he knew what it would bring. Instead, he hid the letter."

She knew it.

In Antioch.

Durov was hunting for an original letter of the biblical book of the Apocalypse.

She shook her head.

How did people still believe this stuff?

It was madness.

"When I was in the US," Jennings continued, his voice now fading in and out, "my wife died. I was born again, you see. Only then did everything make sense. I met my brothers in Jesus – like-minded people. My life developed purpose, and I understood the time was drawing near. And it is. We have friends everywhere, from the White House to the Middle East. So when the rockets are launched on Damascus, the prophecy will be fulfilled."

Ava was not sure she had heard right. "What rockets?"

Jennings continued, oblivious, the blood now staining his trousers and the chair, his voice growing slower and fainter. "After such an act of aggression, Damascus will retaliate against Tel Aviv." His breathing had become ragged, and his voice was now more of a whisper.

Ava stepped closer to listen.

"With so many casualties, Israel will feel compelled to respond mercilessly. The Arab world will not stand by and watch. There will be riots in their streets. The atmosphere is already febrile, and will become more so when evidence emerges that Israel most likely sank the Saudi oil tanker. The US will come to the aid of Israel. The groundwork has been carefully laid. The Americans are incensed by all the attacks on them – even the website of the White House. They are poised to take the war to the jihadis. There will be strong public support. At the same time, Russia is at breaking point with Israel. The Kremlin will be pushed over the edge, and will side with the Arabs. It will be regional chaos in a matter of hours, and that is when we will open the seventh seal."

This was insanity.

"When?" Ava bent down to hear him. "When will this happen?"

Jennings coughed, a weak rattling wheeze, and let go of the blood-sodden cushion to reveal that his whole front was sopping with blood.

Ava picked up another cushion, her sleeve still pulled over her hand, and placed it over the ragged stab wound, pressing hard. "Which rockets?" she persisted.

Jennings looked up at her, his eyes struggling to focus. "He's not perfect. But he will be."

She frowned.

What?

"Which rockets?" she repeated. "What do you mean, 'he's not perfect'?"

Jennings's hands dropped to his sides as his body went limp.

"You need to tell me." Ava bent low to his face. "Which rockets?"

His mouth began to bubble with saliva, but no sound came out.

She put her ear to his mouth.

He was breathing, but only barely.

She checked her watch. It had been eight minutes since she entered the house. The ambulance would be here soon. And the Police after that.

She needed to get out of there, or she would be dragged into hours of questioning. And right now, her priority was to find out which missiles were to be fired, when, and how to stop them. If she was questioned by the Police, it would take days to confirm her story, especially as she could not contact MI13. With Swinton gone, who would believe any of what she said?

Jennings was staring into the middle distance, his breathing inaudible.

She carefully wiped down the gun and placed it beside Jennings, then slipped out into the hallway.

There was nothing she could do for him. The ambulance would do their best, but he had lost a critical amount of blood.

There was going to be all hell to pay when the Police arrived. Jennings was a senior public figure, and she assumed Swinton would show up on some system somewhere.

She let herself out of the front door, and left it open a fraction for the emergency services.

As she closed the gate behind her and stepped onto the pavement, the rear window of a large black limousine in front of Swinton's house slid down.

"Dr Curzon." It was a man's voice. "Won't you get in?"

--- ◆ ---

CHAPTER 53

National Defence Control Centre
Frunze Naberezhnaya
Moscow
Russian Federation

TWO MILES SOUTH-WEST of Red Square, on the left bank of the River Muskva, the National Defence Control Centre gleamed under the security lights.

Aside from the military staff who worked inside the heavily fortified ultra-modern building, few people had ever been behind its doors.

Only recently, images of the interior of the vast three-decker main situation room had been beamed all over the world for the first time. Media-friendly broadcasts had showcased the serried ranks of analysts on the ground floor, and the banks of political and military command-ers in the dress circle, all gazing intently at the megaplex cinema-style wrap-around screens dominating the situation room. But the rest of the military nerve centre was shrouded in secrecy.

In an ops room several floors below ground level, deep in a part of the building belonging to the GRU, a committee of four men and a woman sat around a board room table. In front of each of them, in a plain brown folder, was a photograph of the strike coordinates document recovered from Donetsk, along with a report from the city's GRU chief.

It did not make for comfortable reading.

The report confirmed that the strike coordinates document was a genuine Russian Air Force target list that had been filed with a Mossad crest and a sixteen-digit number in Hebrew. The circumstances surrounding its discovery had been investigated, and everything pointed to Mossad having passed the target list to one of the moderate groups fighting the Syrian regime – exactly the groups who were being targeted by the airstrikes detailed in the list.

The star phone in front of the burly man at the head of the table rang. He punched the answer button, and the line was diverted to the speakers set into the room's acoustically shielded walls.

Nearly two thousand miles away, in the south of France, Oleg Durov's secure telephone connection went live.

"*Gospodin* Durov," the chairman began, his voice picked up by the microphone embedded into the table in front of him. "We are grateful for your contribution to the deliberations of the committee."

"I have been made aware of the Donetsk documentation," Durov began. "And I have information on who is behind it."

"You have our attention." The chairman leaned his bulk back in the chair, tilting it backwards.

"The responsible party is a senior military figure," Durov continued. "One who has developed close links with the Israelis – cemented during our President's visit to Israel in 2014 to unveil the statue to the Red Army forces who defeated Hitler."

"Are you able to share the name with us?" The chairman sounded less than pleased.

"I am", Durov replied. "General Gennady Zhurikov."

The chairman leaned forward in his chair, and towards the microphone. "That's a very serious accusation."

"His men carried out the attack on the Saudi tanker that was damaged on leaving Ras Tanura three days ago," Durov continued. "His actions were strictly contrary to Russia's interests, which are not to openly antagonize the Saudis outside the battlefields of Syria. I need not remind you that damaging Saudi's economic petrochemical interests remains a key priority of Israel."

There was silence in the room.

"You won't get anything from General Zhurikov," Durov continued. "He's been doing this for too long. But you might want to ask his men about it. They will confirm that they were there."

"We will investigate this matter," the chairman confirmed. "And what about the Donetsk papers?" He tapped the folder in front of him with a large finger.

"Photographs have been passed to me of General Zhurikov meeting with a known Mossad officer," Durov affirmed.

It had been so easy to arrange.

The world of Russian intelligence was worse than cats in a sack. The GRU, the FSB, the SVR – all with overlapping interests and heated rivalries. All had separate networks. And all virulently distrusted each other.

Durov had brought in Yegor, his loyal ex-FSB follower, who had instructed an FSB man to contact a known Mossad officer in Moscow and pass him Zhurikov's description and daily routine. It had not taken long for the surveillance team to get the necessary photos. When interrogated, Zhurikov would say that the man was a stranger who had approached him. But by then, no one was going to believe him.

However, the evidence that would seal his fate was the copy of the exact same Russian Air Force coordinates strike list that the GRU would find in Zhurikov's house when they searched it.

He was so Old School he did not even have surveillance cameras on his property.

The chairman scowled. "Very well, we will take the appropriate action."

Durov smiled to himself as he hung up.

That's the last anyone would hear of the general.

CHAPTER 54

Belsize Park
London
England
The United Kingdom

ON HER GUARD, Ava peered through the limousine's open rear window.

It was dark inside the car, but she started as she made out the hooded eyes, full lips, and heavy jaw of the occupant in the back seat.

What on earth was he doing here?

"People don't just waltz in and out of my palace without me making further enquiries."

The man indicated for her to join him.

Ava was not in the habit of getting into strangers' cars at night – even if the occupant was a Prince of the Church and Grand Master of the Sovereign Military Order of Malta.

She was thinking fast, trying to work out why he was outside Swinton's house.

Was he linked to Swinton?

Or to Jennings, and his mad apocalyptic movement?

Or had he been following her?

His face was impassive, revealing nothing.

She glanced swiftly up and down the street.

Was this a trap?

She could see nothing out of the ordinary – just empty parked cars on either side of the road.

"I want to talk to you about Oleg Durov," he continued.

Her mind flashed back to the entrance hall of Torquemada's palace, with its displays of weapons and flags celebrating the Order's thousand years of survival in an ever-changing world.

Her instincts were not to get entangled with Torquemada.

Last time she had seen him, he was hosting Durov in his palace.

"You might be interested in what I've found out," he added, leaning across and opening the passenger door.

She peered into the car.

What was his involvement in all this?

Jennings said that he had friends everywhere.

Did that include the Order of Malta?

She could not be sure, but she doubted it.

If Torquemada and Durov were working together, then why would Durov have called off his bodyguard in the chapel at the Palazzo Malta? And why would Torquemada have allowed her to leave?

In the distance, she heard the wail of sirens.

She had no intention of hanging around. All she needed to do was walk quickly up to the next junction and collect her bike.

She glanced back at Torquemada.

Things were complicated enough already.

Even if Torquemada was not linked to Durov or Jennings, she still had no desire to get mixed up with the Order of Malta.

On the other hand, she had no further leads. With Swinton and Jennings dead, the trail was cold. Durov had the fragment of vellum from Jerusalem. And she had nothing to go on except an icy dread at what Durov might be up to.

If Torquemada genuinely had new information, it might open up a new way to get to Durov. And at the moment, that was her number one priority.

Breathing out deeply, she climbed into the car, and closed the door behind her.

She needed to know what Torquemada knew.

And now she owed it to Swinton, too.

The limousine pulled away smoothly into the road, and Torquemada turned to her.

"I received Mr Durov yesterday at my palace as a courtesy to his government," he began. "I also confess to a certain amount of self-interest. My Order has houses in Moscow and Saint Petersburg, and I have no intention of being the Grand Master who loses them."

He pursed his lips. "But Mr Durov is a complex man, and I confess that his real motivation in visiting my residence is still unclear to me." He paused. "As is yours. So maybe we can start there?"

Ava had no desire to open up to Torquemada without knowing what he really wanted. But she also knew that the meeting was going to go nowhere unless she gave him something.

"He's interested in your icon," she answered. It was a safe bet. Torquemada had no doubt worked it out for himself already. "Our Lady of Philermos."

"Which you also asked about." He looked out at the darkened houses sweeping by. "So you'll forgive me if that leaves me equally distrustful of you both."

"What did you want to tell me?" Ava had no appetite for games. If Torquemada just wanted to spar with her, she had better things to do with her time.

"I'm aware you were badly treated in my palace by Durov's men," he answered sombrely. "But the appearance of things can be deceptive. If I'm to help you, I need your assurance that you're not connected with him, and that you mean my Order no harm. You may choose, of course, to mislead me. But I will eventually find out. And there will be consequences."

Ava did not appreciate the threat.

"Two men are dead in that house because of Durov," she pointed angrily back down the street, "And he's been trying to kill me ever since I met him. I entered your palace because I was following him. You can draw your own conclusions."

Torquemada gave a shallow nod. "Very well," he answered. "Then we have an understanding."

He settled himself more comfortably in his seat. "You may or may not know that my Order is a very large organization, spread across the world. Our medieval forebears were celibate knight-monks and nuns, living a religious life in our commanderies and nunneries. Some of us still live this way. We are an unbroken link to the past. In addition, the Order also numbers knights and dames who live ordinary lives – an arrangement that is perhaps more adapted to the modern world. Beyond these loyal men and women, we are further strengthened by a vast network of associates and helpers. All together, these faithful servants are our eyes and ears – the spreading leaves of a tree that nourish the trunk. As you can imagine, there is not much we do not know about once we make it our business to find out."

He paused. "And so we have come to learn that Durov leads a religious group, known as … "

"The Skoptsy," Ava completed his sentence.

"You know what they believe, and what they do to themselves?"

Ava nodded.

"What happens in the steppes of Russia is beyond our influence. But if these monstrous beliefs start to spread west from Orthodox lands, then they become all of our problem."

Ava was listening intently.

"We are informed that Durov is coordinating the arrival of a large number of his Skoptsy followers at a small private airfield in south-west France. They are arriving from Russia and elsewhere."

He turned to Ava again. "That is what I had to tell you. And I'm hoping you may be able to explain to me why this might be happening."

"I'm afraid not." She shook her head.

There had been nothing on the vellum fragment to point to France.

And Jennings had not mentioned France, either.

It was all news to her.

"What do you and Durov want with the icon of Our Lady?" he asked, changing the subject.

Ava was still not sure what Torquemada wanted, and there was no way she was going to tell him about Rasputin's notebooks.

"I found the original," she answered. "The real one."

He nodded. "In Cetinje, at the National Museum of Montenegro. That's not a secret."

She shook her head. "In Jerusalem," she corrected him. "In the Church of the Holy Sepulchre."

"You're mistaken." He smiled apologetically. "The icon's history is well known."

"Up to a point," Ava agreed. "The Romanovs looked after it until the dowager empress smuggled it out of Russia at the Revolution. But the rest of the traditional story is wrong. The icon didn't go from Belgrade to Berlin, Dedinje, Ostrog, and Cetinje. It was taken to Jerusalem. I've seen it."

Torquemada shook his head. "You're not the first to hunt for our relics. There are dozens of copies – old and new. Not even experts can tell some of them apart."

"Well, I'm not an expert." Ava shrugged. "But the original is in Jerusalem. I'll guarantee it."

"Certainties unnerve me," he smiled. "I prefer leaving them to men like Durov." He looked out of the window and then back to Ava. "What makes you so sure?"

"Because," she answered confidently, "one of your medieval knights left a message inside it – which I found."

Torquemada's eyes widened.

"Although, Durov took it," she added quietly.

His breathing grew noticeably faster. "And was there any mention of," he paused, his tone dropping, "the Apocalypse… of Saint John?"

Ava nodded.

"Then it's true," he whispered, his eyes now shining.

He leant towards her, barely able to contain his excitement. "In the dark days after the crusades, the Order's greatest relics were the icon of Our Lady and the arm of Saint John the Baptist. Our brothers and sisters took great comfort from them. But there has always been a persistent rumour down the ages that we once possessed something else of great significance." His voice dropped lower. "One of Saint John's original letters of the Apocalypse." He stared at Ava expectantly. "And it is rumoured that the icon of Our Lady holds the clue to it."

Ava pushed the button to wind the window down an inch.

So it was not all in her imagination.

It really did look as if the piece of vellum had been written by a medieval Knight of Saint John.

She took a gulp of the night air, trying to understand what it all meant.

Why had a medieval knight left the message?

And why was Durov assembling the Skoptsy in the south of France?

"The rumours of the hidden Apocalypse letter originated in Toulouse, during the crusades," Torquemada continued. "Back then, long before our Order moved to Rhodes and Malta, our European headquarters was in the south of France – at our commandery in Saint-Gilles."

Now it was Ava's turn to be surprised.

That was the territory of the crusader warlord, Raymond of Saint-Gilles, who played such a crucial role in the drama at Antioch with Peter Bartholomew.

"The counts of Saint-Gilles were also the counts of Toulouse. And we had a very important commandery there, too. In those days the Languedoc was a separate country from France, and the counts of Toulouse who ran it were immensely powerful. But it was a turbulent time. From the early 1100s, vast swathes of the Languedoc abandoned the Catholic faith and embraced a virulent heresy."

"The Cathars." Ava nodded.

"Relations between the counts and the Church became fraught. When the pope's special envoy was assassinated by one of the count's men, Rome unleashed a dreadful crusade against the heretics. A massive army from northern France marched south, keen on spoils and plunder. The inhabitants of the Languedoc were massacred in their thousands. You must know the apocryphal story of the papal legate accompanying the crusaders, who told his forces ranged against Béziers not to bother enquiring which of the locals were Catholics and which were Cathars. 'Kill them all,' he is alleged to have said, 'God will know his own'."

Ava nodded. The story rang a bell.

"An apocryphal anecdote. But it shows how strongly people felt about the crusade. Terrible things happened – like at Montségur, where the Cathars preferred to commit mass suicide rather than renounce their beliefs. Anyway, the Languedoc was savagely conquered, and eventually annexed to the kingdom of France."

"You said the rumours of the Apocalypse letter came from Toulouse." Ava was intrigued.

Torquemada nodded. "There have always been legends that the Cathars possessed a treasure or secret knowledge. Many people say they were in league with the Templars." He shot Ava a meaningful glance. "But I think you'll find they had nothing very much to do with the Templars. The Cathars' real connection was to us, the Knights of Saint John."

Ava raised an eyebrow.

It was a pretty big claim.

"Many of the local nobility – including the counts of Toulouse – supported the Cathars. The count who ordered the assassination of the papal legate was excommunicated several times for his Cathar sympathies." Torquemada's tone became more confidential. "But what has been overlooked is that he was a very close friend of our Order. In fact, he was a member. He joined first as an affiliate-knight, then finally, on his deathbed, as a full knight-monk. He was duly buried according to ancient custom, wearing our Order's habit, in our commandery at Toulouse."

Ava frowned. "How did a Catholic order of crusader-monks allow an excommunicate heretic who had murdered the pope's legate to join? How was that possible?"

Torquemada shrugged apologetically. "They were strange times, and the whole affair remains something of a mystery. But you have to remember that we look back and see Catholics and Cathars fighting in the Languedoc. In reality, they were brothers and sisters, mothers and sons. You can never underestimate ties of blood and kinship. Anyway, there's no doubt the count of Toulouse was a heretic. He was infamous as one of the *faidit* lords."

Ava felt the word as if it hit her physically. "What did you just say?" She was staring at him, incredulous.

Torquemada seemed taken aback by the force of her reaction. "His lands were confiscated because of his heretical sympathies."

"You said *faidit*." Her heart was beating faster now. "What does it mean?"

"The *faidit* lords were the ones who lost their property and titles as punishment for their heresies," he answered. "They were notorious – especially the count of Toulouse, who some said brought the shattering crusade upon his people. The history books call him Count Raymond VI of Toulouse, but at the time he was widely known as Raymond the *faidit*."

Ava's breath caught in her throat.

Raimundus Faiditus – Raymond the faidit.

"It's a Catalan word," Torquemada continued. "It means exiled. That's not a perfect translation. But it's close enough."

As he said the word 'perfect', something in the depths of Ava's mind sparked, forming a connection.

"That's the same word Jennings used," she whispered, as the full implications dawned on her. "He said that Durov was not perfect, but he will be." She could feel the blood draining from her face. "That was the main Cathar rite, wasn't it? The ritual of perfection?"

She was sure she was right.

Because there was something else, too.

She had not appreciated it before, but suddenly it made sense.

On the vellum, the four groups of three small circles inside the seven-pointed star were not random.

They just needed to be connected in the right way.

And when they were, they formed a familiar shape.

The Cathar cross.

The Grand Master nodded. "Ordinary Cathars were *Credentes,* or Believers. But once they had been through the ritual of Consolation, they became *Perfecti,* or Perfects. From that moment, they lived in simple poverty, avoiding meat, alcohol, and sex. It was a kind of living death that — "

"Oh my God," Ava cut him off, turning pale as she suddenly realized with horror what Durov was planning. "Which airport are Durov's followers arriving at?"

"Saint-Gaudens – it's a small airfield about fifty miles south-west of Toulouse."

"Can you get us to Toulouse?"

Torquemada nodded. He leant forward and tapped the driver on the shoulder. "Biggin Hill. Prepare the plane."

Ava pulled out her phone and dialled Ferguson's number.

From the ringing tone, she could tell he was back in the UK.

He picked up almost immediately.

"Look, Ava, I just wanted to — " he began.

"It's fine," she cut in.

"I just don't want — " he continued.

"There's no time for that now," she interrupted again. "Can you be at Biggin Hill airport in two hours?"

"Sure. What's going on?" He sounded concerned.

"Do you know what tomorrow is?"

"The twenty-fourth of June," he answered. "So what?"

"It's Saint John's day, traditionally the Summer Solstice." She fought to keep back her rising sense of dread. "If I'm right, that's when Durov is planning to stage his own apocalypse."

--- ◆ ---

CHAPTER 55

Prat dels Cremats
Languedoc-Roussillon-Midi-Pyrénées
The Republic of France

DUROV WAS FILLED with a sense of serenity.

He knew it was here.

Waiting for him.

All the clues pointed to this place.

The Skoptsy he had personally selected were gathered around – exactly one hundred and forty-four souls, representing the one hundred and forty-four thousand to be sealed and saved in the Apocalypse. They were drawn from his whole network – from Russia, Europe, the United States, and beyond.

All were zealous in the faith.

They understood what needed to happen.

It was dark in the field, and the only illumination came from the moonlight and two dozen flaming torches planted in a precise circle around them.

Durov gazed up at the large rocky mountain – a *pog*, he had heard the locals call it. His eyes travelled up the vast outcrop, to the point where the peak was lost in the night sky.

He would have to wait until tomorrow to see the castle.

With his excitement building, he turned back to what needed to be done.

Tonight, he was going to come face to face with history.

And with his destiny.

This was all meant to be.

There was a reason why the Holy Mother had chosen him for this task. Thanks to her intervention, he had learned everything about Rasputin's obsession with the Apocalypse, and the message the mystic monk had left for posterity.

Rasputin had been fascinated that John's eschatological vision was never read in Orthodox churches. He had studied it, becoming ever more intrigued by its arcane symbols. His curiosity had led to an obsession, until one day he came across the piece of vellum in the tsar's icon of Our Lady of Philermos. He had not understood it fully, but appreciated that it was of immense Apocalyptic significance. When the Revolution upended the royal family's traditional way of life, he had been privy to the sacred icon being spirited out of Russia, and had carefully recorded for posterity where it had been taken.

Durov inhaled deeply, savouring the still evening air.

Stepping forward, he moved into the centre of the expectant group, and approached the weather-beaten stone monument they were gathered round.

At its base was a plinth under a carved structure shaped liked a sarcophagus. A gravestone rose from it, up to the height of a man. The whole monument was capped by a circular headpiece bearing a five-pointed star surmounting three crosses, the middle one incised deeper and wider than the other two.

In the flickering torchlight, Durov read the simple words incised into the memorial:

ALS CATARS
ALS MARTIRS
DEL PUR AMOR CRESTIAN
16 DE MARÇ 1244

He was not skilled in Mediterranean languages, but it was not difficult to translate the Provençal:

TO THE CATHARS
TO THE MARTYRS
OF PURE CHRISTIAN LOVE
16 MARCH 1244

He watched as five of the Skoptsy stepped forward with spades and trowels, and began to dig out the earth in front of the monument.

He was not worried about interference from locals.

For the next twenty-four hours, the Skoptsy had the area completely to themselves.

Durov had explained to the mayor of the commune that he and his friends were from an astronomical society keen to conduct certain solstice experiments in the castle. He knew that the craggy ruins regularly attracted innumerable solar cranks bent on investigating how the castle's architecture aligned with the sun's rays on the solstices.

He had stressed to the mayor that they needed absolute privacy for their work, and was reassured by the official's practised smile and nod of understanding that all would be well. Durov sealed the bargain with a handsome payment to the local archaeological trust, and an equally gratifying thank you to the mayor for his generous understanding.

As the sound of digging continued, and the hole in front of the monument deepened, Durov was calm.

Fifteen minutes passed, and the men opening up the wide trench were sweating freely.

Durov used the time to prepare himself mentally for what was to come, allowing his mind to savour the words he knew so well:

I was in the Spirit on the Lord's day, and heard behind me a great voice, as of a trumpet, Saying, I am Alpha and Omega, the first and the last: and, what thou seest, write in a book, and send it unto the seven churches which are in Asia.

He felt himself floating in the holy words, until he was brought back to the present by the dull sound of a shovel striking something metallic.

It was the moment he had been waiting for.

He braced himself.

The prize had been deep in the earth for centuries.

Waiting.

The large stone funeral monument was not ancient, but the site of the Cathars' martyrdom had been marked down the ages. The Cathar cross on the vellum fragment was the key, showing the roll would be where they had perished – where their noble souls guarded the scripture for the righteous.

The men began digging around the object they had struck, and soon exposed a metal chest.

His heart now hammering, Durov knelt down and used his fingers to scrape the last of the soil from around its edges.

He summoned one of the men to bring a torch.

When the man returned and held the flames directly over the hole, Durov could see that the container was iron, around a yard long, and bound with a number of irregular horizontal and vertical reinforcing bands. It was blackened with age, heavily rusted in places, but still visibly intact.

His eyes lingered lovingly on the heraldic shapes embossed on the sides of the chest. They were plain equilateral Latin crosses – the unmistakeable symbol of the medieval Knights of Saint John.

Brushing aside a clod of earth, he carefully examined the medieval barrel padlock hanging from the chest's front, then stood and beckoned for the nearest man to pass his spade.

Placing the tool's point against the box's rusty hasp, Durov stamped down hard on the upper edge of the spade. With a dull scraping sound, the aged hasp and plate sheared cleanly off the chest, snapping the corroded weld, taking the padlock with them.

Durov knelt down again, and allowed the smell of freshly turned earth to fill his nostrils.

Steadying his hands, he reached in and raised the box's lid.

It lifted easily, revealing a single object inside.

It was a smaller container, lighter in colour.

He offered a silent prayer as he took hold of the box and lifted it out, feeling the weight of the mission with which the Holy Mother had charged him.

By the light of the torch flame, he could see the container was made of solid lead, sealed tight with a thick band of tar covering the join where the lid met the body.

"*Raduysya, Blagodatnaya!*" he prayed quietly, "*Gospod' s Toboyu.*"[3]

---

3 "Hail, though that art highly favoured, the Lord is with thee."

The words filled him with power as his eyes settled on the emblem stamped into the lid. It was the Cathar cross – the cross of Toulouse – just as the vellum fragment had described.

There could be no mistake.

This was the box Count Raymond VI had instructed the Knights of Saint John to bury here for safekeeping, on the site of the Cathars' martyrdom.

It was the Cathars' treasure.

One of the men handed him a trowel. He knocked the earth off it, then gently forced its point into the tar, carefully working it around the length of the strip, cracking open the ancient sealant.

His heart was pumping hard as the lid came away.

He closed his eyes.

"Blagoslovenna Ty mezhdu zhonami, i blagosloven plod chreva Tvoego." [4]

When he opened his eyes again, he saw, nestling in the cold lead case, a thick roll of light-tan-coloured parchment. It was around fourteen inches high, and six inches wide.

His nostrils flared in triumph.

The Holy Mother had not deceived him.

As he gazed at the roll in rapture, his eyes were drawn to the spot where its outer flap was fixed down, holding the manuscript firmly closed. They settled on the large irregular plain black seal.

It was unbroken.

---

4 "Blessed art thou among women, and blessed is the fruit of thy womb."

---◆---

CHAPTER 56

Toulouse
Languedoc-Roussillon-Midi-Pyrénées
The Republic of France

TORQUEMADA HAD BEEN as good as his word. An Order of Malta liveried plane had been fuelled and readied at Biggin Hill, and the pilot had taken Ava, Ferguson, and Mary to Toulouse.

On the flight, Ava had told them all about the vellum fragment she had found in Jerusalem, and how the clues referred to Saint Polycarp hiding his original copy of the Apocalypse in Antioch. She had also told them about Swinton's murder, Jennings's confession, and her conversation with Torquemada.

On landing, a car had been waiting, and it had driven them to the centre of Toulouse, to a large residence that Torquemada had arranged for them. A housekeeper had been waiting, and now they were sitting in the garden, in the warm and fragranced night air, under the ancient gnarled trees, enjoying a homemade spread of local food.

"How does Polycarp hiding the letter in Antioch lead to Toulouse?" Mary asked. "I don't see the link."

"The key is Peter Bartholomew," Ava explained, taking a fresh fig. "I looked him up. It's an amazing story from the crusades."

"Go on." Ferguson nodded. "I could use a good war story."

"It's more of a mystery, really," Ava continued. "During the First Crusade, the pilgrim armies marched on foot through eastern Europe, across modern-day Turkey, down into the Lebanon, and finally into Israel. It was gruelling. Along with the frequent battles, there was constant illness and starvation.

"When they arrived at Antioch, they found a city with a massive wall and four hundred towers. They immediately realized that they had to capture and control it in order to protect their rear and their supply lines.

"After eight months of siege, they'd made little progress, but had stripped the surrounding land of all food. So they rapidly began to starve. Eventually, they managed to bribe a local captain called Firouz to let a small group of crusaders into the Tower of the Two Sisters. Once inside, the raiding party immediately crept down and opened the city's main gates for the whole Christian army to pour in. But, no sooner had the crusaders overwhelmed the city than a vast Muslim relief army arrived, and promptly started besieging them.

"The crusaders soon began to starve again. Morale plummeted to an all-time low. But, miraculously, at this crisis point, a simple pilgrim from Provençe had a wondrous vision. Saint Andrew appeared to him in a dream, and told him that the Holy Lance of Longinus was buried in the Cathedral of Saint Peter – Antioch's ancient rock-cut church – where both Saint Peter and Saint Paul had been bishops before moving to Rome."

Ava paused to top up her wine glass with chilled local rosé. "This divinely inspired pilgrim was called Peter Bartholomew. Guided by his visions, he led a party to dig up the floor of the ancient cathedral. After they had been at work for a while, he suddenly jumped down into the trench and triumphantly put his hands on a piece of iron protruding from the earth. The crusaders were convinced it was a sign of God's favour, and rode out joyfully to attack the Muslim army, which they smashed.

"Peter Bartholomew's discovery of the Holy Lance went down in history as a miracle – certainly one of the most important events on the road to Jerusalem. He was not so lucky, unfortunately. Some of the crusaders began a whispering campaign against him and his continuing visions, so he volunteered to undergo a biblical Trial by Fire to prove his truthfulness. On the appointed day, he walked between two walls of flame, convinced God would spare him. But he was so dreadfully burned that he died within days.

"Now," Ava continued, "here's where it gets interesting. The chronicles say that Peter Bartholomew gave the lance to the one-eyed Count Raymond of Saint-Gilles and Toulouse. He was the leader of the Provençal army, and the richest and most battle-hardened of all the crusaders, having spent much of his life fighting the Reconquest in Spain. He was so powerful that when the crusaders finally conquered Jerusalem, they nominated him as their first choice to be king of Jerusalem – but he turned it down."

"So Peter Bartholomew gave the Holy Lance to Count Raymond." Mary frowned. "But what's the connection with Polycarp?"

Ava leant forward in her chair. "I wonder if, while digging in the cathedral in Antioch, Peter Bartholomew discovered something more than the Holy Lance."

"The Apocalypse roll," Ferguson said, "hidden by Polycarp centuries earlier."

"And you think Peter Bartholomew gave the roll to Count Raymond along with the lance?" Mary asked.

"It makes sense of the other clues," Ava continued. "If Count Raymond of Saint-Gilles sent the Apocalypse roll back home, to Toulouse, it would have passed down from father to son, until it was finally entrusted to his great-great grandson, Count Raymond the *faidit*."

"So that's the Toulouse connection." Ferguson leant back in his chair. "Makes sense."

"Only part of it." Ava smiled. "There's more."

She had finished eating, and stood up to leave. "If I'm right, tomorrow's going to be a big day."

DAY SEVEN

———— • ◆ • ————

CHAPTER 47

Ariège
Languedoc-Roussillon-Midi-Pyrénées
The Republic of France

THEY SET OUT early, heading south towards Spain.

For the first half hour, the countryside was flat as they followed the *Autoroute des Deux Mers*, before turning off onto the *Ariégeoise*, where the landscape soon started to roll.

By the time they were approaching the ancient cathedral city of Pamiers, the foothills of the Pyrenees were clearly visible, heralding the start of the rugged mountain range that cut Spain off from France.

"What's so important about the Apocalypse anyway?" Ferguson asked, turning to Ava and Mary. "Why does this all matter so much to Durov? I found a Bible on the bookshelves in my room last night, and read it." He pulled a face. "What on earth's it all about? The whole thing's totally psychedelic. When — "

"It's prophetic," Mary cut in. "A vision. About the End Times."

Ferguson took the small Bible out of his pocket. "It's certainly dream-like. Look."

He opened it at the Apocalypse, and began flicking through as he spoke. "It starts by saying that John heard the voice of a man who was wearing a long robe with a golden sash around his chest. His hair was white as snow. His eyes blazed like fire. His feet were like bronze glowing in a furnace. His voice sounded like rushing waters. He was holding seven stars. A sharp two-edged sword was coming from his mouth. And his face shone like the sun." He looked up. "That's not the usual sort of thing you get in the Bible. It's more like that Beatles film, *Yellow Submarine*."

"You're not the first person to find it trippy." Ava smiled.

"And it goes on like that for twenty-two Chapters," Ferguson continued. "Seven angels with seven seals. Seven trumpets. Seven bowls. Seven plagues. Beasts with many heads, crowns, and horns. Angels rolling up the heavens like a scroll. A woman on a scarlet horse holding a cup of her adultery – whatever that is. It's like the Twelve Days of Christmas on acid."

"True," Mary agreed. "But there's a basic story running through it."

Ferguson closed the book. "I got that. If you leave aside all the scrolls and seals and trumpets, you get a hundred and forty-four thousand people being marked with a seal in order to be saved. There's an almighty battle between God and the Devil, after which the Devil is cast into the pit for a thousand years. Meanwhile, the people with the seals reign with Jesus. Then the Devil is freed, and there's another almighty battle, after which the Devil is defeated and thrown into a lake of sulphur for all time. God then judges everyone. The good people go to heaven. The bad people are thrown into the lake of sulphur. Is that about right?"

Mary nodded. "Although, as you can imagine, everyone has a different view on what it all means. Many people muddle it all up by throwing in other Bible books, like Thessalonians, which says that a load of people rise up into the air and are saved in what they call the Rapture. That said, no one is really clear when it all happens, or how it's linked to the time of the Tribulation or the Last Judgement. And no one agrees on how the Rapture and the Tribulation fit into the thousand years. Or even if the thousand years is literal or symbolic. Almost every Church has a different view."

"A holy mess." Ferguson shook his head.

"Saint John's Gospel and the Apocalypse have always been seen as a bit different to the rest of the Bible," Ava added. "They have a mystical Gnostic feel to them. Some early churchmen refused to read John because the heretics loved it so much. There was even a widespread belief that the Apocalypse wasn't written by John, but by a Gnostic heresiarch called Cerinthus. The Cathars – who were part Gnostic – relied entirely on John's Gospel, and rejected the rest of the Bible."

As the hills started to turn into small mountains, the landscape became greener, more forested, and wilder. The road dropped down to two narrow lanes, and started to wind along the contours of the ancient hills of the Pays d'Olmes.

After driving a while in silence, each of them lost in thought, they rounded a bend, and the view was unexpectedly dominated by a striking sugarloaf mountain about a mile and a half ahead. It rose high above everything, dominating the skyline.

Clearly visible at its dizzying peak was the shell of a medieval castle.

"What's that?" Ferguson asked, awe-struck.

"That," Ava replied slowly, "is Montségur. *Mons Securus* in Latin. Safe Hill."

She slowed the car so they could all look at it. "And I'm pretty sure that's where Durov is – at the location of the last stand of the Cathars."

---————— • ◆ • —————---

CHAPTER 58

Château de Montségur
Languedoc-Roussillon-Midi-Pyrénées
The Republic of France

THE MOUNTAIN LOOMED in front of them as the road snaked to the right, hugging its base.

Ahead, the tarmac widened, and there were spaces on either side of the road for several dozen cars to park.

Slowing, Ava spotted tourist information panels about the site, and the start of a footpath leading up the side of the mountain to the castle at the top.

But she could also see that the start of the path had been roped off, and three bulky men were guarding the access. It was not possible to tell if they were armed, but there was no doubt they had been chosen for their muscle.

"Don't stare," Ava ordered, and carried on driving, slowly increasing her speed.

As they left the parking area, the road narrowed, and Ava drove on through the village of Montségur, before rounding the mountain and heading north, up its east side.

Out of the windows, they could see the mountain's sheer cliff face rising up to the top of the crest. "That was how the crusaders took the castle in the end," Ava said, straining to look up at the dizzying rock face.

"Up that?" Mary sounded incredulous. "But it's vertical."

Ava nodded. "The Cathars hadn't even put a guard on this side as they thought it was unclimbable. But the crusaders brought Basque mercenaries, who knew exactly how to get up it. In the dark."

Mary's jaw dropped.

"Anyway," Ava turned the car around. 'Let's ditch the car back in the village. We're going to have to approach on foot."

CHAPTER 59

West Syrian Desert
The Syrian Arab Republic

THE MLRS MOBILE missile platform had been resprayed a dirty sand colour, and all Israeli markings had been removed. The tech team had ripped out all tracking and control devices, and it was now an independent weapons unit – unaffiliated, and off the grid.

The mid-morning heat was already baking the west Syrian desert when the lethal vehicle moved off purposefully across the sands, its silhouette shimmering in the heat haze.

Inside the forward personnel cabin, the two men knew exactly what they had to do.

Although they had trained on nothing remotely similar in the Ground Forces of the Russian Federation, the system had turned out to be child's play to operate.

It was, after all, designed for soldiers.

Once they were clear of their temporary base, the navigator punched in the destination coordinates, and the vehicle rumbled west, towards the Israeli border.

--- • ◆ • ---

Chapter 60

Château de Montségur
Languedoc-Roussillon-Midi-Pyrénées
The Republic of France

AVA HAD PARKED the car in the village, and they headed north on foot, keeping off the road, making for the base of the mountain.

They had avoided the official car park and three guards, and instead started climbing through the brush and scrub, scrambling higher until they were no longer visible to any of the occasional cars passing along the road below.

"We need to rejoin the path on the western slope," Ferguson announced, pointing left. "Even if we stay a few yards away from it, the climb is going to be easiest on that face."

They nodded and followed him, skirting west around the side of the mountain.

As she walked, Ava was left to her own thoughts, which turned to Ferguson and Mary.

Nothing had been said since they had all met up.

Ferguson had tried to raise the subject on the telephone beforehand, but Ava had cut him off. She had kept her resolve to just accept whatever was happening. All of them had to concentrate on what Durov was up to.

After about twenty minutes, Ferguson halted and dropped to the ground. Ava caught up with him and crouched down low beside him. Mary was immediately behind her.

"Down there," he whispered, pointing.

Ava looked where he was indicating, and made out the car park area they had driven through earlier.

The three men were still there. But now they seemed to be more active. One had binoculars, and was scouring the hillside. The other two seemed to be scanning the area around them.

"They're being cautious, aren't they?" Mary shielded her eyes from the sun as she looked down on the guards.

"Come on." Ferguson pointed to a line of trees a little above them. "There's cover up there. Then we can start climbing again."

They reached the area, and started ascending in earnest. The mountain was rocky in places, and the climb was increasingly slow and hard going.

They continued in silence, and as they neared the top, they passed a low wall with a group of five large round stones several yards in front of it.

"Cannon balls?" Ferguson asked, pointing at them.

Ava stopped to peer at the stones. Then she moved over to examine the remnants of the wall, and the heavy damage it had taken. "Well," she answered, grateful for the moment's break from the hard walking. "You won't see this very often. This looks like part of the original Cathar wall. And these stones are from a medieval siege engine – probably a trebuchet, judging by size. I'd guess they were fired at that wall, and haven't moved in over seven hundred years."

"You mean, they got a trebuchet halfway up this hill?" Mary looked incredulous.

Ava nodded. "Higher. The attacking crusaders got siege engines right to the top."

They set off again, and before long Ava could finally see snatches of the castle's long south-western wall appearing through the trees and shrubs ahead.

Drawing closer, the increasing gaps in the foliage revealed that the castle's wall was solid, with only one small entranceway placed about ten feet off the ground. To access it, a wooden staircase had been tacked to the outside wall.

"Smart." Ferguson peered at the dilapidated steps. "I suppose if they were ever under siege, they just retracted the stairs?"

Ava nodded. "Or burned them. It's a standard arrangement on castles where there's no opportunity for a moat and drawbridge."

When they had passed through the small village of Montségur earlier, Ava had seen numerous postcards bristling on display racks outside the few shops and café-bars. The pictures on them almost unanimously showed the current castle shell, as well as drawings and visual reconstructions of the earlier Cathar buildings.

It seemed the Cathars had topped the mountain with a *castrum*, or fortified medieval village. The settlement was perched on the very top of the mountain, and comprised dozens of houses jammed together, cheek by jowl, in a higgledy-piggledy cluster. Around them, three rings of defensive walls, a barbican, and several towers provided protection.

After the defeat of the Cathars, the village in the clouds had been knocked down, and the stones reused to build a royal castle on the site, whose ruins were the ones still dominating the mountaintop today.

It was a monster castle.

At its west was the great donjon – an ultra-fortified rectangular stone box, at least four storeys tall, with space for a wooden hoarding to be erected on top in time of attack. Its menace was enhanced by numerous arrow slits and only a few small windows.

Attached to the donjon was a large bailey in the form of a high-walled alley-like pentagonal courtyard running the length of the mountain's crest.

Ava was looking forward to getting a closer view.

As they approached the edge of the cover a few yards from the top of the mountain, Ferguson motioned for them to stop. "We need to stay out of sight and watch for a while," he advised. "Let's see who else is up here."

He went off for a few moments, then returned and led them to a small cluster of trees, where he indicated for everyone to sit down in the shade and make themselves comfortable.

The air was crisp, and there was almost no sound apart from the cicadas.

Ava was grateful for the chance to let her mind rove again over the conversation with Jennings.

"He's not perfect. But he will be."

"When the rockets are launched on Damascus, the prophecy will be fulfilled."
What exactly did it all mean?
Was there to be some kind of Cathar ceremony of perfection?
Around a quarter of an hour passed, then Ferguson motioned for absolute silence.

Ava listened carefully, and heard the sound of voices and footsteps coming up the path.

As the voices grew more distinct, she could make out the words more clearly.

They were speaking Russian.

The path was only twenty yards away and, within a few moments, four men emerged onto the rocky plateau, where Ava had a good view of them.

They were weather-beaten, and looked like they spent their lives outdoors.

Two of them were carrying a large steel flight case slung between them. It was sprayed in desert camouflage colours, and she could make out markings of the Israeli Defence Force. The top of the case was unlidded, revealing an all-weather computer console and other controls built around a small screen. Another of the men was holding a large military satellite radio with a long bendy aerial. The fourth was carrying what looked like an external battery pack.

Instead of climbing the wooden steps to the castle's main entrance, they turned left, and disappeared off around the corner of the building.

"That's serious hardware," Ferguson noted.

"What's the range of an MLRS's rockets?" Ava asked, with a mounting sense of dread.

"Depends what it's loaded with," Ferguson answered. "Can be seventy-five miles. Usually around forty-five."

Ava already had her bag open. "You mentioned it, at Ben Gurion." She looked up at Mary hastily. "You said there was a rumour the IDF had lost an MLRS launcher in the Golan Heights." She paused. "Now we know who's got it."

She found what she was looking for, and pulled it out.

It was the tablet she had received in the post from Uri.

She placed it on the ground in front of her and pushed the power button.

"The Israelis need to get people to the Golan right now," she explained hurriedly. "Someone has to find that MLRS before Durov hooks his controls up to it."

Once the tablet had booted up, she entered the same passwords as before, and opened Skype.

The icon for CALEB was still there. And the green dot beside it showed that Uri was currently online.

She tapped the Video Call icon, and was relieved to hear the intermittent ring tone indicating that it was patching her through to him.

After twenty seconds, it was still ringing.

She let it continue for a minute.

Nothing.

She checked the 4G mobile signal reception.

It was fine.

She hung up, and tried again.

It rang for another minute.

"Looks like he's not picking up." Ferguson glanced grimly at the tablet.

Ava's anger was rising. "He's there. I know he is."

She tapped the Video Call button again. The light was still green, with an ONLINE flag by his name.

The tone continued to ring out.

"He's not picking up," Mary concluded.

"Bloody hell!" Ava stabbed the red button to hang up.

It was unbelievable.

Uri had been nothing but a self-centred headache from the start. And now, when there was serious work to be done – not least defending his country – he was playing games with her.

She shut the tablet off angrily.

Or did he know exactly what was happening?

Was he doing more than protecting Durov?

Jennings had said he had friends in the Middle East.

Was Uri working with him?

"We need a Plan B," she announced. "And fast."

"Leave it to me." Mary pulled out her phone and started typing quickly. When she finished, there was a long pause, then her phone buzzed.

"Done." She looked up.

Ava stared at her, wide-eyed with incredulity. "Are you going to explain?"

"The Order of Malta," Mary answered. "We saw them at the airport in Israel, remember? They were on their way to replace the existing UN peacekeeping troops in the Golan." She smiled. "Where did you think I got the guns from?"

"But you said they were an independent Order." Ava challenged her. "You said you couldn't enter their palace."

"All true." Mary nodded. "Five-O-Four has no jurisdiction to enter the Order of Malta's sovereign territory. But ultimately the Knights have been loyal to the pope for a thousand years. They stand beside the Vatican when we need them."

Ava's mind flashed back to the giant painting of the battle of Lepanto on the staircase of the Palazzo Malta. On it, she had seen the galleys of the Papal States and the Knights of Saint John side by side. She had once heard that Lepanto was the largest naval battle the world had ever seen – the last of the great clashes of galleys – and it had definitely halted the westward spread of conquering Islam.

"We all belong to the same organization," Mary continued. "The armed wing of the Order of Malta is the pope's only remaining deployable armed force. And these days their services are becoming increasingly useful to the Church."

"What about the Swiss Guard?" Ferguson asked. "They're armed to the teeth, aren't they?"

"That's a whole different story." Mary shrugged. "You'd need Vatican security clearance for me to talk about that."

"And people don't believe in conspiracy theories … " Ferguson grinned.

They lapsed into silence. After five minutes Ava stood up. "I'm going to check out what's happening on the other side of the building. There's something going on, and we need to know what it is."

"I'm coming." Ferguson stood up beside her. "You stay on stag here," he instructed Mary. "Text if anyone else comes up the path."

The area just below the plateau was covered in rocks, unkempt tufty grass, bushes, and trees. There was no path, and in places it was steep, but it afforded the best cover for circling the building.

As they started to skirt the castle anticlockwise, the southern wall ended abruptly at a sharp corner. They turned it, then followed the next section north-east, until it turned again, this time into the long northern wall.

Until now, apart from the main south-western entrance, Ava had seen no other entry point into the castle – just high solid ashlar block walls. But about halfway along the north wall there was another entrance.

The earth on that side of the castle had been banked up so it could be accessed without steps, and Ava calculated that it was roughly opposite the main entrance in the south-western wall.

After listening carefully for five minutes to check no one was around, she left the cover of the scrub and approached the arched entranceway. Whatever door had once been there had gone centuries ago, and she could see directly through into the long narrow bailey.

The first thing she noted was that it was empty. The smaller buildings that it would once have sheltered were all gone.

It was still impressive, though. The walls were at least three feet thick, with rows of putlog holes running around at varying heights for scaffolding and hoardings in time of attack. She could not see much else, except a rocky floor and the far wall. There was no sign of anyone moving about in the building.

It was deserted.

Returning to the cover given by the shrubs a few feet below the plateau, they continued westwards, until they reached the area where the bailey met the donjon.

Pausing to listen, Ava could now hear the distinct sound of construction work – hammering, sawing, and voices speaking Russian.

It was coming from inside the donjon.

She motioned for Ferguson to follow, and set off again, more slowly and carefully this time, inching her way around the corner until they were now moving down the west wall of the donjon.

There were weathered wooden steps up into the keep, and around the area were scattered piles of timber planks, and other objects concealed by tarpaulins.

From inside the donjon there was the sound of continued construction, and Ava could hear the voices more clearly now. The conversations sounded muted and practical, with none of the banter or pop music she usually associated with building work.

The atmosphere was distinctly sombre.

"They must've brought this lot overnight," Ferguson indicated all the building materials. "Nasty job carrying it up here."

"Think of the people building the original castle." Ava pointed to the castle's massive stone blocks.

Drawing closer, she spotted a pile of canvas sacks stacked up against the exterior wall.

Checking no one was approaching, she broke cover again, and swiftly walked over to them, undoing the rope fastener at the top of the bag nearest to her.

She was not sure what she had expected to find inside.

But it was definitely not dozens of pieces of folded material.

She pulled one of them out, to find it was a white floor-length robe, with wide sleeves and a hood.

There were no other markings on it, and no indication what it was for.

She took out another two, and resealed the sack, before heading quickly back to the cover of the shrubs.

"God knows what Durov's got planned for this evening," she whispered to Ferguson. "But there must be a dozen of these robes." She handed one to him. "We wouldn't want to miss the party."

"And in my colour, too." Ferguson smiled, taking one.

"I've seen enough," Ava announced. "Something's definitely happening here tonight. We're just going to have to wait until later to see what it is."

She set off again, retracing her steps back around the castle in order to avoid crossing the main path just to the west of where Mary was lying up.

But as they approached the clump of trees where they had left her, Ava could clearly see that Mary had gone.

CHAPTER 61

Château de Montségur
Languedoc-Roussillon-Midi-Pyrénées
The Republic of France

MARY HAD NOT seen the men coming until it was too late.

Five of them had emerged silently from the undergrowth.

It had taken her only a few milliseconds to take in the hammers and crowbars they were armed with, and to conclude they were not friendly.

As the shock sank in, she had considered calling out for Ava and Ferguson. But she immediately realized that would only have alerted the men to their presence, risking all three of them being captured.

It was better to hope that she would find a chance to escape. Or perhaps even that Ava and Ferguson might locate her and attempt to rescue her.

As the men had surrounded her, there was nothing she could do. In her days as a Los Angeles police officer, she had seen and learned firsthand when to put up a struggle and when not to. Right now, resistance was going to get her badly hurt. Until she knew what they wanted, her best chance was passive cooperation.

One of the men had stepped forward and confronted her. *"Bludnitsa,"* he spat, as another moved behind and bound her wrists with a short length of twine.

The others had closed in to form a tight group and, when her wrists were secure, they had sealed up her mouth with several patches of duct tape, then shoved her towards the path, and marched her down the mountain.

None of them had spoken.

Once down at the car park, they had taken her to a battered old Citroën 'pig's nose' van, and pushed her inside, onto its dirty floor.

As they had moved off, she had been struggling to keep calm.

Now, after a short journey – ten minutes at the most, she estimated – they were bundling her out, and into the stone outbuilding of an isolated farmhouse.

It was largely empty, except for a few old items of furniture and a scattering of straw on the floor. One of the men pulled a broken plastic chair from a corner, and sat her on it.

They then moved behind her, out of her sight.

Aware something was about to happen, she fought to control her rising levels of panic.

In the van, she had comforted herself with the thought that if they meant to hurt her, they would have done so already. While they had been in transit she had been safe. But now they had her in the middle of nowhere, it was entirely possible that was about to change.

Up ahead, she saw the heavy wooden door at the far end of the room open, and a man entered.

From the broad face, high Slavic cheekbones, and bright blue eyes, she immediately recognized Oleg Durov.

"Who are you?" he asked, entering and stopping in front of her, tearing the patches of duct tape from her mouth.

She looked up at him, then away. She knew that captives should cooperate politely and non-antagonistically. "An American tourist," she answered flatly.

"I see." Durov nodded. "And your friends?"

Mary tried to keep the surprise from showing on her face.

"Which friends?" she asked, playing for time.

Durov stepped back and eyed her slowly. "A pity," he answered, indicating for his men to come forward.

She sensed a movement behind her, and, before she had time to brace herself, was suddenly being lifted off the chair by pairs of hands all over her.

Overwhelmed, she began to lash out with her legs, but strong arms quickly restrained her.

She was dropped heavily onto the floor, and ropes were tied around her chest, knees, and ankles.

Flooding with terror, she watched as two of the men walked to the end of the room. They positioned themselves either side of the barn's thick door, then grunted with effort as they lifted it clean off its hinges.

"Who are you?" Durov asked again, beckoning the men forward.

Her eyes flicked from Durov to the men, unsure for the moment which posed the greatest danger.

"I'm going to call you Margaret," he continued. "Because you shelter my enemies. Do you know what happened to Margaret, who harboured Queen Elizabeth's enemies?"

Mary had no idea, but her heart was racing as she watched, wide-eyed in terror, while the men holding the door approached.

She began to struggle more wildly, but the ropes were restricting all movement, and the hands were still holding her down.

One of the men with the door stepped across her, so the two of them were now standing on either side of her, with the door directly above her body.

Surely they were not going to drop it on her?

It would crush her skull.

"What are — " she shouted, but the breath died in her throat as the men lowered the door onto her, covering her legs and chest, but leaving her head free.

The crushing weight of the thick wood was unbearable.

Before she could breathe in fully, she saw hands appearing from nearby, placing large rocks and stones onto the board.

"I know exactly who you are," Durov continued. "You were seen on the hill with two companions – a woman and a man. From their descriptions, the woman is someone I'm very keen to meet again." He paused. "So – where is she now?"

The weight crushing Mary's ribs was beyond agonizing. She did not even have the breath to scream.

"It's no matter," he turned away. "They'll come for you."

---- • ◆ • ----

CHAPTER 62

Château de Montségur
Languedoc-Roussillon-Midi-Pyrénées
The Republic of France

AVA AND FERGUSON had retraced their steps to the donjon, but there had been no sign of Mary.

They scrambled a little way back down the mountain to a spot where they could get a view of the car park, but there was no evidence of anyone other than the three men on guard, as before. Without binoculars, there was nothing else to see on the low jagged green mountains rising from the surrounding countryside.

Returning to their observation point, they sat down, exhausted, resting against a tree.

There was nothing to do now except wait until whatever was planned for the evening, and hope that there would be some further clue to what had happened to Mary.

Ava leaned back against the trunk of the tree, getting more comfortable.

She reached into her pocket and pulled out a small leaflet she had grabbed off a table when they had passed through the village earlier. It was a history of the castle.

In 1232, Montségur became the official centre – the "seat and head" (domicilium et caput) – of the small Cathar Church that had survived the crusade. However, the end came after a group of fifty men from Montségur and some faidit lords murdered two Inquisition priests and their retinue at nearby Avignonet. In reprisal, royal forces marched on Montségur to 'cut off the head of the dragon'. Aware that a direct assault was impossible up the steep escarpments, they started a siege, pitting around ten thousand royal troops against the hundred or so hired defenders (the Cathars were pacifists who did not fight). Eventually, Basque mercenaries scaled the cliff face at the far end of the crest by night, and took the small citadel known as the Roc de la Tour. The archbishop of Albi installed a trebuchet there, and was able to bombard the Cathar village from close range, forcing those living on the hilltop to move inside the castle. By March, all hope was lost, and the Cathars negotiated for peace. The terms offered to the survivors was harsh. The castle was to be surrendered within fifteen days. All defenders were to be given punishments by the Inquisition. All civilians were to be pardoned, as long as they renounced their heresy. Anyone refusing would be burned. Around 190 Cathars refused to repent, and a number of defenders joined them. On 16 March 1244, following two weeks of prayer and fasting, around 225 Cathars voluntarily entered a pen, mounted the bonfires, and were burned alive. The Cathar castrum was razed. The castle fortifications visible today date from a later period.

It was a terrible story.

Ava put the pamphlet down and looked across at Ferguson, whose eyes were closed.

Typical soldier.

She was happy to take first watch. She would wake him in an hour, then try and get some rest herself.

The time passed uneventfully, and she was grateful for the chance to recharge.

Once dusk fell, things started to happen quickly.

The team that had been working in the donjon all day switched on portable floodlighting, and continued with last-minute adjustments.

Ava could not see what they were doing, but there was the continuing

sound of woodworking and, one by one, flaming torches were illuminated around the inside of the bailey, and on the outside wall by the
entrance.

She closed her eyes for a while, and the next thing she knew Ferguson
was tapping her shoulder, and indicating for her not to make a sound.

She followed his gaze towards the path.

She did not have to wait long before she saw a line of the Skoptsy
appearing, snaking their way towards the wooden steps leading into the
castle's great south-western entrance.

They were all wearing robes like the ones she had found earlier, with
the hoods obscuring most of their faces. They were moving slowly and
purposefully, and were it not for the Russian hymn rising above them,
they could have been a procession of medieval Provençal monks.

As they passed, Ava saw a group of children in the same robes bringing up the rear. She counted fourteen of them, each carrying a large
silver globe the size of a football.

When the procession had disappeared into the castle, Ava quickly
slipped on the robe she had taken earlier, pulled up its hood, and indicated for Ferguson to do likewise.

When his was on, they quietly moved out from the cover of the trees,
and followed the Skoptsy, making for the castle's wooden steps.

Reaching the top of the stairs, the breath caught in her throat as she
got a view into the bailey.

The castle had been arranged like a stage set.

The large group of Skoptsy was gathered to the right, at the far end of
the courtyard. They were facing across the length of the bailey, looking
towards the great wall of the donjon.

Ava lowered her head to obscure her face, and entered, heading for
the group, where she could blend in.

Glancing left, she saw to her amazement that the wall of the donjon
was draped with an immense image of the battered ghostly face of the
Turin Shroud, dominating the courtyard with a macabre sense of fore-
boding.

Ava stared at it in surprise.

Durov had stolen the Shroud from Turin Cathedral in error, believing
it to have been the solution to Rasputin's cross cryptograph. But, from
the disturbing icon room in his house – and the evidence before her now
– it was plain that he had an all-consuming obsession with it.

Either side of the hollow face were flaming torches, and above it was the only way into the keep from the courtyard – a doorway set high up into the thick wall.

She estimated the doorway was at least forty-five feet off the ground, and she was startled to see that a small wooden platform had been built in front of it, jutting out like a mini-stage. Narrow walkways had been attached to the platform, and they branched off to the tops of the adjoining bailey walls. It was pretty much how it would have looked in medieval times, with the wooden stairs and walkways removable when the donjon was under attack.

The doorway and platform were illuminated by small spotlights, but there was nothing to see there, or on the pair of giant flat screens mounted either side of the doorway, each displaying a static image of the icon of Our Lady of Philermos.

It was clear to Ava that the stage was set for something spectacular.

But for now, she had no idea what.

---·◆·---

CHAPTER 63

IN THE SHADOW of the Golan Heights, the MLRS rocket platform was in place.

Up front in the cab, the soldier at the fire control panel flicked the weapons system to STANDBY.

Twenty-five yards away, they had dug a small satellite camera into the sand.

The two men inside knew that the beauty of the MLRS was that they were totally independent. They did not need any defensive emplacements or fire support to protect them. The heavily armoured vehicle was 'shoot-and-scoot'. Once the rockets were away, the half-tracks and five-hundred-horsepower engine would carry them off into the desert again, long before any enemy reconnaissance scouts arrived at the launch zone. By the time anyone was on site to investigate, there would be nothing to see. They would be long gone.

Now all they had to do was wait.

The order would come soon.

———————— • ◆ • ————————

CHAPTER 64

Château de Montségur
Languedoc-Roussillon-Midi-Pyrénées
The Republic of France

IN THE DONJON, Durov kissed the white robe reverentially, mouthing the familiar words in silent prayer.

"These are they which came out of great tribulation, and have washed their robes, and made them white in the blood of the Lamb."

He took off his clothes, and slipped on the robe, enjoying the sensation of the cool material against his skin. It was the last piece of clothing he would ever wear, before his soul would be clothed forever in light.

It had all come together so simply.

By providence, the Rasputin notebooks had arrived in his lap – the gift of '489'. He had tried to investigate the numerology of the name – looking for any clue in the seemingly random digits – but he had drawn a blank. Yet it was of no consequence. The *Panagia* was all knowing, and he felt her heavenly hand in it.

The idea for raining Armageddon down onto Damascus had been a stroke of his own genius.

A new researcher at the Ministry of Energy had shown him an early draft of a working paper on the instability in the Middle East – highlighting that the Israeli-Syrian fault line was the most volatile. The researcher had given as an example the likely disastrous consequences if any of Israel's weaponry in the Golan Heights was accidentally discharged.

The innocent discussion had lit a spark in Durov's mind that had given him the answer he had been seeking.

It suddenly all became clear, and he knew how he could do what the Holy Mother had asked.

The rest would make history.

He draped the prayer shawl about his shoulders, and looked around the donjon critically, ensuring everything was in its place. This was to be a night unlike any other, and everything had to be right.

The world would remember tonight.

Satisfied with his preparations, he strode across to the far wall, and stepped through the doorway onto the platform suspended over the bailey.

As he emerged, the view took his breath away.

He was high on the wall of the donjon, looking down over the courtyard far below.

At the far end of the bailey, the Skoptsy were gazing up at him – their hooded faces thrown into sharply contrasting pools of light and shade by the flaming torches running the length of the top of the courtyard walls.

He saw again in his mind the image of the Blessed Mother.

This was what she wanted.

His heart swelled with pride.

And she had chosen him to achieve it, giving him riches and power – not for him, but to make it all possible.

He ran his eyes over the one hundred and forty-four Skoptsy below.

He did not have to count them. He knew they would all be there.

They all wanted this.

They had never said it to him. Perhaps they did not even realize that it was what they craved.

But he knew it was their innermost desire.

He had been sent to guide them, and the Holy Mother was showing him the way.

She wanted to be reunited with her children.

He smiled at them as they looked up expectantly, then held up his hands, and began.

"We are *Urha* – the Way." His voice rang out clearly in the still summer evening. "We are the Elect, honoured to carry the torch of the *She-liahin*, which we bear with awe and humility."

He gazed around. "Faith has built many fine temples down the ages. Yet none is as great as this hallowed place. These stone blocks were fashioned by the hands of holy martyrs, who laid each one in the unshakeable knowledge that their labours would one day be rewarded with crowns of heavenly gold."

He paused, before resuming more sombrely. "The builders of this place look down on us now, and they bless us as we prepare to reconsecrate their chapel of grace."

He clapped once, and the children with the silver spheres filed solemnly out of the bailey's north doorway.

---◆---

CHAPTER 65

Château de Montségur
Languedoc-Roussillon-Midi-Pyrénées
The Republic of France

AVA HAD HER head bent low, listening to Durov's homily. His voice
was commanding, and seemed to float down onto the crowd assembled
in the bailey. It had the same slightly detached and mildly hypnotic effect
she had noticed during his speech at the Russian embassy, except this
time there was an excitement she had not heard before.

"The *Katharoi* – the pure ones – offer us a burning example of faith.
They did not dwell as fully in the *Meshiha* as we do, but they understood
many things that are only known to the Elect."

Ava was listening intently.

"When ready, each of them undertook the *consolamentum* – the great
consoling. Thenceforward, they vowed perpetual celibacy. Like us, they
knew that the act of sex cuts mankind off from God. Every instance of
fornication kills our divine spirit a little more, until we are empty shells,
no longer in God's image – merely animals."

He glared down at the audience.

"They also understood that only the Spirit is pure. They saw something evil in Yahweh of the Old Testament – the Hebrew god of conquest and pillage. For them he was the wicked Demiurge. The world and

everything in it was his foul creation, and people were his lustful servants. Yet the Cathars were blessed with the knowledge that the *Meshiha* had spoken of a different God – the Trinity – a fountainhead of justice, love, and light. And they were forever grateful that inside each of them resided a spark – a soul – a sliver of that divine light. They understood the eternal conflict between their spiritual essence and their base matter. As do we."

It was the usual cult formula – the saved and the lost, the blessed and the damned. Us and them.

But it was powerful. And Ava could see that the Skoptsy around her were soaking up his every word.

"By the *consolamentum* ceremony, the ordinary Cathar became a Perfect. And here, tonight, we shall follow in their noble footsteps. We, too, shall be Perfected. We shall say with them: *Benedicite. Parcite nobis.*" [5]

Out of the corner of her eye, Ava caught sight of movement over by the north door.

As she watched, the children filed in again, bearing the silver spheres in front of them.

They approached the crowd, and untwisted small caps, revealing that the spheres had openings.

"And did all drink the same spiritual drink," Durov intoned, as the children passed the silver decanters to the crowd. "For they drank of that spiritual Rock that followed them: and that Rock was Christ," Durov recited, as the crowd began to drink deeply from the spheres. "For I am already being poured out as a drink offering, and the time of my departure is at hand."

Each member of the Skoptsy took a deep draught, then passed it on.

He indicated the vast death-mask of the Turin Shroud, "Like the *Meshiha*, we must take the cup that is offered to us, if we desire truly to live."

In no time, the silver spheres were circulating freely among the crowd.

"This is the divine plan," he continued. "Today is Saint John's day – and there is no more fitting time for it to come to pass."

He disappeared through the doorway, then returned a few moments later, dragging something behind him, dropping it at his feet.

As it moved slightly, Ava realized it was a person that Durov was pulling by the hair.

---

5   "Bless us. Have mercy upon us."

"Babylon was ever the Anti-Christ." His tone was now darker. "Never more so than since deceiving the nations from its nest in Rome. Here," he took firm hold of more of the person's hair, "here is the abomination."

As he yanked the hair upwards and backwards with a flourish, Ava froze as she found herself looking at Mary's battered and bloodied face.

Durov was still quoting from scripture, but Ava was barely listening as a white-hot anger began rising in her.

His voice floated over the crowd. "I saw a woman sit upon a scarlet coloured beast, full of names of blasphemy, having seven heads and ten horns. And the woman was arrayed in purple and scarlet colour, and decked with gold and precious stones and pearls, having a golden cup in her hand full of abominations and filthiness of her fornication. And upon her forehead was a name written, *Mystery, Babylon the Great, The Mother of Harlots and Abominations of the Earth*. And I saw the woman drunken with the blood of the saints, and with the blood of the martyrs of Jesus."

Ferguson was staring at Mary, his face ashen.

"Christ," he whispered, taking a step forwards.

Ava grabbed his shoulder, pulling him back.

"You'll be lynched," she whispered, lowering her head again to obscure her face.

She gripped his shoulder tighter, sensing him struggle to restrain himself. "We need to be clever," she urged. "There must be a hundred and fifty of them."

From Ferguson's left, someone tapped him on the arm.

He turned slowly, his eyes narrowing.

The man was proffering one of the silver spheres.

Ferguson took it, then raised it to his lips.

With a rush of panic, Ava jabbed her heel hard into the top of his foot.

He held the sphere to his lips for a moment longer, then lowered it.

"If Durov wants people to drink, it's got to be a bad idea," she whispered.

Ferguson wiped the back of his hand across his lips. "I worked that one out," he replied, passing the sphere to the person behind him.

"It's wine," he whispered to Ava, tasting his lips, "with something else in it."

As he was speaking, a light misty drizzle started to fall.

Grateful for her hood, Ava focused back on Durov, and realized something was not right.

It took her brain a moment to work it out.

It was not raining on Durov or around the platform.

As the mist formed droplets on her face, it started to trickle down her skin.

She looked around, and saw that the flaming torches mounted along the top of the walls also seemed unaffected.

Ferguson had noticed where she was looking.

"What the hell is this?" he asked, holding out his hands to catch the fine droplets.

Ava was squinting at the wall, shielding her eyes from the brightness of the torches.

Suddenly, she saw it – a thin grey tube tacked to the wall about a yard under the base of the torches.

"There," she pointed. "A hose."

Some of the liquid trickled onto her lips, and she suddenly realized with horror what it was, and what Durov was planning.

"Oh my God," she gasped. "It's petrol."

CHAPTER 66

Château de Montségur
Languedoc-Roussillon-Midi-Pyrénées
The Republic of France

ABOVE THEM, DUROV disappeared into the keep, and re-emerged a moment later. He paused, then surveyed the Skoptsy, his eyes bright.

Ava peered up at him, and her heart started beating faster as she caught sight of the thick roll of papyrus in his hand.

She heard Jennings's voice in her head.

"Durov's far cleverer than you. Then again, he knows what he's looking for. You see, he knows that the prize is one of the original letters of the Apocalypse."

She peered through the mist of petrol at the roll of skins.

Could it really be an original Apocalypse letter?

It was too far away for her to make out any details.

Could one of the copies have survived all these years, or was it just a cheap stage prop?

Durov had proved himself to be many things. He was undoubtedly clever and resourceful. He had solved the same clues she had.

The vellum fragment had said PARSEMA.

He scattered.

Had Durov really found one of the scattered letters?

Up on the platform, Durov was addressing the crowd again.

"For two thousand years, we have waited for the Second Coming of the *Meshiha*." His face was shining as he held the roll out in front of him.

"And here is the map, dreamed in a cave on the island of Patmos – the holy vision of Yohanan the fisherman: the beloved disciple, leader of the Way, and sacred apostle of the true believers."

He held it up above his head. "And the angel took the censer, and filled it with fire of the altar, and cast it into the earth." He stared about, his eyes widening. "The time has come for the Elect to take their rightful seats around the throne."

He returned into the donjon.

Ava took the opportunity to look about surreptitiously, and was struck by how the robed figures around had become noticeably less animated. Their eyes had dulled, and a number were looking unstable on their feet.

A moment later, Durov remerged, without the roll, but with something else in his hand.

On either side of the doorway, the television screens displaying the icon of Our Lady of Philermos dissolved to black, then came to life again with blurry green images.

Ava recognized that look.

It was a feed from a night vision camera.

Both screens showed the identical image of a long military vehicle in a desert. The camera was around twenty-five yards from it, and each screen showed the same timestamp in its bottom left-hand corner.

It was one hour ahead of France.

Ava went cold.

So was Israel.

"Fire is divine. Fire is love. God is fire." Durov's voice was rising in volume and intensity. "Since time immemorial, fire has been the purifying force through which base substances have been refined. When King Solomon's Temple was ready, fire came down from heaven, and the Lord filled the house."

He reached down and grabbed Mary's hair again.

"But what is bliss for the martyrs is hell for the damned." His voice became more strained, as a rage began to take hold. "While we enter the kingdom, the harlots of false faith will be consumed by the flames of everlasting torment."

He started raising Mary up by her hair. "Babylon the great is fallen. For all nations have drunk of the wine of the wrath of her fornication.

And she shall be utterly burned with fire: for strong is the Lord God who judgeth her."

Ava could see the pain on Mary's face as Durov tried to pull her up off her knees.

His voice was now screeching across the courtyard. "These shall hate the whore, and shall make her desolate and naked, and shall eat her flesh, and burn her with fire."

Without warning, he let go of her, and she slumped heavily to the floor beside him.

He opened his arms wide in triumph to embrace the crowd. "And again they said, Alleluia. And her smoke rose up for ever and ever. *Benedicite. Parcite nobis.*"

"I've seen enough." Ferguson turned away in disgust. "Let's end this."

———————— • ◆ • ————————

CHAPTER 67

West Syrian Desert
The Syrian Arab Republic

A MOMENT EARLIER, inside the MLRS, the encrypted line on the secure satellite radio link had crackled into life.

The soldier at the fire control panel had listened carefully to the voice in his headphones, repeating back the string of letters and numbers being dictated, then typed them directly into the keyboard in front of him.

When he was done, he reached for the small sealed plastic cylinder hanging on a chain around his neck, and cracked it open, pulling out a slip of black card with a twelve-digit alphanumeric sequence.

He typed the code into the fire control computer, and – after a moment's pause – the MLRS's remote weapon guidance and international linkup went live.

There was nothing more for him to do, except watch the target coordinates appearing on the screen as they were entered from a terminal nearly two thousand miles away.

When complete, the numbers melted from the screen, and the targeting map appeared, plotting the trajectory of each rocket to its destination.

They were all clustered on one small area.

Al-Mazzeh district, western Damascus.

The soldier knew it well from briefings.

It was the most upmarket area of the city – home to international businesses, embassies, the university, and a population of several hundred thousand people.

It was also the location of the government's principal military airport, the base of the elite Republican Guard, and – overlooking it all – the President of Syria's headquarters and palace.

---- ⋅ ◆ ⋅ ----

CHAPTER 68

Château de Montségur
Languedoc-Roussillon-Midi-Pyrénées
The Republic of France

AVA LED THE way out of the bailey's northern doorway, then began running around towards the donjon.

As she and Ferguson sprinted towards where Durov was holding Mary, the surrounding peaks melted into the night sky under the stars. On any other evening it would have been spectacular. But it was treacherous running in the dark. The narrow mountaintop path was uneven, and dotted with clumps of wild grass and loose lumps of rock and masonry. To their right, the mountainside fell away sharply.

Arriving at the castle's north-western corner, Ava stopped and tucked herself against the wall. Conscious of every passing second, she motioned for Ferguson to fall in beside her as she looked across towards the entrance into the donjon.

It was exactly as it had been earlier that afternoon, with the old makeshift wooden staircase leading up into the keep. The only difference was that now the building materials and sacks had been removed, and there was a white-robed figure with a shotgun standing guard at the bottom of the steps.

Ava stepped round the corner, and indicated with her fingers for Ferguson to follow in ten seconds.

Bracing herself, she strode directly towards the guard, keeping her head low, and shielding her face.

As she approached, the man raised his arms and levelled the shotgun directly at her.

She pulled her hood back and approached the guard, as if on official business, making sure she stopped on the far side of him.

The guard turned to face her and, right on cue, Ferguson launched himself at the man from behind, throwing a heavy circular punch to the guard's temple.

As the violence of the blow transferred to the soft matter of the guard's brain, the sensitive tissue crashed into the inside wall of his skull, and he blacked out instantly, dropping to the floor.

Ava bent down and removed his belt. Then, together with Ferguson, she dragged the unconscious man to the staircase, before hooking his arms around the wooden post of the banister rail, and lashing them together with the belt.

Once satisfied the coast was clear, Ava was the first onto the donjon's rickety wooden stairs. She took them two at a time, quickly arriving at the walkway that led directly into the stone keep.

Ferguson was right behind her.

Up ahead, inside, the scene was lit with yet more torches, which cast a macabre dancing light around the crumbling fortification.

Without pausing, Ava entered the ancient fortification, noting that the old walkway was supported on tall wooden stilts rising high above the stone floor below. In front of her, the planks continued for several yards, then met another walkway crossing the width of the keep, forming a T-shape of gangways, seemingly floating in mid-air.

Directly ahead, the Skoptsy had built an additional shallow flight of steps leading up to a new platform, which entirely filled the farther side of the donjon.

On it, to the left, was a table draped in purple. To the right was the MLRS remote command unit, which had been plugged into the battery pack and the large satellite radio. Above the hardware, mounted on the wall, was a small flat-screen monitor showing the same night vision image as the two large flat screens on the outside of the donjon.

But in the centre of the far wall, silhouetted in flame and moonlight, standing out on the platform over the bailey's courtyard, she could see

Durov's back.

He was addressing the crowd of Skoptsy below – his arms outstretched in a messianic gesture.

"And there followed hail and fire mingled with blood," he declared, holding a small olive-green metal box in his hand. A black cable protruded from it, and ran back to the MLRS launch controller.

Before Ava could do anything, Durov held up his hand, and pressed the remote unit's single button.

On the monitor, the image came to life as the MLRS kicked into action.

Ava felt herself go numb.

Clearly visible in the green haze, the end of the MLRS's large rectangular missile pod rose until it was pointing over the top of the personnel cab, then swung out, angling itself sideways.

A moment later, the vehicle shuddered for a second, before being engulfed in a swirling billowing cloud of grey smoke, obscuring it completely. Simultaneously, a fireball erupted in the middle of the rolling smog as a rocket shot out at forty-five degrees.

Ava's eyes were locked on the screen in horror.

Durov was insane.

He had actually done it.

Out on the balcony, he was holding the manuscript roll high above his head, bellowing, "The time is here. The dead will be judged, and the faithful rewarded."

Mesmerized, Ava watched aghast as his fingers found the ancient black seal, and cracked it open.

A moment later, on the monitor, there was another searing blast of light within the smoke cloud, and a second missile launched.

Ferguson was already up on the platform, throwing himself towards Durov, who had turned around at the commotion and was striding into the donjon.

Durov's eyes widened in surprise as Ferguson landed a heavy blow to the side of his jaw, sending him reeling back against the wall. Durov slumped, and his hand opened, releasing the manuscript onto the floor, where it rolled under the purple-draped table.

Ava snapped out of her paralysis, and flung herself towards the satellite guidance system, crashing onto her knees on the floor beside it.

She stared at the controls.

Above her, on the monitor, the MLRS continued to judder as it spewed out its lethal payload.

In no time, all twelve rockets were airborne.

Over by the doorway to the bailey, Durov had recovered, and was now charging forward. But Ferguson was quicker, and took him down hard to the floor.

Ava stared wildly at the equipment in front of her.

None of the buttons were labelled, and the embedded mini-screen was blank.

Unsure what to do, she spun the black trackball beside the keyboard, and the dark blue screen illuminated with a single green word:

LOGON

Underneath it, eight boxes appeared.

"Password?" she yelled over to Durov.

Ferguson was kneeling on top of him, pinning him face-down to the floor with his arm behind his back.

Durov stared defiantly across at Ava.

Ferguson leant harder on Durov's bent arm, straining the shoulder joint to its limit.

"You have no time," Durov gasped through the pain. "Your time has ended."

"Speak up," Ferguson ordered, leaning even harder on his arm.

Durov clenched his teeth, his face draining of all colour. "We're approaching the end of time."

"Password?" Ferguson grimaced, digging his knee down between Durov's shoulder blades. "Now."

Ava frowned.

Something about the way Durov had said the last words was not right.

She looked at him, and saw the corners of his mouth twitching into a smile.

He was teasing her.

Behind Durov, through the doorway, she could see Mary out on the platform. She looked even worse closer up. Her face was puffy and bruised, covered in small cuts.

Ava stared desperately down at the control screen again. If Jennings had been correct and the rockets were trained on Damascus, they would soon be touching the edge of space, and preparing to drop.

She did not have long.

She went over Durov's words again.

No time. Time has ended. End of time,

The sweat was starting to sting her eyes.

How could he make a password out of that?

Eight letters.

She wracked her brain.

CHRONOS? No. That was seven.

APOCALYPSE? No. Ten.

Mary shuffled slowly into the room, staring at Durov with loathing.

Ava screwed up her face in concentration.

JUDGEMENT? No. Nine.

RAPTURE? No.

Think!

She turned her mind back to Rasputin's cryptographs.

Was there anything in those that might have inspired Durov?

She pictured them in her mind's eye, cycling through the images to see if there was anything related to the End Times.

She focused in on the images and words, then suddenly realized there was one clue left.

The cross Rasputin had drawn in his notebook had eight corners. And each one had a letter beside it:

ESHTNOAC

It was eight letters!

She visualized the cross in her mind, trying to see it in the context of everything she now knew about Rasputin, the icon, and the Apocalypse.

And then she saw it.

Oh God.

How could she have missed that?

She had rearranged it to make CHASE NOT. But that was ridiculous. Rasputin did not speak English.

Now, it made sense.

She had to read it line-by-line off the cross, not clockwise.

Durov had even said the word, back in Rome.

And it was exactly the sort of word that would appeal to him.

"We are approaching the eesatton."

It was a threat he had made in the Palazzo Malta, and she had not understood him. She had misheard it because of his accent.

But now she got it.

The Eschaton.

She punched the ancient theological word for the End Times into the keypad.

The screen cleared immediately.

There was no time for celebration, as the LOGON screen was immediately replaced with a radar scanner.

It showed the rockets inbound to their target, with only eighteen seconds to the impact of the first.

In the bottom left of the screen, in a red box, was the single word:

ABORT

Ava jabbed it hard, praying she was in time.

Nothing happened.

Then a new prompt appeared across the bottom of the screen:

RETINAL CONFIRMATION

"Get him over here," she yelled at Ferguson. "Iris check."

Ferguson yanked Durov upwards, and dragged him to the flight case, holding his head over the control panel, positioning his right eye above a dollar-sized lens surrounded by a circular steel rim.

Durov was bellowing as Ferguson forced his eye down over the lens.

The readout on the screen remained unchanged.

Ava glanced at the radar screen again, feeling the adrenaline hammering around her system as she watched the cluster of twelve dots move eastwards.

In desperation, she reached her hands down around Durov's sweaty face and found his right eye.

It was scrunched tightly shut.

With no attempt at gentleness, she pinched the skin above and below the eye-socket, and pulled his eyelids apart hard.

For a second nothing happened, then the controller beeped, and its screen cleared.

"Get him away," she yelled to Ferguson, who lifted Durov's head and dragged him aside.

The screen flashed up a single word:

ABORTING

A moment later another word appeared below it:

DISARMED

Ava's shoulders sagged with relief as she slumped back to the floor.

The rockets were deactivated.

The tracking system would find a patch of land away from the built-up area and bring them down. They would make a nasty hole in the ground, but nothing like the damage of detonating in downtown Damascus.

A few feet away, Durov snarled, and tore his head free of Ferguson's grasp. Seizing the opportunity, he hammered his shoulder into Ferguson's chest, and wrenched himself away, pulling something from behind his watch.

Before Ava had time to react, Durov was on her – one powerful arm around her chest, the other holding a small black triangular blade to her larynx.

His thumb knife.

She felt the point of the blade pushing hard against the soft flesh of her neck.

"Now. Right hand on her jaw," Durov ordered Ferguson, nodding towards Mary.

Ferguson hesitated, then took a step closer to Mary. Watching Durov closely, he slowly and gently took her jaw in his right hand.

"Take the back of her head with the other," Durov ordered.

Ferguson stared at Durov, without complying.

"You don't want to play games with me," Durov growled, pushing the blade harder into Ava's neck.

Ava felt it cutting the skin.

She clamped her jaw down tightly, shutting out the pain.

Ferguson slowly complied, taking the back of Mary's head in his other hand. He whispered something to her that Ava could not hear.

Mary's eyes were darting from Durov to Ferguson.

"Now," Durov addressed Ferguson. "I open this deceiver's throat from ear to ear, or you snap the heretic's neck. You decide."

A flash of contempt passed across Ferguson's face. It was gone in a second. But Ava had seen it.

"A price must be paid. Now – choose."

Ferguson's eyes were locked on Durov, monitoring every micro-signal of his expression.

Ava concentrated hard, trying to feel exactly where the point of the blade was.

She sensed it was at least an inch from her carotid artery – which meant it was dangerously near her larynx, oesophagus, and trachea. A puncture to any of those was not going to be pretty.

She focused back on Ferguson, who was staring ahead, granite-faced, assessing his options.

Opening her eyes wide to attract his attention, she suddenly jerked her head forward in a lightning-fast movement.

The pain in her neck was excruciating as the blade cut deeper into her. Then she whipped her head backwards with all her strength.

As she had anticipated, it connected with Durov's face, and she heard the sound of the cartilage in his nose crunching.

She carried on driving her head backwards, then hammered her elbow into the soft flesh of his stomach.

His grip around her chest relaxed, and she seized the opportunity, tearing free and diving for the military radio. Her hands closed around the bendy aerial. "The Apocalypse is a symbolic story," she grunted, swinging the unit in a wide arc hard and fast at Durov's head. He sidestepped, and the radio smashed against the wall. "You're not supposed to take it seriously."

Durov glared at her.

She took a step forward, whipping what was left of the radio unit back at him again. "I mean, there are dozens of apocalyptic books." The shattered radio unit caught him a glancing blow on the side of the head. "Even in the Dead Sea Scrolls ... "

Durov reeled from the impact, and she could see blood on the side of his head. Oblivious, he recovered and began advancing on her, holding the thumb knife out menacingly.

Suddenly there was a blur to her left, and Mary was charging towards Durov.

She slammed into him, wrapping her arms around his chest in a body lock.

As she did so, she cast a look back at Ava and Ferguson.

Ava took a moment to process the unexpected emotion radiating from Mary's face.

It was triumph.

Durov was far taller than her, but Mary had momentum. He staggered backwards from the impact, and Ava watched in horror as Mary drove Durov's body through the open doorway, and out onto the small platform suspended over the bailey.

Ferguson was already running towards them, but in the next instant they were both gone, over the edge.

Ava had also started running, and arrived on the platform at the same time as Ferguson, only to gaze down with horror at the two bodies lying on the rocks far below.

Durov was sprawled partially on top of Mary, his head on her chest.

Mary's neck was broken, and even from over forty feet away, Ava could see by the light of the torches that a dark pool of liquid was spreading out from under her cracked skull.

CHAPTER 69

United Nations Disengagement Observer Force (UNDOF)
Mount Hermon
The Golan Heights
Israeli Occupied Syria

A MINUTE EARLIER, Major Annibale Della Torre of the Order of Malta's *Corpo Militare* stared in disbelief through his high-powered night vision binoculars.

Down below in the valley, a second rocket was thundering from an MLRS.

"Mother of God," he whispered to himself.

That afternoon, he had received an unusual order from a senior officer tasking him to keep an eye out for a rogue M270 MLRS that was suspected to be moving about in the area – intention hostile. When he located it, he was to report back.

He had spent the last few hours scouring the territory beyond the Purple Line, scanning for any irregular movements.

He had seen nothing except miles of desert.

But now there could be no doubt he had found the missing MLRS.

And it was too late to report anything useful.

It had started live firing.

All hell was going to break loose.

He prayed the Syrians had a functioning missile defence system.

This was going to get very ugly, very fast.

There would be reprisals.

The IDF units embedded around him in the Golan were going to be engaged in no time.

This sleepy area would go hot in minutes.

"Call it in," he shouted to his radio operator. "Rockets away. Into Syria."

Who the hell was launching ballistic missiles?

He stared at the vehicle through his binoculars.

It was pretty much on the Bravo Line – but close enough to Israel for anyone in Damascus to assume that Tel Aviv had a hand in this. If past encounters were anything to go by, all parties would shoot first and ask questions later.

Della Torre wiped the sweat from his eyes.

Damascus would have to take care of the incoming rockets. Perhaps Russia would be on hand to help. Dozens of radar screens would already be tracking the inbound warheads – but downing state-of-the-art missiles was never an exact science. It took special equipment on high readiness, and somehow Della Torre doubted that Damascus had the infrastructure or hardware.

He watched, powerless, as the rockets continued to roar from the mobile platform, the intensity of the fireballs burning white against the night sky.

The stark reality was that there was nothing he could do about it. This was going to escalate way beyond the resources he had.

But one thing he did have to make a decision about was what to do with the MLRS.

There was no time to get further orders from HQ UNDOF, or to liaise with the Israeli chain of command back at Camp Rabin in Tel Aviv. Going through the official channels would take hours. By then the MLRS would have disappeared into the desert and be long gone.

This was down to him.

He peered through the binoculars, and watched as the smoke cleared sufficiently for him to see the missile pod slowly swing back into alignment and slot into place on top of the chassis.

As the MLRS began to move off, he was acutely aware that he could not delay the decision any longer.

Could he be certain that the M270 was not going to reload somewhere and be deployed again?

It would be a brave person who made that call.

But what if the occupants were friendly forces? Maybe this was part of some wider covert operation he did not know about?

He could feel the sweat soaking his back.

The fact was that he had all the information he was going to get. And making tactical decisions with imperfect information was part of what he was paid for.

No one expected him to do anything other than rely on the evidence he had – and on his gut instinct, and his considerable experience.

He put the binoculars down on top of the observation post's hessian-clad wall, and turned to his radio operator. "Call in fast air," he ordered. "Give them coordinates, bearing, and speed. I want it taken out."

The corporal nodded, and transmitted the message to the US 39th Air Base Wing at Incirlik in Turkey. They would have something in the air nearby. They always did. If there was a friendly operation under way, they would probably know about it.

Over to them.

Down in the desert, the MLRS was starting to pick up speed.

It was not long before Della Torre lost sight of the vehicle, as the grainy night vision image struggled to distinguish between the M270's sandy-coloured camouflage and the Syrian dunes.

In what seemed less than a few minutes, he heard the deep boom of heavy ordnance, and saw way up ahead the flames licking high into the air, and the telltale billowing plumes of oily smoke.

He breathed out deeply.

Job done.

Tango down.

———————— ◆ ————————

CHAPTER 70

Château de Montségur
Languedoc-Roussillon-Midi-Pyrénées
The Republic of France

AVA LOOKED DOWN at the two bodies, and suddenly realized that – although battered and bloody – Durov had started to move.

He slowly pulled his body up onto all fours, and hauled himself off Mary, dragging one leg behind him.

Reaching over, he took one of the flaming torches that had been mounted low on the wall. Holding it out ahead of him, he began to drag himself on his other arm, moving away from Mary, and towards the Skoptsy huddling at the far end of the bailey.

With a rush of horror, Ava realized what was about to happen.

The Skoptsy were drenched in petrol.

She stared around, her mind whirring.

She could not jump out of the doorway to tackle him. She was far too high above the courtyard below.

Ferguson had also seen what was happening, and was already on his way out of the donjon. But Ava already knew that he would not get to Durov in time. He had to get out of the donjon, run round the keep, then along and into the courtyard, and finally to Durov.

There was no way he would make it.

By the time he got there, the Skoptsy would be a holocaust.

Her rational thought process confirmed what her intuition had already concluded.

It was down to her.

She ran back into the donjon, desperate for a weapon.

She could not see anything – just the MLRS launch control unit, radio, and battery pack. But they were all far too heavy.

She ran over to where Durov had been standing. His thumb knife was on the floor, but it was useless.

Choking with frustration, she ran back out through the doorway and onto the platform.

Durov had now covered half the distance to the Skoptsy, holding the torch out in front of him, its yellowy-orange flames dancing in the night air. The crowd was sheltering at the far end of the bailey, subdued and passive from whatever Durov had put in the wine.

Ava was keenly aware she was running out of time, when her attention was caught by some cabling and a length of grey hose tacked to the bottom of the doorway. Following it, she saw that it ran out of the donjon's doorway and under the small wooden platform jutting out over the bailey.

Dropping to her knees, she peered under the boards of the platform, and saw that the electrical cabling was feeding the two large flat screens. Beside the electrical wires, she could make out that the hose was plugged into a T-joint which fed two tubes running out towards the walls of the bailey. She followed them, and with a rising sense of excitement saw that they were the tubes she had spied up on the wall when she had been down with the Skoptsy.

As traced the route of the hoses, she saw they were fixed to the bailey's walls several yards beneath the row of flaming torches at the top. At the far end of the bailey, where the Skoptsy were gathered, they must be pierced with holes, which were still spraying a fine flammable mist over the crowd.

Glancing over her shoulder and back into the donjon, she saw that the hose ran down below the old walkways to the original stone ground floor far below, where it was connected to a pump and a tank of liquid.

The Cyrillic words stencilled on the side of the container were meaningless to her, but she recognized the international hazard sign of an orange diamond with black outlined flames.

Flammable liquid.

Crouching down in the doorway, she grabbed hold of the tube under the platform and pulled as hard as she could. The screws holding its small fastening clips tore easily out of the wood, and the hose came free of the T-joint.

The air was suddenly filled with the smell of petrol, as she held up the tube, which was now gushing liquid.

Down in the bailey, Durov was still dragging himself towards his followers – the flame edging ever closer to their petrol-sodden clothes.

Ava stood up on the platform and pinched the end of the hose together with her fingers.

Immediately, a pressurized jet arced out from its tip, sending a sparkling rainbow of flammable fluid high into the night sky.

It landed a few yards behind Durov, spraying a wet patch of petrol onto the courtyard's floor.

She squeezed more tightly and angled the hose a fraction higher, watching as the stream of fluid jumped forward and hit Durov's back and shoulders.

She let it continue to pour directly onto him, soaking his body from his shoulders to his feet.

As the liquid hit him, his head turned to follow the jet of petrol, and he raised his glance to the platform where Ava was standing.

His eyes locked onto hers, and his expression twisted into a mask of animal rage.

She looked at the torch in his hand, and then at the crowd ahead of him, unsure if she could do what had to be done.

It was one thing killing in self-defence – she had done it before. But it was quite another making a cold calculation about who lived and who died.

Her mind flicked back to the photographs Jennings had shown them back in MI13, of the Skoptsy man and woman who had undergone the ceremony of the Great Seal.

She looked out over the courtyard, at the mass of Skoptsy huddled at the far end, and at the children sitting in a line in front of them.

Durov was a monster.

The Skoptsy were not the first, and they would not be the last, to fall under the spell of a charismatic cult leader. She had no sympathy for their views, but whatever they had got themselves into, they did not deserve to be the victims of Durov's perversions.

He was the one responsible for mutilating them.

And now he wanted to incinerate them.

He was still snarling up at the platform as she took another look ahead at the crowd of Skoptsy huddled in the shadows, then gently inclined her wrist a fraction.

The parabola of petrol inched forward from Durov's back, and – as if in slow motion – hit the flaming torch he was carrying.

Ava watched, transfixed, as Durov erupted into an orange fireball. The conflagration started at the torch, then moved back to engulf his entire body.

She let the hose keep pouring for another second, fuelling the blaze, then squeezed the tip closed, and allowed her arm to fall to her side, pouring the petrol harmlessly down onto the rocks at the foot of the donjon wall.

Up ahead, Durov was rolling on the ground, a flailing inferno in the middle of the ancient courtyard.

Through the sound of the flames roaring, she could clearly hear his screams.

Down to the left, Ferguson ran into the courtyard through the north doorway. He made straight for Durov, who continued spasming for what seemed like an age, until eventually he lay still at the heart of the lapping flames.

Ava looked away.

It was over.

CHAPTER 71

Château de Montségur
Languedoc-Roussillon-Midi-Pyrénées
The Republic of France

AVA RE-ENTERED THE donjon, and made for the old walkway.

From there, she could see a long ladder down to the original stone floor of the keep and the tank of petrol. She quickly climbed down it, and shut off the pump.

There had been enough burning for one night.

When she had turned the tank's tap off as well, she climbed back up and out of the donjon, and headed round into the bailey.

Up ahead, Ferguson was standing a few yards from Durov's still-burning body.

She approached, holding up her hands to shield herself from the heat.

It was a horrific sight.

Inside the orange flames, she could clearly make out a body curled into a foetal position. Most of its face and hair had gone, leaving skull bone visible inside the rolling flames. The rest of the body was equally ravaged, with the torso and limbs little more than smouldering chunks of scorched meat.

She pulled off the white robe she was wearing over her clothes, and tore off a strip. She wound the narrow material carefully around her neck as a bandage to staunch the bleeding where Durov had cut her, before throwing the remainder of the robe onto the fire, where she watched it disintegrate in the flames.

"But the fearful, and unbelieving, and the abominable, and murderers, and whoremongers, and sorcerers, and idolaters, and all liars, shall have their part in the lake which burneth with fire and brimstone," Ferguson pronounced over the burning cadaver, reading from the small pocket Bible he had brought from the residence in Toulouse.

Ava looked at him quizzically.

"It's from the Apocalypse," he answered ruefully. "I read it last night, and the image kept me awake. I've seen too many bodies burn. It's not something you forget."

He closed the Bible, and started walking towards the rocks at the foot of the donjon wall.

Ava followed, stopping beside him next to the still form of Mary.

Whatever damage had been done to her skull to cause all the blood was not visible. Aside from the impossible angle of her head, her body was unmarked by the fall.

Ferguson bent down and gently closed her eyelids. "Rest in peace, Mary. May perpetual light shine upon you."

"I'll tell the Vatican," Ava added quietly after a pause. "They'll make arrangements with the French authorities to fly her back to Rome. I'm sure they'll want to bury her with full honours."

Ferguson nodded and stood up.

Ava pulled out her phone, and looked across to the Skoptsy at the other end of the bailey. Heaven only knew what drugs had been in the wine Durov had fed them. They were all likely to be in shock, and in need of medical attention.

She dialled 112, and informed the operator that there was a large group of people in the Château de Montségur in need of blankets and first aid.

"There's just one more thing before we go," she called over to Ferguson, then turned and headed for the northern doorway out of the bailey.

--- • ◆ • ---

CHAPTER 72

Château de Montségur
Languedoc-Roussillon-Midi-Pyrénées
The Republic of France

BACK IN THE donjon, Ava approached the table, and knelt down beside it.

Reaching underneath the floor-length purple drapery, she felt a tremor of excitement as her fingers brushed the familiar texture of old vellum.

Thank God it had not gone up in the flames.

She pulled the roll towards her, and gently took hold of the soft bundle. It was heavier than she had imagined, with densely furled thick leaves.

Lifting it up, she placed it carefully onto the table and stared at it for a moment, trying to calm her emotions.

It was definitely not a stage prop.

The pale washed-out colour, the inconsistencies in the sizes of the stitched vellum sheets, the overall squashed look, and the irregular discolourations caused by the centuries, were not the sorts of details found on even the best theatrical replicas.

She found her eyes irresistibly locked onto it, as she wondered if she really could be in the presence of an original manuscript of one of the most famous religious texts in the world.

Ferguson approached, and stopped beside her. "Go on then," he encouraged.

"Before we do this," she looked up at him, "you need to know that, if this is real, then it predates any known copy of the Apocalypse by over two hundred years. It will also be the oldest-known biblical book by far – one of the most important physical links between apocalyptic Judaism and early millennial Christianity."

She took a step closer to the table, suddenly mindful that the roll was perhaps contemporary with Professor Amine Hamidou's extraordinary pottery shard with the names of the disciples.

Was that a coincidence?

It did seem extraordinary that she had come across both – in the same week – each capable of rocking the world's understanding of early Christianity.

She pushed the thought aside.

There would be time for that later.

"How come it's a roll?" Ferguson asked. "I've seen really early Bibles. They're books."

Ava nodded, focusing back on the manuscript in front of her. "Books only really started around AD 300, as did the first Bibles. When John was writing, at the end of the first century, people still used rolls."

Ferguson peered down at it. "Which way does it open – horizontally or lengthways?"

"The answer will tell us a lot," Ava replied, moving the roll carefully to the middle of the table top. "If it's sideways, then it's a *volumen*, which is what it should be. If it's lengthways – like royal proclamations in Hollywood films – then it's a *rotulus*, which was much more common in medieval times, and usually for ceremonial purposes."

"Let's find out then." Ferguson inched closer to the table.

Ava took a deep breath and placed both hands on the roll.

"Look." She pointed to the outer leaf, where Durov had cracked the brittle black seal. "On most rolls, the first leaf is heavily worn and damaged because readers always have to handle the roll there to open it, regardless of which section they want to read. It's also where readers start winding the skin around the baton that they insert to make it easier to handle."

They both peered at the outer leaf, which was in pristine condition. The leading edge was still straight, with no sign of any damage or wear.

Ava held the end down, and started to roll the ancient cylinder out. As she did, she gasped.

The inside surface was covered in small clear black Greek letters with no spaces between words. The text was meticulously arranged in four-inch columns of writing running from the top to the bottom of the skin.

It was stunning.

And it was unequivocally a sideways-opening *volumen*.

She stared at the immaculately spaced regular blocks of letters – fully justified on the left and right margins – not quite believing her eyes.

She began to read. "*Apokalupsis iesou christou hen edoken auto ho theos deixai tois doulois autou ha dei genesthai en tachei kai esmanen aposteilas dia tou aggelou autou to doulo autou ioanne.*"

"What does it say?" Ferguson asked quietly.

Ava looked up at him, her eyes shining, before turning back to the text. "The revelation of Jesus Christ, which God gave him to show his servants the things which must soon occur, and which he made known through his angel to his servant, John."

She turned to Ferguson again, her face flushed. "It's the opening of John's letter." She swallowed to stop her voice from trembling, and added with awe. "I think this is one of the seven original copies of the Apocalypse."

Ferguson reached out and held his hand just above it.

Ava smiled, breaking the tension. "You can touch it. You don't need gloves. The oils from your skin are actually good for it. They'll stop the skin from drying out."

She watched as he gently unrolled it further. "It's a work of art," he marvelled. "How did one man write seven of these?"

"Eight, if he kept his own copy," Ava peered over his shoulder. "John was an illiterate fisherman. There's absolutely no way he would have known how to read or write. He would probably have dictated it in his native Aramaic. A professional scribe would have translated it into Greek then copied it out. Just look at it. This is definitely a skilled scribe's writing."

"Wouldn't a scribe have been expensive?" Ferguson unrolled a little more.

She nodded. "And vellum cost a fortune."

"So, probably not written by a fisherman in a cave?"

Ava smiled. "To make eight of these took someone with very deep pockets."

They gazed at the ancient words, hidden from daylight since they were sealed up on an Aegean island almost two thousand years ago.

After a few moments, Ferguson broke the silence. "What are you going to do with it?"

Ava hesitated.

It was not the most important artefact she had ever handled. How could anyone rank one over another?

She had worked on the tablets of the Epic of Gilgamesh – the first known story in human history. She had handled the treasures of Nimrud and Babylon. They were all unique and irreplaceable for what they preserved of the ancient world.

But there was no doubt that an original book of the Bible was going to create one of the biggest storms archaeology had ever seen.

The media frenzy would be intense.

Scholars and theologians were going to pore over it, letter by letter, to see the actual words the writer used, and correct the proliferation of errors that had inevitably crept into subsequent versions as it had been copied down the centuries.

The ramifications would be immense for Christians, and for scholars of early Christianity and its writings.

The results would be electrifying.

It was going to be a sensation. The museum that held it would be on every front page, and the tourists and researchers would come flocking for years.

She looked at the doorway out onto the platform, and saw again in her mind's eye Mary bundling Durov over the edge.

"Our friend gave her life here – partly for this manuscript," Ava answered quietly. "She once told me that she felt Rome had everything, if only people knew where to look. The Vatican was very important to her, and that's where it should go – on condition they lend it to all the world's great museums, starting with London."

"I think she would've liked that." Ferguson nodded slowly. "Maybe they can call it the 'Mary Apocalypse 504'."

"I'll make sure of it," Ava replied quietly. "And I'm sorry – about Mary."

Ferguson looked at the doorway she had hurled herself out of. "It was her choice."

"I know," Ava replied. "But you and she were…"

"Were ... ?" He looked confused.

Ava chose her next word carefully. "Close."

He frowned.

"In Rome, when you both came to the library ... "

Ferguson shook his head. "Back in London, when she told me about the child killed by the gang, and how she came to be working at the Vatican, I ended up telling her I joined the army when my parents died." He paused. "The guilt of the child's death weighed on her mind. It was something she wanted to talk about. She thought I might understand. She needed someone to tell her it was okay. That these things happen."

"So you weren't ... "

"Weren't what?" Ferguson looked bewildered.

Ava could not believe she had got it so wrong. "But I thought you two ... "

Ferguson put his arm on her shoulder, a grin spreading across his face. "Well, you thought wrong. I wondered why you were being a bit odd."

"I wasn't," she blustered.

He slid his arm around her shoulders. "Still, it's nice to know you care."

Ava felt her ears heating up. "I didn't say that."

"No." He smiled, pulling her into a hug. "No. You didn't."

Without thinking, she wrapped her arms around him, and placed her cheek next to his, feeling a warmth and calmness settle over her for the first time in longer than she could remember.

There was a sound over by the entranceway, and Ava turned to see two armed French *gendarmes* standing on the wooden walkway at the top of the stairs.

"Dr Ava Curzon?" the one in front asked, stepping forward.

She nodded.

He held up an official-looking piece of paper with the word 'INTER-POL' stamped across the top. "This is an Interpol Red Notice. I'm arresting you for the murders of Sir Mark Jennings and Alan Swinton."

---— ♦ — ---

CHAPTER 73

The Old Town
Sana'a
The Republic of Yemen

IT WAS LATE in Sana'a, one of the oldest inhabited cities in the world. Tradition said it had been founded by Shem, son of Noah, who had settled on the Yemeni plateau after the waters of the great flood subsided.

Al-Irlandi headed through the ancient walls and into the Old Town, oblivious to the mad beauty of the brightly coloured adobe houses, plastered in exuberant geometric designs and wiggly white cake-icing decoration.

The anarchy across Yemen suited him well. The civil war of the Arab Winter kept the place awash with fighters – rival governmental factions, foreign forces, militias, *mujahideen*, al-Qa'ida, Islamic State, and endless bands of mercenaries.

Society had broken down completely.

So no one looked twice at another foreigner. No one monitored his phone calls or e-mails. No one cared what he bought and sold. No one was interested in who he associated with. And no one had any idea who he was.

It was a free-for-all, and it provided him with everything he needed in an operational base.

As he headed deeper into the warren of buildings – some over a thousand years old – his phone rang.

Glancing down, he saw the country code was +507.

Panama.

He knew immediately who it was. And also that the call was coming from somewhere far east of Panama. Far to the east even of Sana'a.

From Guangzhou.

He answered the phone smartly.

"*Wanshang hao.*" The familiar Chinese voice was polite but distant. It was being processed through a pitch shifter.

Al-Irlandi knew that the caller would not identify himself.

He did not need to.

It was the Dragon Head.

He would not stay on the phone for long. His carefulness was one of the reasons why he and his organization were so effective – and had been for centuries.

Al-Irlandi was not a member of the Dragon Head's sworn brotherhood. Far from it. But one of the Dragon Head's lieutenants had been the first to recognize al-Irlandi's special gift – all those years ago in Northern Ireland, in Lisburn's notorious Maze prison.

Since then, the Dragon Head had taken an interest in al-Irlandi, helping him find his feet when he had finished serving his sentence.

For that, al-Irlandi would always owe him a debt of gratitude.

The Dragon Head sounded agitated.

"Something highly unfortunate happened tonight," he began. "One of the Invisible Brothers of the Red Crane has been killed. In France."

Al-Irlandi was listening attentively.

"We had invested much time in certain events due to transpire in Damascus this evening. We had set them all up very carefully."

"I can be in Syria in a few hours," al-Irlandi replied.

"No. The moment has passed. But the French *gendarmes* arrested an English woman at the scene. They have placed her into Police Nationale custody in Toulouse. This is not the first time she has interfered. There was another occasion, before, at Wewelsburg Castle. I now require *bao chou.*"

"I will avenge you," Al-Irlandi replied. The line went dead.

A few seconds later, a photograph arrived by SMS.

Al-Irlandi studied it carefully.

It showed a woman with brown eyes and long dark hair. She could have been anyone.

Pretty, though.

Unusually, she was standing beside an old-fashioned-looking motor bike.

He swiped the photograph away and pulled up his phone's address book.

He had good men in Marseille.

Reliable. Ex-military.

They had done a good job with him in the Paris catacombs against that pathetic professor.

They knew what to do.

He would rendezvous with them in Toulouse at first light.

TO BE CONTINUED …

POSTSCRIPT

◆

Turin Shroud

The Turin Shroud remains one of the Catholic Church's most controversial relics. Despite its fame, it is only exhibited on special occasions. The Church's official view on its authenticity is cautious.

MI13

By the end of World War Two, the UK War Office's Directorate of Military Intelligence had seventeen 'MI' sections. MI13 was responsible for Special Operations. Today, only the domestic Security Service (MI5) and the foreign Secret Intelligence Service (MI6) have known functions.

The Apocalypse

The last book of the Bible has many titles, usually involving the word 'Apocalypse' or 'Revelation(s)' and a name such as John, John the Apostle, John the Divine, John of Patmos, John the Elder, John the Theologian, and other variants. Christian tradition says that its author was John the Apostle (son of Zebedee), who is usually believed to be 'the beloved disciple'. He is also credited with writing the Gospel of John and the three letters (epistles) of John. Nowadays, mainstream scholars think this is unlikely. The Greek writing style in the gospel and letters is refined and uses a similar vocabulary, whereas the Greek in the Apocalypse is different, rougher, and contains errors. The Apocalypse recounts that it was written on the Aegean island of Patmos, whereas the gospel and letters are generally thought to have originated in the Christian community at Ephesus. Parts of the Apocalypse may date from AD 60, with the majority likely to be from the time of the Emperor Domitian (AD 81–96). The Gospel of John is the latest of all the gospels, usually dated to AD 90–110.

Skoptsy
The Skoptsy were a real group of castrati from Oryol in Russia. They flourished from the late 1700s into the 1930s. Some small pockets of believers remain, and they continue with their ancient faith and rituals.

La Santa Muerte
La Santa Muerte is an increasingly popular religion in Mexico and the southern states of the US. It is based on a syncretic fusion of Catholicism and indigenous Mexican religions. There is no single gang called *La Santa Muerte*, although the cult is strong in the world of organized crime. Individual members of various gangs worship *La Santa Muerte*, and bold tattoos showing allegiance and devotion are commonplace.

Knights of Saint John | Order of Malta
In over a thousand years of continuous history, the order has had many names, including the Hospital, the Hospital of St John, the Knights Hospitaller, the Knights of Saint John, the Knights of Rhodes, the Knights of Malta, and the Order of Saint John, It's official name today is the Order of Malta. It still exists as a military order of the Catholic Church, and it is an independent country with observer status at the United Nations. Its armed wing is the Military Corps of the Association of Italian Knights of the Sovereign Military Order of Malta (*Corpo Militare dell'Associazione dei Cavalieri Italiani del Sovrano Militare Ordine di Malta*), whose soldiers serve with the Italian military. Its recent military peacekeeping deployments have included Albania, Kosovo, and the former Yugoslavia. Its Prince and Grand Master is answerable directly to the pope. The last two knights to hold this position, from 1988 to the present, have both been English.

Our Lady of Philermos
The icon of Our Lady of Philermos is real, and is the most sacred relic of the Order of Malta.

Cathars

The Cathars were first recorded in Europe in the early 1100s. Although they appeared in Germany, Italy, and France, the epicenter of their activity quickly became the Languedoc. Pope Innocent III launched a crusade against them from 1209–29. It was the only Crusade ever called against Christians. The Cathars were destroyed, and the Languedoc was annexed to France. The last traditional Cathars were gone by the 1320s. The mass burnings at Montségur in 1244 are commemorated by a monument in the *Prat dels Cremats*, as described in the book.

Count Raymond VI of Toulouse (1156–1222)

Raymond was count of Toulouse, Saint-Gilles, Rouergue, and Melgueil, duke of Narbonne, and marquis of Provence and Gothia. He was also a grandson of King Louis VI of France. He was excommunicated in 1208–9, and again from 1211 until he died excommunicate. Despite his ongoing excommunication, he became an affiliate (*confrater*) of the Knights of Saint John in 1218, and was received as a full brother of the order on his deathbed in 1222. He was buried in the Knights of Saint John's chapel of Saint-Rémi in Toulouse. There is a mural of him in the Supreme Court Chamber, Saint Paul, Minnesota, USA.

Arnaud Amalric (died 1225)

Arnaud Amalric (or Amaury) was abbot of the great abbey of Cîteaux. When the crusader army assembled before Béziers in 1209, he is alleged to have told a crusader, "Kill them all, God will know his own." However, most modern historians do not take this as accurate history, as it was recorded by a monk called Caesarius of Heisterbach, living miles away in Germany, who wrote about it in a book of stories for novices. Caesarius also admitted that he had no source for the story, except that "it was said" that Amalric spoke the words. The exact phrase Caesarius ascribes to Arnaud is: *Caedite eos. Novit enim Dominus qui sunt eius.* (Kill them. For the Lord knows who are his.) The second part is a direct reference to Saint Paul's second letter to Timothy: *cognovit Dominus qui sunt eius* (the Lord knows who are his, 2 Timothy 2:19).

Peter Bartholomew

The story of Peter Bartholomew is told by many chroniclers of the First Crusade. They relate how, in 1097–1098, Peter Bartholomew experienced visions which led him to find the Holy Lance at Antioch. They also relate how, the following year, Peter failed a Trial by Fire to prove he had been honest about the visions, and died of his injuries.

Saint Margaret Clitherow (1556–1586)

Margaret Clitherow was caught harbouring Catholic priests in Yorkshire during the reign of Queen Elizabeth I. Despite being pregnant, she was stripped, laid onto a sharp rock the size of a fist, and the door from her house was placed on top of her. It was piled with rocks until her spine broke and she was crushed to death.

ARAMAIC

— • ◆ • —

Aramaic was the mother tongue of Jesus and his earliest followers. It first appeared around 1000 BC as the language of the Aramaeans, and was later taken up by the Assyrians, Babylonians, and Persians. It became widespread across the Middle East, where for a while it acted as a *lingua franca*. When the Hebrews were carried off to Babylon in the sixth century BC, they switched their day-to-day language from Hebrew to Aramaic, and Aramaic remained their common spoken language throughout the centuries of their return, the Roman occupation, and the early diaspora. Therefore, in Jesus's times, Aramaic was the ordinary language of Jews in Judaea and Galilee.

The Aramaic words used in the book are listed below in alphabetical order. As Aramaic had its own alphabet, the words are written as pronounced. (The apostrophe represents the letter *ayin*.)

Knista | **Synagogue**
The Aramaic word *knista* means 'gathering' or 'assembly' (originally the people rather than the place). The Greek word *synagoge* (συναγωγή) is a translation of the Aramaic and Hebrew word meaning 'gathering'. The Aramaic and Hebrew words have the root KNS, which gives the name of the modern Israeli parliament: the Knesset.

Meshiha★ | **Messiah or Christ**
The original Hebrew word is *Mashiah*, and its Greek translation is *Christos* (Χριστός). In all three languages it means 'the anointed one'.

Rabbuni | **Teacher**
This Aramaic/Hebrew word is used in the Bible in Mark 10:51 and John 20:16, where it appears in Greek letters as ῥαββουνί. Scholars do not agree whether it is Aramaic or Hebrew.

Sheliah (**pl.** *Sheliahin*★) | **Apostle**
The Aramaic word *Sheliah*, and its Greek translation, *Apostolos* (ἀπόστολος), are both based on a meaning of people being 'sent forth' or 'dispatched'.

Urha★ | **The Way**
The Acts of the Apostles records that the earliest Christians in Jerusalem called themselves 'the Way', or *he hodos* (ἡ ὁδός) in the biblical Greek. The original Aramaic names used in the book are:

Bartalmai | **Bartholomew**

Matai | **Matthew**

Shim'on Kepha | **Simon Peter**
Kepha is Aramaic for 'rock'. The Greek for rock is *Petros* (Πέτρος), and the Latin is *Petrus*. They are the root of the modern name, Peter.

Shim'on Qan'ana' | **Simon the Zealot**
The Aramaic word *Qan'ana'* means a member of the Zealots (political group). In biblical Greek this is *Zelotes* (ζηλωτής) or *Kananaios / Kananites* (Καναναῖος / Κανανίτης). See the text of the book for a fuller discussion.

Tauma | **Thomas**

Ya'qov | **James**
The literal translation of *Ya'qov* is Jacob, which later evolved into James. For example, the followers of King James II of England and VII of Scotland were called Jacobites.

Yehuda Siqari' | **Judas Iscariot**
The Latin *sicarius* (pl. *sicarii*) means dagger man. The Aramaic word is *siqari'* (pl. *siqarin*). The traditional etymology of Iscariot (Ishkariota) is

Ish Kerioth, meaning a man from Kerioth. See the text of the book for a fuller discussion.

Yehuda Thaddai | **Judas Thaddeus**

Yeshua | **Jesus (Joshua)**
The correct translation of *Yeshua* into English is Joshua. But, traditionally, people have always used the Latinized version of the name, which is Jesus.

Yohanan | **John**

Andrew and Philip
These two apostles had ordinary Greek names: *Andreas* (Ἀνδρέας) and *Philippos* (Φίλιππος).

* The last 'h' in the words *meshiha, sheliah, sheliahin,* and *urha* is pronounced with a guttural sound like the 'ch' in the Scottish word 'loch' and the German name 'Bach'.

SOURCES CITED

———————— • ◆ • ————————

Bible references

For consistency, all biblical quotations are taken from the King James Bible. Quotations by Danny Aronov are taken from the English edition of the Tanakh by the Jewish Publication Society.

Chapter 11. The reference to prophecies of the End Times in the Tanakh are in Nevi'im: Isaiah 24–7, 33–5; Jeremiah 33:14–26; Ezekiel 38–9; Joel 3:9–17; and Zechariah 12–14. 'As I looked on' is from Ketuvim: Daniel 7:9–10 (JPS).

Chapter 19. 'For there are some eunuchs' is from Matthew 19:12.

Chapter 24. 'For if we believe that Jesus died' is from 1 Thessalonians 4:14–18.

Chapter 31. The Biblical accounts of Jesus's siblings are from Matthew 13:55–6 and Mark 6:3.

Chapter 33. 'From Lebanon come with me' is from the Ketuvim: Song of Songs 4:8 (JPS).

Chapter 51. 'There was war in heaven' is from the Apocalypse 12:7–11.

Chapter 55. 'I was in the Spirit on the Lord's day' is from the Apocalypse 1:7–11.

Chapter 55. 'Hail, thou that art' is from Luke 1: 28, 42.

Chapter 56. 'I John, who also am your brother' is from the Apocalypse 1:7–11.

Chapter 64. 'These are they which came out of great tribulation' is from the Apocalypse 12:7–11.

Chapter 65. 'And did all drink the same spiritual drink' is from 1 Corinthians 10:4. 'For I am already being poured out' is from 2 Timothy 4:6. (New King James Version). 'I saw a woman sit upon' is from the Apocalypse 17:3–6.

Chapter 66. 'And the angel took the censer' is from the Apocalypse 8:5. 'Babylon the great is fallen' is from the Apocalypse, 18:2, 3, 8. 'These shall hate the whore' is from the Apocalypse 17:16. 'And again they said, Alleluia' is from the Apocalypse 19:3.

Chapter 67. 'And there followed hail and fire' is from the Apocalypse 8:7. 'The time has come for judging the dead' is from the Apocalypse 11:18

Chapter 69. 'But the fearful, and unbelieving, and the abominable' is from the Apocalypse 21:8

Chapter 70. 'The revelation of Jesus Christ' is from Apocalypse 1:1 (my translation)

CPSIA information can be obtained
at www.ICGtesting.com
Printed in the USA
BVHW051538010323
659464BV00011B/364